WAYWARD

THE FORBIDDEN HEIRS

1

BECCA N. DRAKE

DWP

For the crowd, the clan, the gang,
whatever else we call ourselves.

PRONUNCIATION GUIDE

Athrú	uh - THROO
Atlarand	AT-lah-rand
Babandodd	BA - buhn - dodth
Braidac	BRAY - dack
Cael	KALE
Caeradin	CARE-uh-din
Calibor	KAL-ih-bore (a as in cat)
Corandul	kor-AN-dool (a as in cat)
Draas	Drahss
Elfryth	EHL - frith
Emlyn	EM - lihn
Eoin	pronounced Owen
Ethelfled	EHTH-uhl-fled
Gildio	GIL - dee - oh
Ioan	YOW-uhn
Irminric	ER-min-rick
Itis	EYE-tis
Jaccius	JACK-ee-uhs
Jeiosach	JAY - oh - sach (Scottish ch, as in loch)
Lleogren	llee - OH - gren
Lorhurst	LORE-herst
Oedolyn	oh-WED-uh-lin
Orrtha	OR-thuh
Priodas	PRY-oh-dus

Rhys	REES
Righnách	RIG-nach (a as in cat, Scottish ch)
Rivariar	rih-VAH-ree-ar
Rodd	ROD
Rodhin	ROH-din
T'aesea	TAY-jzah
Tylysk	TIL-ihsk
Vespar	VEHS–par

PROLOGUE

Heldran's steed charged down the dirt path and deserted the crammed city street. The pelting rain made the journey more laborious, but the young Mage Master hurried his sodden mount. Heldran didn't even think to pull up the hood of his cloak. The chilly downpour drenched him, mud splattered him and his mount, and he didn't care.

Word of his sister harried him, demons come to grasp his throat.

The news left Heldran dazed. His limbs moved on their own while the little messengers' words halted his foggy mind. His assistant, Alric, tried to shoo the two begrimed children from Heldran's presence, but their persistence forced Heldran from his office work. The lad spoke over the weepy girl.

Mention of the river stopped Heldran's heart. Even Alric couldn't silence himself.

"Fool boy, you know not to go near the river when the water is so high—"

"It wasn't s'posed to be as high this year," the boy said. "We just wanted to look. We stayed on the bridge and everything."

"My sister went with you?" Heldran demanded.

The girl hid her face. The boy nodded.

As the understanding struck him, Heldran stumbled from his office and out to the courtyard. He had no memory of retrieving his horse nor mounting it. He hastened down the road to the Old North Bridge.

It wasn't true. His sister was home practicing her letters or rescuing her cat from the servants' scorn. Her governess would never let the children out alone, nor let them near the waters at spring flooding.

Heldran realized he had passed the turn on the road in his daze. Wiping the drip from his eyes, he yanked his horse about, abandoned the path, and spurred his steed through the field to the north.

The aged wooden bridge soon emerged from the mist. The high water lapped its underside. The figures of his servants, short Hilda and gangly Rufus, stood at the bank, ghostly in the fog, watching the water's flow.

Heldran dismounted a distance from them. He led his horse along the sodden bank, scouring the flooded grass for some disturbance, some sign of the children's presence. Rufus took the horse's reins as Heldran passed unnoticing. Finding nothing on the banks, Heldran moved to the bridge. To his dismay, forsaken by the middle post, a child's fistful of pebbles waited to be cast to the water.

He backed away. He searched the length of the river, her name scalding his throat.

Heldran recoiled from Hilda's hand on his arm. She stood away, handkerchief to her nose. "My lad, please, come away from the water."

His face grew hot despite the unyielding rain. "How? Why?" Heldran furiously motioned to the river. "She knows better. She's afraid of the water. Why would she come here? Why did you let her?"

They gave no answer.

"And she can't have…gone so far?"

"The river is swift, sir," Rufus murmured. He stepped forward. "'Tis all I could save of her, sir."

Heldran looked at what lay across Rufus's calloused hand. A precious red silk ribbon. Her favorite ribbon, the one that had dressed her hair that morning.

Not again.

Heldran succumbed to the familiar numbness. He sank to his knees. This time, so hideously alone, he crumpled. His servants stood by and watched him weep.

VIII

ATLARAND
The Adriel
IRMINRIC
Norcrest
Fallewel's Ridge
PRIODAS
ETHELFLED
Scethecael
Talck
ELFRYTH
LORHURST
Gildio
LLEOGREN
Windborough
GILDIO
The Adriel
The Mystic's Lake
Babondodd
RHODIN
Rhovani Desert
ITIS
RIVARIAR
JEIOSACH
TAESEA
The Southern Wall
CORANDUL
Lydan

I

CHAPTER 1

Rhys

A stall keeper swore at me as his barrel of potatoes toppled across the cobblestones. A horse reared, and an old woman's deafening geese scattered as I bounded through the gaggle. Behind me, four Ordinary guards, three mages, and one household knight stumbled upon the wreckage, hardly slowed in their pursuit. Though it hindered my escape, the congested market street made a decent enough cover while I weaved my way to freedom.

Or, rather, evaded my incensed would-be escorts, who'd see me back to the Manor by the scruff of my neck. Being Master of the Claytherdon Manor, I doubted I'd be dealt more than a figurative slap on the hand for my stunt. But such escapades out of the castle were restricted—for me, at least, which is to say, unless I accompanied my mother somewhere, I never set foot outside its walls.

I ducked into a side street, where I slammed my back to a brick wall and caught my breath. If I could make it the last few streets to the city square, I could disappear altogether.

In the square, the summer sun beat down on the assembled T'aesean tinker caravan, where a ring of ornamented wagons camped. Masked actors performed on a makeshift stage. Musicians gamboled alongside ribbon dancers and tumblers. Children galloped from one wagon to the next in search of toys and exotic sweets. Others with more than a quib to spare perused the rarer merchandise—spices and wines from Rodhin and Rivariar, the latest fashions from Priodas, a spectrum of jewels mined in Irminric and Jeiosach.

The mage spell tightened like a noose around me. I tripped out of the alley to escape its conjuror. I merged into the flow of the throng, slinking along without catching too many eyes. The mages breathed down my neck.

On the far side of the square, a squat two-story inn sat deserted beyond the crowd. The familiar sketch of a yellow knife under the words "The Golden Rogue" on the tavern's weather-beaten sign caught my eye.

I ducked around a tinker pounding a drum. The dark-eyed dancer behind him grazed me under the chin with her ribbon and winked. I turned from her to meet a haggard tinker woman spewing some premonition from the slightest glance at my palm. Veering aside, I collided back to back with another stranger.

The man reprimanded my peasant recklessness before we turned to eye each other. The nobleman went red from his chin to the brim of his velvet cap. The woman on his arm gasped.

"Master Rhys!"

My name spread faster than fire through the square.

The nobleman bowed. "Beg pardon, my lord. It was my mis—"

I sprinted. A pair of guards closed in. I bobbed around the wagons, through the dizzying spread of caravan colors. As I loped away, the crowd closed off to stare after me, providing me enough time to escape into the tavern.

I halted inside the door. A boy arranged the chairs and tables around the silent common room, and the tavernman polished flagons at the bar. Before either looked up, I bolted for the nearest hallway. The tavernman called after me.

The boy dropped his chair when the door burst open. I slammed my back to the wall, concealed in the shadows. The men stormed the common room, the tavernman protesting their carelessness with his tables and benches.

"Where's the boy?" an intruder demanded.

I cringed. The knight stood an arm's length from my hiding place.

The tavernman blustered. "Bolted clean through. Hopped the counter and out the back door. Most appalling—"

The knight cursed. He hurried through the kitchen while the others back-tracked to the front door. The knight ordered his men to go around, to search the alley.

I waited, heaving for breath, until the nervous boy spotted me again. I grimaced at him and the tavernman and crept out of the corridor.

"Sorry."

Eyes on me, the tavernman nodded sideways to the lad, who skittered to straighten the crooked tables. He smiled at me as he would any other tavern goer. "Skin and bones, we've not had the honor of a young lord through our door for a fair many years."

The boy dropped another chair. "Dad," he hissed.

The barman silenced him. "Quiet now, no trouble. Mind your brothers."

His shoulders sank, but casting a look at me, the boy slipped into the kitchen. Once his son slinked out of sight, the tavernman took a flagon to a keg before setting it on the bar. "If Master Claytherdon will take old Brac's humble offering."

I inched toward the bar. "Why didn't you turn me over?"

Brac shrugged his broad shoulders and pushed the flagon closer to me. "I won't spoil our young lord's schemes. Hate to see what they've done to my kitchen, though." He gestured toward the front door with a cock of his head. "The crowd will be in before long. Ah, sit, Master Rhys. You have a moment. Drink."

I took a sip of the cinnamon-red brew. Sweet cider, cooled for the summer day.

"What has our young master so stirred as to leave the comforts of the Manor and duck into my little abode?"

I thumbed the handle of the flagon. "Nothing, really."

Brac laughed. "Alone and into trouble, no less." He fiddled with the end of his red mustache. "The good Lady wouldn't like it, and I should think less of her if she did."

I grimaced.

"But I can't keep my own boys in sight longer than a tail's wag. They'll do as they will, as they say. But my lads haven't the same ransom you could have on your head, m'lord."

I took another drink to avoid his eye.

"Ah, well. The Lady may as well turn you loose now, seeing as you're almost of age. In happier times, you might not be hunted yourself."

"What makes these times unhappy?" I asked crossly. "I thought these were better times than most."

"I don't disagree, sir, but your good mother perhaps does." He shook his head. "I can't say I envy you. I'd not be called Master of the Hunt for all the gold in Caeradin."

I looked away. Neither would I.

Brac took my empty flagon from the bar. "But someone must do it, I suppose. The witches must be brought to justice."

"So we're told."

He peered at me sidelong. "Should I be concerned by your indifference, Master Rhys? Or should I be more concerned about the gentlemen coming to my door?"

I stiffened, not daring to look. Brac chuckled at the plea on my face, then nodded over his shoulder. I careened around the bar and dove to the floor. My back hit the cabinet as the door squealed open. I recognized both sets of footsteps crossing the common room floor, one the careful click of a boot, the other with more shuffle.

Brac shifted his feet. "Might I help you, sirs?"

My pulsing heart filled the silence.

"My men say Master Rhys passed through here not long ago."

I knew his civil voice better than I wanted to. Lord Mage Vespar, adviser to the Claytherdon Household and my lifelong tutor.

"He did, as I said, m'lord," said Brac.

"He said nothing to you?" the second, keener voice asked. Mage Master Tylysk.

"No, sirs."

I could sense the Lord Mage's expression—his steely green eyes sharp with focus, the stony blankness on his features, the slight downward curl of his thin lips. Vespar had a falcon-like aptitude for striking down a lie. "My men were not far behind him when he came here, yet they've found no sign of him since."

Brac shrugged. "If you'll not take my word for it, come and see the state of my kitchen."

I caught my breath as the tavernman opened the bar's swinging door and welcomed the mages in with a gesture.

The inn door flung open. "My lord, come quickly!"

Tylysk hurried to the door, but Vespar lingered long enough for the ruptured quiet to meld again. I held my breath, waiting for his clawed hand to snag me over the bar.

"My lord," Tylysk said.

Vespar stepped away. "Thank you for your time, Mister Brac."

The barman bowed. He watched the mages until the door shut and waited a breath before pulling me to my feet. I sauntered back to my stool.

"I can't say I envy you for them, either," said Brac.

"I haven't the slightest what you mean."

Brac smiled. "Indifferent to them as you are the Hunt?"

"Not indifferent. I can't honestly say there was ever a person who'd met Master Tylysk and not been galled by his presence."

He laughed. "No, indeed. But I do believe Master Vespar shouldn't be crossed—even by you, if I may say."

I glared at the door. Brac had witnessed the gentle side of my demanding, perfectionist tutor. For all the influence granted by my title as Lord-to-be and future Master of the Hunt, my power ended at Vespar's feet.

"All the same, I wouldn't turn him away if he sought to protect me," the barman said. "Say what you will of his demeanor, you couldn't be in safer hands."

No. Not unless you were a witch.

Brac saw the thought cross my face. He returned my gaze, leaning with both hands on the bar. "What's taken such hold of you that a Claytherdon should doubt the Hunt?"

"You said yourself you wouldn't be Master of the Hunt. You don't like it, either."

"I don't like it, and I don't have to like it, same as I don't like the dreadful tonics the physician orders. But I drink them all the same."

"Do they do you any good?"

Brac shrugged. "I should think so. Would I risk my good health to find out?"

I fingered the grain of the wood bar. "What a terrible waste if you discovered they did nothing at all."

The barman eyed me. "Nothing has befallen me since I started them. Isn't that enough?"

"If you keep letting the physicians force them on you, you may never know."

"No, but I'm safe for now."

I stepped away from the bar. "I hate to think an innocent woman was murdered without any proof of whether I'm safer for it."

Brac shook his head. "Aren't centuries of security from dark magicks proof enough?"

"Security." I weaved through the tables toward the door. "From women and children who most often know as little of the workings of Magic as Ordinaries themselves. Centuries of a Hunt based on a theory of women's 'tainted magic' yet to be proven."

"Or disproven."

"No one seems terribly inclined to attempt either."

"Except you."

I smiled, gripping the door handle. "What gave you that idea?"

CHAPTER 2

Rhys

By the time I sneaked out of the tavern, the knight and mages had moved off, with a few Ordinary guards keeping watch at intervals along the road. With Master Vespar and his lackey drawn away from the square, I thought it safe to venture out again.

The tinkers danced and performed to the constant prattle of music. Endless travel darkened their naturally tan complexions, sun-bleached those with rusty-brown hair and darkened the others' raven locks. While their gracious affability appeared sincere enough, tinkers were the sort to give an actor's bow while hiding a dagger behind their backs.

I kept to the outer ring of wagons, away from another fortune-teller or cheeky dancer. Vendors scrambled over each other to catch a young nobleman's eye. More than once, I turned away from a string of pearls or an amethyst ring to give a sweetheart I didn't have. One woman forced a sample of her fresh cinnamon bread into my hands, claiming that girls won't take such skinny lads even if you tempt them with pearls.

The most striking wagons belonged to those who claimed to produce poultices and talismans for protection against dark magicks. One tinker offered pocket-sized books of spells even Ordinaries could cast to perform the simplest protective charms. To prove its worth, he would have settled for the five lor instead of the tine he asked for, but he got nothing from me.

Turning my back to him, another wagon caught my attention, this one blue with scarlet stars and a painted gold sun on its door. It carried the same sort of wares: a pouch of charmed spices on a leather cord to be worn about the neck for two lor. The tinker proprietor attested to his product's effectiveness by shaking it in a little girl's face. Gagged and roped to a wagon wheel, the girl cowered as far from her tormentor as the binds allowed. It convinced some onlookers, and they steered away from the child. A few departed with a pouch.

With the last lor tight in his fist, the tinker swung to the girl and bellowed in his own sharp tongue. This time, she made no effort to retreat from the pouch dangling her face. She may have feigned the pains the fake poultice didn't inflict, but real tears dribbled down her face. The girl endured her captor's reprimand, and he clutched the front of her dress and rattled her. She slumped out of his grasp. He left to entice another passerby.

I followed the line of wagons, eyes on the tinker until a customer distracted him. As I drew close enough to study the girl, I spotted bloodstains beneath the dirt caked on her bare feet. For all the painful raggedness of her hair, the girl must have endured her captor dragging her about by it. She raised her sunburned face in my direction, her soft, blue-violet eyes dim.

Keeping behind the wagon, I knelt beside her. She drew her knees up and whimpered.

"Don't be afraid," I whispered. "I'll help you."

The girl cowered, pushing away with her heels.

I reached for her binds, but snapped my hands back from a fiery sting lancing through my arms. I glanced at the girl again, half thinking she'd done some spell herself. A closer glimpse, and I found a crooked dirt circle ringing the girl. The faintest red mist hovered above the outline. I ground my teeth. Why the ropes if a mage trapped and stifled her in a magic circle?

"It's all right," I said. "I'll find some way—"

"She not for sale."

The tinker's rumbling voice yanked me to my feet, and his height almost sent me back down. He stood four hands taller than I, with a dark, rugged beard and his hair tied up. The ridiculous mismatch of his red waistcoat, teal breeches, and purple knee-high boots hardly detracted from his height and brawn.

"She is not to buy," he said. His T'aesean accent sharpened his rugged voice.

I stood away from the girl, pretending to glower. "Where did you find this witch?"

"Babondodd. We take her to the Lady for reward."

I gaped. The girl had been abducted for several weeks, suffered the seventy-some miles north to Gildio and every stop in between. "Why didn't you turn her over to the Hunters?"

"What reward would we get? No, we take her to Lady."

"Lady Orrtha, you mean?"

"Aye."

Nodding, I drew a handful of coins from the pouch on my belt and fingered them across my palm. "Allow me to take her off your hands. I'm Master Claytherdon."

The tinker eyed me, then flung around to the girl. She whimpered at the sound of my name. The tinker's string of foreign words silenced her. He centered his skeptical attention on me again.

"You are Master of Manor?"

"I am."

"Prove."

I pretended to sigh. I gave him my handful of coins and upended my pouch over his palm. Whatever the assortment of tine, silver, and a few gold amounted to, some fell from the tinker's hand before he got the other up to catch them.

The tinker gawked. He called over his shoulder, eyes on his fists. Another lanky tinker approached. A rapid exchange in their own language, and the newcomer glared at the girl. He uttered a sharp incantation. The girl squeaked as the red mist of the magic circle bled into the ground around her. One more incredulous look to me, and the mage tinker stalked away.

The seller pocketed his spoils, freed the girl of her binds, and redoubled them once he hauled her to her feet. A hard shove to the back of her head sent her reeling into me.

"Take her, Master Claytherdon." He exaggerated a bow. "Apologies for doubting." The tinker retreated to boast to his companions.

The girl tugged against my grasp, cries choked by the gag. I lightly gripped her arm, but feigned the repulsion witnesses expected to see on anyone handling a witch. She wilted, the last of her strength sapped by her terror. I scooped her over my shoulder and moved.

We escaped the ring of wagons and abandoned the square. With a glimpse for any onlookers, I swept the girl down a few alleys before we veered out of sight. I lowered her down. She crumpled to the ground, hid her sobs in her aching arms.

"I'm sorry," I said, kneeling beside her. "I didn't mean to hurt you. We just had to make them think so." She shrieked when I reached to remove the gag. "No no no, it's all right. Let me help you." I peeled the gag from her raw mouth.

"Please, sir, *please*, don't take me to Lady Orrtha!"

"You're not going anywhere near Lady Orrtha."

I unraveled the binds from around her blistered wrists. Once freed, the girl scuttled a few feet away before collapsing from the pain in her feet. She cried facedown on the road.

I dropped beside her and lifted her from the dirt. "Easy. Let's rest here a moment," I said. "Tell me your name."

She shook her head. "Please, Master Rhys…"

I leaned against the wall and cradled the girl as she rested. I brushed the dirt from her cheek. Aside from her exhaustion and doubtless hunger, she showed no other signs of grave injury. Her soiled, tattered dress, once long, exposed her scraped knees. Dried blood flaked off her wrists, the gag left her swollen lips raw. Gashes in her sleeves exposed yellowing bruises discoloring her arms.

I drew the tinker woman's bread from my pocket. She nibbled at it and licked the crumbs off her fingertips.

I watched the streets beyond our hiding place, waiting for the knight and his dogs to saunter past. We'd stood still too long, but where would we go? Not to the castle, where wolfish mages stalked and preyed. But if I stayed away much longer, the search would redouble, and the girl and I would be discovered, and she dragged before the Lady and her council like a mere lamb to slaughter. What choice did we have?

Scooping the weightless girl close, I stood and pressed my back to the wall. "You're safe with me, I promise," I said. "Let's hurry before someone comes around."

We inched down the backroads, hidden from the sun under the shadows of the aged structures on either side. I stayed pressed to the wall and peered around the first corner. The next alley opened wide into the busy main street beyond, still too close to the square of tinkers and their audience. We cut across the road and swerved left into the closest side road. Forward, snaking down the grimy alleys, behind a putrid butcher shop, past another tavern where a sprawled drunk stirred to consciousness as we sprinted by.

Before long, we reached the main road with nowhere else to turn. The knight was nowhere to be seen, nor the Lord Mage and his men, but a few Ordinary guards prowled through the townsfolk. To our left, the Manor towers soared above the city a distance off. The girl whimpered at the sight of them.

We merged into the bustle beyond our backstreet sanctuary. Most paid us no mind, while some eyes followed us through the throng. I held the girl close, shielding my familiar face with her presence.

Bobbing around one last corner, we came face to face with the castle's southern wall. Beyond the massive barricade spread the Manor gardens to the south, the bailey on the north side. Sentinels stood guard on each watchtower, where Gildian banners of the black eagle on green hung lifeless in the windless air.

The girl squirmed free. She sprinted as soon as her feet touched ground. I snagged her arm and bundled her away, a hand clamped over her cries. We huddled in the shadows, she dangling in my hold, smashed tight to my chest until she exhausted herself.

"Y-you said you w-weren't bringing me here," she sobbed.

"I told you I won't take you near the mages or anyone else. This is the only place I can protect you until we find somewhere better."

"You're lying!"

"If I were lying, I would've left you to those tinkers. Please, you have to trust me."

The girl eyed the barricade down the road. She shrank away, shook her head.

I knelt in the dust, kept an arm around her. "You know who I am, don't you?" I said.

"Y-you're Master Rhys."

"That's right. And that means you're safer with me than anywhere."

The girl scrubbed her eyes with her wrist. "But…I'm a witch. You hate witches. Everyone does. Witches are bad."

She believed it. Her hopeless gaze told me.

I drew her hand from her face. "I don't think you're bad," I said.

"But I'm a witch."

"So?"

Her brows drew together. "But…you're Master Rhys."

"Even I don't have to believe what everyone thinks about witches. You're proof, right here. What have you ever done wrong?"

She didn't return my smile, uncomprehending.

"Trust me. I won't let them hurt you."

The girl eyed me, tears clinging to her chin. One last glimpse at the Manor, and she faced me once more. "Promise?"

I gripped her tiny hand. "Promise. I won't leave you."

The tumult in her blue-violet eyes calmed a little. She smeared the tears from her cheeks. She nodded.

I tousled her hair. "Come on."

She curled her arms around my neck and held herself close. A quick search for a patrol, either in the street or atop the castle wall, and we sneaked on.

The nearest gate stood on the eastern side and led into the garden. An obsidian black eagle statue perched atop the archway glowered down on us. As expected, the latched gate refused to budge. The girl clung to my waistcoat when I set her on her feet and peered between the gate's crossbars, through the long archway of the dense wall.

Far toward the west end of the garden, tucked against the southern wall, stood a little stone garden house. Mage gardeners maintained the ancient, two-windowed structure for appearances alone—otherwise, it no longer had any use except filling the corner of the lawn.

I showed the girl. "That's where the gardeners used to live a long time ago," I said, "but no one goes in there anymore. We'll be safe for now. Just...how do we get in?"

She studied our dilemma, tugged my sleeve. She cowered when I looked, but regained her courage. "Master Rhys, I-I can get us in."

I glanced down the wall in both directions. "That sounds dangerous."

"I can do it," she said, with no real confidence. "I've done it before."

"The mages."

She swallowed. "I can do it fast."

A flicker of movement caught my eye, and I whisked the girl into the cover of the archway. I peeked again. A herd of lazy sheep roamed the faraway hillside to the east.

Slowing my racing heart, I said, "The mages would sense your spell, wouldn't they?"

As I spoke, a dull thrum of hooves rose over the cobblestones a street away. The main road led straight past us, around to the bailey.

The girl whimpered. I turned her about and hoisted her up to reach the lock. "Fast, then."

She laid a trembling hand over the keyhole. The cobblestone din drew closer.

She flung her hand from the lock. "It's not working!"

"Concentrate." I bounced her into place. "What are the words?"

"There aren't any words."

"Every spell has words, an incantation, something."

"This one doesn't!"

"Try again. Concentrate."

She squeezed her eyes shut and pressed her palm to the keyhole. The ancient latch creaked. She gritted her teeth. The keen sound of hooves echoed an alley away.

"I've got you," I said. "Don't be afraid. Come on."

She yelped when the gate swung out of her reach. We slinked in and latched it shut. The riders passed as my back slammed to the archway wall. A whirl of green behind a white destrier, another behind a tan stallion—Lord Mage Vespar and Master Tylysk.

The girl and I stayed hunched to the wall while she caught her breath. We hadn't made it through the Manor walls, and someone nearly spied us out. Vespar, no less, the man to worry about more than any other mage in the Manor.

What had I done?

I tiptoed to the far end of the archway. Watching the castle windows, we darted for the line of oak and Melys trees along the southern wall. We took shelter behind each, tree after tree, until we came to the garden house.

What had long been a groundskeeper's hovel had aged to a dank, filthy pit. Soiled windows filtered little sunlight into the cramped chamber. A rotting chair fell forward on its snapped legs near the tiny, blackened hearth. A slight counter bore the remnants of vermin-infested dishes.

The girl squealed as a few rodents skittered out of the moldy blankets decking the narrow bed. A spark of yellow flared across the room. The pests scattered from their burrows, and with a few chilling squeaks, the light swallowed them up.

The girl watched the rodents' fatal evictions with horrified eyes. "I'm sorry, Master Rhys, I didn't mean to!"

I pressed a finger to her lips. "It had to be done one way or another." I raised the girl higher from the grimy floor. "This won't do at all."

"Master Rhys, I can, I mean…"

I frowned. "I think more of your magic will catch attention."

She bowed her head. "The mages at home never felt my magic."

The idea rattled me, but it was either that or risk getting caught sneaking her needs from the castle with nowhere else to go. One wrong move meant her death.

I relented with a sigh. "Only what you need."

She nodded.

I placed her on her feet. "And the first thing you'll do is put a lock on that door, yes?"

"Yes, Master Rhys."

I crouched beside her. "Just Rhys. You don't have to call me 'master'".

Her lips flickered with a smile for the first time. Evening sunlight dusted her sweet face. She glanced at her feet. "My name is Emlyn."

"Emlyn. What a beautiful name."

She beamed, and it warmed the room. I tousled her hair. She ducked away at first, then turned into my palm like a kitten to a stroke. I left my hand on her cheek until she blushed and dropped her gaze. Emlyn starved for a tender hand as much as food.

I peered out the window to where the Manor lay in turmoil. "I have to go, Emlyn. They'll look everywhere for me until I get back."

"No, Master R—I mean—"

"I'll be back as soon as I can. I'll bring you supper and some sweet cider, shall I?"

"Don't go…" Emlyn crumpled. She stood hunched into herself and cried.

The lightest touch on her arm, and Emlyn launched herself at me. I staggered a step, surprised, and lifted her up again. I held her tighter as she wept, unsure what else to do.

I watched her first few enchantments. Emlyn remade the ancient lock with a simple charm and alighted a lantern on the counter with a pinch of her fingers to its wick. A flick of her arm banished the filthy debris. Once she set to work, I slipped out with a promise to be back as soon as I could.

Hands in my pockets, I strolled up the path to the castle, as if the day had been absolutely uneventful.

CHAPTER 3

Orrtha

"**G**uard."

The mage outside her chamber door entered and bowed. "Anything?"

"No, milady."

Orrtha steadied herself into her chair, knuckles white from gripping its arms. "Search the library again."

The guard exchanged weary glances with his comrade by the door. "Yes, milady." He closed the door behind him.

Orrtha drummed her fingers on the arm of her chair. Sunlight brimmed the chamber, cooled by a breeze through the open window, yet the room suffocated her. What use was she trapped behind her desk while Gildio's capital and the Manor upended themselves in their confounding pursuit? Confined to her chambers, she felt time slipping through her fingers, as her son had.

Despite her appeal for yet another scour of the library, Orrtha knew Rhys would not be there. She stumbled to the window again. She'd done little more than scrutinize the garden's walks and hedgerows below the entire day.

Orrtha peered over the city, seeing nothing more than a mass of slate roofs. She couldn't blame her son for his restlessness, if the incident truly was a matter of his behavior. But the boy knew his bounds, knew full well the perils beyond them, what he risked venturing from the sanctuary of the Manor alone.

The Lady banished the thought, though her guards placed careful surveillance over her, too, as many worried the circumstances behind Rhys's disappearance might prove more dubious than she let herself believe. Too many sought the life of Gildio's Lord-to-be, the next Master of the Hunt, her sole heir.

Orrtha forced herself to face her husband, though he was only a portrait now. It disconcerted her how little it resembled him. Those were his features, the dark sweeps of his hair, his sharp jaw and warrior's build. Yet those stormy blue eyes showed none of the cool streak of his lightheartedness, nor the warmth of love. Some severe, unforgiving lord stood in that portrait, not her Ioan.

"Don't laugh at me," she scorned. "You would. You would think this is all nonsense, and you would scold me for having our son on a chain."

Orrtha couldn't imagine whoever stood in the portrait capable of laughing. She looked away from the keenness of the beloved stranger's eyes. She spied the likeness of the silver trinket dangling against his chest, the polished Gildian eagle framed by three gleaming emeralds. The Lady gripped the pendant where it rested on her heart, thumbed its ancient jewels.

The knock on the door jolted her. "Enter," she called.

Lord Mage Vespar stepped in. He bowed as he shut the door, straightened and rubbed his eyes. Orrtha found no sign that he'd been out—unruffled, not a ripple in his rich green mage cloak, shoulders square. Weariness dulled the stark contrast between his sharp green eyes and dark hair. Orrtha sank into her chair at his apologetic look.

"The troops have yet to return, my lady. A search has been conducted in the Lower Side. A precautionary measure, milady." He raised a calming hand.

"Rhys knows not to stray so far."

"He does, my lady. I've started another round about the Manor as well." Vespar came forward and held his hand out to her. She let him grip her trembling fingers. "We'll find him, Orrtha. He'll be home before the day is out. Have no fear."

She yearned to believe him, but Master Vespar knew better than most what dangers awaited her son beyond the Manor. He dealt with witches face to face. Their beguiling, superficial innocence was nothing new to Vespar, but Rhys had never confronted a witch before. Her son's inexperience frightened her more than most anything he might encounter.

"He is as prone to trouble as his da," she said.

Vespar's smile strained before broadening. "They are enough alike in the face."

Orrtha spared the portrait another glimpse. Its features resembled Rhys's as much as his father's, and one could mistake the portrait as the boy's. They contrasted in size, however—Rhys never trained as painstakingly at swordplay or sported a hunting bow as his father had. The thought saddened Orrtha.

Vespar watched her study the painting. "He has his father's head," he said, "and his mother's heart."

Orrtha offered the sentiment a bleak smile.

After a silence, Vespar reached into his cloak pocket. "However, our search has not been fruitless." He produced a scroll and held it out to her.

Orrtha grasped it hesitantly. Without glimpsing at the document's contents, a vile taste rose in her mouth. Her soldiers accomplished this, but they couldn't retrieve her son? The parchment felt especially weak, and Orrtha wished she'd let herself shred it apart. But Master Vespar stood by, waiting. She unfurled the parchment.

It bore the same concise message as ever: a declaration of the order of the Claytherdon House, Lords of Gildio, Masters of the Hunt, a reminder of the Hunt's vow to bring witches to justice and guard Caeradin from wicked forces of magic. Orrtha skipped to the following paragraph. She mouthed the words until she came to the stunning discovery.

"Eight witches?" she breathed. "*Eight?*"

"Found in a cellar in the Lower Side, my lady."

Orrtha pressed her knuckles to her lips. Eight. Eight witches awaited the mindless scrawl of her pen to seal their fates. The Lady understood the necessity of the Hunt and her role in presiding over it, but she loathed it. She'd tried not to think on it before, but eight lives were too many to overlook.

She swallowed. "Were there children?"

Vespar lowered his gaze. "Four, my lady."

Orrtha's heart stopped.

"They are witches, my lady," he said solemnly, seeing her despair. "None are exempt, regardless of age or standing."

Yes, so the document in her hand stated. Orrtha laid the parchment on the desk before she crumpled it. She fingered the pendant on her heart. "How young?"

"I would guess the youngest is eleven."

Her hands shook. She fretted over her own child's well-being when she would as soon send another mother's daughter to her death. How could she consider taking her quill from the drawer?

Orrtha laid a hand on the parchment, unsure whether to inch it closer or shove it away. She glanced out the window and thought it better that her mages apprehend these witches before they discovered her son. Tenderhearted Rhys was not immune to a child's tears. A meager plea for help would snare him.

"It is your duty, milady. As Mistress of the Hunt, it falls to you to perform this task. If you do not, who can?"

Orrtha matched her eyes to Vespar's. He spoke true, however downcast he appeared by his judgement. What would come of her household should she let these witches sift through her fingers? Children or not, Gildio's allies would not care.

She retrieved her quill. Vespar politely took the inkbottle from her trembling hands and unstopped it for her. The Lady dipped her pen.

Orrtha dropped the quill when the door opened unannounced. "Rhys!"

The boy slipped into the chamber, eyeing the guards outside. Unlike Master Vespar, Rhys displayed signs aplenty of his escapade—dirt dusted his crooked blue waistcoat and white tunic. He smoothed his ruffled hair when he spotted Vespar near the desk. But Orrtha spied no signs of injury, and Rhys let her clamp him in her embrace, hunched so she could reach to kiss his cheek.

"Why are there guards outside your door?" he asked.

"What happened to you?" Orrtha demanded. "Where have you been?"

"Just in town to see the caravan." Rhys strove too hard to ignore his tutor's presence.

Orrtha massaged her eyes. "Sun and stars, Rhys Ioan—"

"What does it matter? I'm home. Nothing happened to me."

"Would it have been so terrible to take an escort instead of vanishing before our eyes? To have told someone instead of leaving the entire household to think the worst of…to think someone had…oh, Rhys—"

"I sense nothing, my lady," Vespar said from his stance behind them. "Rhys is untouched, as he says."

"I didn't meet a witch," said Rhys, glowering at his tutor. "I didn't meet anyone."

"Rhys, please," Orrtha said. "If something has happened, listen to Master Vespar. He will help you. He always has."

The boy steadied his glower until Orrtha spoke his name a touch stiffer. "Yes, Mam." Rhys withdrew and shoved his hands in his pockets.

Vespar watched the exchange between mother and son. The boy flitted contrite glances at her, as to be expected, as was the contempt Rhys seared in his tutor's direction. Vespar had no doubt that even if Rhys had indeed suffered from some enchantment, he would fight his master's aid with every bone in his gangly body.

Less than content, the Lady sent Rhys after his belated supper. Excusing himself, Vespar bowed and followed the boy out. The guards at the door took their dismissal. Neither tutor nor pupil had taken a step before Orrtha's stifled sobs met them through the door. Vespar arched a brow at Rhys's guilty glance and marched down the hall.

"I hope you enjoyed yourself, for the mayhem you put the Manor through," he said evenly. "I hope your mother's distress was worth it. Get your hands out of your pockets."

Rhys scowled but obeyed. "Forgive me, sir. Some days, I'd prefer some better company than those books you always throw at me or your escorts stifling every step I take." The boy hurried down the long staircase. "But you'll be glad to hear I didn't deal with anyone."

"Anyone but a tavernman. Did you spend all afternoon stowed behind his bar?"

The boy glowered.

"You may have evaded my men well enough, but you cannot hide from me." Vespar turned down the corridor of darkening windows ahead of Rhys.

"Why did you leave me there?"

"You were safe enough cowering in your corner. Other vital business called me away. You might have noticed I set escorts along your path home."

"Yes, *sir*, I did. What could possibly have made you abandon me?"

Vespar strode on, though Rhys slowed to demand his attention. "In our desperation, we conducted a search in the Lower Side and discovered eight witches hiding in a cellar."

Rhys halted. Vespar turned to watch the color drain from his face.

"You what? *Eight*?"

"Do you see? The danger is real and a footstep away. How easily you could have been beguiled and fallen subject to their cruelty."

Vespar's matter-of-factness produced a gratifying anxiety in the boy's eyes. "You've said that before," he muttered.

"You had best remember it."

"May I ask you something, my lord?"

Vespar turned and eyed him.

"What makes their magic any more merciless than yours?"

Vespar raised his brows in feigned surprise, and Rhys saw through it. The boy frowned again, irked.

"If I recall, it was not a mage who brought about Caeradin's downfall and slaughtered thousands for the sake of having the power to do it. In fact, I believe it was a mage who gave his life to apprehend the culprit."

"But—"

"And what have they become since?"

"You condemn them for a reputation," Rhys rebutted.

"Reputation? Have you ever faced a witch, Master Rhys?"

The boy glared. He stood his ground as Vespar stepped nearer.

"If you could see their malice for yourself, hear how they curse and spit upon your father's memory, how they crave to be your murderers, Master Claytherdon, and squabble like dogs over who should have the honor."

Rhys swallowed. He avoided his master's eye.

"If it is only a reputation, it's certainly accurate. If they were not wicked to begin with, they have molded into this monstrous repute of their own accord. They have allowed their magic to be corrupted."

"I don't believe it," Rhys said. "Neither do you. Not really."

"Why should I not? The evidence abounds."

"And if it didn't?"

Vespar offered a hollow smile. "You would not be Master of the Hunt, would you?"

Rhys was unmoved, but Vespar knew he'd broken the lad somewhere. His eyes sparked with busy rumination.

"Go on. I have work to do." Vespar grasped Rhys's shoulder as he passed. "I trust today's events won't happen again."

Rhys stared ahead until his master released him. Vespar watched him move down the hall before returning to his own chambers. If nothing else, Vespar startled the boy more than he showed. Yet such a shock had never swayed his father's radical ideals, either.

Vespar had never seen such resolve in Rhys's eyes. Once, Vespar might have disregarded his claim as the outburst of an insubordinate teen. Now, the sincerity of his conviction troubled Vespar. He long believed he could slow Rhys in his revolutionary endeavors, but the nearer he drew to coming of age, the stauncher he became. The abruptness of this argument, however, was what Vespar could not overlook.

Something had happened during the boy's escapade. Vespar would get it from him.

CHAPTER 4

Rhys

Once Vespar disappeared up the stairs, I stopped to breathe. I'd expected some reproach for my rashness, a slap on the hand, so to speak. But I had never considered my potential murder until my tutor reinforced it this time.

I glanced out the corridor windows, where dusk shrouded the vast gardens. Little Emlyn waited in the growing dark, probably thinking her makeshift hovel was a dungeon and I'd return with a troop of mages at my flank.

Vespar was wrong. Even if every other witch in Caeradin proved as corrupt and wicked as he claimed, one little girl was not.

I moved down the hallway before I stared at the garden too long. Evening shadows crept into the corridor, up the dark marble pillars to the high arched ceiling. They swallowed the aged tapestries ornamenting the cold gray walls until the magelight candelabras flared to life, alighted by a mage's distant touch. Heatless, silvery flames licked the darkness.

I massaged the back of my head, where the familiar pain spiked at a mage spell's appearance. No healer had discerned how I, an Ordinary, sensed magic's use. Of course, Ordinaries were as susceptible to magic's potency used against them as those who wielded it, but something as unobtrusive as starting a magelight should have gone blissfully unnoticed. Vespar and the healers had long abandoned their search for a cure when they concluded I suffered no real harm. Magic's constant presence left me accustomed enough to the pain to tolerate it.

I examined the candelabras as I passed. The crisp, blinding magelights contrasted with the ethereal glow of Emlyn's lanterns. I reached a hand through one of the flames, let its tendrils caress my fingers. Nothing but the dull thrum of magic forced my hand away. But Emlyn's charms did me no harm. I sensed nothing of her magic at all.

Corrupt magic. As if Vespar's powers were any purer. What an excuse to carry out the systematic slaughter of a magical counterpart.

Vespar would never convince me of his view. Da had eyed the Hunt the way he would a snake, and despite what little I understood of it as a child, I loathed it as much as he.

Few controversies had stood between Da and Vespar other than the Hunt. Otherwise, they had remained as close as brothers until Da died. Back then, Vespar acted more like my uncle than the austere, exacting tutor he'd become. But nothing vexed him more than Da's resistance to his own duties.

"Will you not defend your kingdom?" Vespar argued once. I watched him and Da bicker from my hiding place in the council chamber balcony, peering down through the railings. Da leaned with a hand on the hearth mantle and stared long into the fire while Vespar paced the length of the table. The unusual heat between them unnerved me. "You'll send your armies to aid another weak lord's numbers, yet you won't secure your own people against the perils of the home front? Master of the Hunt, indeed."

"If I can't mount it on my wall, I won't Hunt it," Da said.

"Then you will be hunted yourself, by our allies who would replace you with a more emboldened commander. The other lords will not stand for your tenderness."

"Tenderness?" Da turned on Vespar, such fire on his face, it frightened me. "If you saw a child being beaten in the street, would you not rescue her? If a widow pleaded you for a crust of bread for her starving children, would you not take pity? Is that tenderness or decency?"

"Your duty is to guard them against wicked forces they cannot battle themselves. I don't wish death on anyone, my lord, but the welfare of our people must take precedence over what is or isn't decent."

Da coughed hard into his fist. When he caught his breath, he said, "Are witches not our people, too? Can't they be saved from their corruption? Are they still so far gone?"

"If they were not, you wouldn't ask me so."

I wriggled closer to the edge on my belly, gripped the railing bars when Da coughed again. He shook his head. "You are not heartless. I've seen you. You would save them."

"If there were a way, yes," Vespar returned, "but the evidence—"

"*Evidence.* If you let them prove themselves, your evidence would lead to a different end. You are governed too strictly by your head."

"And you by your heart, my lord."

They eyed each other, each as unwavering as the other. Da turned back to the hearth, the orange firelight glaring on the sharp line of his mouth.

"I'd be better satisfied if you searched and found no evidence to the contrary than if you didn't look at all," he said. "You're determined to disregard any proof of their innocence."

"You said it yourself—I would help them if I could."

"And yet, you divert my every attempt to do so," Da's voice raised.

"Because of your haste, Ioan! Because your pride and obstinacy will have the other lords at your throat!"

Da choked, slammed a fist to his rattling chest. He sank into the chair at the end of the table, each unrelenting cough sapping his strength.

"Da!"

They spotted me. I stumbled to my feet and ran.

"Rhys Ioan."

I halted. I crept to the railing, a prisoner peering between the bars.

Da heaved for breath, and at last the fit subsided. He stared me straight in the eye through the dark. He pointed to the floor beside his chair.

I plodded down the stairs until Da said, "Sometime before the sun is up, boy." I stood on the spot where he pointed, head hanging.

Da set his elbows on his knees and met me face to face. "Your mother will be sore to hear you're out of bed."

"I was waiting for you," I sort of lied.

"I told you I'd come, didn't I?"

"You were taking too long."

It eased the disquiet from Da's face. He gave a smaller cough, shifting whatever filled his lungs.

"Da—"

"Easy, chap. It's no worse than it's ever been."

"Is too. You sound like old Master Wulfric when he wheezes."

Even Vespar laughed. I scowled, my seven-year-old pride pricked. Da stuck out his hand, and I heaved him from his seat. Vespar ruffled my hair as we passed him and made for the door. He and Da exchanged good evenings, again as convivial as brothers, but it wouldn't be long before their dispute rekindled.

Da said nothing on the way to my chambers. I didn't dare make a sound. He knew I'd overheard every word, and there was no point in more excuses for eavesdropping.

Once in my chambers, Da knelt at my bedside, smoothing my hair from my brow. His sudden seriousness churned my stomach.

"Will you remember something for me, chap? Will you promise?"

I did.

He smiled, dispelling all my unease. "Remember that no one is made wicked by any means but his own."

An odd thing for Da to say, and I understood little more than that it was important to him. I kept my promise.

Not a fortnight later, his fever claimed him.

After ten years, Vespar still hadn't detracted me from accomplishing what Da couldn't.

I glanced over the garden one last time, toward Emlyn's tiny dwelling hidden by the hedgerows. Just a few months until I came of age and could instigate all Da strove for. Until Emlyn and all her kind could go free.

Two servants waited at the table in the private dining hall. Dark-eyed Theresa bobbed an angry curtsy, and shy little Aria shakily did the same. I veered out of the range of Theresa's wrath as she made for the kitchen. I took the chair across from the girl seated at the table, my mother's Atlarandian ward and, though plans had since gone awry, my once bride-to-be.

Isabelle popped a plump grape in her mouth as her brown eyes met mine. "Rhys," she lilted over my name. "Nice to see you back. Hope your adventure was worthwhile."

"I'm not sure."

"You've been rewarded for your stunt, then."

The trencher slammed on the table in front of me. Spiced soup slopped over the edge of the bowl. Theresa stood back, glowering, daring me to comment on the food's lukewarmth. When Isabelle dismissed her, she dipped another stiff curtsy and stalked out of the hall.

"If you'll forgive her," Isabelle said. "The uproar had everyone on edge, what with half the household out looking for you. Captain Perreth had patrols outside the city. Aria made rounds about the castle all day too." She tucked Aria's hair behind her ear, but the girl returned to its cover with a shake of her head. Isabelle glanced between me and my platter. "I hope Theresa or the cook haven't done something to that."

I rolled my eyes.

Isabelle took her napkin from her lap and laid it on the table. "Where did you go?"

I dunked a bite of buttered bread in the cold soup.

"Sounds fun."

"I found the caravan."

"You ran off to see the tinkers." Isabelle raised a brow. "Was it everything I told you it'd be? Loud and hot and crowded?"

"Mm."

"You didn't get your fortune told, did you? They always nab lads like you to scare." Isabelle grinned. "What else?"

I shrugged. Offering a nervous curtsy, Aria gathered Isabelle's empty platter and whisked herself to the kitchen. Isabelle watched her close the door before leaning over the table.

"Nobody's listening now. Tell me honest, where did you go?"

"I told you. The caravan."

"A rumor's gone around that you went to the Lower Side."

"I'm not that stupid."

"And that you rampaged a tavern."

"Nobody was there."

"Was this before or after too many drinks?"

I cocked a brow at her. I finished the last of my bread as Isabelle followed me from the dining hall. She waited, but I made no sound, watching the darkening windows.

"You never could keep secrets from me." She bumped my arm. "You went through a lot of trouble for a drink and a palm reading. And you're not usually this sullen after Master Vespar's reprimands."

I grimaced. "You heard him?"

"No, but no one else could put you in such a mood."

The conversation fell away, a feather ready to drift up at the slightest breath. Isabelle's innocent nagging prodded more than she knew. She strode backward in front of me, never taking her eyes from mine. Her smile coaxed me.

"He said they found some witches today."

Isabelle frowned. She fell into step beside me. "I might have guessed. You can't blame him or the Lady for being suspicious of what happened. You're not one to disappear. Whatever you think of him, Master Vespar cares about you."

"He used to. Not anymore."

"Which is why he spent the entire day in the heat and mob to be sure you made it home in one piece. You're unfair to him and you know it."

I avoided her eye.

"And I know what you'd say about your Da and witches and all, but that doesn't mean your mother thinks the same."

"Mam can't bear it any more than I," I muttered.

"There's a difference between loathing the sentencing and understanding what she and most of Caeradin believes is a necessity."

"Do you think the Hunt is necessary?"

Isabelle pursed her lips, swept her long curls over her shoulder. "No one's given me a reason to think so, nor a reason not to." She eyed me. "You won't get far without proof, Master Claytherdon."

"How can I find proof when all the evidence is shunned into hiding or slaughtered? Believing that all witches are corrupt is as absurd as believing all mages are guiltless, or that every Ordinary is a thief and a cutthroat."

She jabbed a finger at my ribs. "I didn't say I didn't believe you, fool." I squirmed away, nearly knocking over a magelight in my retreat. Isabelle laughed. "You could weasel your way into a crown, charming as you are. No lord will stand a chance against your batting eyes."

I didn't answer. I looked out to where the sunset left the garden to purple twilight.

Isabelle jabbed me again. "Ash and flame, you are dismal this evening, aren't you?" She followed my stare. "Do you miss it out there already? Is that why you're so grim?"

I moved away from the windows. I kept few secrets from Isabelle, she being my longest friend, but I couldn't risk endangering her with knowledge about Emlyn. Better to be ignorant should things go awry.

Isabelle halted at the door to her chambers. She looked me over, frowning. "I'm just glad you're home safe. You scared me, little fool." She swatted my arm. "Keep out of trouble, will you? The wheels in your head are spinning too fast for my taste. I expect you to be better company tomorrow."

I stared at my feet. "You'd be dismal too, if you knew something you did led to the deaths of eight innocent people."

CHAPTER 5

Vespar

By midafternoon, Vespar had yet to return the Mistress of the Hunt to her duties. The warrant for the witches' executions remained untouched. When Orrtha continued to resist his pressure, Vespar let it be. The witches no longer posed a threat, confined under the watch of capable mage wardens, shackled against the use of their own powers.

As the Lady hadn't called on his guidance for her duties, and he had tended to his own, Vespar found himself at his desk while business at the Manor carried on around him. The Claytherdon House sustained an eerie silence after yesterday's calamity. The knights and garrison trained with Swordsmaster Perreth. Mage Masters carried on their busy work, managing the estate, reestablishing order after the previous day's bedlam. Rhys was, his mother said, studying.

Vespar sat back in his chair. Orrtha's noncompliance oddly coincided with Rhys's outburst the night before. Curious, he supposed, but he doubted Orrtha's delay was more than her typical hesitancy. Vespar twisted Rhys's words in his mind. The boy boiled long and hard before an eruption, and perhaps he had merely lost his head to his temper and demanded attention.

Vespar doubted it. Rhys had grown to be a treacherous clash of his thoughtful, deliberate mother and his imprudent father. Something was whirring in that brain of his. Vespar saw it in his eyes, the way he used to see it in Ioan's.

He twisted the gold ring on his right forefinger. Rhys, as his father had, tinkered with affairs that expanded far beyond the realms of his own kingdom. Every province in Caeradin would fall prey to his obduracy. Vespar knew the lad meant well, but his rashness would turn every lord on his head. Friend would be foe, foe would become feeble allies. Gildio may have been one of Caeradin's greatest realms, but the world was greater than Rhys's inheritance.

But the matter of magical affairs, over which the Ordinary boy had insignificant power, concerned Vespar at least as much as the other lords' wrath. Rhys and his father scoffed at such worries, so Vespar asserted the diplomatic upheaval into every argument instead. Yet no matter how Vespar strove to deter him, Ioan's stubborn son ever emerged from the depths of logic. Vespar rubbed the ache from his eyes.

If Rhys refused to believe what he was told, perhaps he would believe if he were shown.

A precarious endeavor sprang to mind, perhaps Vespar's last chance to tug the reins on the boy.

All the better the Lady hadn't yet signed the order.

Vespar left his chambers and moved down the stairs to the western wing of the castle. Far at the end of the last corridor, two Ordinary guards stood at attention at the dungeon's barred entry. They bowed and let the Lord Mage pass. Vespar followed the silver thread of a mageglow torch down the spiral staircase and to another iron door.

Three cells made up the first dank chamber. Four guards stood at the ready with their sentinel wands drawn, two by the door, two at the occupied cell. The witches huddled together on the grimy floor stones, further snared in a scarlet pentacle that rendered their magicks powerless. The three women hushed the four little ones' whimpers, though

Vespar saw more fear in their eyes than the children's.

The last witch, a redheaded teen, might have been lovelier but for her scowl. Her girlish figure had yet to bloom—thin and shapeless, the virtual rags she wore all but spilling from her shoulders, but her delicate features and vivid green eyes somehow detracted from much else. She was the quietest of her group, but the fiercest by far.

Vespar dismissed the guards at the cell. He gave each witch a long look. Two of the little ones burst into tears. The redhead returned his stare, hers as steady as his.

He stepped forward, ending his inspection with her. He motioned for her to stand. One of her elders hauled her to her feet when she refused.

"Your name?" he asked.

She gritted her teeth. "What does it matter, unless you have the decency to mark my grave properly?"

"Flannery," one woman warned.

"On the contrary." Vespar squared his gaze to match her unshaken stare. "You may have better luck than the rest of your troupe."

Flannery clenched her fists. "They're my family."

"As you like it. I have a request for which I may be willing to spare your life."

The girl scoffed.

"It's simple enough, I believe, for a vital matter. You could save Caeradin from the throes of war, and its greatest household from collapse."

Flannery's face compacted to scarlet rage. Vespar didn't flinch when she rushed to the cell bars and flailed through them. "Greatest household of liars and murderers! How dare you ask for my help. How *dare* you!"

Vespar raised a brow. "Why let that keep you from your reward?"

"Nothing I could do would provoke such mercy from you."

"It is a desperate matter. Surely you wouldn't see Caeradin torn apart again."

Flannery clutched the bars. The corner of her lips quirked up. "And Lord Mage Vespar himself comes groveling for a witch's aid."

A guard standing by readied his wand at the girl with a command to bite her tongue. Flannery no more reacted to his rebuttal than Vespar had reacted to hers, but the other witches cowered and pleaded for her to take care.

Vespar studied the other witches. He gestured to the child with her arms constricted about Flannery's waist. "Your sister, perhaps? You have the same features. Her name?"

Flannery rested a hand on the child's flaming hair. "Abigail. What do you care?"

"I should think it's quite clear."

A new ferocity clouded her gaze, yet now, she dared not counter him. Flannery searched each face within the cell, spied their desperate terror, their betrayal. She may yet survive, while no hope remained for them.

"If you succeed, Abigail may go free with you," Vespar said. "Let that, if nothing else, be your incentive."

The heat in Flannery's glare dwindled to a strand of smoke from a doused fire. The guards stood ready as Vespar unbolted the cell. Abigail clung to her sister until another witch gathered the wailing girl away.

Flannery halted at the edge of the confining pentacle. Vespar extended a hand over the flickering red boundary. Gritting her teeth, Flannery rested her fingers on his, and she passed through the barrier unmarred. The cell door locked behind her.

Vespar anticipated some outburst, one of either magic or words, but Flannery stilled her weaponry. He motioned to the stairwell. Flannery kept her back to her sister's sobs and followed.

Once the dungeon's iron door barred behind them, Flannery loosed her tongue. "If anything happens to her, I'll spoil whatever you're concocting."

"Her welfare rests on your end of the bargain."

The girl shielded her eyes from the glinting magelights and stalked up the steps after him. Vespar poised a defense charm on his lips but showed no unease. He'd subdued Flannery for the moment, but despite what his previous investigation gathered of her meager strength, he knew little of her capabilities. A flare of her temper could unleash any unintended attack, if she hadn't yet learned to prevent it.

"How old is Abigail?" he asked.

Flannery set her jaw. "Ten. But that's never stopped you before, has it?"

"And you?"

"I don't see why it matters."

"Your abilities are what concern me."

Flannery snorted. "Looking to get deeper into trouble?" She gave in to his narrowed brows with a huff. "I can do enough. I'm not useless."

"Certainly not. Might I assume you've had training?"

"A year's worth."

"And I might guess you are…fifteen, sixteen? When did your magic manifest?"

She rolled her eyes. "What does it matter?"

"Your powers will have grown alongside you regardless of your training."

Flannery tossed her arms out. "I might not be a match for you, *milord*, but I can make do."

Vespar continued up the stairs. Whatever her abilities, her task would be simple enough. But no precaution could be left unconsidered while so much hinged on this undertaking.

He doubted Flannery was concealing anything. Granted, witch magic was quieter than mage magic, the way a woman was meant to be the gentler, but quiet had no bearing on strength. Vespar sensed nothing to fret over, but neither did she promise any greater help beyond this task.

"What am I doing?" she demanded.

Vespar studied her harsh expression in the magelight. The lilt of her words drew his attention. "Rivariar," he said. "Need I ask what brought you to Gildio?"

She glared.

He considered. "A year of training, perhaps with those women downstairs. About that long ago, a Hunting party had a scuffle outside our gates. A few witches escaped."

"Clever, aren't we?"

"So it seemed."

Flannery almost appeared daunted. "Are you going to tell me?"

Vespar hushed her as they reached the next door, and he ignored her remark about skulking around. He led Flannery past the guards and into the empty corridor. He took her by the elbow.

"The issue is delicate. As I said, Caeradin stands at the brink of war."

"What's that got to do with me?"

"It concerns Master Rhys."

Flannery halted. She stiffened, resisting Vespar's grip.

"Get me anywhere near him, and I will kill him."

"Abigail would be sorry to hear it."

A sharp tug on her arm set the witch moving again. "I won't," she growled. "Kill us both. Kill us all. I won't help you."

"Who are you to offer your sister's life? Will you turn from her as she waits for you to save her?" Vespar tightened his grip. "Surely you have a mother waiting for you."

Flannery stumbled. Her eyes fixed to his, inverted to despair and disbelief.

"If it suits you better," he said, "consider this. You would help one mother save her son's life in exchange for saving yours. A child for a child."

Flannery made no sound the rest of the way down the hall, past the library, past the door to the garden, onto the staircase leading to the mage quarters. The witch recoiled, wrinkling her nose. Vespar had quite forgotten the steady pulse of magic through the Manor, which must have beat upon the girl. He stalled long enough to let her steady herself. Flannery's scowl dissipated, the bleakness in her eyes exposing more astonished grief than fear.

Vespar slackened his grip on her arm. "I will explain all soon enough. You have nothing to fear on your part. Do it well, and you'll have your reward."

"I don't believe you."

"Do you not think I'm as skeptical of you?" Vespar raised a brow. "So long as you keep your end of the bargain, I will keep mine. Nothing will befall your sister if you succeed. Mind yourself, and all will fall into place."

Flannery met his eye, tightening her lips. She squared her shoulders. "For my mother."

Vespar gave her sentiment a slight bow of his head. "For Caeradin."

He hesitated a moment longer. The dungeon had done Flannery no more damage than a year in the Lower Side had, which was enough to make her unpresentable to anyone, let alone the Lady.

As the thought crossed him, his second, Master Tylysk, rounded the corner onto the stairs. He halted midstep, brows narrowing on the witch at his master's side. His fingers curled around the hilt of his dagger as he descended the last few steps.

"Master Tylysk," Vespar said, "I trust you remember Flannery from yesterday."

Tylysk eyed the girl, his green eyes cold. She glowered back. "I do, sir," he said.

"She will be our guest here until we see fit," said Vespar. "I believe she may be able to assist us with Master Rhys."

A hint of a smirk teased Tylysk's mouth. "I'm intrigued, my lord."

"In time. There is much to see to."

Tylysk grasped the girl's wrist before Vespar released her. Flannery restrained her recoil with a scowl.

"I must speak with Lady Orrtha," Vespar continued. "I will leave Flannery in your capable charge, Tylysk. If you will see that our guest is accommodated. Join us when she is ready."

"Yes, my lord." Tylysk set off toward the guest chambers, mindful of his roughness in towing the girl along. The witch flickered a glance over her shoulder at Vespar before he made his way to Lady Orrtha's study.

This would do it. Flannery would shake him. Rhys needed proof of the peril at his doorstep. Enough to make him hesitate, make him pliant in Vespar's hands.

For a moment, Rhys's words plagued him again. Vespar truly took no stance of his own against Ioan or his son. Rhys's claim about Vespar's disbelief may not have been too shy of accurate. But for now, the lords remained appeased and subdued. For now, the sad reality was, only the Hunt stood between Master Rhys and his kingdom's demise.

At least he had no power yet. Until he came of age, Rhys could do nothing but sit on his hands and watch his mother and tutor rule his inheritance in his stead. Vespar had time to slow him.

Still, Rhys's claim haunted him. Vespar hesitated at Orrtha's door, spun the ring on his finger.

The Hunt was not a furnace. It was a sieve.

CHAPTER 6

Rhys

Guarding my napkin of breakfast spoils, I hurried for the garden. I collided into the servant girls Lizzie and Violet as they rounded a corner. They stared while I shifted my bundle behind my back and burst into giggles when they thought they'd escaped my hearing. I waited until they went on their gossiping way before I slipped outside.

Late morning warmed the fragrant garden. A glimpse around showed me no one else amid the hedgerows. Swordsmaster Perreth, his knights, and some of the garrison took to the bailey to train. Beyond the wall to the east, the shepherd and his dog drove their flock down the ridge.

I followed the hedges to the garden house. The creaking scrape of the lock met me at the door, and it swung ajar at my touch. I slipped in, shut the door, and gaped.

The tiny structure expanded within, separating a kitchen and sitting room to either side of the cottage. The minute hearth had grown twice as wide. A dining table sat in view of the broad window, set with bowls of sweetmeats and fruits. A few plain wool carpets covered the packed earth floor. The old lanterns we'd found dangled from the rafters, glowing with the delicate light of Emlyn's enchantments.

I tiptoed in, expecting to ruin her spell. Emlyn was nowhere in sight. I crept through the sitting room and halted at the foot of a staircase. How far did she think she could take this?

I sneaked up the curving stairwell to the loft. A fireplace took up one narrow wall, and a wardrobe stood against another. A chest bordered the end of her bed. A glistening, feathery orb of light bobbed over the bedside table, casting soft gold across Emlyn's sleeping face.

I crept up one more step. Emlyn jolted upright. She flashed me a wide-eyed glance, clung to her doll, and burrowed beneath her quilt.

"Just me, Emlyn. Told you I'd be back."

She peeked and emerged from her covers, scrubbing her drooping eyes.

"I brought you some breakfast." I laid the napkin open on her blanket. Emlyn sheepishly took a piece of peppered sausage.

I sat beside her, though she still avoided my gaze. Faint freckles speckled her nose where grime had blemished her face. Though bedraggled with sleep, her soft brown curls shone, clean and brushed. A plain nightgown replaced her tattered clothes.

"You must feel better," I said. "How are your feet?"

She shifted out from under the quilt. Aside from the bruises, her cleaned feet bore no sign of more terrible injury.

"Better. I brought something for that, but it looks like you don't need it."

Emlyn tucked her knees up and avoided my eye by nibbling on a heel of bread.

"You don't seem to need much from me at all, do you? You have food, clothes, everything. Far better than what we found last night." I scanned the loft, glimpsed out the window displaying the spread of immaculate green, out to the unsuspecting castle beyond. "It must have been hard. It took a lot of magic, didn't it?"

She raised another bite to her mouth. "The mages didn't feel it."

"Why is that?"

"I don't know. No one ever feels my magic."

I studied her again. Emlyn was stealthy, talented, strong. Little. So small, holding her apple in both hands.

"How old are you, Emlyn?"

"Six."

I startled. "And you can do all this? Where did you learn it?"

"Books."

"You can read?"

"Yes. I had teachers at home. And Mama taught me." Emlyn lowered her sad eyes. She smeared the juice from her chin.

"You miss her," I said.

"She and Papa were very sick," she recited, perhaps the way her tutors explained it. It made me ache.

I stroked her arm. "So was my da."

Emlyn watched me fold the napkin. "My brother takes care of me. When he was at work, I used to sneak into his room to read his books."

"Does he know you're a witch?"

She shook her head. She sucked the sticky juice from her fingertips.

"When did you find out you have magic?"

"I read one of the spells out loud. I was just pretending, but it worked."

"How did you read those difficult spellbooks so well?"

Emlyn shrugged. "Magic helps me. And I'm good at it."

I beamed at her. "Did you practice your magic at home?"

"Sometimes. Sometimes, Magic just does what I want. I don't always need spells."

I understood little of magic, but I knew that was unheard of. Vespar and Tylysk used magic without uttering the incantation all the time, but every spell required some specific command, spoken or not. And they had decades of training behind them, while Emlyn might not have had one year. How did she tame the wild force that was Magic?

The charmed gold light drifted nearer when Emlyn peeked at it. She squeezed it to her chest, pillowed her head on its feathery form.

"It's beautiful," I said.

She stroked it, avoiding my eye.

"See, look at all the wonderful things you've done with your magic, Emlyn. You haven't hurt anyone or done anything wrong. You're a witch, but you're not bad, are you?"

Emlyn peeked up at me.

"Having magic doesn't make you or anyone else bad," I said. "Just because the mages say it, it doesn't make it true."

Emlyn's rosy lips quirked. Voice thick, she said, "Promise?"

"Promise." I tapped a finger to her heart. "You are not a bad witch."

Emlyn laid her hands there, holding my words close. Clinging to her courage, she crawled closer. She ducked when I reached an arm around her, then huddled in my embrace.

When she finished her breakfast, Emlyn led me by the hand through her little hovel, explaining all she'd done. She had everything she needed, from my perspective, but she complained of the barrenness of her bookshelves, wardrobe, and toy chest.

"You did put a lock on the door, yes?" I asked.

"Yes. The charm will let *you* in, but no one else."

One step toward the door, and the lock unlatched. A step back, and it secured itself again. Emlyn beamed at my approval.

I left her to her work before anyone at the Manor grew too suspicious of my absence again. I merged onto the garden path from behind the last hedge. A cool breeze whisked away the afternoon heat, and clouds loomed in the northern sky. I wondered whether a coming rainfall would prevent a visit to Emlyn's.

"Shouldn't you be in lessons?"

His smirking voice made my skin prickle. I glared at Tylysk to find him swaggering up the path, a wrist resting on the hilt of his sheathed dagger.

"After your stunt yesterday, I'd imagine you had work to catch up on," he said. "Or are you thinking of bolting again?"

"Not that you could catch me. I evaded your highly developed senses well enough."

"Not my senses I'd worry about. I'm surprised Master Vespar didn't have you out from behind that bar by the scruff of your neck." Anyone else might have seen his smile as genuine. His handsome face had that unfortunate way of concealing his transparent sarcasm.

"Speaking of," Tylysk turned aside, "he sent me to fetch you."

"Well done. Isn't that what dogs are supposed to do?"

His smile darkened. "I'd take care, Master Rhys. Master Vespar isn't in the mood for your…wit."

Tylysk turned on his heel and wandered back to the castle door. I watched him through the windows. His green cloak made a sickeningly gallant flourish as he swerved up the stairs.

I found Vespar's door open a crack. He sat at his spotless desk, thumbing the ring on his right forefinger. Parchments and ink tinged the room with an unrelenting mustiness, with permanent stacks of pages poised on the corner his desk and the nearby table. His deep green mage cloak, stiff and pressed, hung on a hook by the far door.

I shifted for a glimpse of whatever Vespar studied. A bulky leather-bound tome with brass yellow delineating the cover. It bore no title, but I recognized the book enough to dread what was coming.

"Come in, Master Rhys. Close the door."

I obeyed. I took my hands from my pockets when he glanced at them. "You wanted to see me, sir?"

Vespar met my eye and thumped the book shut. "Sit."

I took the chair opposite him. He put the book between us.

"Haven't we discussed this enough, Master Rhys? Clearly, you're still unconvinced."

I could guess his game, and I decided to play. "Of what, sir?"

He wasn't amused. He flipped the book open without taking his eyes off me. He dropped a finger on a paragraph and shoved the tome toward me. "Read to the end of the section."

I checked for the segment break. Not terribly long, I supposed.

"Aloud, if you would."

I grimaced, but obeyed.

"Not many generations after the High Kings began their reign over Caeradin, the first Wizard and Enchantress were named. As distinguished Authorities of Magic, they wielded the greatest power of all mages and witches. The Wizard, Praed, and the Enchantress, Blodica, were both young, fair, and beloved.

"Lord Praed remained faithful to his gifts and mastered them for the benefit and learning of others. With the help of his most trusted followers, he founded the Academy for magical students. Praed served the High Kings all his days.

"Lady Blodica did not remain so loyal. Her unbridled power corrupted the Enchantress, and Blodica grew to use her magic for her own gain. Many, including several Dragon Lords, succumbed to her guile and malice."

Vespar rose and paced around his desk. I continued at his gesture.

"Blodica brought about Caeradin's dissolving with her insatiable lust for power. She crushed the forces of the High Kings and remaining Dragon Lords and brought the monarchy to its knees. Blodica meant to claim the crown for herself.

"Praed, having made every effort to tame the Enchantress, had no choice but to end her life for the well-being of the faltering nation. Expending all his strength, Praed sacrificed himself and silenced his magical companion forever. Caeradin fell into leaderless turmoil.

"After long months of struggle," I read when Vespar waved me on, "wealthy heads of noble households recreated Caeradin with provinces linked by the High Kings' ancient capital in Elfryth. The forming of the Caeradin Council was later celebrated as the Welding.

"Through careful debate among the nobles and the renowned Academy headmasters appointed by Praed himself, they concluded that Blodica's wrath and corruption, and those of her witch followers, could not be risked again. Therefore, all witches, regardless of age or status, were to be executed.

"Many argued that this would not resolve their apprehensions. Magic would forever claim more witches and Enchantresses without discrimination for the demeanor, motives, or character of those women. Such powerful evils would rise again if not vigilantly prevented. Thus, Cerdic, first Lord of Gildio, proposed the establishment of the Hunt until such time as the Council deems it unnecessary.

"After some generations, many lords concluded that whatever dark magic Blodica possessed had died out, and it was safe to allow witches to live alongside mages once more. Others disagreed, claiming that Blodica's magical bloodline lingered within her witch descendants, assuring the lasting impact of her malice, as exemplified in the misdeeds of many witches before their capture."

"And the Hunt continues." Vespar examined the rest of the section and, seeming satisfied, flipped the cover closed with a thick thump. He put a hand on the back of my chair and the other on the desk and leaned closer. "I don't see what your qualms are with this." He tapped the cover. "Enlighten me."

Well, it was the most succinct, unbiased, and uninteresting version of the history he'd ever given me. Every other rendition was at least compelling while they favored the Hunt.

Thinking on it, I couldn't recall many texts providing a thorough explanation for Blodica's betrayal. Something about Blodica's dark witchcraft had to be true to put such a hideous idea as the Hunt in someone's head. Centuries later, they still believed witches "inherited" whatever corrupted their first Authority.

"It's accurate," I reported. "On most accounts, anyway."

"Most?"

"I'm struggling with the idea that witches and mages are so different. Isn't magic just magic, regardless of who wields it? Aren't witches and mages claimed by the same source?"

"All magical beings are claimed by the same source. But could it not be that mage and witch magicks differ in the same way the magicks of plants and creatures differ?"

"I'd think they'd be identical compared to other magicks." I tapped the book. "No one's ever concerned that mages will catch whatever contagion Blodica passed down. They say the crimes of some witches since Blodica prove their corruption, when as many mages could be convicted themselves. It seems nobody could be bothered to come up with a better excuse to continue the hunt."

Vespar frowned. "But it was not Praed who went astray."

"Blodica lived over seven centuries ago. Isn't it unreasonable to still look to her as the model of witches? And if it is true that magic differs between mages and witches, what makes witch magic more sinister? Maybe it wasn't Blodica's powers at all—there could be any number of reasons why she went…well, mad."

"Granted," Vespar returned, to my surprise, "but, as you observed, she lived long ago. Since then, it has been proven that there are significant distinctions between the magicks of mages and witches."

"Such as?"

He released a deep breath. "For one, witch magic is quieter and less detectable. There are certain skills for which either party tends to have a greater aptitude. Magic often manifests in mages at younger ages than witches. There are many ways."

"Then what makes witch magic corrupt and not mage magic?"

"What corrupts anything, Master Rhys? How is a tool broken?"

I pursed my lips. "Using it wrong. So one woman using magic poorly corrupted it for every other witch, and Praed behaving himself keeps mage magic pure?" I met Vespar's eye. "Or is it that witch magic was corrupt once, and you're afraid it will be again?"

"If it wasn't still, would it need purging?" Vespar awaited another rebuttal I didn't make. "Did you not think the Council would have considered and tested your theory in the past? Perhaps one day they will find a different answer, but for now, the fact remains. If they had proven otherwise, why would the Hunt continue?"

"I don't know." I fingered the gleaming outline on the book's cover.

"Perhaps for the same reason this book says Blodica went mad."

Vespar frowned at my implications. "What would such a Hunt offer us if not security?"

I had no answer.

He moved around the desk to his seat. "I will not deny that there may be witches among them who are innocent, and to your credit, perhaps more than we can yet see. But there are dangers that you underestimate. Your hasty endeavor is not one to be taken lightly."

I studied him as hard as he studied me. "Did you mean what you told Da?" I asked.

Vespar's brows narrowed.

"When you told him you would save witches if you could. If you knew how to help them, would you?"

"Do you think me so heartless?" he asked evenly. "Do you think I enjoy this tragic duty, that I relish the deaths of our peoples' daughters?"

I looked away. Yes, part of me believed that.

"I don't deny how lamentable it is. We can agree upon that." Vespar waited until I met his eye. A sadness touched his features. "You mean well, Master Rhys, and I commend you for it. But until we find a way to save them, we cannot risk Caeradin's security and peace."

He studied me a moment longer, then broke the growing silence. "We have further matters to discuss. If you will wait for me downstairs. I'll join you shortly."

Vespar followed me as far as Mam's chambers. I plodded down the stairs.

My head churned, dissatisfied. Admittedly, I'd always suspected Vespar of deriving some depraved pleasure from the Hunt. Nothing else explained why he restrained Da and me. If he loathed this tragic duty, why not work alongside me to see its end in a way he saw fit? A way that would appease the other lords and purify this so-called corruption? Why did the Lord Mage stay his hand when he and Lord Ioan could have ended the Hunt together?

Vespar didn't believe it. As sincere as he pretended to be, and as logical as he made it sound, he knew better than I that there was no corrupt magic. If there were, and if he cared, he would have been scouring for a remedy long before Da died. Whether he believed in dark witchcraft or despised its consequences, Vespar wanted the Hunt to carry on.

I turned toward the stairs at my mother's call. Vespar came a step behind her with his obedient lackey, Tylysk, at his flank.

At Mam's side, a girl with long fiery hair pinned from her freckled face treaded down the steps. The dark blue of her gown accentuated the creamy tint of her skin. She held an elegant pride with her head high, displaying a gold-and-sapphire pendant at her smooth throat. The scarlet in her cheeks warmed the longer she looked at me.

"Rhys," Mam said, leading the girl to my side, "this is Countess Flannery."

I bowed. The Countess's hands balled into fists.

"She's come all the way from Rivariar," Mam went on. "Her company was overrun by bandits, and she found her way here to safety."

I stopped my jaw from going slack. "I'm sorry, my lady. Rest assured the matter will be thoroughly investigated," I said, glancing at Vespar. "But I'm glad you are unharmed."

Countess Flannery clenched her jaws.

"She is to stay as long as she requires," said Mam. "Be sure to make her welcome."

"Of course."

Mam reminded Flannery of the directions to her guest chambers, then excused herself. Vespar looked between Flannery and me before following her, smirking Tylysk not far behind.

I shifted to the Countess. "I—"

"If you'd show me to my room, please?" she said in a whisper that could shatter glass.

"…Right. This way."

She moved off before I motioned which way to go. She refused to look at me as I fell into stride alongside her.

"So, you're from Rivariar?"

Flannery set her jaw. "Yes."

"I can tell now, by your accent," I dared to say. "My father always promised to take me there one day. He told me how beautiful it was, the Realm of a Thousand Waters, with its endless rivers running over the full green. He said the mountains to the north look like a crown on the Mystic's Lake."

Flannery's eyes narrowed. "Yes."

"My father joked how his journey there was as steady as the rainfall. You must not be used to this Gildian heat."

Nothing.

"Speak of," I rescued myself, "what brings you to Gildio?"

"I'm traveling to Atlarand. To see family."

I nodded and thought of nothing else to say.

A discomfiting silence loomed over us before we reached her chambers. I stepped forward to open the door. The Countess bobbed a hasty curtsy. "Thank you, Master Rhys."

"Rhys," I said. "Just Rhys."

She forced a hard smile. "Then just Flannery."

The door locked before I could bow.

CHAPTER 7

Rhys

At supper, the Countess spoke to Mam and Isabelle when she wasn't glowering at Tylysk or me, and she altogether ignored Vespar's presence. She stayed long enough to stir her food, make as little conversation as possible, and excuse herself for her exhaustion. She cast me yet another fiery glare before curtsying and hurrying from the dining hall. Sending me a sorry frown, Isabelle followed her.

Little changed over the next week or more. While Vespar claimed most of my time in lessons, Flannery contented herself either in Isabelle's more welcome company or losing herself in the library. She still scowled and refused to speak in my presence, but with Isabelle's coaxing, the Countess crept from behind her high-headed barricade. Night by night, our conversations eased, if and when she spoke to me.

To my pleasant surprise, I found Flannery and Isabelle sometimes came to watch me practice with tyrannical Swordsmaster Perreth.

Impossible as it seemed, whatever association she had with Tylysk deteriorated. Flannery bristled at his arrogance. He preoccupied himself with restraining his remarks from the cusp of anything distasteful, but his presence was distasteful enough. A least whatever the severest misgivings she had for me had slowly transferred to him.

I managed one brief visit to Emlyn's without drawing attention. To my surprise, she'd restricted her renovations in her little cottage. A few dolls sat around the table, each with a serving of fruit and cider. Her bookshelves had room to spare.

"Most of these are magic books," I observed.

Emlyn blushed.

"You've gotten a lot of practice, haven't you?"

Her eyes twinkled. "I'm going to be a good witch, like you said. But I'll be *careful*."

"That's right. And soon, you won't have to hide anymore, and you can do all the magic you want. Then we'll get you home, too."

Emlyn nodded, but an uncertainty touched her eyes.

Once the Countess had time to recuperate from her tragedy on the roadside, the court arranged a customary banquet to welcome the visiting noblewoman. Being Master of the Manor, I escorted Flannery to the feast she appeared less than eager to attend.

As she came through her chamber door, I bowed and extended an arm. "M'lady."

Her emerald eyes were still the thorns to her rosebud lips, the same hue as her green satin gown. She all but scoffed at my compliment on her beauty.

"You're dashing," she said dryly, taking my arm. "If you had a crown, you'd be the spitting image of a prince."

"I hope you'll forgive the delay for a proper welcome," I said after a silence.

"I wouldn't have minded if you'd forgotten altogether." Flannery's disapproval reappeared in the line of her mouth. "We don't have many banquets at home. Just Midsummer and Winter Dawn. The Welding, if we want to. You like the Welding up here, don't you?"

Gildio took the autumn festivities seriously. We took pride in our significant part in rebuilding Caeradin after the Great War all those centuries ago.

"Most of it," I said. "There are a few things to be said against it."

Flannery's brows drew together. "Against?"

"Don't get him started," Tylysk's voice came from the hallway ahead. "He won't stop."

Isabelle swatted his arm. "You told me you'd stop that."

Tylysk passed a smirk between Flannery and me. The look he sent me made it clear how unimpressed I left him. I gritted my teeth. Tylysk grabbed Isabelle's arm and set off down the corridor. She rolled her eyes and tagged along.

Flannery set her jaw. "Gutless pig."

I stumbled.

She swung her glower to me. "Don't you think so?" She graced the mage with another glare. "He's worse than the rest of them."

"The rest of who?"

She shook her head.

The heat in my face intensified as the silence set in. Flannery and I opened our mouths at the same time.

"Sorry, you—"

"You."

I stared ahead, away from the glint in her eyes. "I was going to say, you surprise me, milady. You're not like other countesses I've met."

"You're not like other lords."

"I'll take that as a compliment, as mine was intended."

"It's as good as any, coming from me."

"I don't believe that. You've put up with Tylysk. That's a compliment to us all."

Flannery's look wasn't too dissimilar to Tylysk's.

In the great hall, we took our seats on Mam's right on the dais, where her handmaid Aria awaited her needs. Isabelle planted herself between Flannery and Tylysk. Vespar kissed Mam's fingers before seating himself on her left.

As noblemen and women, Mage Masters, and household knights arrived, most with an escort in tow, they filed past the dais and bowed to Lady Orrtha before greeting Flannery and me. I recognized the man I butted into while on the run. He and his wife skittered to their table without meeting my eye. I ignored them, the way Flannery mostly ignored everyone else.

With each table full, servants presented a feast of boar and venison, sturgeon with ginger, a spread of meat pies and sauces, herbal bread and cheese, plump pears and candied plums, spiced nuts, and sweet pastries, all with wine and berried water. Flannery's eyes widened as they placed a full roasted swan in front of us.

Once the meal began, the court musicians sneaked to their platform in the corner of the hall to our left. The viol and lute players tuned while the piper exercised his fingers across the keys. The fourth readied his hand drums and bells. The piper led the group into the first tune. Flannery watched them, her hand seldom going to her mouth.

I leaned as close as etiquette allowed. "I would've thought you'd never heard musicians before."

I made a quick apology—Flannery startled and dropped her fork. She snatched it up when it clattered on her plate. "Don't be silly, of course I have." She took a drink and steadied herself. "A good song always captures me, and they are especially good."

The players swayed to the beat, their nimble fingers making the rapid performance look as easy as breathing. When the song finished, they merged into another ballad, one Da sometimes sang to us.

"'The Mirror of Hilidou,'" Flannery said, frowning.

"Don't you have musicians in your court?"

"Of course, but it's always an honor to hear a musician play."

"They would be glad to hear your admiration, Flannery," said Mam. "I'm sure they know some Rivarian tunes we would all enjoy, should you request one. Perhaps Isabelle will accompany you."

Isabelle, grateful for any excuse to escape Tylysk's company, rose and beckoned the Countess along. Flannery's cheeks flushed. The way her hair moved with each step held my gaze so Mam's voice jerked me back to her.

"She's a lovely girl. As pleasant to look on as she is witty. Don't you think, love?"

I battled to keep from looking at Tylysk. His stare seared into the back of my head. "Er, yes," I said.

"Is that all, my Rhys?"

At least my glance only flickered down to Vespar, not around to Tylysk. Mam's expectancy compelled me to say, "I haven't known her long enough. There's not much more to think."

"Perhaps not." Mam fingered the silver pendant on her heart. "But I've noticed an easiness to your smile since she arrived. Of course, as you said, I can't expect more yet." She raised her goblet to her lips.

I watched the musicians bow to Flannery. Isabelle requested another song, and they followed the lutenist's lead into the next tune. A real grin bloomed on Flannery's rosy face.

"She tells me she's heading north to Morwick, in Atlarand," Mam said, eyes on her drink. "I don't know her rush, but again, we won't send her away as long as she wishes to stay. At any rate, her visit has done you some good."

Tylysk's stare came so hard, he might as well have been breathing down my neck. I welcomed my mother's dismissal as much as Isabelle had. I spared the mage a glance as I left the table. He sat with the same professional air as his master, fingers laced together. His eyes stayed on Vespar, but he aimed his smirk perfectly.

The lutenist bowed to me, plucking an aimless melody, and the others followed his example. "We're honored to have such a captive audience," he said. "We seldom have visitors at our stage."

"There are too few players as fine as you," Isabelle said when Flannery found no words. "One more, before someone begs for a dance."

The viol player took the lead, immersing the group into the next tune,

"Mosey Bard," one of Da's favorites. It jumped, climbed, spiraled. Flannery's eyes shimmered. She mouthed the words in spite of herself.

Flannery caught Isabelle's contagious delight and applauded when the players bowed to her. Pink bloomed in her cheeks when she matched her smile to mine.

Quick as it came, her expression soured. Isabelle rolled her eyes.

I turned and jolted. Tylysk was hovering over me like the vulture he was. The mage stepped back and grinned, too pleased to see the heat crawl up my face.

"Have you always been so childish, or are you putting on a show for my sake?" Flannery asked, cocking a brow.

Tylysk dared to laugh. "No, indeed, milady. It's not my concern whether you like what you see."

Isabelle made to scold him, but Flannery interrupted. "Perhaps not me, but if Isabelle wasn't forced to endure your company, you wouldn't have any girl on your arm."

"If it wasn't for your pity, neither would he."

"Tylysk!" Isabelle hissed. I tried to draw Flannery away. The musicians stared.

Flannery shook my hand off her arm. "Does Master Rhys scare you, sir? You yap at him like he's stolen your favorite bone." Tylysk's easy grin slipped. "If not, you should let him alone. Your charm is as alluring as a pig's backside."

Tylysk somehow regained himself. "Forgive me, but I don't remember being in your charge, milady, and I'm certainly glad I'm not," he said, then gestured to me. "It's quite enough to be in his."

Tylysk flung himself backward when her fist met his face. Flannery toppled him with a foot to his gut. She swerved out of my reach and pinned him with a stomp on his chest, thrusting the air out of him. Isabelle screamed for them to stop while the musicians behind us stifled their snickers behind their hands. All other eyes turned to us. Mam and Vespar rose.

Tylysk's fingers scrambled at his belt for his dagger. I swiped an arm around Flannery's middle and wrenched her off him as the blade came free.

Isabelle's gasp made Tylysk sheathe his dagger before anyone else saw it, particularly Vespar, who hurried to separate us. Tylysk stood down when Isabelle hauled him to his feet, but Flannery yanked to free herself from my restraint.

"Enough!" Vespar hissed. "Will you make such a scene while the whole city watches?"

Flannery froze. She glared her bloodied victim down and ordered me to release her. She stayed beside me, head high, shaking the ache from her hand.

"Apologies, milord. Master Tylysk's behavior was so juvenile, I thought I'd return it in kind."

Tylysk cupped a hand under his dribbling nose. "I did nothing, my lord."

"You said plenty—"

"We're sorry, sir," I said, putting a hand in front of Flannery. "We—"

Vespar's stony expression shut me up. He looked to Isabelle, who bobbled between which side to take. He softened his tone. "Go get him cleaned up."

Tylysk slashed us with another glare, most of it striking Flannery. He let Isabelle guide him from the hall.

Flannery appeared more bored with the situation than I was stricken. She caught me staring and sent back a demanding glower.

Vespar rubbed his eyes. "I thought we'd settled this, Master Rhys. Several times."

I swallowed. "Yes, my lord."

"It wasn't his fault," Flannery scoffed.

Vespar's jaw tightened. "I'll speak with Tylysk. I presume other measures will be taken in the future."

"Yes, my lord," I said before Flannery opened her mouth. I thought she might smack me next, the look she gave me.

"Now," Vespar reclaimed her attention, "it is not my place to discipline you, milady, but had it been anyone else, there would have been consequences."

Flannery gritted her teeth and refused to look at him.

"I will say, should anything else occur during your stay, your family will hear of it."

"…Yes, milord."

As soon as Vespar turned aside, Flannery spun on her heel and stalked to the nearest door. I followed, ignoring Mam's calls.

"Milady—"

"That's it, then?" Flannery stormed down the hall. "You just let him win?"

"What was I supposed to do? Tylysk's a Mage Mas—"

"So? You're Master Claytherdon. I don't care who he is; he has no right to kick anyone."

"I'm sorry to offend you," I retorted. "Had I not come between you, he would've sliced you open without a second thought. I'd rather he kick me before that even crossed his mind."

Flannery slowed. She looked away. "At least he'll think twice before doing it again."

"If Master Vespar's censures haven't stopped him, neither will you, my lady."

"He kicks you regularly, I gather."

I fell into step beside her. "Ever since he went to the Academy. Tylysk hasn't left Vespar's side since."

"Now he's a Master and still as mature as the snotty boy that school made the mistake of accepting. Told you he was a pig. He needed a good beating."

"Is it just him, or is something else the matter?"

Flannery halted midstride. She put a bit of distance between us.

"It wouldn't be our mages, would it?"

The Countess watched the darkening windows. "Your mages are different from mine."

"Mine aren't terribly obedient to me yet." I braced myself. "Don't let Tylysk be the model of Gildio's mages."

She rolled her eyes.

"My lady—"

"It's nothing." Flannery strode ahead to her door, didn't slow for me to open it for her.

"I apologize for everything," I said. She paused in the threshold. "I hope I, at least, haven't offended."

Flannery's mouth tightened. She held her head high, but her gaze stayed on the floor. "Sorry I got you into trouble."

I offered her a half smile. "I was going to thank you next."

"Don't. Tylysk seems the kind to retaliate."

"True, but he has his pride to nurse, and who knows how long that will take?"

Flannery's brows rose. The corner of her red lips flickered upward. Saying nothing more, she closed the door behind her.

CHAPTER 8

Rhys

After I slept through breakfast the next morning, my lifelong, unflappable chamber servant, Stephan, brought a platter of buttered bread and jam, a summons from my tutor, and a warning not to keep him waiting. Much as I would've liked to, I scarfed down the meal and rushed into my clothes. After the incident with Flannery and Tylysk last night, Vespar's steely mood was bound to be more so.

As I moved down the hallway, I inspected myself, relaxed my shoulders, straightened my collar and cuffs. As long as Vespar found nothing amiss with my appearance, our discussion could at least start with just a remark on my punctuality. He answered my knock.

"Have you misplaced your comb again, Master Rhys?"

I smoothed my unruly fluff of hair down. "I woke up late."

"Apparently." He beckoned me inside.

I took one of the uncomfortable chairs in front of his desk. I waited for the fire and brimstone, as straight backed and poised as my nerves allowed. Vespar dropped into his chair, steepled his fingertips, and set his stare on me. A silence eked by until I thought the skin of my knuckles might tear from my grip on the arms of the chair.

"You're not a liar, Rhys."

I blinked.

"Certainly not a very good one."

"Sir?"

"We've both had time to ponder on your recent escapade." Vespar folded his fingers together. "Have you decided to come clean?"

"I have nothing to come clean about, sir."

"In other words"—he clipped the end of my sentence—"tell me where you went and what you did while you were out."

My mouth came ajar, but I said nothing. Emlyn and the garden house sprang to mind. I drove them from my head—the back of my neck started to tingle.

"I went where we used to go. To the market and the square. And the tavern."

"And what did you do?"

"Went to the tavern."

"What else?"

"Nothing." When he frowned, I added, "I wandered the square and watched the tinker performers."

"Did you meet anyone?"

I thought fast. "Some tinkers tried to sell me trinkets. They didn't recognize me."

"Did anyone?"

"One of the courtiers," I said, remembering the nobleman I barreled into in the street.

Vespar held another intense stare on me. He could see through me with his hawk-keen eyes. My heart pounded.

He shifted to the other arm of his chair. "And that was all."

I nodded.

He waited for me to reconsider. "If you wanted to see the caravan, why didn't you ask? Your mother or I would have accompanied you, or would have sent an escort at the very least. It would have spared us all of trouble, and your mother of grief. If nothing else, sun and stars, tell someone you're leaving," he said, voice as straight as ever.

I looked away. "Will I still have to hold my mother's hand when I come of age, sir?"

Vespar considered. "Fair enough," he said, to my surprise. "But how can I think to let you out alone when I myself take the precaution of at least one companion?"

I didn't answer. Tylysk wasn't a precaution. He just followed his master around like a strutting pup.

Vespar shifted back to the other arm of his chair. "I understand your need to escape, being a lad of your age." Something changed in his eyes—dare I say, they softened. "And you are your father's son, after all."

The strange gentleness of his tone made me smile. "Da was always out."

"He couldn't stand not to be." Vespar rolled his eyes upward. "Always restless, looking for adventure, finding trouble, always dragging me into it." He smiled at the memory. "Praises be, you inherited your mother's discipline rather than his. We'd be in far greater trouble had you not."

At least he still had no idea.

Vespar's face emptied, slipped to something downcast. "In fact, some argue it was your father's restlessness that took him."

My stomach flipped. "What?"

He shook his head. "Rumors started around the court that Ioan might have unwittingly crossed paths with some unsavory sort. For the kind of risks he took, the idea was not implausible. Rumors say he was cursed, and that is what brought his early death."

"That's not true. Da died of fever."

Vespar twisted his ring. "That we both know, but what made this fever worse than the others he overcame? Why did few else contract it?"

Ridiculous. Da was always sickly—even as a child, I knew some illness would take him. Everyone did. These rumors bruised his name.

"No one can prove or disprove there was such a curse," Vespar said. "Most never know they are cursed until it is too late."

His gaze intensified. A breath caught in my throat.

"Sir?"

The magical touch stung the back of my head and thrust me forward. Vespar extended a hand in front of him, his ringed finger calmly aimed at me. Then he tensed, brows narrow. He searched me, disregarding the pain he inflicted.

"Sir—"

"Did you meet anyone else?"

"No, I—"

His magic grip tightened. "No one?"

"No!"

"You lie. There's something there. Another magic." Vespar's spell coiled in the back of my neck.

"I would have felt it if someone cursed me. You know that!"

The surge brought me to my knees. Vespar moved from behind his desk, hand outstretched. "You've failed to detect this one. Stop resisting."

"I'm not—"

"Look at me!"

I obeyed. Vespar knelt at my side, his ringed hand inches from my face.

"I can remove it." Sweat beaded his brow as the grip in my head strengthened. A cry escaped me. "Listen to me. I can remove whatever holds you fast, if you will let me. Stop resisting. Let me help you."

His spell clawed through me, slashing to reach whatever it thought it had found. Vespar's fingers twitched. He shoved, driving a spike into my skull. I made no defense, resisted nothing. The agony doubled me over.

"Master, please!"

Vespar flung his hand away. The pain subsided. I collapsed on my side, hands clamped over my neck. A hot bitterness filled my mouth. I dabbed my lip with my sleeve and glared up at Vespar.

His jaw tightened with every heaving breath. "You feel nothing," he said, "but I know it's there."

I staggered to my feet and walked out.

I stormed down the hall. What had come over him? Had Vespar really used a curse himself to dispel what he imagined lurked there? Had he stooped to torture to find what I wasn't hiding? Torture. Vespar had tortured me. His superior, his Lord-to-be.

I halted midstride.

That was why my every conviction plagued him. This fatherless boy, young and malleable, whom he raised, was his superior. This boy who grew steadily unlike him until they stood face to face in ardent opposition was his Lord-to-be.

The pit of my stomach roiled with a matched hatred toward him, and it left me small and scared. For all the criticism and austerity my condescending mage tutor could deal, I had never hated him. Da loved him as a brother, and once, I thought of him as an uncle. Part of me wanted to believe that man still existed. But now I knew he didn't, nor ever would again.

Only then did it cross my mind, while I stood alone in the corridor, shrinking in on myself, that I was on the wrong side of Caeradin's most renowned mage.

Flannery waited for me at the bottom of the staircase with a book tucked under her arm. I dabbed the blood from my lip and twisted my sleeve from her sight. Still, her brows narrowed as I approached.

"What happened to you?" Her jaw clenched. "Tylysk."

"It wasn't Tylysk."

Flannery's lips tightened, her voice small. "It wasn't because of me, was it?"

"No, of course not."

My inquisitive look convinced her. "You should tell the Lady. Maybe she'll get rid of him."

"I don't believe she would, milady." I bowed. "Excuse me."

"No." Flannery stood in my path. "You told me you'd show me your garden today."

"My lady—"

"*Flannery.*" She emphasized each syllable. She waved me toward the door.

A breath of rain lingered on the breeze and glistened in the cloudy sunshine draping the greenery. It shimmered on Flannery's warm red hair. I shoved my hands in my pockets and let her lead the way. A few larks and swallows filled the silence between us until Flannery peered over at me.

"Isabelle says you like to hide out here."

"It's away from everything else," I said.

"It's nice. It's a different world out here." Flannery stooped and pinched a blossom, making its dragon's jaws gape. "I've never seen those in blue before. They're beautiful. And the lilies. Bleeding hearts, winter's craft, larkspur, rainveil…you have everything." She gazed out across the hedgerows. "I didn't know most of these could grow here."

Though she wouldn't like it, I said, "Anything can grow here if a mage makes it so."

"Then there's something good out of them after all." Her candor made her eyes sparkle. She shifted her gaze away too soon, to the spread of trees along the southern wall. "Come on."

Flannery thumped her book to my chest and led me to the nearest Melys tree. She wedged her foot on a protruding knot and hoisted herself onto the lowest branch. She peered down through the patch of broad leaves. "Are you coming?"

I stowed her book in my waistcoat pocket. "I haven't climbed a tree in…ages."

She rolled her eyes. "Hurry up."

Flannery scaled from one limb to the next, nimble as a cat. I clambered after her. We went high enough to find a settling place among the branches, and Flannery crawled into a pair of cradling limbs. I eased into a spot across from her.

She laughed. "Look at you, all scuffed up."

The precarious height beyond the reach of the world somehow relaxed me. The dark leaves emitted a warm, sweet scent. Flannery twiddled one between her fingers as she scanned the acres of garden, squinting in the late-morning light.

"That's a pretty garden house."

My heart lurched.

"It's perfect. The bluebells in the window box, the dainty red door." She watched Emlyn's hiding place until I thought she might leap from the tree and run for it. She lay back, plucked her leaf apart. "You really want to see Rivariar someday?"

"Absolutely."

When Flannery spoke of her home, she soon lost herself to it. She told me of her village, the orchard where she and her brothers and sister played, the geese they'd chase out of their yard, and how in the summer their father took them to a secret place near the Mystic's Lake. How, if you got high enough in the mountains to the north, you could see the White Towers of Elfryth, the points of a crown rising from the marble-white city.

I had far less to tell her of Gildio when she asked, but Flannery laughed at the tales of the misadventures Isabelle and I often found ourselves in when we were young. Unprompted, I wandered into memories of Da, speaking of him in ways I hadn't since he died. My mouth moved on its own, taking advantage of how sincerely Flannery listened.

"Master Rhys, sir?"

Flannery motioned to the ground when I failed to notice the tiny voice below us. I glanced down through the branches. Aria peered up at us, her cheeks blooming pink. She tucked her hair behind her ears and curtsied.

"My lady sent for you, sir."

"Thank you, Aria."

Another discomfited curtsy, and Aria ran to the castle.

Flannery watched her as we scaled down the branches. "I haven't met her yet."

I lifted her down the last leap. "Aria's my mother's handmaid. You'll have to forgive her. She's shy and…well…"

"Odd?"

"Well, no, she…" I stumbled, but Flannery understood. "She doesn't speak much, and hardly anyone but Isabelle and my mother see her often."

Flannery spotted the girl sprinting past the castle windows. "What is she, twelve?"

"Thirteen."

As we moved onto the garden path, she asked, "Would she, you know, be upset if I tried to talk to her?"

A smile crept up on my face. "No, I think she'd like that."

Flannery took her book back before we parted ways at the door. I watched her go. She hugged her book tight to her chest, and her shoulders inched up to her ears. She hurried away.

CHAPTER 9

Flannery

Flannery followed Isabelle through the stables, where they found Aria prancing about the bailey with Rhys's four hounds. The girl hurried over when called, but fidgeted when Isabelle introduced her to the "Countess." Flannery pretended not to notice. She asked about the dogs at Aria's heels, if she had a favorite of the horses in the stable, anything to get her to speak. Aria answered little more than a single word for each, peeking out from behind her hair.

"Odd" was a harsh word for her, Flannery soon understood. It seemed her mind had forgotten to grow alongside her bones. A young child's mind in a thirteen-year-old's head, troubled with compulsive curtsying and nerves. A clever girl—not at all slow, just impaired. Little wonder why Lady Orrtha loved her.

With Isabelle's coaxing, Aria's anxious fidgeting subsided. She let her dimpled smile appear. She never threatened to bolt. Isabelle had compared her to a skittish fawn, but Aria never proved the resemblance.

The girls sat out on the lawn, watching the dogs wrestle when Aria could no longer keep from touching Flannery's hair. The girl blushed and retreated.

"I'm sorry, milady."

"Not at all. You can play with it, if you'd like."

Aria scuttled back to Isabelle. She hid in the curtain of her straight brown hair. Isabelle hooked it behind the girl's ear, but Aria turned away.

"Tell Flannery how well you can dress hair," Isabelle said. "You dress Lady Orrtha's and mine for the banquets."

"Do you?" Flannery lured Aria's gaze with a gasp. She combed her fingers through her hair, which, after showing Rhys how to climb trees, better resembled a bird's nest than the curls she had conjured that morning. "Would you dress my hair for supper tonight, Aria?"

The girl's excitement escaped in a jittery curtsy.

Flannery had no inkling what brought her to take Aria under her wing. She doubted she'd last much longer at the Manor. When Vespar finally grasped the absurdity of his scheme, away Flannery and Abigail went, and Aria would be back to her virtually friendless life.

Not that Flannery cared, but she wondered whether the mages would think her friendship with Aria suspicious. As if the whole affair wasn't suspicious. As if Vespar could hide Flannery as long as he planned before someone found her out, and oh no, how could the Claytherdon mages not realize a witch stood right under their noses? Or what would the Claytherdon House think when he unveiled his trick and revealed her himself?

That was the perk of being Lord Mage, she supposed. He got away with everything.

Flannery led Aria to her chambers and thought no more of it. She sat at her vanity while Aria studied her array of jeweled hairpins. If despicable Tylysk deserved any credit, it was in the decency of what he charmed up for her wardrobe. He could have left her looking like a fair idiot, and she could've done little about it.

Aria had barely gathered a layer of Flannery's hair when a knock came at the door. As quick as the intruder entered, they might as well not have knocked at all.

Aria blanched. Before Flannery thought to stop her, she skittered under Vespar's arm and out the door without a curtsy. Vespar watched her burst down the hall, then dropped his gaze on Flannery, heavy as stone.

She ignored him. She loosened the unmade layers of her hair from the preparatory pin. Splendid timing, spooking Aria. If Rhys had spoken true about her lengthy disappearances, Flannery wasn't sure when, or if, she'd see Aria again.

Vespar shut the door, maintaining his usual coolness. "Is Master Rhys not charmed by your wit and pretty face?"

Flannery regarded him in the mirror. "Sorry?"

He came nearer. "Did you cast some spell before I asked?"

"Why would I? My sister's still downstairs, isn't she?"

"Someone has a hold on Master Rhys. You'll forgive my skepticism," Vespar said, matching her underlying sarcasm.

Flannery faced him, tapping her pin on the desk. "Someone? You don't know who? And you don't know what kind of hold, either. If you couldn't decipher it, *milord*, I couldn't set it."

Vespar's eyes reminded Flannery of flint in use. "No, not with a year's worth of training in a pit of thieves. Mind your place, girl."

Flannery stood, but had nothing to hurl back at him. She fisted her pin until the jewels pinched her palm. "Then why couldn't you?"

Vespar gave no answer. He rotated his ring. Though his eyes focused on her, his mind didn't. Flannery saw the busy work there, the flint striking for a flame that wouldn't come. In time, he looked down at his ring. Flannery glowered as he drew nearer, eyeing his magic trinket.

"He won't fight you," he said. "Do what you must. Find it."

Flannery snorted. "That's it? Rhys won't fight, but what about the other end?"

"If his captor thought to strike, he would have when I hunted for him."

"Him. Splendid. Not a witch."

"Whoever it is," Vespar interrupted, "will be slow to try anything more than block you. They risk doing Rhys harm."

"And you know that's not what they want?"

"You're going to find out, aren't you, my lady?" Vespar pressed his ringed finger under her chin and raised her face. The gold warmed against her throat. "Nothing more," he said.

"For my mother."

He released her, the gold grazing her jaw. He moved to the door. "He isn't what you thought, is he, milady?" Vespar turned back, his face empty. "Are you still inclined to kill him?"

Flannery faced the mirror, glowering at the mage's reflection as he moved through the door.

Long after Vespar had gone, Flannery moved. He demanded more than her confidence guaranteed. If she slipped because the force in Rhys's head resisted her, would Abigail hear of it? A scream hung leaden in Flannery's throat. She stormed down the corridor.

Rhys hadn't yet returned from his errands with Lady Orrtha. Flannery paced the long hallway twice, from the kitchen down to her chambers. She rammed into the servant Dom when she closed her eyes, trying to remember the words to the blasted spell. Dom bowed and asked if she was all right. Flannery suppressed her curtness long enough to reassure him. Truth told, she couldn't breathe.

On her third loop, she spotted him coming up from the stables. Rhys hadn't noticed her yet, as he fumbled a hand in his waistcoat pocket. Flannery hurried to meet him, heart threatening to break through her ribs.

Rhys peeked up when he heard her footsteps. He revealed that half grin of his and stuck his hands in his trouser pockets. The slight slump of his shoulders completed his gentle casualness, and Flannery almost liked it. He wouldn't fall over if she breathed wrong, unlike the other stiff-backed highborn they'd forced her to mingle with over the past two weeks. She fought to ignore the twinkle in his blue eyes.

Rhys bowed and graced her with a delicate "M'lady."

She flourished a curtsy. "How was your outing?"

"Wonderful." He slipped a hand into his waistcoat pocket. "I brought you something."

Flannery's stomach flipped. She smoothed a hand down the book's plum cover, traced the gold coiling border boxing the front. On the first page, a crescent moon bejeweled with stars created a letter *C* to begin the story.

"Even when you can't keep me out of your library?" she asked.

"You don't have to put this one back. The shopkeeper said it's popular. I thought you might enjoy it."

Flannery hugged the book to her chest. "Thank you," she said, and meant it. "You surprise me, too, you know. You're not what rumors make of you."

"Ah." His eyes twinkled all the more. "Good or bad?"

"Depends." Her eyes locked to his longer than she wanted them to. The spell itched her tongue. "Some people adore you. I've heard them say how you'll make an excellent lord, and they think you're ready. And of course, you could never escape a whispering girl's fancy."

Rhys laughed uneasily.

"And some people don't like you at all."

"Because I'm a Claytherdon."

Flannery blinked. That was it? The conversation shift made him comfortable. He wanted to have this discussion.

Rhys shrugged. "A name doesn't decide who I am for me."

Flannery acted before her curiosity piqued. Magic arose, a tingling mist swelling from within. It awaited her will, still as a breath. She centered the incantation in her mind, fixed her gaze to Rhys's.

"And who is that?" she asked.

Rhys stood frozen, unblinking. It spooked her, how suddenly empty he became. Nothing, not a thought, not a move. At least she found no pain in his eyes, unlike whatever Vespar had dealt him.

The fierce pulse of her heart quivered through her magic like a plucked string. But Rhys took no notice. Never blinked. Flannery's face warmed. She refocused and willed the spell to sink deeper.

The ghostly threads of magic drifted along the dark paths of Rhys's thoughts, caressing each piece it encountered. Images appeared in her own mind, seemingly unlinked, as they made no sense to her. A patch of hollyhocks, fingers dancing on a viol, a flagstone road, a book with no title, magelights, a tankard, a brass eagle door knocker, a child's face.

Then nothing. Deep, vaporous darkness, transparent and giving as a wall, halted the charm. But...as Vespar had said, something lingered behind the shadows. Flannery saw nothing, but detected some massive presence. She sensed what Rhys couldn't—a grip. Shackles, chains, hands clenched on a throat. An oath, perhaps a judge's sentencing, irrefutable, binding. No magic she'd ever felt before.

Rhys put up no resistance. Flannery took the risk and shoved. She had to find it. Whatever gripped him, Flannery had to get it, see it, anything. She had to take *something* back to Vespar. She had to know who gripped him.

Rhys blinked.

A spark of blue, and the shadow wall recoiled with a bowstring's force. It flung Flannery, spell and all, out of his mind.

Rhys put tentative hands on her arms when her knees slipped. "Are you all right?"

"Just tripped."

"You're shaking."

"No, I'm fine." Flannery regained herself. She smiled, though she wanted to scream. Though she had nothing to tell Vespar, and who knew what would happen to Abigail now? She smiled at Rhys, though it was his fault, his stupid fault, for getting her stuck doing this in the first place. Skin and bones, his fault any of this happened.

Why had Vespar unleashed her on Rhys instead of subduing the matter himself? What did Flannery care if it tormented the Claytherdon Lord-to-be? Let Rhys get what he and his slaughtering forebears deserved. Let that ignorant, stupid, despicable boy fall. With his ridiculous charm and hateful wit, his pathetic grins and outrageous faces that stole her breath. The horrid way he teased her with his "M'ladys" and the vile way her arm fit too well when looped through his. And the stupid way his hair brushed his brow and made her want to touch it.

Looking at Rhys, the clench in her stomach rose up and squeezed her heart until it suffocated her, and the tears started at her throat before welling in her eyes. She wanted to bury her face on his stupid chest and cry.

"You're sure?" he asked, taking his hands away.

"Yes. I'm wonderful." Flannery hugged the book tighter to her chest. "What were you saying?"

"…What were we talking about?"

Flannery strained to remember. "Your name," she said.

"And you asked…" She nodded, and Rhys considered. "Someone new. Someone unexpected."

Flannery tilted her head. "I didn't expect you to bring me a gift."

"Then you prove my point."

Rhys's bashful grin was so precious, Flannery could've stolen it.

She blushed and stared at her feet. "Thank you again. It means a lot to me."

"I…hope you like it."

They both shuffled awkwardly until Flannery couldn't bear to stand under his kind gaze any longer. "I should…go wash up for supper. It shouldn't be long."

"No, it shouldn't." He looked away.

Flannery tucked her hair behind her ear and remembered. "Oh, Aria…I had her all excited to do my hair, but— something scared her."

Rhys flickered between surprise and gratitude. "Really, you did?"

"Yes, but…"

"I'll find her. Isabelle can help me if I spook her."

Flannery copied his side smile. "She's not scared of you. She told me so. She likes you."

His grin brightened. He moved down the hall. "I'll find her, m'lady."

Flannery hurried toward her chambers. When she no longer sensed Rhys's eyes on her, she shook her head. It cleared nothing. She wondered what Abigail would think of her swooning over Master Claytherdon himself, while she cowered and starved in his dungeons, trapped by his mages ready to throttle her. Then Mother, and Papa. Her brothers, who would've disowned her if they found out.

Flannery halted at the unanticipated sight waiting outside her door. Tylysk slouched against the wall, a hand gripping the hilt of his dagger. The healer he saw the night before had worked wonders; to her disappointment, no sign of the black eye she'd dealt him remained. But she doubted it would've detracted from the prettiness witless girls gossiped about behind their hands. A shame he was so handsome. His good looks were wasted on him.

Whyever Vespar kept this tactless, immature lout in his good graces, Flannery would never know. Tylysk lacked the strict decorum Vespar demanded of everyone else, at least when Vespar wasn't looking. Poor Tylysk must've been terribly lacking in his master's attentions.

Tylysk eyed her figure. "That blue really is your color. Dare I say, you've caught my eye, milady."

"Then I'll be sure never to wear it again." Flannery held her head high. "You can tell your master it didn't work. Whoever it was pushed me out, and Rhys didn't last long, anyway."

"I noticed."

Flannery glared.

Tylysk crossed his legs, perfectly comfortable in his role as courier pigeon. "I think the mess in his head could be used to our advantage, don't you?" Tylysk's eyes sparked. "You're doing well. He's smitten."

Flannery turned away before she swatted him with her book. She reached for the door. Tylysk put a hand to it, held it firm. He stepped closer, towering over her.

"Keep it that way."

She found nothing to say. Tylysk slunk to the wall, challenging her with the raise of his brow. Flannery slammed the door behind her.

CHAPTER 10

Rhys

After the incident with Vespar and my "curse", the Manor fell quiet for several days. Once Vespar dismissed me from lessons, and I'd taken a proper beating in Swordsmaster Perreth's training ring, Flannery and I spent the afternoons roaming the garden or chasing the dogs across the bailey. Whenever Isabelle and Aria claimed her attention, I sneaked to Emlyn's hideaway. My first chance, I stowed my new gifts for Emlyn in my waistcoat and slipped out.

Fumes of lavender and herbal beles overwhelmed the cottage. A yellow haze choked the dry air. Emlyn leaped at me, her arms about my middle.

"Ash and flame, what are you doing in here?" I waved a puff of yellow from my face.

Emlyn pointed to the cauldron on the hearth. "I'm practicing." She grasped my hand and pranced to the kitchen. She stepped onto her stool to peer into the huge pot. Fresh lavender heads bobbed on the watery concoction, and strips of blue-green beles leaves surfaced between boiling bubbles.

"I just started." Emlyn gave the potion a churn. "It'll take a while."

I went to the open book on the counter. It was as big as she, leather bound and fraying. I squinted at the scrawl.

"Lindilum Fuil," I sounded out. "A Resilience Potion."

"It says, if you take a few sips, you won't have to eat or drink for a whole week. And it makes you strong, so you won't get hurt as easy." Emlyn waited for my approval with batting eyelashes. I lifted her onto the counter.

"Why'd you pick this one?"

"Just because."

"Have you ever made a potion before?"

"No."

I ran a finger down the list of ingredients. With measurements beside them, the tiny scrawl took up an entire page. "You know what all these are?"

"Some of them. Magic gets me the rest."

"How?"

Emlyn shrugged. "I tell it to."

I wiggled a finger over the book's scribbles. "You know what all this means?"

"Uh huh." She giggled at my expression, swinging her legs. I tickled her nose with the end of her braid.

"You're to clever for me, Emlyn."

Her blue-violet eyes glistened.

I took the tin from my pocket and opened it for her. She grinned and plucked up a hard strawberry candy. She gave the first to me and popped the second in her mouth.

"This, too," I said.

Wide-eyed, Emlyn took the storybook as though it were sacred and propped it on her lap. She leafed through its pages, admired each intricate illustration. Her candy had melted on her tongue by the time she clasped the book to her chest. "I'll keep it by my bed and read it every night." She sealed her promise with an embrace.

Emlyn sat back. "I saw you yesterday. You were with a girl. Who is she?"

"Her name is Flannery."

"She's pretty."

Emlyn's expression made me smile. "I think so, too."

"Do you like her?"

My brows shot up. Emlyn blinked at me, finding no fault with her frankness.

"I see you with her a lot. Do you?"

I leaned on the counter and said nothing.

Emlyn sucked on another candy. "You should take her a flower," she said.

"You think so?"

"Mm-hm." She scringed her mouth to the side and considered. "A daisy. I like daisies. They'd be pretty in her hair."

So when I went to meet Flannery, I brought her the fullest, brightest daisy the garden had to offer. Pleasant pink touched her cheeks when she took it. Our conversations became remarkably easier after that.

We both kept our distances from Tylysk. He never dealt any retribution for his bruised pride, but his smirks unnerved us as much as the anticipation of reprisal. I hardly expected him to go to the lengths Flannery had, but if he spied any chance to humiliate us, he'd leap for it.

Tylysk redirected his hostility from me to Flannery. She ignored him, and he happily accepted, for all it irritated her. But his petty attacks no longer provoked a testy counter. The Countess who first came would have sneered and spat back, not turned away. Tylysk wouldn't taunt her so, not while his pride should still be tender.

Though Flannery successfully disregarded him, something roiled within me each time he crossed my path. Some sore stirring in my chest, as though it physically pained me to see his ghastly face. My flesh stung and prickled at the mere mention of his name.

Mam kept a closer eye on me. She never dropped the idea that something lurked in my head. She'd grimace and ask about my headaches. When she got a quiet "Fine, Mam," she turned her worried frown to Vespar.

I slouched over the library writing desk, much to my tutor's chagrin, but he averted his attention to his parchments and strolled in slow, mind-numbing circles about the table. I stroked my feather quill up and down the stacked spines of the tomes towering over me and muttered whatever answer Vespar demanded of me.

"The weather has taken a turn, and the crops in Dellhaven are failing. Whom do you consult?"

"Master Gaige."

"Your delegates to Jeiosach?"

"Master Thorn and Mistress Renna."

"In a trade dispute with Itis—"

"Countess Cerda in the north, Count Aedmon in the southwest, Master Holm in the southeast…"

Vespar pursed his lips.

"We've only gone over these more times than I can count, sir."

"I've failed to notice," he said.

I watched him gather his books one by one. "May I ask you something?"

"So long as it's not for another parchment for you to waste on aimless scribbling." He swiped the page from under my arm.

I cleaned my quill. "You tell me that as Lord of Gildio, my most important duty is to the Hunt, yet you never speak anything of it."

"You've been less than interested in the subject."

"That's never stopped you before."

Vespar raised a brow. "At least you don't dispute other subjects, regardless of your interest in them."

I followed him about the library as he returned his texts to their shelves. "Then what will I do when I'm Master of the Hunt and know nothing about what I'm doing?"

"You know as much as is needed for now. As long as you can wield a pen, your task will not be too taxing."

"Just like that, you'd have me sign a woman's life away?"

"You know she is a witch, and you know her fate."

"And nothing else. Not her name, not where she comes from, how many children she may have left behind. How can you not see how merciless that is?"

"Again, you blame me for heartlessness, while the one misunderstanding anything is you and the Hunt's necessity." Vespar spun on me, shaking a book in my face. "Until you accept that, you are not ready for anything further."

He turned to the shelf, thumped another book into place. I took my dismissal. I made it as far as the end of the aisle, then turned back.

"When I become lord," I said, "I will find a way to save them, rather than standing by and waiting for someone else to."

Vespar didn't look at me.

Early the next morning, I sneaked to the library before lessons. I was bound to find something more about the Hunt than Vespar cared to share. Whatever he concealed, he must have thought I could wield it against him. I might, if it proved as valuable as he made it appear.

A magical Watch charm met me at the double doors. The too-familiar spell prodded more like a finger than a spike anymore. I cleared my thoughts and pressed on. The charm crawled through my head, sending shudders through my bones.

I wandered through the musty-sweet of books and parchments. The vast second-story window illuminated the narrow aisles of the tremendous room, while mageglow lamps mounted on the ends of bookcases gave way to sunlight. An elderly Mage Master shuffled about the balcony with an assortment of tomes riding on some spell over his shoulder. I followed the passage to the desk in the back, where the curtained windows opened to the bailey.

A stack of ready parchments stood on one corner of the desk, a magelight on the other. A quill already rested in an open ink bottle. I plucked up the slip of parchment pinned under a pair of unspectacular books and scrolls.

Study:

Basic Ethelfledian customs, including societal roles and rituals
Hunters and their roles

I glanced around. How did Vespar beat me here?

I tossed the slip back. Neither assignment would offer me anything new. I knew as much as I wanted about Ethelfled's grim warrior lifestyle—how every mother handed her infant, girl and boy, over to Hunting camps. Children never knew their parents, parents rarely knew each other. Hunting troops provided the bleakest semblance of family, if it could be called that. Most had gone on their first Hunt by fourteen. The few weak and unable settled for dishonorable tasks like breadmaking or tailoring. Wretched, but they bred those hard and cruel enough to execute the Hunt.

For the sake of saying I did as Vespar asked, I skimmed through the scrolls for the second topic.

Scouts located witches, retrievers captured witches, sentries guarded witches, captains gave orders and led the crew to Gildio. First Commander, Ethelfled's Lord Calibor, oversaw the ordeal. Master of the Hunt, me, organized, funded, and "finished" the job.

The Watch spell scuttled through my head, sent a judder up my spine.

I set the scrolls aside and cleared my mind. I wandered the aisles, empty, half hoping I might stumble upon something useful without trying. The mage holding me fast gave no sign of his presence, slinked about the way I did. I made a show and studied random texts, straightened spilling scrolls. The strange, painful roiling in my chest churned, and a ripple of chills tingled across my skin.

The eerie lurking game went on until I found myself at the foot of the staircase leading to the balcony. Anything helpful to my research would be up there.

The magic thread coiled low in the back of my head. It forced me through an oddly puppetlike motion, flopping backward and spinning toward the bookshelves. I took control of my limbs and steadied myself.

Tylysk twisted his invisible magic thread between his forefinger and thumb. I put a hand to my neck, where the charm squirmed.

"Do you mind?"

His fingers stilled. "Getting better at clearing your mind, Master Rhys? Or perhaps you're growing more empty-headed."

"Maybe if you didn't spy on me so often, I wouldn't be so practiced."

"Perhaps if you weren't so prone to trouble, I wouldn't need to spy."

"Oh, you took it upon yourself to look after me. How thoughtful."

"No, actually, the Lady asked me."

I glared.

"She worries when you won't watch over yourself," Tylysk said. "She'll take the measures you refuse to."

I rolled my eyes. "Not you too."

Tylysk shrugged. "You have no evidence to the contrary."

"For the hundredth time, I am not cursed." I brushed past him and moved down the aisle. "And why you would remotely care is beyond me."

Tylysk watched me walk away. "All you can deduce from not sensing the curse is that a mage is not responsible for it."

I glanced back.

"You only know how mage magic feels," he said. "How would you know if your captor were a witch or anything else?"

"Unless you've let a witch slip through your fingers, I can't imagine how that's possible."

"Unless you stumbled into one during your escapade."

I swung on him. I drove Emlyn from my mind before Tylysk spotted her. He interrupted as I opened my mouth.

"How coincidental that your curse should present itself just days after such a stunt. They say the same thing happened to your father."

Rage readied my fist to meet his teeth, but a firm hand clinched my wrist.

"Enough, both of you." Isabelle faced Tylysk. "Master Vespar will have both your hides if you make a mess in the library."

Tylysk's face softened within a flicker of his eyes between us. "There you are, milady," he said, sincere as the smiles he sickened her with. "You always know when you're needed."

"I was suspicious when I saw you coming in here," she said. "I'd always assumed you thought your mountain of knowledge surpassed the library's, as seldom as you visit it." Isabelle grasped my wrist. "Come on, Rhys."

Tylysk caught her hand. "Let me. Master Rhys has a mountain of studying to do himself."

I gritted my teeth and drew Isabelle away. Tylysk clutched her fingers. She stood caught between us, arms widespread. Tylysk reached his other hand to draw her nearer.

Isabelle yelped when I wrenched her aside. It jostled Tylysk backward. I thrust Isabelle behind me and squared the mage with a glare.

"Leave her alone."

Tylysk's smirk vanished. His hand inched toward his dagger.

Isabelle touched my arm. "Come on, boys, this is getting—"

I swiped at Tylysk and missed. Isabelle shrieked. The dagger came free, but went no higher. Tylysk glanced at Isabelle. She minded his warning and stepped back.

"Rhys, stop. Leave Tylysk alone."

"He should leave."

Tylysk studied me hard, the way his master would. The remainder of his Watch charm fizzled, but his dagger hovered at his hip. "If you lay a finger on her—"

"Don't. Touch her. Again."

He stood his ground. Red humiliation crossed his face, but with one more glance at Isabelle, he retreated, no doubt to tattle on us.

Isabelle touched my back with trembling fingers. "Rhys, what are you doing?"

I turned. She ducked away, eyes wide. Seeing her terror, I relaxed my fists and tightened limbs. Sudden exhaustion swept my knees from under me. Isabelle caught me before my head cracked on the floor. She propped me against a bookcase.

"Sun and stars, what's wrong with you?" she demanded.

I had no answer. I hardly remembered what happened, that Tylysk had been there. My head pounded with every hard, short breath. I gawked at Isabelle.

I must've looked pitiful. She put her arms around me. "Easy. Calm down."

"What was he talking about?"

"It doesn't matter."

"I frightened you."

"You're frightening me now, the way you are. Rhys, breathe, will you?"

I couldn't with my heart smashing against my ribs and my body trembling, sweat coursing in cold trickles down my brow.

Especially not when Flannery found me in a pathetic heap on the floor. She rushed to our side. "What happened?"

"Nothing." I sat myself up from the bookcase.

"I saw Tylysk leave."

"They had a scuffle," Isabelle blurted.

Flannery cinched up her sleeves and stood.

I took her hand. "Forget him. It was nothing."

She snorted. "Nothing, my—"

"Please. Let's…go out to the garden."

Flannery relented. I refused either of their help to stand. Flannery looped my arm through hers and kept me on my feet. Isabelle followed us to the back door before Flannery assured her she had things in hand.

"Isabelle," I said, "don't tell Mam. She's worried enough."

She searched for Flannery's opinion before she yielded. Flannery grabbed my wrist and pulled me out the door.

"Come on," she said.

"Where are we going?"

Flannery dragged me down the path without an answer, not noticing how I watched the sun on her autumn hair. Something in her steadying grasp eased my breath. She said nothing until we lost ourselves deep in the hedges.

"Aha. There. Sit."

We dropped on the stone bench we found. Glancing over the flower beds, Flannery spotted a single stray daisy rooted in a patch of foxgloves and iris. She pointed to it.

"Watch that flower and tell me how much it's grown when I ask."

I raised a brow. "How?"

"Not by looking at me." She turned my face back. "Watch."

Silence collapsed on us, Flannery content in whatever scheme she had concocted. I stared at the drooping flower. A breeze tousled its petals.

"I don't see—"

"I didn't ask yet." Flannery stood and crept a distance down the hedges. When she caught me staring at her gathering windswept blossoms, she waved me back to the daisy. After several long minutes, she turned from her work of bunching the blooms into a tiny bouquet. "Well?"

I shrugged.

"You're not concentrating hard enough." She knocked her knuckles against my skull. "Forget everything else. *Watch*."

I planted my elbows on my knees and watched the daisy. It had a dainty beauty, despite its raggedness. Its bright white fingers and gold face shone stark against the deep fuchsia and indigo crowding it, and it lacked the elegance of the other flowers. Perhaps that was what made it more beautiful than the rest.

One of its petals fell away.

"Well?"

I shrugged. "A petal fell."

"What do you gather from that?"

"…Er…"

"The flower has changed, yes?"

"Yes."

"Do you think the flower did that on purpose?"

My brows knitted together.

"Do you think the daisy did that because you were watching?"

"No."

"Do you think the daisy itself had anything to do with the petal falling? Or was it an outside force, like the wind?"

"Both, I suppose."

Flannery nodded sideways, agreeing. "So what part did the daisy have?"

I stared.

She knelt at the flower bed and rested a hand under the daisy's head. "What if the petal was hurting the flower?" She plucked the white blade from the soil. "Maybe it hindered the flower's growth, and maybe there was no other way to cure the problem."

Flannery moved her hand from the blossom. Somehow, the daisy stood noticeably straighter, rid of some indiscernible weight. A tiny difference, but its face raised higher toward the sunshine.

Flannery made a plucking motion next to my temple. "Let the petal go. Holding onto it won't change what was or is or will be. You have to let go"—she released the white petal to twirl down at my feet—"before you can move forward."

I blinked. How did she…

"With what, my lady?"

She straightened. "Anything, I suppose."

The daisy swayed in the wind, sighing, its face upward to drink in the sun.

Flannery took the seat beside me. "They rip petals off in there," she said, nodding toward the castle. "But that harms a flower worse."

"Are you calling me a daisy?"

She wrinkled her nose. "A dainty little daisy."

"Then are you the wind?"

Flannery's eyes glistened. "The wind can coax, but it can't catch the petal until the flower lets it go."

She went pink under her freckles. She chewed her lip and turned away, her long autumn hair between us. I looked down, my heart thudding hard.

"Up to the flower now," she said, and stood.

I watched the daisy a moment longer before following her. "Where did you come up with that?" I teased.

"My mother showed me when I was small." Flannery frowned. "She told me keeping my head down is always worse than raising my voice. Silence lets the wound fester."

We meandered through the hedges. Flannery kept her fingers on the rough green, caressed it as she walked. I wasn't sure whether she held her other arm that way to invite me to take it. I stuffed my hands in my pockets, cringing at myself.

"Vespar thinks someone's gotten into my head," I blurted. "He thinks it's a witch. I can't decide if I believe him."

She frowned. "Why?"

"I've never met any witches," I said, looking away from the garden house. "I don't feel anything wrong. Nothing out of the ordinary. Except, today, when Tylysk…"

"They say you can't remember meeting a witch," said Flannery. "They say witches know spells to take your memory of them. Of course, you know that, don't you?"

I couldn't tell whether frankness or contempt came through her voice. I shrugged. "I think it's all exaggerated. They make witches sound worse than they are."

Flannery spun on me. "What? You're serious?"

"Yes. And I don't think one has a hold on me. I don't know why they're so insistent."

She folded her fingers tight around her tiny bouquet of stray blossoms. "That's what you meant by someone unexpected."

I plucked a flower from the hedge.

Flannery's lips pinched. "That's why Tylysk beats on you and Vespar hammers down on you. Why haven't you told me?"

"Force of habit, I suppose. I'm always scolded when I tell someone."

"You thought I'd scold you?"

"You'd think I was mad."

"I do." She walked backward in front of me. "Wonderfully mad."

Her smile emboldened me. I stopped her as she made to fall into step beside me. "Flannery, I want to tell you something."

Vivid pink bloomed on her face. "Finally," she teased, but gave a discomfited laugh. She fell serious, matched my sorry frown.

"A few weeks ago, Vespar found eight witches hiding in a cellar in the Lower Side of the city. He said there were children with them. Little ten or eleven-year-old girls. Ten years old—what could a ten-year-old have ever done to deserve…"

Flannery stared at her feet. I tossed the flower aside so I wouldn't crush it.

"I can't do this. The entire country expects a brutal Master of the Hunt to lead the troops to slaughter. I'm not. I won't. I can't be a lord of murderers. I have to stop the Hunt."

Her bouquet fell from her fingers. Flannery staggered. She stepped away when I moved to catch her.

"Flannery?"

She paled. Her hand pressed tight to her mouth, her freckled knuckles white.

"I'm sorry. I didn't mean—"

She sprinted through the hedges.

I heard the door open and shut. Flannery glided past the windows, her fiery hair streaming behind her. I scrubbed my watering eyes and roared at myself.

CHAPTER 11

Flannery

lannery smashed herself to her antechamber door. For all the agonizing strain of her stifled sobs, nothing escaped her. The knot in her throat swelled with every wracking breath.

That was what he'd been hiding all this time. Vespar had never said a word. How perfectly Flannery fit into his plot. Get a good grasp on Rhys's heart, and when everything unraveled before his unsuspecting eyes, give it a nice shattering. Let Rhys see for himself all the ruin and anguish a witch would leave in her wake.

Flannery sank to the floor.

Why tell Vespar? He already knew Rhys's mind. Flannery would betray Rhys's ultimate trust, and Vespar knew it. Then came the unraveling, the world plummeting out from under him, when no one but his Lord Mage could save him.

How dare she be the wretched child to tattle on him and spill his soul when Rhys had every power to save her? It wouldn't be long before he brandished his blade. Flannery believed it—she'd never seen such fire in the soft pools of his eyes. He'd try, whatever came of his beautiful rashness. Rhys could save her, and ash and flame, he'd see it done.

But what of Abigail?

Flannery buried her face in her lap. What did her freedom matter if they denied the most precious soul the same? How could Flannery exchange her sister's life for Rhys? No matter what choice she made, they had no hope. Stay her course and be a good slave, and only Abigail would live. Desert to Rhys's side, and only Abigail would die.

Flannery's heart had never felt so empty, yet ready to burst. And ached, like the hollow of starvation, swollen with bruises from too many hands casting it back and forth.

She wanted him. She couldn't leave him. If Vespar didn't kill her, that would.

But Abigail. Their mother.

She'd be brave, that precious girl with cinnamon freckles and eyes so green Papa always said the hills never compared. Abigail would face those mages for every other lost child. For every other parent mourning for their daughters.

Flannery sobbed until her teeth ached and salt stung her cheeks, until her stomach couldn't take the brutal pounding from her lungs anymore.

The knock at the door jolted her.

Flannery remembered to bother with her tears and ugly nose before she stood. Here he'd come to apologize for no wrong, and she'd pounce him. Smother herself in his chest, gulp up his nearness until her heart emptied out her throat and he knew everything. Until she was no longer Countess Flannery, but just Flannery.

She flung the door open. Tylysk blocked her from slamming it in his face.

"Don't you come in here," she screeched. "Get out!"

She had no strength to stop him. She moved aside before the door squashed her to the wall. Tylysk stood in the threshold, brows pinched.

"Should I come back later?"

The softness of his taunt didn't fool her. "Don't come back at all."

Tylysk shut the door. Flannery stood far from him, put the table between them.

"Did he hurt you?" he asked.

"How dare you suggest?"

"Then what's the matter?"

"You."

"Have I made you cry?"

Flannery glowered at him. Tylysk avoided her gaze, oddly discomfited. He roughed the front of his dark blond hair when she squinted at him too long.

"You haven't yet, you never could," she said, head high. "You're not worth tears."

"Your tears, anyway." Emboldening himself, he met her eye and squared his shoulders. "Anything to tell me? Rhys is a poor lost pup out there."

"Not in the least."

Tylysk examined her with Vespar's intensity. Flannery blushed at his expression, waited for him to pat her head. He leaned with the heels of his hands on the table, and his fingers drummed the underside. He as good as sneered, that pitying glimmer in his eyes and all. He stooped his head to catch her low gaze.

"Oh, you poor lamb. That wasn't supposed to happen."

Tylysk might as well have had a hand around her throat. "Go away," she breathed.

"What now? Have you told him?"

"'Course I haven't."

"You should."

"Why? So you can gut him when I'm through with him?"

He tilted his head back and forth, eyes raised. He crossed his ankles. "Did you think something could come of the two of you?"

Flannery was tempted to topple the table on him. "I said, go away."

"How would it look, Master Claytherdon and a witch? Would you disgrace him?"

"He wouldn't think it a disgrace," she burst. "He wouldn't care what anyone thought. He'd love me all the same."

Tylysk cocked a brow. "Ah, that's what he said."

If her glare could set fire, he would've been ablaze.

The mage dared to wander around the table, a finger following the grain of the polished top. Flannery gave him no satisfaction in a retreat.

"You didn't think to keep it from us, did you?"

"You already knew, you noxious lout."

"Oh, but now you do too. And knowledge is power, so they say, and a witch with power is what got us here in the first place."

Flannery might've tackled him, but she faced him alone without Rhys to rescue her from her blind rage and Tylysk's dagger. The vulture towered over her, a full head and shoulders taller, she with no strength to lift her gaze. She sulked like a child, dreading his hand on her head.

"Master Vespar won't be surprised by your feelings," he said, "nor that you think something can be done about them. What I'd love to see is how Lady Orrtha will take it."

"You leave his good mother alone."

"You'll even defend the Lady before yourself, and she'd have you out before the hour. Has Rhys changed you so much?" Tylysk leaned with a fist on the table. "She'll hear of it, and you watch her stiffness with you."

"You have what you want, now leave me alone." Flannery thought of a thousand things to deal at him, but her foot stomped on its own and missed his entirely. Furious red surged up to her ears. Tylysk said nothing but with a silent laugh through his nose.

"You'll come tell them yourself."

"Touch me, and I'll break your arm."

"I'll believe it when you prove it."

Flannery swung a backward fist to knock his arm out from under him and have him face down on the table. He put one foot back, and she missed. Tylysk clutched her flying arm as the other fist shot forward. He snatched the other as easily. Flannery stood trapped, arms crossed, and her brothers would've smacked her for her stupidity.

Her fingers tensed close to Tylysk's face. The mage thrust her backward and lurched away. His dagger came free. Flannery drew one hand to her cheek and extended the other.

"Don't you dare," Tylysk hissed. "You'll die where you stand."

"Then don't touch me."

He directed his knife between her eyes. Though he stood halfway across the room, it seemed close enough to see her breath on its gleaming steel. "Don't ruin it now," he said. "Not when you're so close."

"To what? Ruining him? To abandoning him? Escaping this prison while he stays?" The spell prickled Flannery's fingertips.

Tylysk shifted his feet, hands quirking. He licked his pale lips. "Whatever you do to me, your sister will get in turn. Think, girl."

The words sat square on her tongue, ready to bend the threads of magic. Heat blazed on her palms. Tylysk eyed every twitch of her fingers. Concentration beaded sweat on his brow.

"Think."

Flannery drew her hand back. The other fell leaden at her side.

Tylysk kept his stance until her tears puddled in the corners of her mouth. He took slow steps toward her, one hand ready, but he sheathed his dagger. His shining leather boots almost touched toe to toe with her slippers. He raised a finger an inch from her face.

"You'll come now, or I'll have you over my shoulder."

Flannery glared.

Tylysk doubled over.

"Don't, don't you dare!" Flannery leaped back. "Hands off, pig, I'm coming."

He motioned for her to lead the way. Only his threat kept Flannery moving when they found Vespar in Lady Orrtha's council chamber.

Strange, how quickly the Lady exchanged one demeanor for another. The sight of Flannery's tear-brimmed eyes stood her up with worry. With Tylysk a stride behind, the witch approached the Lady's desk and relayed what had happened in the garden, struggling against her thick, scalded throat. Lady Orrtha's keen eyes and womanly intuition read enough into her few words. Her expression then: delicate pity, kind, but as if she looked on the child she never wanted.

Vespar said nothing. He and Tylysk exchanged glances. Tylysk beckoned Flannery away.

"My lady," she blurted, "I'm sorry. No one deserves this, Rhys especially. I've never known someone so kind, and no doubt from his good mother. I would never, *never* hurt him. No one has been better to me than your son."

Lady Orrtha pressed her white knuckles to her lips.

Tylysk seized Flannery's wrist and dragged her out the door. Before Tylysk closed it behind her, she spied Vespar kneeling beside the Lady's chair. He gathered her hands in his as she wept.

Flannery ripped from Tylysk's grasp and stalked away. "You're cruel to her. Not a thing you can do to a soul without breaking a mother's heart."

"She'd be worse if we did nothing to save her son."

"Saving him from compassion, is what you are. From kindness and mercy and all the good in the world."

"What is good in the world with another lord at your throat? Master Rhys would find no compassion from anyone of importance."

"So security is what this is? Ha. Instead of your armies, you put women and their daughters on the front lines."

"How unfortunate Magic claimed you and affluence didn't, poor girl," Tylysk smirked. "You would have made an intriguing diplomat."

"Had I been a man claimed by magic and no affluence, it might have happened all the same."

"A shame we'll never know."

Flannery swung around, halting Tylysk in his tracks. Her eyes stung, and her wretched nose muted her voice, but she faced him.

"Then what am I to you?"

He looked down on her with an unimpressed twitch in his cheek, as if mud and filth drenched her entire being, dripped from her hair and crooked limbs. She was repulsive, and he was far too much a gentleman to expose his true disgust.

He stooped, came eye to eye with her. The hair on the back of Flannery's neck prickled.

"You are a witch. You are a temptress, a deceiver, and as callous as any there was. You feign your guiltlessness and lure away blind innocents, soil Magic with every kind of vulgar deed, until the light that might have been in you is dark, and all that might have been good is disgraced, and with all your power you would ravage everything without thought, until either there is nothing left, or another good man gives his life to see you ended."

Flannery was a child then, fragile, not knowing what to do. He so much greater than she.

And the world just like him.

CHAPTER 12

Rhys

Between lessons, Emlyn, and Flannery's stay, time escaped me before I knew how much of it had gone.

A step into the castle reminded me. Servants hefted banners and tablecloths about, balanced stacks of dishes and platters to dress the banquet tables. I peeked into the great hall. A handful of mages made quick work of setting out the long tables and benches and freshening the candles in the iron chandeliers. One mage charmed the Gildian black eagle banners to drape from the high arches once a pair of women finished pressing them. Lizzie and Violet huddled on their knees, polishing the oak floor until their faces gleamed back at them.

The Midsummer feast. Flannery and Emlyn had been at the Manor for two months.

Thinking back, I might have suspected the Countess of traveling to stay with relatives for the festivities. She never mentioned her family in Atlarand, nor any of her travel plans. Not a word on leaving. Curious, but I said nothing about it. The thought of her leaving was a gulp of water to the lungs.

I squeezed out of the way of the women lugging baskets of goblets and silverware. I trudged down the corridor, hands in my pockets, heart under my feet.

Mam hurried in my direction, not noticing me until I veered out of her way. Haste reddened her face, and a lump bubbled in the front of her hair from fiddling with it too often.

"There you are." Mam caught her breath. "Wash up and get changed. Stephan has a new set of clothes for you. He'll be in to see they fit you."

"Yes, Mam."

She froze, gaze flickering between floor tiles. "What was I doing?"

"The rushes, Mam." I steered her toward the great hall. "You sent Dom with the rushes."

"That's right. Off with you." Away she went, her bustling chamberlain close at her heels.

The leather jerkin Stephan brought me fit well enough over the crisp white shirt, if a touch loose. He cinched up the straps and polished his fingertips from the silver buckles. A step back, a brief inspection, and he smiled.

"You are your father, indeed, my lord," he said. "Your mother's been saving this for quite some time."

I stood with my arms out, forgetting to breathe. "This was Da's?"

"Yes. He rather liked this one. He thought he sported it right well, indeed." Stephan straightened the jerkin on my shoulders. "She hoped it would help you stand as tall and proud as he always did."

I glanced myself over. I'd wondered why the ensemble seemed familiar. The faint scent off the leather collar was Da's, the blend of fresh earth and cider. Part of me warned to take it off before I somehow tainted it. Another clung to this piece of Da strapped about me.

Stephan cleared his throat. "Your boots there are polished. And don't forget that wet fluff on your head, my lord." He bowed and closed the door behind him.

The novelty of Da's jerkin didn't distract me for long. It entangled my nerves all the more. The comfort Mam hoped for became the reminder of what lay ahead, what I had to prove. I spared myself a glance in the mirror. No one but Mam would understand its significance, but wearing it brought the eerie sense of the world watching for my next move.

My heart thumped against my ribs as I plodded to Flannery's door. I had no idea what to say to her, since I'd gone and ruined the past two months. What had I said wrong? Shouldn't she be glad to hear my stance? Shocked, yes, but wouldn't a Rivarian Countess be pleased to know I planned to end the Hunt?

I frowned. Too pleased, perhaps? A good explanation for the hesitancy my mother strove to conceal around Flannery. The same happened with Isabelle, when her Atlarandian parents called off our engagement until Vespar set my rebellious ideals at bay.

I understood Mam's wariness. The political clash between Rivariar and Gildio was unsavory, but that would soon change. Mam tried and extended an awkward hand of fellowship in helping and protecting Flannery.

And Rivariar stayed. Flannery stayed.

The door opened as I raised my hand to knock. Aria emerged and blushed to the tips of her ears. She shut the door, offered a delicately clumsy curtsy.

"She's almost ready, sir," she said, voice breathless.

"Did you dress her hair, Aria?"

The girl let her chestnut brown tresses hide her face.

"Flannery told me she likes to have you dress her hair. She's glad you're her friend."

Aria curtsied. She shifted from one foot to the other, ready to bolt. I followed her gaze up to the damp fluff I'd forgotten on my head. I bent down.

"Here. I can't have the court see me like this."

Panic crossed her face, but Aria inched nearer. I kept still as stone, and she swept my hair from my brow. She stepped back to curtsy.

"Thank you, Aria."

She smiled at me for the first time. She burst down the hall and out of sight.

I leaned against the wall and waited, twiddling my peace offering between my hands. I tucked the gift behind my back at the sound of the door latch. Flannery crept out, inspecting herself uncertainly.

"Well?"

She grinned—my face answered for me. She was a sunburst of scarlet and gold in shining satin. Teardrop rubies glittered on her throat and ears. Garnets pinned her hair from her face, and a gold diadem nestled on the back of her pristine curls. She spun a circle, giggling a little.

"M'lady." I bowed and kissed her fingers. "I'm glad to see you so cheerful."

"Why shouldn't I be? I love Midsummer. And I feel fit for the White Towers."

"You are," I said. "They'd think you were a princess of the High Kings."

"You're a right handsome High Prince, like Caedbed himself." Flannery smoothed my collar.

I told her about Da's jerkin. She studied me closer.

"I wondered if you'd leaped out of the portrait in your mother's chambers."

It warmed me a little. I extended my peace offering. Flannery brightened and held the tiny bunch of flowers to her nose.

"I always liked forget-me-nots. Are you trying to tell me something?"

I grimaced. "I'm sorry."

"That would be a hyacinth. But I like these better." Flannery petted the blue blossoms. "You have nothing to apologize for, anyway."

"I upset you."

"You astounded me. But I should be sorry. I shouldn't have run and left you out there."

"Then…you're not upset?"

"Relieved, actually."

I finally breathed. Flannery hid her laugh behind her flowers. She hooked her arm through mine.

We took the long way to the great hall, circumventing the massive double doors where the mob of guests filed from the bailey. The steady court chatter drowned the musicians' tunes already pouring from the hall. With the doors wide, the tangy smoke of Midsummer bonfires wafted in from where they speckled the hills beyond the Manor walls.

Flannery twirled a lock of her hair around her finger. It glistened intermittent silver and gold cast by awakening magelights and the sunset through the windows. "My brothers always make the biggest bonfire in the village," she said. "Everyone else stopped building them, and they just come to ours." She looked me over. "They'd like you. And Abigail would adore you."

Flannery always hesitated when mentioning her sister, but this time seemed to pain her. She swept her gaze across the garden beyond the windows.

"Did you mean what you said? You'll try to end the Hunt? How did they not beat it out of you?"

I told her how Da would have done the same had Vespar not stifled him, and if his relentless fevers hadn't taken him so soon.

"What about the Lady?"

I shook my head. "Mam hates it, but I don't think she ever felt the same as Da. Besides, she'll do anything Vespar says. As long as he's in favor of it, so is she."

Flannery frowned. "She doesn't have much choice, does she? I admire her courage, though, to go it alone without her husband. At least she has you." Flannery's smile brightened the shaded corridor. "If anyone can see this wicked Hunt ended, it's you. And you'd better, else I'll haunt you the rest of your days."

A tease rode her laugh, but a heavy grief dimmed the spark in her eyes. She looked away when I stared too long. I stopped her, glanced down the corridor for any onlookers.

"Flannery, is Abigail…"

She blanched.

"Ah."

"Rhys."

"No, it's just…that's why you hated the mages and never wanted to be here, and…well, you wouldn't even look at me at first."

Flannery gripped my arm. "Rhys, please—"

"It stays here. No one will know."

We strolled on, neither of us able to meet the other's eye. We said nothing more until we came to the side door into the great hall. I reached to open it, but Flannery grasped my hand. My heart pounded. She stared at her feet.

"You're right. I had no idea what to make of you. I wanted you to be like them, so I wouldn't feel guilty about what I thought of you," she said. "It's easy to hate someone cruel. But I was cruel to you when you offered me every possible kindness. You've even rescued me from Tylysk."

As terrible as it had been in the moment, I rather relished the memory of Tylysk's bloody nose. Flannery's temper both terrified and thrilled me. I brushed a thumb across her pale knuckles.

"What's cruel is what you expected to find here. No one else would have thought or done anything different. I'm a Claytherdon."

"But you said so yourself. That name does not define you. Neither you nor your father deserves the reputation that comes with it."

I shook my head. "If the rest of Caeradin would think the way you do."

"You have to change their minds, too." Flannery straightened the collar of Da's jerkin, avoiding my eye. "When you do, you'll be the greatest lord that Gildio has ever seen, Rhys Claytherdon."

"M'lady."

I suddenly tasted her tears on her mouth. Stunned, I caught my breath, overtaken by the sweet violet perfume of her hair. A flare of heat rushed through my entire being and prickled my skin. Succumbing, I took her face in my hands. Her blushing cheeks were soft as dewed rose petals.

Flannery stood away, scarlet rising to her ears. "Sun and stars…" She hid her face in her fists, turned her back.

I grasped her hand, determined not to let her bolt again. I dabbed the tears from her freckled cheeks, drawing more from her. Her quivering smile had never been more beautiful, nor had it tempted me like this before.

"I should have told you sooner," I said.

She laughed. "If only you had."

I kissed her, this time savoring it. The thrill of it, the shape of her supple mouth, her resolve. Her trembling fingers on my jerkin, tugging me closer, climbing up my chest, my neck, skimming along my jaw. My palm followed the line of her taut throat to the nape of her neck, and my fingertips explored the soft curls of her fiery hair.

Flannery and I staggered apart when the door opened, knocking me aside. To our horror, Master Vespar himself halted in the threshold. He glanced between us, seeing our squashed mortification, but graciously ignored it.

"Master Rhys. My lady. If you would join us at the table. The hall is full already."

"Of course, sir." I motioned for Flannery to enter ahead of me. I followed her red-faced scurry past Vespar.

"And, Master Rhys?"

I turned back, face burning worse. Vespar examined me, from my polished boots to the damp fluff Aria had fixed on my head. He nodded.

"That looks very well on you."

I blinked. For all my astonishment, I almost didn't say, "Thank you, my lord."

Flannery and I hurried to the dais and peered across the hall. Four long tables edged close to the walls left room for dancing. Glistening serving platters bore as many roasts, meat pies, and dressings as there were baskets of fruits and pastries. A mixed aroma of herbal seasonings, fresh baking, and wine set our mouths to watering.

Mam sat in her high-backed chair, nervous Aria at her side. She stroked a hand down the shoulder of Da's jerkin, beaming brighter than she had in years. The words she longed to say refused to come. She turned her cheek for me to kiss.

We took our places to the Lady's right, Vespar to her left. Tylysk and Isabelle claimed the last two seats on Vespar's side. Isabelle rolled her eyes as Tylysk towed her along, but winked when she noticed Flannery's hand resting on mine. Despite Tylysk's distracting efforts, Flannery exchanged a frequent girlish glance with Isabelle and ignored Tylysk altogether.

The last of the guests trickled in and looped by the dais before taking their seats. The nobles bowed to the Lady before greeting us. Tylysk's Mage Master friends were polite enough, besides being too loud and eyeing Flannery too long.

One kindly, senile old woman who used to pinch my face when I was small grinned and stepped up to the table. "Is there to be an announcement, you two?"

Flannery and I reddened, but she squeezed my hand.

"Oh." The woman covered her mouth and winked. "Must be a surprise. Don't mind me." We kept quiet long enough for her to hobble out of earshot before we broke out laughing.

Flannery spoke more during the feast than she had any meal her entire stay. She laughed, set her emerald eyes to glittering. She paid the musicians their share of attention, as always. Her fingers followed their melodies, pressing lightly on the back of my hand.

Halfway through the second course, a wave of applause and cheer overtook the hall as old Mage Master Quil rose from his seat. He raised a hand, waiting for quiet so he could begin his annual epic. Each segment of the story of Farawl Silverblade's quest to retrieve the lost crown of the High Kings grew more magnificent every year, with ravaging beasts and battles against the wicked Lady Blodica's forces. Master Quil prowled the hall, a lion stalking to mesmerize the court.

"And so, weary, having suffered many wounds, and having found no fortune in the lairs of the Enchantress's minions, Farawl made to return to Elfryth," Master Quil said. "He longed for the sight of the splendid White Towers again, for his kin, for all he had sacrificed to take on his perilous quest. He only hoped it all remained standing when he returned.

"Yet, what should await him at the gates of the ancient city but the forces of Lady Blodica herself." Master Quil relished the gasps across the hall. "Yes, the wicked Enchantress with her treacherous army, their siege machines and trebuchets, militias of bowmen, witches and mages armed with hideous curses, the legions captained by the traitorous Dragon Lords and Ladies she beguiled. Oh, how it pained Farawl to see them! The noble greens, the steadfast blues, the valiant reds, the regal purples, all once magnificent to behold, all once wise and gentle creatures, glinting beneath a despairing sun. And their lords, Farawl's once-trusted allies—nay, his friends—fallen hard and cruel, swords raised against the throne they had sworn to uphold."

Master Quil lowered his raised fist, scanned a hard eye across his audience. "Leading the horde," he said low, "astride the Defiled Beast, its hide the black of death and decay, poisoned by the temptress's guile, with her ivory staff raised high: the Lady Blodica."

The Mage Master smirked, eyed his colleagues about the hall. "It is said the Lady Blodica's followers succumbed as much to her beauty as her guile. It is said she was as pale and fair as the full moon on the coldest winter night, her hair the black of such a sky. Tall as a man, they say, and endowed with a perfect loveliness and form. What a terrible thing that such tremendous powers should be bestowed upon a wicked creature with such beauty as to drive the greats of Elfryth to treason."

Flannery squeezed my hand, her lips pinched.

Master Quil stood taller. "And yet, Farawl took heart, for holding firm between the Enchantress and her prey poised the armies of Elfryth, for hope was not lost so long as the white banners of the golden dragon stood. He took up his silver sword and, in the name of the High Kings, the lost princes, and the once-true order of the Dragon Lords, Farawl plunged into the fray.

"Never had Farawl fought so mightily, nor so valiantly," Master Quil said, raising an invisible blade. "Victory lay but one stroke away. If the Lady Blodica could be struck down here, peace would reign once more.

On he pressed to the front, his foes heaping upon the battlefield as leaves in autumn, until at last he came upon the Defiled Beast and its dismounted rider.

"For but a moment," Master Quil said quietly, "Farawl was seized by the terrible sight of his smitten comrades, fallen upon the ground as densely as the heather which made their final resting places. Neither Blodica nor her terrible beast spared any fearless soul who dared challenge them. Farawl watched the polluted dragon stoop over its latest prey. Farawl recognized the fair face of the High King's eldest son and heir, the last remaining High Prince."

Master Quil let the gasps die away in solemn silence. "Determined to avenge his liege lord or to lay down his life, Farawl charged the Defiled Beast. But the creature was swift. A swing of its long neck, and Farawl heaped as quickly as the foes he had slain. He stirred himself before the beast clamped its monstrous jaws about him. Again, the creature struck him down, its neck like an iron whip.

"Farawl knew dragonhide was not easily penetrated, for so thick were its scales, they shieled it as armor upon a warrior. Yet like the armor of warriors, they bore their weaknesses. The creature had sustained few wounds, none of which seemed to slow him. So great was the beast, the wounds which would have slaughtered a man left a nick in its flesh. No weapon could slow the creature.

"But he was Farawl Silverblade," Master Quil cried, "whose sword was forged in dragonfire and blessed by Lord Praed himself. Once more, Farawl raised himself, but again was stricken down upon his back. As the Defiled beast advanced upon him, Farawl slashed his mighty blade across its underbelly. The creature reared, spitting golden flames toward the sky. Farawl lunged. His silver sword hacked into the beast's neck, sparking in the fire surging up its throat. The beast writhed until its weakened limbs gave way. At last, Farawl raised his sword high and smote off the head of the Defiled Beast!"

A roar went up, cups raised to cheer. Even Vespar silently raised his goblet.

"And yet," Master Quil quieted his listeners, "we know this was not the end of Lady Blodica's grievous reign. The Enchantress escaped before Farawl could turn his blade upon her. Caeradin would suffer many more months of terror before Lord Praed sacrificed himself to secure her demise." The Mage Master returned to the table for his goblet, which he raised high. "To Praed, the first Wizard." He turned to the dais, bowed, and met my eye. "And to a household sworn to prevent the rise of another wicked creature of such power."

Master Quil drained his goblet to the sound of cheers. Flannery and I exchanged glances. We took a sip from our cups as the entire hall followed Master Quil's example.

The musicians set to another tune when the Mage Master reclaimed his seat, and couples rose to dance. Flannery sat back, frowning.

"Well," she said, "I've never heard that one before. Nor do I believe Blodica was a Dragon Lady herself."

"She wasn't," I said. "She took that dragon by force. I read he was one of noblest dragons at court, until Blodica murdered his Dragon Lord and claimed him for herself."

Flannery drummed her fingers on the stem of her goblet. "It's a shame we only hear the stories of Silverblade and Tenbur and Praed instead of how many witches stood against their own Enchantress. I suppose that'd change too many minds about things, wouldn't it?"

Mam sent us a sidelong glance. She thumbed the Gildian pendant at her chest and returned to watching the swirl of gowns and ceremonial steels weaving along the hall. Vespar never shied from requesting a dance, and I knew better than to think every invitation was meant to rescue Mam from missing Da. He made no move, but it was early yet.

"Those boys are staring again." Flannery leaned closer, hiding her remark in her cup. "Now that Tylysk has Isabelle down there, his friends will be up here if you don't move fast."

The mages in question fixed their attention on the Countess, shoving and daring one another to approach the dais. Their rather suggestive searches of Flannery's figure set that inexplicable roiling force in my chest to a furious boil. I swallowed hard, shoving the sensation aside before Flannery noticed it.

"I'm not one for dancing," she said. "If it doesn't suit you either, let's go over there."

I excused us from the table, and we made for the musicians' corner. Mam's glance followed our quick retreat down the dais steps. We squeezed through the idle throng chattering away as they awaited their turns to dance.

"Ahem. Milady, if I may." The slick voice halted us, and one of Tylysk's friends slithered his way through the mob. He might have been handsome enough, if not for his crooked teeth he exposed with a haughty grin. He bowed. "If I could have the honor of the next dance, milady?"

Flannery clutched my hand. "Er, thank you, but I—"

"There's been a happy rumor in town regarding your extended stay, milady. I believe it's been exposed to the court by one particular guest tonight," he said, glancing sidelong at the excitable old woman whispering loudly to anyone who would hear her.

"She is mistaken," I said.

"Oh, terrible shame. The Countess would make such a lovely addition to the court. Unless, of course, it's only a matter of time, in which case it would be customary for gentlemen to seek the Mistress as a partner."

I stiffened, but Flannery struck faster. "I'm afraid Master Rhys has claimed the next several dances. In fact, the hall may be empty before the dances run out."

"Master Rhys wouldn't deprive the court of the privilege of making your fair acquaintance more intimately, my lady. And for Midsummer, surely he could spare you for a few tunes."

"Even if he would, I would be as disinclined to leave his company, *sir*," she said. She scanned the hall, finding Isabelle and Tylysk, and sent them a subtle plea for rescue. To my surprise, Tylysk moved to answer. I sensed Vespar rise from his seat behind us. I made to steer Flannery from another dismal encounter.

"Indeed." The mage stopped us with a laugh. "It may take but one dance to change your mind." He dared to reach for her hand. She recoiled, but he caught her fingers in an uncouth fist.

Tylysk grasped the mage by the shoulders and urged him aside. "I'm afraid the Countess isn't the agreeable partner you're looking for," he said. "If you remember what happened the last time someone crossed her."

Flannery escaped to the musicians' corner before the mage rebutted. I shot him a glower and followed her, but the mage fixed his gaze to her. He shook out his hand, as though he'd dealt some painful blow rather than having grasped Flannery's hand. He and Tylysk bickered low for a moment longer. The mage stormed to his table, red-faced, to endure the torment of his goading friends. His stare followed Flannery about the hall for the rest of the evening.

CHAPTER 13

Rhys

"I'm fine, Mam."

"You always say that, yet you grow worse," she snapped.

I refrained from reminding her that the incident with Tylysk and Isabelle in the library had happened a week before, and nothing came of it. "It was nothing," I said. "Just a dizzy spell."

Mam shook her finger in my face. "One potion. One potion would have saved your father's life, and he refused it. Do not make that mistake. He was not that strong, and neither are you."

She kept from looking mortified, and she made no apology. She startled me, at least. Even if she convinced me, why would I take the issue to a healer whose powers would torture me before they accomplished anything? Da never had that excuse. Besides, how could he know the difference between a fading fever and the one come to claim him? He rarely took his useless potions anyway.

Mam watched the rationalization in my eyes. She took my face in her hands. "Just this once, will you not be like him?"

She sat back in her chair, heartsick. She clutched the Gildian pendant to her chest.

Vespar stood at her side, where he'd stayed since dismissing me from lessons for the Midsummer festivities for the next short while. Whenever I saw Mam, there he would be, holding her hand, neglecting to use her proper title. I thought to remind him how he'd tried all that years ago, and nothing had come of it. I'd made sure of it.

Then again, he never stopped trying.

Vespar followed me to the door, closed it behind him. "She means well," he said, "but I fear she may be right. If you will let me—"

"You've tried." I backed away. "You'll really frighten Mam if you do it again."

He glanced at the door, twisted his gold ring. He stopped me from turning. "I see you and the Countess have been inseparable since the feast," he said. "Surely you're aware, talk of you and Flannery has spread. Your subtle affections have been more overt than before."

My face warmed. "There…we…nothing's happened."

"Nothing officially."

"Nothing at all."

"Indeed." Vespar showed a rare smile. "Why are you ashamed? She's won your mother's favor, and the court's."

I glowered. "You're supposed to dissuade me."

"Then you have no doubt of my opinion." He watched me fumble for words. "It may not be the most ideal match, perhaps, but I don't suppose she would shun a place in the most formidable household in Caeradin."

"That didn't stop Isabelle's father."

"Isabelle's father is a headstrong braggart who believes his daughter has ascended the chain as far as she can. He will soon regret dismissing you."

I stared.

"Any further excuses? You seem to want to dissuade me yourself."

I stuttered. Vespar patted my shoulder, sent me on my way, and returned to his post at my mother's side.

❧❦❧

Flannery and I wandered the garden most of the afternoon, or lounged among the Melys tree branches. She curled up at my side and told me of home, of games she played with her brothers, stories she spun for her sister. Whenever I peeked over her head at the garden house, I almost thought I spotted Emlyn watching us through her window.

We swung around Captain Perreth and his men training in the courtyard to the bailey. We chased the hounds out of the stable and rushed them across the lawn. Two little beasts tangled under my feet, and I dropped into a wrestling swarm of cold noses and dirty paws. Flannery sank beside me, rolling with laughter. She lured a pair of pups onto her lap. She was beautiful, cheeks ruddy, hair disarrayed, grass stains on her white skirts. She wrinkled her nose at me when she caught me staring.

"You're quiet today," she said. "Something the matter?"

"No. Just thinking."

"About what, dare I ask?"

"Vespar and I had an intriguing conversation this morning."

"Intriguing—that's a new one." The smile in Flannery's voice didn't show on her face. "I've been thinking, too."

"Hm?"

The pup on her lap whined and nosed her chin. She cradled him on her arm. "I've decided I have something to tell you."

The pile of hounds on my chest tumbled as I sat up. Her sudden discouragement made my stomach ache. Flannery's hand fell limp in mine. The color seeped from her face.

"Now, this is secret," she said. "You don't tell a soul."

"You have my word."

I watched the struggle in her eyes, as if she were facing Tylysk in another fistfight. But her opponent terrified her, almost to retreating.

"Darling?" I said.

Flannery blushed when I said it, but she squeezed my hand in return. She glimpsed around the lifeless bailey, the silence broken by Captain Perreth's roars to his trainees in the far courtyard. A deep breath, and she met my eye.

"Milord, milady."

The dogs leaped aside when Flannery and I startled. They barreled over to Aria's heels, jumbling her wobbly curtsy.

Flannery took her hand from mine. "Hello, Aria. The dogs were waiting for you to come and play."

Aria giggled at the hounds hopping about to greet her. They obeyed her command to sit, and she patted each of their heads before turning to us with another curtsy.

"Isabelle's looking for you, milady," she said.

Flannery blanched. She rushed to her feet, dusting grass from her skirts. "Oh. Of course. Sun and stars, I forgot I'm supposed to meet her. I'll be right there, Aria."

The girl darted to the stable, the dogs a step behind.

I grasped Flannery's hand. "You were saying?"

"It doesn't matter. I'll tell you later."

I tucked her hair behind her ear. "Isabelle can wait a moment."

"So can this."

I hesitated, but she avoided my gaze. "Well…hurry back, m'lady."

Flannery's cheeks bloomed pink. She stood on her toes and kissed me hard. Never looking at me, she turned aside and hurried to the castle.

I circled to the garden. A glimpse at the castle windows, the hedges, and finding no one but the shepherd far away on the hill, I cut across the lawn and crept into the cottage.

Emlyn sat at her table, dunking strawberries in a bowl of cream. She scrubbed her lips with the back of her hand and popped up from her chair.

"Look, Rhys, look!" She pulled her lip back and wiggled a tooth with her tongue.

I gasped, scooped her over my shoulder and tickled her ribs until she grew breathless. I set her on the table and took the chair in front of her. Emlyn bit back a giggle each time she met my eye.

"What's so funny?" I asked.

Emlyn smothered another laugh in her hands. "I *told* you, you like that girl."

"What?"

"That girl you're always with. What's her name again?"

"Flannery?"

"Yes, her." Emlyn leaned closer and whispered, "You *kissed* her!"

I reddened. "I…well—"

"Are you going to marry her?"

My heart stopped. I tried to laugh. "It's a little soon to be thinking about that, isn't it?"

"But you want to, don't you?"

I stumbled for an answer. Emlyn burst into giggles.

"Oh, wait. I have something you should give her." Emlyn slid off the table and pranced to the staircase.

"Emlyn, wait, Flannery and I—"

"Just wait." She disappeared to the loft for a moment, shuffling overhead, then she skipped to the table. "Here."

Emlyn cradled a woven silver ring on her palm. The light from its polished emerald cast a glowing jewel across her brow.

My breath caught. "Where did you get this?"

She shrugged. "Mama had one like it. Papa would bring her these all the time."

"Was this one your mother's?"

"No. It just looks like it."

"Did you make this?"

Emlyn scringed her mouth to the side. "Sort of. It came in the chest with the clothes Magic got me. Isn't it pretty?" She slipped the ring onto her forefinger. "It's probably too small for Flannery, but I can make it so it'll fit when she puts it on."

"Emlyn, I can't take this."

"Why?" She sank. "Will she not like it?"

"It's not that. It's just—this is very special, and—"

"Well, she's special to you, isn't she? That's what Papa always said about Mama." Emlyn held the ring out to me. "I want her to have it."

I grimaced. Emlyn grasped my hand, laid the little band on my palm, and closed my fingers around it. She clambered into her seat to return to her strawberries, and that was that.

I pocketed the jewel. "Well, I'm not making any promises about marrying her."

"Even though you want to," Emlyn remarked around a mouthful of cream.

"But if I did," I said, "that would mean things would change. If Flannery stays here, I'll have to tell her about you."

Emlyn's eyes widened.

"She'll keep it secret. She likes witches. She's going to help me change things."

Emlyn sucked the juice from her fingertips, frowning. "But I still have to stay in here?"

I lifted her onto my lap. "For a little longer, until my birthday. When I'm lord, you won't have to hide anymore. Flannery and I will take you home."

"But..." Emlyn blushed. She curled her arms around her head.

"What?" I tugged her arms down. "What's wrong?"

She stared at her fumbling fingers. "Nobody wants me at home."

"That can't be true, Emlyn."

"Is too. I'm a witch. They don't want me anymore."

"But they wouldn't give you up, would they? They love you."

Emlyn's gaze distanced toward the hearth. A shudder ripped up her spine, and she huddled against me. "I want to stay with you. Please? You still want me, don't you?" She turned to face me. "You love me, don't you? You'll always love me."

I brushed a thumb along her cheek, sighing. "Of course I will, Emlyn. Of course I'd want you to stay—"

"Then I can?"

My heart lurched in a thousand directions. Toward her, the quiver in her voice, all the desperate hope in her face. To the danger looming over her, an axe poised at the ready, and how much longer she could endure it. To her family, no doubt sick with worry for her, and how, even if Emlyn wanted it, I had no right to take her from them. Unless she spoke true, and they'd abandon her because of her magic, then what else could I do?

"Please?"

I tucked an arm around her. Emlyn cuddled up and gave a tiny, triumphant giggle. The warmth of it filled me from foot to crown.

"Oh, you have to see my potion!" Emlyn wriggled off my lap and yanked me toward the hearth. Halfway there, she squinted through the window. "Rhys, who's that girl? I see her sometimes. Who is she?"

"Oh, that's…"

Aria stumbled down the garden path, pallid and crying, searching wildly about.

"Stay here," I said without thinking. When Aria turned her back, I darted out the door. She squeaked as I came up behind her. "It's me, Aria. What's wrong?"

Tears trickled down her ashen face. I'd never seen her too afraid to bolt. A red welt swelled below her left eye.

"Aria, who hit you?"

She touched the wound. She stared with glassy eyes. "Master Rhys, you have to help me."

"Tell me what happened."

As the understanding dawned on her, her breaths came sharp, and her brows knitted over clear eyes. "It's Milady. They took her."

CHAPTER 14

Rhys

I blinked. "What?"

Aria stopped herself from sprinting away. "Milady. Isabelle and me…" She fingered the welt on her face. "But the guards came and took her."

I staggered. I grabbed Aria's hand and charged into the castle. She clung to my arm, but I steered her toward the staircase.

"Go find Lady Orrtha. You'll be safe with her."

Though frightened to go, Aria sped up the stairs. Not thinking, I made to run for Flannery's chambers. Aria's shriek flung me back around.

"Milady!"

I bounded up the stairs. Aria screamed and bolted for Mam's chambers. Tylysk advanced from the next corridor, dagger in hand.

"Don't!"

He halted. He watched Aria escaped, redirected his blade toward me.

"Don't you dare touch Aria," I snarled. "Where's Flannery?"

Tylysk kept his dagger poised. If I took one more step, he would have impaled me and thought nothing of it. "Tread lightly, Master Rhys. She's beyond your help."

"Let me through."

"You—"

I ducked, smashed Tylysk into the railing, and swerved into the hall-way. A burst of scarlet struck me from behind, locking my feet to the ground. The spell released once he seized me by the arm. He hauled me into Vespar's chambers.

Two mage guards took stance on either side of Flannery, sentinel wands ready. She stood in shackles, motionless before the Lord Mage, hiding behind her disarray of half-made curls and braids. I lunged for her. Tylysk snagged me again. Flannery never moved.

"Stop this! This is outrageous. Let her go!"

Vespar made no move. As ever, his austerity was clear, empty, and hard as stone. But his eyes lingered on the floor, a troubled line to his mouth. I looked between his feigned remorse and Flannery, more infuriated.

Beside him, the tactless, crooked-toothed Mage Master from the Midsummer feast glared down his nose at me.

"What is he doing here?" I demanded.

Vespar motioned for me to join him.

"Not until you let her go."

Flannery bowed her head. Her shoulders trembled.

Tylysk released me as Vespar approached. He grasped my arm, led me around the guards. Tylysk and his scowling friend joined in their stance, Tylysk with his dagger raised.

She stood still. Through the curtain of her autumn hair, I spotted a line of crimson trickling from the corner of her mouth.

Vespar didn't stop me as I stepped toward her, but Flannery's cringe did. She turned away. My throat knotted.

Vespar put a hand on my shoulder. I was too stunned to shake him off.

I felt I'd known it all along, since the first moment we spoke. But despite everything I stood for, all I promised her, everything I planned to set right, it was a knife in the chest.

For a moment, the way she refused to look at me, how her bedrag-gled hair fell about her face, shackles tight around her inflamed wrists and her white gown soiled and tattered, she was wild and terrifying, the wicked temptress everyone believed her to be.

"You're a witch."

She finally looked at me. Her emerald eyes shone with tears. Not a temptress's eyes. My Flannery was in those eyes.

"I don't care," I said. "Let her go."

"She tried to curse me," the surly Mage Master spat. "At the feast. I felt it."

"If you hadn't assaulted her, she wouldn't have touched you. And she wouldn't waste an ounce of strength on the likes of you."

The mage made to rebut, but Vespar raised a hand. He took his dismissal and stalked to the door. "Be glad I exposed her, Master Rhys," he said. "You'll finally be free of her guile."

I stalked after him. Tylysk wrestled me back to Vespar's side.

Vespar grasped my shoulder. "Master Rhys—"

"Stop it!" I lurched out of his reach. "I won't hear it. Yes, I *am* Master Rhys, and I said, let her go."

"It's hardly that simple, and you know it."

"Why? It has been so far." I motioned to Flannery, so enraged, I laughed. "All this time, you never noticed? This whole time, my Lord Mage, and you never detected her? Of course you did, and you did nothing."

Vespar watched me with the same pity he would offer a whining child. "Yes, I did detect her, about the same time I detected your curse."

Flannery's head came up. The guards thrust her backward when she took a step. She stammered, livid scarlet rising in her face. Tylysk pressed his dagger to her throat.

"There is no curse," I growled for the thousandth time. "And even if Flannery set it, you always said you'd get rid of it."

"I had to be sure of her motives," he said. "I had to be sure she acted alone, of what kind of hold she placed on you. Worse might have happened had I acted too quickly."

My hands clenched. Tylysk came between his master and me. He tipped the point of his dagger up, dimpling Flannery's chin. "Don't make a mess," he said.

"I don't believe you," I said, jabbing a finger at Vespar. "This is a trick. Your game to turn me around."

I wanted to strangle that apologetic look off his face. How dare he pretend to be sorry? How dare he pretend he cared?

"Tell them." I stepped up to Flannery, though she recoiled. I tucked her hair away from her face, thumbed the blood from her bruised lip. "Darling, tell them you haven't done anything. You'd never curse me."

Her glance wavered between the mages behind me. I turned her face to me.

"Don't look at them. Look at me, and tell me they're lying. *Tell me.*"

A tear rippled down her cheek, under my palm. "They have Abigail." My hands fell from her face.

"I'm sorry," she said, as bitterly as when we first met.

I crept back, my vision misting. "Flannery, you didn't."

She hid behind her hair.

Vespar came to my side. "She acted alone," he said quietly. "She hoped to manipulate you into returning her witch sister. What would have come of you had she succeeded? Do you believe she would have kept up this pretense for your sake?"

Flannery's shame doubled her over. The guards slackened their grip and dropped her on her knees.

"But everything you said this morning," I faltered. "You told me... you said..."

Vespar pursed his lips.

To see Flannery broken, overtaken with soundless sobs, groveling at my feet, should have convinced me. But I doubted.

The guard snapped her upright at Tylysk's motion. "Now remove the curse," he ordered.

Flannery's tears gave way to scarlet rage. "You do it," she hissed. "All you mighty mages, you glorious cowards and murderers. Save him, if you're so powerful. Break me. Cast me out. Have your victory."

She spat beads of red to Tylysk's face. The guards dragged her out of his reach when she thrashed. She hurled one harmless curse after another, until her gnarled words became fluid under her breath, and I understood nothing of them except they were brimmed with power.

"Flannery, don't!"

Tylysk slashed his dagger. She reeled back. Red soaked the waist of her white gown.

Vespar locked me in place with a spell of his own. He put an arm in front of me to block my reach.

Tylysk paled, teeth gritted. He waved her own blood in her face. "Remove. His. Curse."

Flannery stared at him, trembling, a strangled gasp escaping her. Sweat drenched her brow, her murmuring lips. She gave a weak nod.

I crumpled. Vespar caught me before I hit the ground. He lowered me down.

"Away with her," he said.

I shoved him off and lunged. Tylysk pinned me back until Vespar interceded.

The guards took no pity for her wound. They hauled Flannery away, her bare heels skidding across the floor. The pain tore a ragged cry from her. A nod from his master, and Tylysk followed them out.

Vespar stayed behind, pinning my flailing arms from meeting him. I wished, for once, for the hideous strength lent by the rage that had leaped at Tylysk days before. Now, when I needed it, it wouldn't come. I battled all the more.

But she was gone.

My limbs wilted. Vespar slowly released me and sat back. I swerved out of his reach when he meant to tousle my hair.

"How could you? Why did you let him…"

"Tylysk has every right to defend himself. It won't kill her."

"Then what will?"

He gave no answer. He put a hand to my chest when I made to rise. "Rest a moment. That was not gentle on you."

I glared.

"Her removal," he said. "Whether you felt it or not, magic is never gentle on the mind."

"That explains a lot, doesn't it?"

Vespar pursed his lips. "The Ordinary mind."

He meant to make a healer's inspection over me, but I swatted his hand away. "You did this. You're trying to break me so I'll come crawling to you and your cruelty. I won't let you make her some pawn in your wretched game."

"If not for her curse, you would never have known Flannery," Vespar said. "What you call cruelty is saving your life, Master Rhys. The real cruelty is how she used you to her own ends, how she enslaved you with her affected love. She would have shattered you and left you and your kingdom to fall in her wake."

I shook my head with every word. "She would've stayed. She would've helped me."

"Then you are blinded by her guile."

"And you are blinded by your hate!" I lurched to my feet. "I won't bow to your mercy, my lord, and I will not let you murder her."

A wave of his arm, and the door slammed and locked in my face. I glared at him, hands shaking. His gaze never wavered.

"Then you will bring ruin upon yourself and all of Gildio, Master Rhys."

I fisted my quivering fingers, fought to breathe.

"The Council will not heed you. When the other lords hear of your rashness, they will come against you. Yes, you are Master Rhys, but you have no power yet."

"I won't surrender to you," I spat.

"But you will surrender to a witch who would see your destruction. You will defend this temptress who made *you* her pawn. You will still declare your love for a creature who never loved you."

It struck me. Despite Da's convictions, despite little Emlyn cowering in the garden house, despite every oath I had made to end what Flannery faced, I doubted. Was it really her trick? Had she ever loved me?

I sank to my knees. Vespar joined me at the door, knelt beside me.

"I want to see her," I said.

He frowned. "After all she did to you?"

The knot in my throat refused to give way. Emlyn's ring weighed heavy in my pocket. My hand gripped Vespar's sleeve on its own.

He took a deep breath. "Not now. You need rest." He pulled away, but I held his sleeve tighter.

"Will that be too late?"

He met my eye, but didn't answer.

After a lasting silence pervaded the Manor, the softest knock came at the door. Vespar opened it to Mam clutching the Gildian pendant to her heart. One glimpse at me, and she stifled a sob with a hand. I refused Vespar's help to stand. He bent and gripped my shoulder, his edges soft, the stone invisible. He joined my mother, and they exchanged a few words too low for me to distinguish. I couldn't watch him kiss my mother's cheek before he left.

CHAPTER 15

Rhys

"Master Rhys, you're still here."

I peered up at the mage warden. He stood over me where I sat against the wall outside the dungeon door. By midafternoon the next day, I had yet to see Flannery. "If you go to Master Vespar, he'll give you his consent."

"I'm afraid I can't stray farther from my post, milord."

"Then I'll wait."

The warden glanced between his men standing guard, shook his head, and descended the long stairwell to the dungeon.

Vespar had yet to make an appearance after I contended with him that morning. He ignored my every word, made no sound. Carried on tending to his parchments as though nothing had happened. Even when I begged him to, he didn't look at me.

Mam watched me while I paced her chamber and fumed and quarreled with everything Vespar might have said, or the council, or any soul who condemned Flannery. She offered little more than her own heartache.

"Then you'll do nothing?" I challenged. "You won't speak with him?"

"Rhys, they believe Flannery has committed a crime everyone fears of witches," Mam said. "Even if witches are not all bad, they believe she is proof of the danger they strive to remove."

"They should start hunting for wicked mages too. I've seen more heart in Flannery's contrived kindness than I find in the likes of Vespar and Tylysk."

Mam winced. "I wish it were as simple as you think it is."

"If Da were here, it would be. He would save her."

"If Da were here, it would be no different." The strength in her voice sent me back a step. "You think you know your father's mind so well. What he understood that you do not is, being a witch makes her no more innocent than it makes her guilty. Ioan would not have liked it any more than you, but he would have accepted the consequences."

Tears sped down her face. Seeing them made my own fall.

"She's not like that, Mam. She can't be."

But I couldn't believe it even as I said it.

I leaned against the chilled wall, watched the guards change shifts again. Emlyn's ring stayed tight in my clammy fist. Its woven pattern imprinted into my palm.

Isabelle came, and Stephan, and Dom. None of them so much as got me off the floor. I touched none of the food Theresa brought. Isabelle tried to persuade Aria to draw me out, but the girl refused to take a step nearer to the dungeons. She gave up when Aria looked about to bolt, which she did anyway.

The sun shifted across the windows in the corridor beyond. The guards changed twice more. Afternoon fell to evening, evening stole to night. The spreading dark convinced me Vespar would never show. Whether he did or not, I'd wait. Someone would give in.

The magelights flared before he came. Mam followed him, but stayed in the hallway beyond at his few words. I stowed the ring in my pocket and stood.

"You took long enough," I blurted.

The way Vespar looked at the guards, I thought he wouldn't let me in. He motioned me away. I stood my ground.

"To speak with you," he said.

I met him halfway. Mam watched me over his shoulder. Vespar positioned us out of Mam's and the guards' earshot.

"Consider the risk you're taking." He held up a hand and silenced my rebuttal. "Your affection for her changes nothing. She may attempt to convince you otherwise."

"Is this what you're going to tell the court when they find out? That you were running an investigation and put me at risk?"

"Do you think I would have let her hurt you?"

I'd never heard him sound so stupid.

Vespar frowned. If nothing else, he was an excellent actor. He tried to lay a hand on my shoulder.

"Don't. Not from you."

He drew back. He stared at his feet. "Hurt. Grieve. Be stronger for it. It will pass."

He fiddled with his ring, eyed me expectantly. I returned his gaze in kind.

"You have your mother to thank for persuading me," Vespar said, marching to the door. "Whatever you gather from what she shows, she is the bravest woman I have ever known."

I looked back. Stephan brought her a chair and set it at the end of the corridor, beyond the splice of shadow and magelight. She dismissed him. She was alone.

At Vespar's gesture, the guards let us pass. He led me down the stairwell and through the iron door. Mage guards stood ready within, though the empty cells bore nothing to guard. What a pretty show—they'd forgotten to grab their dice from the nearby table.

Vespar motioned for the warden to stay behind and led me on. Beyond the door on the back wall, the dungeon forked in three different directions, off into a labyrinth of cold, rancid corridors and cages. We took the tunnel straight ahead, passing a dozen barred cells on either side, all of them empty. Why all this room for no prisoners? Had they found that many witches back in the day?

The passage spilled into another crossing pathway. Instead of bars, an iron door sealed each cell. Chains hung from the locks of the one closed door. The guards standing watch stepped aside. A wave of Vespar's hand, and the chains fell, the door unbolted, and the pain of what had to be an imprisoning pentacle dissipated. Vespar blocked the door.

"Steel yourself," he said. "She is not as you knew her."

"She can't be putting on as much of a show as you are." I brushed past him.

"My lad, listen to me."

I wedged the door open.

The sound within froze me. Ghostly rising and falling, delicate and childlike. I glanced at Vespar, heart pounding. He frowned. I stepped into the cell.

"Flannery?"

She didn't acknowledge me. She paced along the back wall, a little girl cooing to herself. The grate overhead cast a grid of moonlight at her feet. Flannery watched her shadow pass across it as she tiptoed over the squares, arms out to keep her balance. A chain jarred her wrist. She turned about and strolled in the other direction until it stopped her again.

I watched her, unsure what to think. Her ragged white gown hung off her shoulders, shredded down her back, the skirt hanging in ribbons. She'd used a length of it to tie up her hair, or perhaps the sleeve torn off her arm, but much of her autumn hair draped in tangles about her face. If her bloody waist agonized her in the least, she gave no sign of it. She went on pacing.

She doubled over and shrieked with all the force her body could muster. She clutched her side, whimpering.

"Flannery, be careful."

She froze. She gazed in my direction, glassy eyed. A hollow smile spread across her face. "You came," she breathed.

"I wanted to see you," I said.

"Wanted to see me." Flannery sang it to herself over and over, set to pacing.

"I…I brought you something."

She swung around. "A present? You brought me a present?"

I stepped back, unnerved by the emptiness in her bloodshot eyes. Flannery laughed a little, but pressed a hand to her wound and whimpered. When the pain subsided, she gasped and scooped her hair off her neck. Sweat dribbled down her freckled shoulders and back, visible through the slashes of her gown.

"So hot," she moaned. "Let's go to the garden. It's too hot here."

My heart ached. "We'll go to the garden soon," I said. "But I have something for you, first."

"A present?" Flannery put her back to the moonlight and tiptoed as far as the chains allowed. "Yes. Because you wanted to see me."

I held the ring on my palm. Flannery stared with a ghostly smile.

"Pretty," she cooed. "Pretty. Is it for me?"

I slipped the ring onto her finger for her. She turned her hand about, watching the moonlight glitter on the emerald, caught sight of the green reflection on the wall. She giggled.

I reached for her hand again. "Flannery—"

She jumped away with a scream. I staggered. Her wild eyes widened. "Cold. You're cold." She snagged my hand and pressed my palm to her cheek. "Too hot. It's too hot, too hot."

A breath caught in my knotted throat. Flannery's glassy eyes followed my tears. "No," she said. She cupped her blazing hands on my face. "No no no. Don't cry." She dabbed my tears away. "Cold. Cold." She swiped them from my face, gasping for breath, catching anything that could soothe her. She wrenched aside and shrieked. She wailed, clutching her wound.

"Darling," I said.

Flannery's sobs warped to laughter. She propped herself against the wall. "*Darling*," she sneered. "What a silly thing to call me. What a silly thing you are."

I crept backward. For a moment, I wondered what final act she was playing, if it was an act at all. If anything of the past two months had been real. If she had simply made me her fool.

Flannery swept her hair off her neck. She gasped when the moonlight sparkled on her ring. She shined it about the cell, casting quivering green glows on the grimy stones.

"They said you wouldn't come," she said. "They said you'd left me. They said you didn't know me anymore."

"Who said that?"

Flannery directed the emerald reflection to bob around the iron door. She giggled. "Isn't it pretty? It's for me. Don't you think it's pretty?"

I couldn't answer. Flannery stared at her ring, paced under the barred window, humming snatches of tunes the musicians had played for her. The chain snagged. She pirouetted to the other direction.

I shook my head, tears spilling. I made for the door.

"No, don't go!"

I flattened myself to the door, heart pulsing. Flannery cowered to the wall with her arms tight about herself. She dropped to her knees and sobbed.

"Don't let them in. Don't leave me here."

I watched her weep. Flannery pressed her cheek to the chilled bricks, spread her arms along the wall. She tried to sing to herself, interrupted by intermittent sobs.

I crept nearer. She didn't acknowledge until I reached a hand down to her. She laid her fiery cheek on my shaky palm.

"Cold." She sighed and peered up at me, eyes glazed. "Then we can't go to the garden?"

I took a steadying breath, brushed her hair from her dripping brow. "No, Flannery. You need to rest. You'll feel better when you've rested."

She sank to the ground. She scooped her hair off her neck and pressed herself against the cool wall. "Yes. I'm tired. Perhaps it won't be so hot tomorrow."

"Yes, Flannery. Tomorrow will be better."

Sweat trickled down her skin. Her breaths came heavier, shallower. Her hollow eyes widened.

"Make it stop." Flannery's gaze flicked to mine. She gasped for air. "Why are you doing this? Why did you let them come?"

My heart stopped. "No, darling, I tried to stop them. I tried to save you."

Flannery clutched her throat, rasping. "You left me."

"No, I came back. I'm here. I did everything I could. I loved you."

The heat off her skin blazed in her blind, bloodshot eyes. "What?"

"I loved you."

Flannery clinched my wrist with a bloodstained hand. "Stupid boy!" she screeched. "Hateful, despicable beast!" She thrust me away with all her strength. I heaped to the ground.

I groveled out of reach. "Flannery, you're not yourself. I know you. You love me, too."

She tipped her head back and cackled. "How could anyone love such a murdering wretch? No one could even look on someone so foul and faithless."

"Flannery, please, you'll hurt yourself."

She swatted my hand away. She fell to tears once more. "You lied to me. You said everything would be better. Now look what you've done to me."

"No. I swore I would end all this, remember? You and I…we were going to do it together. You were going to help me."

She lunged, screeching. I stumbled away, too horrified to breathe.

"Wicked, vile, *stupid* boy! Rot you! You deserve that curse upon you! May it haunt you the rest of your miserable life! Curse you! *Curse you!*"

The door burst open. Vespar hoisted me off the floor. The guards piled into the cell. Flannery cowered to the wall, whimpering, pleading. They advanced.

Flannery's howls drowned the sound of my own begs. She screamed for me to save her, not to leave her alone. Vespar drew me to the door.

The men dragged her up, thrust her to the wall, one pinning her to the bricks with a hand around her throat. The other ripped Flannery's head back by her hair. His other hand clawed around her chin to pry her jaws apart.

Vespar shut and blocked the door. Flannery's shrieks quieted for a breath. She wailed. She called my name.

Her cries dwindled to silence.

Rhys

I stared at the cell door on my knees, too overcome to grasp what had happened. Vespar came away from it, held out his hand to me. A long moment passed before I looked up at him.

"That's it?" I said. "She's gone?"

He didn't speak.

My fingers tingled in fists. "What did you do to her? That was not Flannery."

Vespar drew me aside as the door opened. He tried to block my view of the executioners hauling Flannery away like a slaughtered animal. I turned away from her broken body, the sweat still glazing her skin, the blood on her lips and side. Her last words to me pierced me over and over again.

I steadied myself with a hand on the wall. "What will they do with her?"

No answer.

"I won't let you throw her away. I'll dig her grave myself."

Vespar frowned. "You know that can't be done, Master Rhys."

I stammered, summoning the last of my strength to keep upright. "Of everything else you've taken, you'll take that from me, as well?"

Vespar quietly said, "Such a move, however honorable your intentions, will not go unnoticed by your people and the Council. You cannot afford to turn the other lords against you before you come to power. If you wish to see the Hunt ended, you will hinder yourself by paying your last respects to a witch charged with cursing you."

I shook my head. I peered into the cell, to the chains no longer shackling her, to the pool of blood on the stones. That tortured creature was not my Flannery. But then, had the Flannery I loved ever existed? Had she ever said one true word to me? Or had I succumbed to a snare I never believed anyone capable of setting?

Vespar looked at his hands. "You believed Lady Blodica's example was obsolete," he said. "Is this not proof enough?"

It buckled me. I dropped, hid my face, and wept.

Vespar knelt at my side. He roughed my hair. "Little boy," he whispered, as though I were seven again. "Little boy."

For that briefest moment, he was my uncle again.

He drew me up. "Your mother is waiting."

I hesitated. "I'll never see her again?"

Vespar gripped my shoulder and led me on.

Aria was asleep with her head on my mother's lap. The sound of the dungeon door startled them both awake, and the girl darted. Mam stood and waited for me beyond the corridor. Her arms hung heavy at her sides, but the set of her shoulders spoke of how she needed them around me. She cupped a hand to my face and kissed my brow when I bent down.

She sent me to rest. I made my way down the hall, too numb for the spark of the magelights to reach me. I couldn't tell how long I'd been in the dungeons, but the stifling pall of slumber hung over the castle.

Isabelle paced in front of my chamber door. I watched her fluid stride from the end of the hall until she noticed me.

"Sun and stars, Rhys Claytherdon, I've been worried mad about you."

I said nothing. Isabelle opened my door for me, eyeing the disheveled mess I was.

"What happened to your face? And your hands?"

I'd forgotten my cheek was handprinted with blood. It stained my hands, cracked with the lines of my skin.

Isabelle followed me into my room. "It was…quick," she said. "I know it's no comfort, but she didn't suffer long."

I scoffed. "No? Wait, what did you say?"

"She—she didn't—"

"How would you know?"

Isabelle's brows pinched. "You didn't?"

She ducked away from me. "How did you know?"

"I thought you did. You're supposed to know these things."

"Does everyone know, then? Hm? Everyone but me?"

"No, Rhys, of course not." Isabelle dabbed her nose. "It was an accident. I overheard the Lady and Master Vespar talking about it once."

I stood down.

"I'm sorry. I would've told you if I'd known."

I sank into a chair. It sickened me to think the substance I'd watched them pour down Flannery's throat had set her to madness. If they hadn't come when they did, she might have endured the agony for days, weeks. I couldn't bring myself to believe it, nor much of anything anymore. A howl stayed clenched in my chest, ready to burst. I reached up to rub my face.

"Don't," Isabelle said. "Wash first. You don't know what the poison could do to you, too."

She endured my unintentional glare. She kissed the tip of her finger and pressed it to my nose, how she used to when we were young. She retreated.

I soaped and scrubbed my hands and face until they were raw. The water's crispness bit my hot skin, soothing nothing. I changed clothes and left the bloodstained assemblage by the hearth. If not for sheer exhaustion, I would never have slept.

I talked myself out of avoiding Flannery's chambers the next morning.

I crept to the guest quarters to find her door hanging on one hinge. I tiptoed inside, heart in my feet.

Her apprehenders had spared nothing in the demolished chambers. The chairs and table sat upended, curtains and their rods torn from the wall and the four-poster bed. The writing desk lay in shambles, broken straight down off its legs. Parchments carpeted the floor. Jeweled hairpins sparkled amid shards of mirror. Burns and residue dusted random surfaces from fired, recoiled, and misdirected spells.

Blue glass speckled the floor near the upturned nightstand. The book I brought her lay lopsided on the fragments. The daisy I gave her rested on the purple cover, still in full bloom. Odd, that they should be unmarred by the surrounding mayhem. I tucked the book in my waistcoat and took the daisy to my chambers. I tossed it in the hearth.

Isabelle's roars echoed down the corridor, drawing me into the hallway to find her. Tylysk was already there, calmly dealing back everything she gave him. He recoiled when Isabelle raised her fists. She had no strength behind them, and he let her hit him until she crumpled. Sobbing, Isabelle teetered into his arms. Tylysk shielded her, his cheek on her hair, and stared exhaustedly across the hall.

I didn't know what to do. There would be no funeral, though Flannery deserved the dignity of a burial, at the very least. But Vespar's words reeled through my mind alongside my mother's terrors and Tylysk's warnings. I couldn't fathom how the Flannery I had loved had been an act, and everything that had sprouted between us was only in the mind of the pawn she made me out to be. Yet all the evidence stood against me.

However much I loathed to admit it, Vespar was right. One compassionate move toward a convicted witch, and I would lose the respect of Caeradin's most influential lords, the Hunt's most tenacious supporters. To them, Flannery's strike against the Gildian Lord-to-be proved the Hunt's necessity tenfold.

It eased none of the pain. I was just a pawn. I had been snared.

I ignored those who passed me in the corridors. Most turned on their heels, either ashamed of my falling for a witch or terrified of my curse.

I gave Aria a few moments. She followed me, skittering between pillars along the hall until she summoned the courage to call my name. Her eyes shone dry, but wild.

Her features softened. For the first time, nothing plagued her, none of her gentle fidgeting or curtsies. She tiptoed close and drew her arms about me.

As I returned her embrace, she ripped away and bolted.

The dogs followed me out to the stable without any coaxing. They stayed at my heels, sensing something amiss, and wondered why I came without the playful girl who used to chase them. They tagged behind me toward the courtyard behind the armory. Swordsmaster Perreth had his men dueling as he counted beats. The captain wandered their ranks, barking orders.

Watching them put strange vigor in me. Something urged me to snatch up one of those discarded blades and charge something. I sneaked away before the Swordsmaster's beady eyes squared on me.

A hot, dusty wind kicked across the sun-beaten garden. Out on the hill, specks of white roamed the green, and a dog herded them to their pen.

I stared at the garden house from my perch in the Melys tree, hoping the sight of it might wheedle me into seeing Emlyn. What would I say to her? That in the course of a few hours, our plans were dashed? And if I had no power to save Flannery, how could I protect Emlyn?

I took Flannery's book from my waistcoat. I leafed the pages against my thumb. It was the way her hair moved, how she twirled in her Midsummer gown.

A page fluttered from the book and slipped through my fingers. It fell apart, and its pieces floated to the grass. I clambered down the tree to gather the fragments before the breeze whisked them up.

I reorganized the numbered pages and took them behind the Melys tree, out of view of the castle windows. I soaked up Flannery's rushed scrawl.

M'lord,

If you've found this copy, then someone else found the original letter I intended to give you. I cannot tell you how sorry I am. Though I wish with all my soul that I could save you, we can't undo what is done. It was never meant to go this far.

I wrote you a story. It isn't very good, with what little time I had to write it. But despite my unfavorable writing skills, I think this will do you good.

CHAPTER 17

Flannery

Our village was months from its regular Hunting. The Council must have grown tired of taxing their homelands for fruitless raids. My parents went to great lengths to hide their daughters during "hunting season." But we had no defense against the troops this time.

In broad daylight too. I was going to meet Papa and my brothers in the orchard when the boys spotted two of them ready to pounce. A huge, broad-shouldered boar of a man, muscled arms near as big around as my head, a length of bearskin down his back, charged after me. To my disgust, a wiry, skulking woman lurked behind him.

Papa and the boys advanced against the Hunters' broadswords with rakes and pruners and hatchets. Papa dropped so quickly, and he collapsed under the plum tree, as crumpled at the fruits he fell upon. I begged the Hunters to stop before any of my brothers dropped. The boar hefted me over his shoulder while the Huntress kept any followers at bay. I never saw Papa and the boys again.

Abigail already huddled in the wagon, still drenched from the laundry. Our mother's shrieks carried over the entire village standing by to watch. When I dream of her, that's all I hear—our names mangled in her throat. The Hunter tossed me into the barred wagon and blocked my every attempt to catch one last glimpse of my mother.

They'd hunted three other witches before us, all older than I. Five more joined us on the way. One was a new bride, by the way she played with her gleaming ring. One in her early teens, and one the same age as my nine-year-old sister.

They carted us off, surrounded by a few scrawny mages who followed the Hunters around and kept watch. Despite their glinting armor and soldiers' wands, they were laughably small compared to the war-bred Hunters they claimed to defend against our magic. But at least one of the Hunters was a mage, himself.

The journey took weeks. The Hunters never let us out for more than a few moments a day, if we were lucky, and one at a time. They tossed food and tainted water pouches through the door. Why they bothered to cart us away, I'll never know. It seemed an absolute waste to me.

But the Hunters enjoyed the long road. They loved spitting and cursing and laughing at us. Some dealt me a crude tease once in a while, and I amused them with a few biting remarks of my own. If I overstepped, they turned on Abigail, which shut me up. But the silent, apathetic indifference, revulsion, from the warrior women stung as much.

We came through Gildio city's northern gate. Abigail cowered at the sight of the lofty castle, how its three towers spiked to the sky, black eagle banners adrift in some sinister majesty. Personally, I'd always imagined it being bigger.

The woman beside me grasped my hand. She hadn't spoken a word the entire journey.

"Save these little ones."

I glanced to the other five women clustered within the wagon. Each woman's face paled, set with fearful determination. Abigail huddled close. Twelve-year-old Anna curled an arm around little Grace's shoulders. The four of us had the bleakest chance of escape if the others bought us time.

I hesitated, dreading to think of the heavy price these five strangers, these innocent women, would pay for our freedom.

The wagon lurched to a stop. The woman beside me uttered an incantation. A mage unbolted the door.

A crack of red crumpled him. The women propelled spells and curses through the bars. Two piled out the door and assailed the Hunters on either side. I jumped over the soldier's slumped form at the door, the girls close behind, and we sped for the nearest road. I turned in time to watch the new bride collapse, making no sound as she sank motionless to the flagstones. Her Mage Master slaughterer charged after us.

We ducked through strangling hordes in the streets, skittering through seams in the crowd. Mages smashed through the throng. They drove us on until we cut into a backstreet severed by the narrow river. Our pursuers drew in. With nowhere else to run, we plunged into the rushing water. Abigail narrowly escaped the Mage Master's swipe for her arm. He cursed and ordered his men to follow us over the bridge.

We clambered onto the opposite bank, shaken and soaked. We tripped onto the dirt road of the impoverished Lower Side. I kept the girls close, steering clear of grasping strangers and beggars, our wariness slowing us as we snaked through the maze of teetering shacks. The Hunters closed in.

I spotted a high stone wall with an overhanging roof to one side of a ramshackle hut and yanked the girls behind it. The mage and his men darted past. When he realized he'd lost us, he split his men up to search in every direction. I peeked around the wall.

"I'd not come out yet."

The girls covered their mouths to quiet their shrieks. I scoured the road for whoever had spotted us. A man swung back and dangled from his perch on the overhanging roof, upside down, low enough to hang nose to nose with me. He winked.

"Not quite yet, loves. Hush hush."

Another troop rushed past our hiding place. The man went stone still, some refined gargoyle hanging there, fingers steepled, brow raised, and lips pursed. He held up a finger when I made to stand. Another pack of Hunters charged by. The stranger nodded.

"You've a few moments till they make another round."

I grasped Abigail's hand, she continued the chain with the other girls, and we moved toward the next road.

"Ah ah ah, not that way," he said, his voice disarmingly silken. "That's the scary part down there. Just a few pickpockets up here. Down there, that's where it gets gruesome."

I glared at him. He dropped from his outrageous perch and dusted his mock highborn attire. His grungy shirt mismatched his waistcoat under a dark long-coat, paired with threadbare breeches and holey knee-high boots, topped off with a soiled feathered cap. Scruffy, but as tidy as a man without a quib could be, he was gallingly attractive.

"What would you suggest?" I hissed.

"Would you trust a kindly stranger?"

"Not you, I think."

He pouted. "An exchange of introductions might remedy that."

"You first."

The stranger tipped his hat in a theatrical bow. "Sir Thackery J. Bright, m'ladies. Don't ask what the J stands for. Bit of a mouthful, so I'm attuned to Thatch, if you like." He winked, a spark in his ruddy brown eyes.

"'Sir' Thatch?" I said.

He replaced his cap. "Count works, if you prefer. Or Baron. Always liked that one."

"Sounds sinister to me." I tugged the girls out of his reach.

"Not at all. Sheriff might work too, but it doesn't have the same ring to it. That's what I do, though. Keep things from getting messy over here. Keep boundaries in check, stave off deadly brawls, that sort of thing."

"But you're not friends with the mages."

Thatch spat in the dirt. He wiped his mouth on his sleeve. "Sorry. Can't help it."

Abigail peeked from behind me. "Then…if you don't like them—"

Thatch clamped a hand over Abigail's mouth and yanked her to the dirt. I waited until the marching quieted before I wrenched my sister from his grasp.

"Have I got something against witches?" Thatch guessed.

We all stiffened.

Thatch shrugged. "We're all unjustly doomed criminals. Whatever our motives, we have a common enemy. But the real point is denying the mages the victory."

I rolled my eyes. "That makes you all the better."

"Thought you'd think so. So, I can take you somewhere safe, guarded night and day by yours truly and company."

The girls peered up at me, exhausted, terrified. I glared at Thatch, but with no other option available to us, I gave a stiff nod.

We ducked out of sight of another patrol. Grinning, Thatch said, "Right this way, m'lovelies."

Thatch sneaked under the roof and steered clear of the roads. We weaved through the Lower Side, keeping to gaps between decaying walls and crumbling structures. He waved us into the narrowest opening yet, tucked in a line between forsaken shops. We slinked in sideways.

Halfway down the passage, Thatch stood still until soldiers passed at either end. He reached across to the patchwork wooden wall opposite us, and knocked once, paused, and rapped twice more. A tense breath, then a thick square panel shifted silently to the right. Thatch ushered us through the shadowy entry. The wall closed off behind us, sealing us into total darkness.

"Stairs there, m'sweet," Thatch whispered to the girl in front. "Down— there you are."

Grace stumbled in the dark, but with Anna's help, she groped her way down the steep stairwell. She bumped into a dead end.

"Put your hand on the door, right in the middle," Thatch instructed.

She did. The door swung wide, spilling yellow light across her surprised face.

Thatch winked. "Only friends can get in that way."

The girls crept into the cellar. "Cellar" gives the wrong impression—it was a home, with a kitchen and bedrooms, all dressed with rather comfortable makeshift furniture. The tiny space had two hearths and a washroom. Despite its size, it was cozy and bright, and nothing had felt so safe in weeks.

The girls peeked around the corner into the kitchen, where they heard and smelled some mouthwatering brew bubbling on the hearth. Thatch told them not to be shy. They tiptoed farther, but the unseen figure at the fireplace thwarted them.

"Thackery J., is that you I hear?"

The girls leaped at the sound of the woman's tender voice. Before they made it far, Grace tangled on the floor with another little girl, who might've popped out of the ground, she came so sudden. The girl burst into giggles and pulled Grace to her feet.

"Look, Leona! Thatch brought more friends!"

The girl squealed when Thatch scooped her up and flipped her backward over his shoulder. She locked her arms around his neck and pressed her cheek to his dirty face.

"Lady Liv, how are you?" He made a rude noise against her cheek until she squirmed free. "Yes, I brought you more friends. Be good to them, hear?"

"Sun and stars!" The motherly voice came from the plump woman in the kitchen. "Not but skin and bones, the lot of you, and soaked through. Never mind the floors; they've seen worse than a dripping. Liv, fetch Dela and Mae, and bring some blankets."

Liv pranced from the room. The woman steered the girls toward the fireplace. As she passed Thatch, she planted a wet kiss on his cheek.

"This is Leona, m'lovelies," Thatch said. "Thought you might find a spot for these wandering lambs, ma'am. The wolves were about to chomp down on them."

We gathered at the table near the fire, where Leona inspected the girls' drooping faces before she examined me. "There's hot supper for you. You too, Thatch, if you've got a moment?"

"'Fraid not, ma'am. Best be up to see the beasts have retreated."

The girls sank, but Thatch patted each of their heads, winked at me, and bounded up the stairs.

Liv returned with an armload of blankets, followed by two other women. None of them ate a bite of Leona's stew until we newcomers had our fill. They insisted, remarking time and again how they were just like us.

Dela and Leona had fled to the Lower Side of the city when their magicks manifested around the same time. They knew mages stayed away from what they thought of as a barbarous pit of thieves and cutthroats. The north end was safe enough, they said, but we never ventured farther south, where Thatch warned us not to go.

Mae made her escape not long after. Some years later, she stumbled on a starving, beaten little boy lying unconscious outside their alley. He grew to be their lookout, protector, and provider, none other than Thackery J. Bright.

"They found me too," Liv said, "but they didn't know I was a witch. I got my magic a few months ago. They've been teaching me. Thatch brings us magic books sometimes. Now they can teach you too."

And that was that. No one went hungry or cold. No one had anything to fear with Thatch and his friends prowling about, always on watch. We used our magic as we pleased, and we learned all we could about it. We were no Academy, but we managed.

Sir Thackery became a better friend than any I'd ever had. He came every day before tending to his duties as self-appointed sheriff, and sometimes he took me with him on his night watches. We sat on the roof of our ramshackle hideaway, and we traded off giving stars the most absurd names. He surprised me with books and precious parchments sometimes. He brought me sticks of chalk and graphite whenever he found them.

We were happy. Despite being far from home, not knowing what came of our beaten father, missing our family and the orchard and those ridiculous geese that would swarm our yard and everything else so much we couldn't breathe, we were fine. And yes, it took a while to get used to the Gildian heat. But the winters are like Rivariar's, with pretty scuffs of snow and misty days. We made do. We were happy.

A year passed.

The mages demolished our magical barrier, blasted down the door. Dragged the shrieking little ones from the table and tossed them over their shoulders, hauled Anna along by her hair. Bewilderment paralyzed Leona, Dela, and Mae, and they obeyed the mages' every order. I thrashed, screamed for my sister, for my new family, for Thatch.

He lay crumpled in the alleyway, the way Papa had, facedown in the dirt. The way the mages left him told me not to hope for him.

It was over. My sister and I were going to die.

CHAPTER 18

Rhys

The rest of Flannery's letter revealed her deal with Vespar, related her first grueling days at the Manor. She admitted to any spells she'd performed and news she'd reported. She recounted a few events; her satisfying confrontation with Tylysk during one particular banquet, our visits to the garden, the Midsummer feast.

She confessed to having told Vespar she would kill me. She despised me for everything.

Despite this, and despite everything Vespar forced me through, I fell for you.

After what you said in the garden that day, I wasn't afraid to love you anymore. I decided I would stay at your side and do whatever it took to help you.

Tylysk told me what people think about witches. I won't stain your good heart with what he said, but it had me thinking if I didn't have the courage to stand at your side, Caeradin would forever be of the same mind as that contemptible pig.

Everything was perfect this Midsummer. If we could still be there, swept up in music and bonfires and starlight, forgetting anything else in the world mattered.

Be brave, my Rhys. Make your da proud. Make me proud.

M'Lady

I huddled behind the Melys tree, numb. I couldn't feel the parchments between my fingers. I felt nothing except the streams of cold drying on my face.

It was my fault Flannery and her family had met their deaths. My childish disappearance that day drove the mages into a frantic search of the Lower Side, where she had sheltered safe from all outside cares, hoping perhaps to live out some quiet, albeit guarded life. One foolish choice, and it had cost eight innocent women and children their lives.

A realization battered me in the chest. This story, this letter, was Flannery's condemnation.

Had she not revealed anything to me, Vespar would have kept his word and released her. But Flannery's confession thwarted his plot. I had to believe every word about the curse he had invented and a witch's cruelty. Her exposure by that despicable, crooked-toothed mage might have ended the scheme, and she could have escaped. But when they ransacked her chambers and found the letter, she had no hope.

And it had all been real. She had loved me. She'd given her life to tell me.

How pleased Vespar must have been that he didn't have to set her free.

I skimmed over the pages again, my eye catching on the first line. "Our village was months from its regular Hunting."

I put my back to the tree. Hunters actually scheduled where and when they'd raid? No wonder they'd had so little success the past few years—if the people know the Hunters are on the prowl, they run.

Except, once the people became complacent and learned the Hunting routine, their defenses fell. That was the real hunting season. Then

Hunters swept hundreds of unsuspecting witches away, just as they had Flannery.

Still, something seemed off. Why did they let the people get away with hiding witches? Were they not disciplined for breaking the law? Gildians brutally enforced such punishments. Why had Flannery's family escaped the consequences of harboring their witch daughters? Would the Hunters not make examples of them?

Stowing the parchments in my pocket, I stalked to the library. The answers lay in those books Vespar had me studying days before. I had to get them. Flannery shoved me on, haunted me, as she promised she would at Midsummer. If I didn't fight now, I never would.

No one stopped me this time. No Watch charms, no interference. I went straight up the staircase and scavenged the shelves. The scroll featuring the Hunters' duties proved easier to find than the thick tome Vespar had given his history lesson from some months before. I threw them onto the nearest table and examined the scrolls. I cast the first three aside.

The fourth parchment, complete with an official Elfrythian dragon seal, appeared to be a copy of the treaty signed during the establishment of the Hunt. I skimmed through the first few passages.

> No province or lord or lady shall be exempt from the demands of the Witch Hunt. No lord or lady shall inhibit Hunting parties from passing into their realms, nor shall they expel any such parties from within their borders. No citizen, noble or otherwise, shall inhibit or disrupt these parties in any manner. Hunting parties may take necessary action to defend against and end such attempts. Citizens, noble or otherwise, who are discovered concealing witches shall be surrendered to local authorities for sentencing through due process of law.

So people got away with hiding witches if their Lord or Lady said so. The conviction of those hiding witches lay on the lord's set of laws, and those whose lords opposed the Hunt went untouched. Hunters had no responsibility for punishing insubordination. But once Flannery's family struck back, they received little more mercy than she.

I was still missing something. Flannery questioned why they brought witches to Gildio at all. Who said they had to? But the scrolls mentioned apprehending and executing, not carting across the country to meet the headsman.

I flipped the book open and found the understated tale of Lord Praed and Lady Blodica. Guiding my finger along the text, I searched for the sections arguing the corruptness of witch magic, anything about the Hunt. Again, nothing helpful.

The last paragraph stopped me, though it hadn't seemed important before.

> Enchantresses often evaded the Hunt. After several generations of Magical Authorities, Wizards became more accepting of their Enchantress, as it was the Wizard's and Enchantress's duties to protect and support one another. Some Enchantresses have been captured. Fewer Wizards have been discovered hiding them.

Well, then. There was my answer. If the Wizard himself thought the Hunt was a bad idea, then a bad idea it must be. Leave it to Gildio to think they had the power to impose their laws on the highest Magical Authorities alive.

But the texts offered me nothing to act upon. What did a few vaguely insubordinate provinces, small ones at that, matter to Gildio? Besides that, Gildio and her allies had been counteracting Magic's will by taking out Its appointed Authorities for centuries. Why would anything else matter? Magic Itself didn't, so why should anything else bother them? Nothing would.

Then why did a defiant boy like me vex them so?

I terrified my tutor. But even after I became Lord of Gildio, Vespar would still be the most powerful man in Caeradin. He had all the influence. Each of Caeradin's lords and ladies bent to his will, either in admiration or fear. How could I, the powerless, fatherless Lord-to-be, pose a threat to perhaps the greatest mage in Caeradin?

Why did Flannery have to die for it?

If Vespar dared to take such extreme measures to turn me around, what else would he try when he realized he'd failed? How many more would fall victim to his anxieties? I'd been fooling myself. Sure, I'd have the authority to do what I wanted when I became lord, but ability was another matter. I had to overcome the most influential man in the country to stop the Hunt. Now, without Flannery, I faced him alone.

I would never win.

Clouds loomed to the west, and the wind took a deep breath. An eerie silence stifled the garden, made the air heavy. I trudged to the garden house to escape it.

Vinegary steam choked the cottage from the hissing cauldron. Mangled stalks of herbs crowded the counter after a brutal chopping for the potion. Colored bottles dabbled the hearth mantle.

I called for Emlyn. No answer. I listened close. The fizzing concoction alone broke the silence. I searched the kitchen, around the table and bookcases in the next room. Panicked, I darted up to the loft to find it empty. I peeked under the covers of her bed. She was gone.

I sat on the edge of the bed and forced myself to breath, but my throat strangled every inhale. My mind reeled for what to do.

"Rhys?"

My heart froze. Emlyn stood on the top stair, worry thinning her lips. She tilted her head.

"Emlyn, where were you?"

She startled back from the bite in my tone. "I was looking for something in the closet. I'm sorry…"

Uneasy relief weighed me to the floor. I dropped my heavy head on my knees to hide my tears from her, but she watched my shoulders quake and heard my desperate gulps for air.

Emlyn's bare toes stepped into view, curled under with her feet turned in toward each other. She cradled her arms around my head, planted a tiny kiss on my hair, and rested her cheek there. I scooped her onto my lap. She hugged me tighter as I wept.

Emlyn drew herself up and led me by the hand down to her table. She flitted about the kitchen on the tips of her toes, light as a butterfly. She laid her box of strawberry candies open in front of me and went back for cups of cinnamon cider.

We stared at each other for a long moment. She sat cross-legged in her chair and fiddled with the cuff of her long sleeve. I took a drink to break from her gaze. Staring into my cup, I explained what had happened.

Emlyn's petrified astonishment lodged a lump in my throat. She folded her arms on the table and hid her face. "It's my fault."

"Emlyn—"

"It is too! They know something's wrong, and I'm what's wrong, and if you hadn't found me, there wouldn't be anything wrong, and you wouldn't have found me if I didn't do that stupid spell!" She smothered her face in her arms and cried into the table.

"What stupid spell?"

Emlyn sniffed. "The one that made me a witch."

I sagged, rested a hand on her head. "Emlyn, we talked about this. You promised you'd stop thinking about that."

"But it's true. If I didn't become a witch, the tinkers wouldn't have got me, and then you wouldn't have got me, and none of this would have happened."

It was logical to her, however indecipherable to me. "But if you'd never done that spell, I would never have met you."

"Exactly!"

"But I'm glad I met you. I'm glad you're here with me. I need you."

Emlyn peeked over her arms, scrubbed her tears from her cheeks.

"I would be all alone if you weren't here. You're all I have left to fight for." I lifted her face. "They won't take you, Emlyn. I made you a promise, and I won't break it. I won't leave you." I pressed a kiss to her brow. Her little smile sparkled through her tears.

An enormous bubble burst in the cauldron and splattered cheese-yellow slime all over the hearth. Emlyn hurried to stir the concoction before it expanded again. She drained a vial into it, and the steam fumed bright orange. The potion quieted over the flames. A flick of her finger, and the mess peeled itself off the hearth stones and tossed itself into the fire.

Emlyn cleaned her ladle. "It has to boil and cool overnight. Then…"

I nodded, not listening. I studied her. How she could curl up in that cauldron, small as she was. So young, she was just starting to lose her teeth. But Vespar wouldn't care about her innocence, should something happen. I'd have no power to fight him.

"Emlyn, we have to leave."

She tiptoed to the table.

"It's not safe anymore. Vespar will try whatever it takes to get to me, and that will take him too close to you." I put an arm around her. "We'll go the first chance we get, when things have calmed down."

She nodded.

I stayed until I spotted Isabelle coming up the garden path. Evening sun doused the garden in yellow, and a faint stripe of blue upheld the looming clouds. Emlyn grasped my hand as I left, a tiny squeeze to bolster my courage.

Isabelle waited for me to join her on the path between the hedges. "My Lady was worried when you didn't come to supper," she said, eyes low. "I suspected you wouldn't be hungry."

"I'm not going to sit at the same table with him," I said.

Isabelle stared at her feet. "If you could believe Master Vespar has your best interest at heart—"

I brushed past her. "Don't make excuses for him."

"Rhys." Her soft voice stopped me. "I don't know why you won't listen. You've changed since you ran off. And that Flannery came the next day…it's the only explanation they've had."

"And you think Flannery was capable of this?" I snapped. "You knew her. You were her friend. Ash and flame, even Aria adored her. Do you really think someone could put on such an elaborate act as long as she did? Even when she knew I wanted to save her kind?"

Isabelle shook her head. "All I know for certain is, you did not come back the same that day. Whether it was Flannery, or another charm, or whatever else, you changed." She mustered the bleakest smile. "I thought you said you only rampaged a tavern."

I couldn't speak. The answer to her plea stood one pace from death in the garden house behind her.

For a moment, watching her dark eyes mist and the weary pallor of her face, I thought how we should have been Lord and Lady Claytherdon ourselves. If we had, this would never have happened.

Isabelle said nothing more. I left her and went inside.

My mother waited for me in my antechamber. She sat in the chair beside the hearth, taking in the feeble warmth of the firelight. She massaged her aching brow and sank into the cushions. Noticing me in the doorway, she sat forward and held her hand out to me.

Broken, I dropped to the floor beside her chair. I drooped to the rhythm of her hand stroking my hair.

"I miss Da," I said.

Mam's fingers paused. "He would have handled this better."

I opened my eyes. "You knew?"

Her silence spoke enough. I fought not to feel too betrayed.

"I begged him to find some other way," she said. "I knew what would happen, and I wouldn't see you this way again."

"Vespar won't listen to you. He never has." I glanced up at her. "Do you believe Flannery cursed me?"

Mam didn't answer.

"Do you believe what he says about witches?"

She looked into the fire. "I don't know what I believe."

"Are you afraid not to believe it?"

No reply.

"Even when Da didn't?" I meant to keep my tone straight, but my inflection begged for an answer. Nothing. I rose up on my knees and faced her.

"Has Vespar frightened you to silence? You're the *Lady*. You are in charge of him, yet you let him bully you into doing everything he wants."

"Rhys." Her scold bore no strength. "It's difficult."

"It isn't. Vespar is not lord. You are Lady. He's supposed to do your bidding."

She hesitated, staring into the restless flames. "I try to do what's best for you. Much of the time, he knows better than I."

My mouth fell open. "You're my mother. How could anyone know what's best for me better than you?"

A sorrowful emptiness swept across her face. "I was a young widowed mother, Rhys. I was stricken with grief and unfit to assume the role that had befallen me, as both Lady Regent and a lone mother. Master Vespar was there when no one else was."

I sat back on my heels. Mam truly had succumbed to Vespar and his illusion of power. She gave him every power over herself the day her husband died.

Sinking, I dropped to the floor and scrubbed my eyes. Dreary silence settled between us, dimmed by the first patters of rain. Mam ran her fingers through my hair.

CHAPTER 19

Rhys

The household took up its routines again within a few days. Vespar was gracious enough about my grief, but insisted that all was for the better, and my mother, especially, no longer had anything to fear. I was safe, the household secure. We all had a better appreciation of the true dangers beyond our walls and everything the Hunt stood for.

"Perhaps one day there will be more hope for your cause, Master Rhys," Vespar said. "But for now, our strongest weapons are deliberation and patience. Diplomacy, order."

I said nothing. Just sat in that uncomfortable chair in front of his desk without looking at him. Based on the pair of books under his hand, Vespar hoped to see me back to some lesson today, however brief. He dismissed me instead.

Mam busied herself about the Manor more than usual. Isabelle stayed strong for everyone else, particularly Aria, who'd taken to hiding in whatever nook the castle had to offer. I'd seen little of Tylysk, the one thing I took any comfort in.

I ate nothing at supper, but sat at the table for Mam and Isabelle's sakes. I sipped the cider when Aria filled my goblet herself. For once, Tylysk kept his eyes on his food in silence. Vespar tried to detract me from the sullen disquiet thickening the room by discussing minor affairs of the realm with my mother. He asked my opinion. In truth, replacing the sheriff who'd swiped the silver from Ashroth Castle or the state of the highways into Lorhurst were the least of my concerns.

When I'd taken as much as I could bear, I excused myself. I stooped to let my mother kiss my cheek one last time. Isabelle made to follow me, but Tylysk grasped her hand when she rose.

I locked my bedchamber door and set to packing. I stuffed my satchel with clothes and a spare blanket. Emlyn had assured me she knew spells to, quite literally, conjure up provisions until it was safe to buy them ourselves. I dropped to the chest at the foot of my bed. The leather pouch buried at the bottom held a few gold and silver pieces, and plenty more to see us through the next few months at least. I tucked it in the bottom of the pack and reached into the chest again.

I unfolded the dagger from the old shirt bound around it. Its leather sheath still gleamed. I grasped it gingerly, remembering when Da let me hold it for the first time. While he'd intended it to be for show on a small boy's belt, it would serve its real purpose well enough.

I sank down on my bed and waited for the outside magelights to dim. I tried not to sleep, but exhaustion made my head pound. The fresh rain lulled me.

The sudden absence of pain woke me. The mageglow lamps dulled, and the garden slumbered in darkness. I crept to the window. The wind carried the clouds south, and the full moon glistened on the quivering veil of mist across the green. I bundled my cloak around me and put my hood up.

I dropped my pack outside the window. The grass shushed me as my foot touched down. I plunged and flattened myself to the wall. Taking a deep breath, I shouldered my pack and slinked along the wall toward the hedges.

Keeping watch on the castle, I crept across the lawn and ducked behind the nearest hedge. No light came from any windows, but braziers atop the watchtowers blazed on each corner of the wall. I padded to the next few hedgerows, pausing behind each. The problematic leap still lay ahead, where the garden path severed the hedges and left some fifteen feet of full exposure.

Someone bellowed.

I ducked, smashed my back to the hedge, and snagged my hood under my chin. How had I been stupid enough to forget the guard change?

I huddled in the shade, the moonlight slicing my boot. On the wall, guards marched to their next post. Their dull shapes cut across the braziers and torches, their cloaks curling smoke under the moon. Another call, and the guards took stance. Firelight emblazoned their halberds with hot orange.

I sneaked on. Watching for every possible eye, I bolted over the cobblestone path. I slid for the next hedge. A guard glanced back. He waved to the man nearest him, and they turned. I hugged myself, heart pounding in my ears. When I peeked up, the watchmen had returned to their posts. I summoned the courage to scuttle to the garden house.

Low flames in the hearth cast the darkness out of the cottage, warming the room with a comforting glow. The potion gurgled in the cauldron. I checked the kitchen window. Terrifying—thirty feet above me stood Emlyn's death.

Using the dim firelight, I made my way to the table and deposited my pack and cloak there. I groped the rest of the way to the stairs and stole up to the loft.

Her bed was empty.

Dismay halted me before I looked toward the fireplace. Emlyn lay on the floor rug with her head on her storybook, warm in the firelight. I tiptoed to her side and cradled her up. She jolted.

"It's me, love."

Emlyn rubbed her eyes. "What are you doing here?"

"I thought I'd better stay with you tonight." I held her on my lap and sat on the edge of the bed. "Close your eyes. Back to sleep."

She nuzzled her face on my shoulder. "Is it tomorrow?"

"Yes, Emlyn. We leave tomorrow."

She crawled to the pillows and wriggled down under her blankets. She patted the pillow next to hers. I lay down on the quilt beside her, and she huddled close, curling into my side. I fed her every comfort I could think of.

"Where will we go?" she whispered.

I hadn't considered it. It hardly seemed to matter. "Out of Gildio as fast as we can."

Emlyn yawned, but sleep evaded her.

For the first time since Flannery's arrest, the roiling force in my chest startled me.

It merely arose deep in my chest, this time painless, and stirred like a restless sleeper. I strained to shove it aside, but it persisted. A violent chill ripped up my spine. Emlyn jumped.

"Sorry," I said.

"Are you cold?"

"No, I…" I licked my lips. "Emlyn, can you do something for me? No, stay here. Don't get up."

"What, then?"

I carefully told her of the curse everyone believed Flannery had set. She'd denied having a hand in it, but she never denied that something lurked there.

"Do you think you can find it?"

Emlyn chewed her lip. "I can try."

"But…be careful, right?"

She fumbled, then crawled up the pillows to rest her forehead to mine. "Close your eyes."

I did. Her warm hands cupped my face. I peeked when she made no sound. Her eyes squeezed shut, nose wrinkled, tongue wetting her lips.

I blinked. Emlyn lurched off the bed and thumped on the floor on her backside. I scrambled over and hoisted her up. Shuddering, she coiled her arms about me.

"That was quick," I tried to tease.

"That took forever," she moaned. "How could you not notice? Didn't you feel it?"

I frowned, realizing I'd let a six-year-old use magic to scope through my head. "What did you find?"

"I-I don't know. It's giant, and it's really dark. I didn't want to, but I touched it, but it pushed me away."

My mouth went dry as sand.

"It didn't feel like normal magic," Emlyn said. "It was something else. Not a witch or a mage."

"What else could it be?"

Emlyn shuddered and hugged me.

Vespar was right. Something was lurking in my head, and it had attacked Emlyn. And he couldn't penetrate it, for all his magnificent strength. Thinking back, he'd panicked when he tried. What could have frightened him? And if every magical person who'd made the attempt sensed this presence, why couldn't I?

The force. It had driven Emlyn and Vespar away. It had made a leap at Tylysk. And my inexplicable sensitivity to magic? Was this presence behind that? Whatever it was, it had no liking for other magicks.

"What do we do?" Emlyn whimpered. When I shook my head, she said, "I'll try—"

"No, you won't. I'm not sending you after it. We'll think of something. There has to be someone somewhere who can help, right?"

Emlyn nodded. "Don't be scared, Rhys. I'll protect you. They won't hurt you."

Her innocent determination made me smile for the first time in days. She snuggled under her blankets, cuddled closer, and drifted.

The shock kept me awake. I second-guessed myself half the night and made up my mind more than once to call off our escape. Emlyn's tiny hum in her sleep banished the thought. She had to escape. We'd risked her discovery for far too long already.

As I drifted toward sleep, another call ordered the guards to rotate.

CHAPTER 20

Rhys

"You're sure about this?"

I stood at the table, where the cauldron rested, its yellow contents bubbling as though it had never left the fire. It spouted the same vinegary odor, and the too-smooth mixture had a sickly shine to it. It looked like phlegm.

Emlyn flitted about the kitchen in search of the last ingredient. "Yes. Almost done."

Sunrise peeked through the windows. Emlyn had shaken me awake when its first rays glowed pink across the garden, and by then we were late. She scrambled to finish her potion while I gathered her satchel.

I agreed to taste the concoction, hoping it'd serve as our sustenance for a while. Emlyn was confident, at least. In all honesty, I wasn't looking forward to gulping a cupful of the first magical brew a six-year-old ever attempted.

Emlyn snatched a tin cup from the table and shook a bottle labeled Whitebale over it. Its chalky contents puffed in her face.

"What does that do?" I asked.

"Well, the book says…"

It eased her nerves, but I didn't understand what she said about it working with some sort of salt and another liquid she'd added. The brew blended to pumpkin orange.

"One last thing." She hopped from her chair.

I glanced out the windows. The Manor would awaken soon. Stephan would knock on my door, find it locked, and get no answer when he called. We had to be out of the city before someone told my mother I was missing.

I checked our packs one last time. Emlyn had a few gowns, one doll, her box of candies, and her storybook. She hadn't bothered with anything else. Her confidence in her own powers worried me—then again, she'd made it this far on her gifts alone.

"Emlyn, come put your cloak on, before we..." I gestured to the cauldron.

She stood still long enough for me to tie the little cloak about her shoulders and skittered to the table. She emptied the phial of red liquid into the potion, counted her churns aloud. After the seventh stir, she set her ladle on the table. She put her arms to her sides and clenched and unclenched her fists.

"Done?" I said.

She smiled when I did, though mine felt queasy. She fetched a cup while I pinned my cloak on. I hadn't noticed how badly my hands were shaking until I stuck my thumb.

"Here, hold this."

I took the mug from her. She climbed up to her cauldron and readied her ladle.

I stopped her. "You're absolutely sure about this?"

"Yes."

I peered inside. The potion retained its stark orange shade, but its consistency had morphed from slime to mush. "It's supposed to look like that, yes?"

Emlyn hoisted her book up for me to see. The substance matched both the description and the appropriate hue on the color wheel shown.

It gurgled and fumed vinegar into my face as described.

"I have the an...antee—"

"Antidote?"

"Yes, that. Just in case." Emlyn patted the pocket of her dress.

"What will that do?"

She grimaced. "Give you a bellyache."

I already had one. "Delightful. Let's do it."

I held the flagon while she filled it. One, two and a half scoops. The mixture squelched as it settled to the bottom. Emlyn grasped my hand while I stared into the mug.

"Just a few swallows," she said, like a mother with a spoon of tonic. "Then it'll be all done."

I brought the mug to my lips, blinked the heat from my eyes.

The door ruptured from its hinges. A swirl of green cloaks flurried into the tiny house. Emlyn shrieked. She fell from her chair and ducked under the table as a shot of scarlet cracked over her head. A spark shattered the flagon in my face. I dove to snatch Emlyn out of the invaders' grasps. An arm slammed across my chest and wrenched me backward. I doubled over and sent the assailant over my head. Two more piled on me. They pinioned me and shoved me to my knees.

Curses crackled in all directions as a mage struggled to catch Emlyn. Screaming, she scuttled out from under the table as he upended it. Magic escaped her grasp in her terror, sending spellbooks soaring across the room. Shelves burst from the walls, bookcases caught her pursuer in the shins. He overpowered her involuntary assault with a roar. The arsenal plummeted from where it halted in midair.

Emlyn scrambled for the stairs. He caught her by the ankles, hooked his arm about her middle, and hauled her back to his followers. She sobbed and thrashed to no avail. He dropped her and snagged a fistful of her hair. His dagger pricked her chin.

My chest seethed with fire. I lunged, but the other mages pinned me down.

Tylysk stared at me, heaving for breath. He gazed about the cottage, taking everything in with wide eyes.

"What, ash and flame, is this?"

"None of your business," I spat.

"Shut your mouth." Tylysk clenched Emlyn's curls. "You did all this? Answer me!"

"Y-yes!"

He poised his dagger at her throat and dragged her along as he inspected every inch of the room. Her magic books strewn across the floor, her shattered cases of tonics and herbs, her demolished stash of food. A nod to one of the mages sent the man up to search the loft.

"How did you do it?" Tylysk gaped. "You're a child. How did you do it?" He jabbed the dagger toward me. "Did he help you?"

"N-no."

"You did all this?"

Emlyn wailed and tugged at his fingers in her hair. Tylysk towed her toward the overturned table. The cauldron teetered along the floor, and its contents slowly pooled over its lip. He motioned to it with a jerk of her head.

"What is that?"

"None of your business!" I barked.

"It is now!" Emlyn's tears dribbled down Tylysk's blade. "Tell me what it is, witch."

"A potion."

Tylysk twisted his fingers in her hair. She shrieked. "What potion?"

"I—I don't know—how to—"

He thrust her toward the rumpled spellbooks on the floor. "Find it."

Emlyn scrabbled through the wreckage of leather-bounds, hands quaking, and dropped most of them. She flipped open the potions book and showed the mage.

Tylysk looked from the tome to her, eyeing her narrowly. He sheathed his dagger, ripped the book from her grasp, and flattened his palm to the back of her head. Emlyn wilted. Tylysk lowered her to the floor. Keeping his eyes on her, he pointed to me and ordered, "Don't let him loose."

"Don't, Tylysk, stop it!"

He knelt beside her. He laid her along the floor, moved her arm out from under her back, turned her face toward him.

"Don't touch her!"

"Shut up." Tylysk fingered Emlyn's face, kneaded her tight throat and the back of her neck. He traced her fingers and smoothed his thumbs across her palms. Closing his eyes, he propped her head in his hands. Concentration furrowed his brow.

"Please, Tylysk, stop!" A mage clamped a gloved hand over my mouth.

Tylysk's jaw fell. The way his shoulders hunched, he must have stopped breathing. He turned his stare to me.

Emlyn gasped awake. Tylysk pressed her to the floor with a hand to her chest. "Don't. Move."

She sobbed and massaged her aching scalp.

Tylysk rose and drew his dagger. He directed it at her, but stepped out of her reach. "Where did you find her?"

The mage took his hand from my face. I said nothing.

Emlyn shrieked when Tylysk drove his foot into my stomach. "Tell me!"

"Your master wouldn't be happy to see you behaving so," I grunted.

"He won't care if you have all your limbs the next time he sees you. Answer me." Tylysk kicked me again, but stood down. "This is your worst mistake yet, Master Rhys." He yanked Emlyn to her feet and summoned a heated smirk. "I suspect she'll find more mercy than you."

The fire broke free.

Surging energy forced me to flail. Chilling silence and darkness clouded me. I only the knew the stretching of my muscles, burning as they seemed to tear down my back and arms. I couldn't tell how they moved, nor what motions could have induced that much pain.

But the agony liberated me. A violent resurfacing from the deep, a desperate gulp for air, a roar to rend suffocating chains.

The dark jarred and tumbled. A scream echoed inside out until my hearing returned. I opened my eyes.

The guards were heaped on the floor where I had leaped out of their grasp, one of them unconscious. Emlyn huddled in a pile of broken bookcases, hugging herself, staring with horrified eyes. Tylysk's dagger stuck out of the wood of the overturned table.

I straddled him, hand raised to strike. Tylysk cowered and covered his face with his arms. Slashes ripped through his sleeves and flesh. Blood soaked the both of us. He unshielded his face. A gash slithered through his left brow, down his cheek, through the corner of his lip, and off his chin.

I scrambled off him. Tylysk shuffled backward and tore his dagger from the table.

I stared at my bloodstained hands. My vision blurred, but I knew something more was wrong with them. I smeared the blood on my clothes. Maybe if it went away, it wouldn't have happened.

The room tilted. I called for Emlyn, but my voice made no sound. I staggered toward her. Emlyn floundered out of reach. Tylysk rushed between us, dagger outstretched. The hand raised to his ear crackled with a scarlet spell. Blood ran into his eye.

"Get back."

I looked between them, but my vision lagged. My head swirled. I fell face down on the floor. The corner of a spellbook grazed my cheek.

"Get the healers," Tylysk ordered.

"Emlyn," I moaned. "Emlyn…"

Agony split through my back, my shoulders, out my hands and feet. My sight fell to darkness. Emlyn sobbed.

CHAPTER 21

Emlyn

Rhys fell silent, face to the floor, blood all over him. Emlyn wasn't sure what had happened. Rhys threw the mages aside, tackled Tylysk, and started beating him. Scratching him. It happened too fast for her to see well, and Emlyn didn't want to. She shuddered and tried not to be sick. Everything stank with blood.

Tylysk put his knife away. He dabbed his face with his shredded sleeve. One arm looked worse than the other, and he cradled it to his stomach. He had more blood on him than Rhys. He stood over Emlyn, glaring.

"Get up."

She obeyed. Her mouth opened on its own.

"Hush." Tylysk snatched her arm and faced his men. His voice was slow and runny. "Stay here. You'll be needed when the healers come."

"My lord, your wounds," one said.

"Mind your orders. Bring him to the castle. Alive, if you can manage."

Emlyn panicked. "No, Rhys isn't—"

Tylysk lugged her out of the garden house, his hand hot and sticky around her wrist.

The sunshine stung her eyes after weeks of hiding. Tylysk dragged her up the stone path where she'd watched Rhys walk with Flannery. Emlyn stared at the big wooden door to the castle. The Manor was so huge, she felt it might fall on her if she peeked up.

The guard burst out the door with three more mages. They had green-and-white robes instead of the cloaks all the other mages wore. One of them stopped Tylysk and insisted he examine his scratches while the others ran to the garden house.

"Later," Tylysk said. "Master Vespar—"

"Will not see you like this, and certainly not before the Lady."

Emlyn whimpered without knowing it. Tylysk jerked her arm, hurting himself. The healer glared at her.

"Skin and bones, Master Tylysk." The healer tore off Tylysk's sleeve. "What have—"

Tylysk whispered too low for Emlyn to hear. The healer's face turned white.

"Impossible. It wasn't…" He glanced at Emlyn. She hid her face.

"What do you think?" Tylysk demanded.

The healer pressed the sleeve to Tylysk's bleeding arm. Emlyn sensed his spell rather than heard it. Tylysk sucked a breath through his teeth. When the healer peeled the fabric away, nothing of Tylysk's gashes showed but pink-and-white scars. He did the same with the other arm. Blood dried up to Tylysk's elbows.

The healer gestured to the slash on Tylysk's face. "You'll need a closer look at that, and soon, before you lose your sight."

"If I have a moment, I'll wait."

The healer pursed his lips. "No more than that," he said. He used the same spell on Tylysk's face. It stopped the bleeding, but the gash still gaped. When Tylysk blinked, red tears came out. Emlyn tried not to look.

"That will hold you a few minutes, no longer." The healer glowered at Emlyn. "Mind yourself, girl."

Tylysk marched on, Emlyn in tow. He jerked her arm whenever she let a sob loose. Her knees slipped as they stepped through the castle door. Tylysk growled and hefted her over his shoulder. Emlyn dangled down his back and wailed.

"Put me down! I'm a good girl, I promise! Rhys—"

Tylysk jostled her. His cloak waved around her as he hurried through the castle. She hid her face in her arms and tried to stop crying. Rhys wouldn't want her to cry—he'd want her to be as brave as him. Even when Tylysk kicked him or put his knife to Emlyn's neck, Rhys was brave. Nothing scared him.

Tylysk opened a door. All the noise in the room went silent, then big gasps, and a woman cried, "Tylysk!"

He resettled Emlyn on his shoulder. "We found Master Rhys, my lady."

Emlyn froze. Lady Orrtha stood right behind her, and Emlyn hung over Tylysk's shoulder like an old doll to be tossed in the fire.

"Where?" the Lady demanded.

"Hiding in the old garden house." He dropped Emlyn on her feet. "With her."

Three people standing around a desk stared at her. Emlyn recognized Rhys's friend Isabelle, the one she thought looked like a princess.

Emlyn had never imagined Lady Orrtha being beautiful. She was a queen in her pretty green gown, with a pearl necklace and jewels in her hair. Emlyn sometimes forgot she was Rhys's mama, because she always imagined Lady Orrtha being scary and horrible. She wasn't. She looked so afraid. Emlyn ducked her head when the Lady covered her mouth.

She didn't need to guess who the third was. Rhys had told her all about him, and Master Vespar matched everything he'd said. Hard and terrifying, his green eyes sharp as a knife, but he showed nothing on his face. He glanced between Emlyn and Tylysk, and his brows went down. He didn't seem angry. Somehow, that worried her more.

"Where is Rhys?" the Lady asked, breathless.

Tylysk stuttered. "He's injured, my lady. We're still ascertaining what happened."

Their eyes moved away when he spoke, but Emlyn felt them on her again. She peeked up, right into Lady Orrtha's gaze.

She pointed at Emlyn. "You…you hurt my son?"

Emlyn panicked. "No, no, I didn't! I didn't, Lady Orrtha, I wouldn't ever hurt Rhys!"

"Don't you say his name." The Lady's shaking finger never fell. A wild shine came to her eyes. "Take her away. Get her out. Where is my son?"

Emlyn backed away, ramming into Tylysk's knee. He clawed her shoulder.

"The girl didn't harm Master Rhys, milady," he said. "It was another matter. The healers are seeing to it as we speak."

"I…I don't care. I want her out of my sight. Where are her papers?"

Master Vespar stepped to the Lady's side, his eyes on Emlyn. "Let me, my lady. Go with Isabelle and be there when they bring Rhys in. Master Tylysk and I will see to this."

Lady Orrtha stared at Emlyn. "Why are you stalling? She's here. Do something with her."

"My lady," Isabelle said. No one had ever looked so sorry at Emlyn before.

Vespar held Lady Orrtha's hands. "Yes, my lady, but we must first be sure nothing more has come of your son. The child will be dealt with, but Rhys needs you now."

The Lady peered into his eyes, clung to his hands. "Help him. Please. Help him."

Vespar kissed her fingers. "Go. I'll join you as soon as I can."

Isabelle hooked her arm through Lady Orrtha's and led her to the door. She stopped long enough to touch Tylysk's arm. He grasped her hand, but Isabelle frowned and led the Lady out.

Once the door shut, Tylysk shoved Emlyn forward. She stood in the middle of the room, chin to her chest. She wished the floor would split open and swallow her up.

Master Vespar studied her. "Were you going somewhere?" he asked, his voice empty.

Emlyn bundled her cloak around herself and rubbed her tears on the scratchy wool.

"Was Master Rhys taking you away?"

She didn't answer.

Vespar looked to Tylysk. Something passed between them, but Emlyn couldn't tell what.

Tylysk shifted. "I searched her, my lord. I'll look to your judgment, but what I found astounded me."

Emlyn couldn't stand their stares anymore. She dropped to the floor and curled up as small as she could.

Vespar cleared his throat. "I see," he said, the slightest shake in his voice. Emlyn scooted away as he drew near, but he went to Tylysk's side.

"Go have that seen to," he said. "I'll manage this."

"Sir—"

"I won't have you incapacitated, Master Tylysk. I expect you back as soon as you are able."

Tylysk tried to argue, but eventually, the door opened and closed behind him.

Master Vespar wandered the chamber, his gaze heavy on Emlyn. She peeked over her arms. The way he moved reminded her of how her cat at home used to pace in front of the window when he saw a bird. He twisted his gold ring. Emlyn watched him stride past a painting that looked like Rhys, except sterner and colder. She tried not to look at it.

When Vespar reached the desk, he stopped to face her. The heels of his boots clicked together. "Tell me your name," he said gently.

She sniffed. She answered.

"Emlyn." Vespar said it as though her name was sacred. He stared at his ring. "I'm afraid you've caused some trouble, little one."

She whimpered.

"Have you nothing to say?"

"I didn't hurt Rhys, sir, I promise. He's my best friend."

Emlyn wished she hadn't said it. Master Vespar frowned. "Is he? Why?"

"He…he saved me."

"He made a valiant effort." He watched her, no suspicion in his eyes. "Did you force him to help you?"

"No, I didn't do anything to him!"

"Stand up here. Why are you on the floor?"

Emlyn obeyed. She remembered how Rhys had faced Tylysk, how courageous he'd been. She kept her eyes up and gripped her cloak to keep her hands down.

Vespar smiled. "Better. Now, tell me how Master Rhys saved you."

"What's going to happen to him?"

"That isn't our concern now."

Emlyn tugged on the cuffs of her sleeves. "A tinker brought me here. He was going to take me to Lady Orrtha, but Rhys came instead."

Vespar frowned. "You've been hiding in the garden this long?" He gave his ring another look. "You must have been afraid. Did you believe Master Rhys would help you?"

"I…I don't know."

Then he looked sad. "Did he promise to take you away from here, Emlyn?"

She shut her mouth. If she told him the truth, Rhys would be in even more trouble, if that was possible. But Vespar already knew, seeing her cloak and boots.

"Where were you going?" he asked, sounding more curious than anything.

Emlyn blinked at him. His gentleness spooked her as much as Tylysk's yelling scared her. "He didn't know. Just far away."

"Home?"

She stared at her feet. "No."

He nodded. He licked his lips and twisted his ring. Rhys never told Emlyn he did that.

He suddenly held out his hand to her. "Come, don't be afraid."

Emlyn planted her feet.

His hand fell. He swallowed, gave his ring another glance. "You rather impressed Master Tylysk. Tell me, how old are you?"

"Six, sir."

A spark crossed Vespar's eyes. He squared his shoulders. "Magic claimed you so young," he said. Another look over her, and he asked, "Or has It always had you?"

"I don't know."

He stared again. Emlyn's hot cheeks stung with tears, her head hurt from Tylysk pulling her hair. She didn't feel very brave.

Vespar stepped forward, hand outstretched. "Don't be afraid. Please, come."

Emlyn trembled. Vespar was supposed to be mean and cross and the worst man alive, Rhys said. But his sharp eyes softened, and worry wrinkled his brow.

Emlyn tiptoed closer.

Vespar smiled. "There, little one. I won't hurt you."

She halted, fists under her chin. "But...I'm..."

He inched nearer. "Master Tylysk wonders something about you. Let me see, little one."

"What about Rhys?"

"It doesn't matter now. Let me look."

"I don't want you to."

Master Vespar stood close enough to touch her. Emlyn didn't step away, afraid he'd grab her if she tried. He knelt down. She let him take her hand.

"Please," he said. "If it could save your life, why won't you let me?"

"It hurt when Tylysk did."

"For a moment. Is that not worth it?"

Vespar begged her. She saw desperation in his eyes.

Emlyn swallowed. "If I let you, will you let me see Rhys?"

He pursed his lips. "I can't promise that. It may be unsafe, from what Master Tylysk said."

"Rhys would never hurt me. He loves me."

Emlyn didn't regret saying it this time. It made her strong. No matter what anyone else did to her, Rhys would always love her. He promised.

Vespar focused on her, looking from one of her eyes to the other. "If you do this for me, I will do what I can to let you see him."

That wasn't good enough, but Emlyn doubted she had a choice. He'd do what Tylysk did and make her sleep so he could pry around her magic. Either that, or wait for Tylysk to come back and pin her down while Vespar did it. Emlyn shuddered. She never wanted to see Tylysk again.

Emlyn took a deep breath and closed her eyes.

"Good girl," Vespar said, a smile in his words. He took her head in his hands, his thumbs brushing her temples. He tilted her face up. "Be still, now."

Emlyn concentrated on keeping her knees from hitting together. His magic pierced her. She jumped and clung to his wrists.

"Shh." His thumbs circled her temples. "Be still."

The threads of Vespar's magic crawled through her head, a spider scuttling across her brain. It slinked down her neck and speared into her heart. Tylysk's spell hadn't hurt this bad. Vespar's power was a hundred, no, a thousand times stronger than Tylysk's. The threads of her magic's essence frayed at the ends to make room for his.

Then it stopped. Vespar pressed harder, and though it ached worse, his magic went no farther. The threads wove together and resisted him. Emlyn wasn't making them do it.

He took his hands away. Emlyn stumbled, fingering where his spell had stung her cheeks.

Vespar forced himself to breathe. He stared at the floor. When he could lift his head, he staggered to his feet and leaned with his fists on the desk. He didn't look at her for a long time.

"Good. Very good, dear girl." He smiled on her. "Fateful, indeed. Who knew Master Rhys had such luck?"

Emlyn perked up. "Then he won't get in trouble?"

His face emptied. "That has yet to be decided."

"Please don't hurt him. *Please.* I want to see him."

"In time. It may be some time before he's well enough for visitors."

Before Emlyn opened her mouth again, Master Tylysk barged in after a short knock. Stitches lined the gash on his face. His eye didn't look damaged anymore, but he had to blink blood out of it sometimes. Emlyn found herself cowering closer to Master Vespar.

A silent message passed between the mages. A grin broke across Tylysk's face. Master Vespar struggled to keep his from going too wide.

"Well done, my lord," Tylysk said. "Who would have thought it would come about like this? And you, girl, are absurdly fortunate."

Emlyn hid her face in her arms. Their anger frightened her, but their praises were worse. Whatever she'd done that they liked, Rhys wouldn't, and if Rhys didn't like it, it had to be bad.

Vespar beamed at her for a moment, then his brows narrowed. "Yes, but this must be handled carefully. Any word on Rhys?"

Tylysk touched his face as if Rhys's name stung his wound. "They got him to his chambers, sir. The healers are with him, but they've refused anyone else, including the Lady. They've deemed it too dangerous."

Emlyn's heart stopped. "What happened?" she blurted. "Master Vespar, what happened to Rhys?"

"Hush, little one. Never you mind."

"But—"

"Hush." Emlyn ducked her head out of his reach. "I have much to see to, then," Vespar said. "I'll entrust Emlyn to your care until we decide how to proceed."

"Yes, milord," said Tylysk.

Vespar watched Emlyn once more. "Do as you see fit, Master Tylysk. I trust your judgment. But, gentle, remember—the gem is delicate."

"Yes, my lord."

Emlyn shuddered when Master Vespar set a hand under her chin.

"I will do all I can to keep my word, but for now, behave yourself. Do as Master Tylysk asks."

She was too afraid to say anything but, "Yes, Master Vespar."

Tylysk held her hand until they stepped out of Vespar's sight, and then he gripped her wrist. He whisked her down the stairs and deeper into the castle. She ran to keep up with his stride. Tylysk whipped her in front of him when they turned down another hallway. Voices echoed far behind them. Emlyn recognized the Lady's—Rhys's room must have been down there.

Tylysk unlocked a door and bumped her into the room. Emlyn stumbled aside when he shoved past her. A swing of his hand, and the door shut and bolted itself.

Tylysk draped his cloak over one of the four chairs at the table in the middle of the room. Emlyn noticed a few bookcases, eyed other sets of shelves with dusty magic trinkets. Two more doors on the far wall led to a bedroom and a workroom, she supposed. Tylysk spotted her glancing at them and moved to close the doors.

Moaning, he went and flopped in his armchair. He rubbed his eyes. He forgot his wound and sucked a breath through his teeth when it stung. Emlyn didn't know what else to do but stand where he could see her. Tylysk glowered at her, but she was getting used to it.

CHAPTER 22

Rhys

A dark, rugged voice. A string of indiscernible words in a slick, harsh tongue. A chamber brimmed with shadow. A fire emitting no heat or light. A distant movement of someone turning. A pair of blood-red eyes direct against my gaze. An empty regard. An inhuman face.

I felt nothing beneath my feet, but the darkness upheld me. Smoke thickened the air, but there was no air. My mouth tasted of ash. Far in front of me, hardly distinguishable from the rest of the dark, a pool of shadows lay still as glass, save a single outward ripple with every pulse of my heart. A light with no source rode the ripples.

The eyes hovered above the pool. They paralyzed me. They were no human eyes, a black slash through red. The rest of its being stayed hidden, but its huge, haunting presence towered over me.

It spoke again. I'd never heard anything like its language, all teeth and throat and spit. Breaking glass, crackling fire, scraping plate armor. Frightened, I stepped back. My foot plunged through the murk. I flailed for balance. When I looked at the eyes again, they drew closer, near enough to touch. My heels dangled over the brink.

It reached for me. A gigantic force closed in to crush me. I cowered into the shadows.

I thrashed awake. My eyes stayed sealed shut, my head swirled. My mouth was dry, gritty, and nasty as a swallow of sand.

I overpowered whoever was restraining me. Another came, and I arched and writhed to escape. The effort tore at the muscles down my back. They pinned me down, and another clamped cold iron around my wrists. It took all of them to snap my arms to the wall.

Mam's voice froze me. I called for her.

"No, my lady," a voice ordered. Mam protested, but he denied her again.

"Drink, Master Rhys."

Bitter liquid scalded my throat. I choked, and most of it dribbled down my chin. I forced the next swallow down. My body relaxed. I sagged in the chains.

I recognized the cushion of my own bed when the men moved aside. Several pillows propped me up. The stink of medicinal brews pervaded the room. My hands itched maddeningly.

"Master Rhys," someone said. "Deep breath, Master Rhys."

The expansion of my lungs set them ablaze. I cried out.

"Let me through," my mother snarled. "I can do more for my son than your ghastly concoctions." In another moment, her soft hands cooled my face. "Rhys, my love, I'm here."

I peeled my sticky eyes open, but the dim candlelight stung. Candles, not magelights, praises be. I ventured to see again and shielded my face in Mam's palm.

"What happened?"

"Hush, my Rhys."

I moaned. "It hurts, Mam."

She tipped a cup to my mouth. I gulped every drop of water. My hand moved to wipe the excess from my lips, but the shackles held firm. I glared at them, finding my hands strapped in thick falconry gloves.

"Take these off," I said.

"Sweetheart, the healers—"

I yanked the chain, wrenched to free myself.

"Rhys, stop. Stop. You'll break your wrist."

"Make them take these off."

"Darling, please, it's hard enough to see you so."

I breathed too heavily. Mam brushed my hair from my brow.

"Relax," she said. "The more you relax, the less it will hurt."

I closed my eyes, and Mam rested her cheek on my hair. I slowed my breathing, willed the scalding sedative to do its work. Pain shuddered through my bones. Mam hummed in my ear.

A withdrawal, all the force seeping into my chest to disperse. An ache spiked in my back, hands, and feet. I cried out at the sting.

It stopped. All of it. It left me weak and exhausted, but whatever had gripped me vanished.

"I'm…fine now, Mam. It stopped."

She took the cloth from the bedside table and dabbed my brow. I downed another cup of water.

"What's wrong with me?"

Mam paled. I hadn't noticed how her hair spilled unkempt from her pins and braids, and circles darkened her eyes.

"How long has it been?" I asked.

She looked at her hands. "This is the second night since we found you."

I gaped. "Mam, please."

She fussed with everything to avoid my eye. "They…believe it was the curse."

I might have guessed. "What did it do this time?"

"Not now. Rest."

"Don't do this to me," I groaned.

"Rhys Ioan, don't start. You're lucky your father didn't come and take you from me. I won't hear it."

I looked away from her weariness. My arms tingled from the shoulders down, dangling over my head. "How did they find us?" I asked.

Across the room, the physicians made conscious efforts not to turn their heads. They spoke low. I caught something about a trial, no doubt my upcoming hearing for my crimes.

Angry scarlet rushed to my mother's features. She dropped in the bedside chair. "When Stephan found you missing, we sent another search. Someone came forward." She took the cloth's water dish in her lap. "The shepherd on the hill. He'd seen someone sneak to the garden house sometimes, but he thought little of it till now."

I glared at the ceiling. I hadn't imagined the old shepherd paid attention, let alone saw me. No, he had a lovely view of the Manor garden from his sheep hovel on the hill. How had I been so stupid?

Ignoring the healers puttering about my bedchamber, I asked, "Where is Emlyn?"

The room went still as a graveyard. Mam waved the healers away.

"Be careful. No one is happy to hear of it," she said. "She's in custody. Nothing has come of her yet."

I tugged on the chains to sit myself up. "She did nothing wrong. I don't care what everyone thinks. She used no magic on me."

Mam watched her hands wringing out the rag over the water dish. "I don't believe they think she did. She's too young to know how to manipulate you, they've told me."

"But she'll die anyway because she has the magic to do it."

"Rhys." Mam sank in her chair, a hand to her aching head. "Why did you do it?"

"Why wouldn't I? She came all the way from Babondodd, bound up and displayed by her tinker kidnappers day after day, and no one, *no one*, gave her a second glance. Doesn't that sicken you, Mam? They knew this child faced her death, and no one did anything to stop it. I did." I gritted my teeth. "Da would have done the same."

"Tell me this, then," she challenged. "Did you do it out of pity or to make a statement?"

My mouth didn't stay open long.

"Then no, that is not what your father would have done."

"Maybe it was a statement at first," I confessed, "but not now. She's brilliant and precious and alone. She needs me, Mam. She is all that is good in the world, and they're going to murder her."

Mam's mouth tightened. I twisted onto my side as far as the shackles allowed.

"Please. Don't let them. I'll...I'll take her away. We'll leave. We'll never bother them again. Isn't that what Vespar wants?"

"No, and nor do I," Mam said scornfully. "How dare you suggest?"

"I don't care what happens to me. I'll give up my lordship to see her safe, if they'll just let me take her. And if a price has to be paid, I'll pay it, my life and all."

"Shush." Mam's hands clenched. "Close your mouth. Stop this nonsense."

"What nonsense? She is everything to me. I swore to protect her, and ash and flame, I will die before I break that promise again."

Mam overturned the water dish in my face.

I spluttered. Blinked the dribble from my eyes. Mam calmly ordered someone to fetch more pillows and a fresh shirt. She slicked my dripping hair from my brow. Sitting beside me, she took the rag and dried my face. Much of what she dabbed away were tears.

"If you love me," she said, "you'll take back your word and never speak it again. Perhaps I do believe your father, but I will not let a witch ruin what is left of my family." She sighed, shaking her head. "All this time," she said, "with Flannery here and everything."

I turned aside so she wouldn't see me crumble.

Smaller flareups agonized me the rest of the night. No nightmares, but the pain and swarming force seized. Once Mam calmed me, it dispersed and seemed never to have existed. Healers came and went to pour tonics down my throat. I rested, but not before dawn.

The healers agreed I wouldn't be well enough for my trial for at least two more days. They shifted around me as they would a lion with a stirring appetite. I sometimes felt that way.

Once the healers decided I could make a suitable recovery without their supervision, they dismissed themselves. Isabelle tended to me while Mam rested. My mother never left the room, and she slept in the bedside chair when she could.

Without the healers' guidance, their efforts went unrewarded. My fits never relented. Nothing banished my tenacious headache. Even with Aria's coaxing, I ate nothing.

I never saw any Lord Mage or Mage Master. Sometimes I wished they'd stroll in. I had a word or two I would've liked to tell them.

CHAPTER 23

Tylysk

"Will you—" Tylysk took a deep breath. "Stop. That."

Emlyn ducked her head, but stared at him. She stayed on the sofa in his study, hugging her knees. Her weepiness had lessened over the past few days, at least in front of him, but those blue-violet eyes always shone with the threat of tears. After three days, it still set his teeth on edge.

"Now, are you listening?"

She nodded.

Tylysk approached, dagger drawn. Emlyn didn't flinch. "I have late business," he said. "I won't be long."

She buried her face in her lap. At least she'd learned not to argue and beg. Finally.

"So go to sleep." Tylysk knelt at the sofa and pointed his dagger to the floor. "I'll stop the circle when I come back."

Emlyn didn't budge.

"Do as you're told."

She bundled her blankets around herself, tipped onto her side, and faced away from him.

"Don't let me find you awake when I get back."

Nothing. Good.

Tylysk touched the point of his dagger to the chalk ring on the floor. Emlyn braced herself as he murmured the incantation. A pale red glow emitted from the dagger's tip and followed the circle around her sleeping place. Bland preparations, but detaining a scared little girl required little more. Tylysk sheathed his dagger and stood.

The girl sniffed.

"No. Stop that. You're not getting out of it."

She curled her arms around her head and mewled like a miserable cat.

Tylysk made it to the door. He raised a hand with a spell to douse the magelight. She huddled as close to the cushions as she could wriggle herself. Tylysk ground his teeth.

"All right, all right!" He turned back. "Stop it. What's the problem?"

The girl scrubbed her tears away. She hiccupped.

"Well?"

Her tiny voice said, "Where are you going?"

"None of your business. What's the matter?"

Another hiccup. She stayed silent too long, and he turned to leave.

"When will I get to see Rhys?"

Tylysk swallowed a groan. Even if she hadn't said a word about it since Master Vespar left her to him, the anticipation that she would was as bad as if she'd done nothing but pester him. "I don't know. He's…he's starting to get better. Now, if you're a good girl and you stop crying and go to sleep, I'll ask Master Vespar about it tomorrow."

Emlyn peeked over her shoulder. Tylysk grimaced at her pink-rimmed eyes, but it didn't deter her. "Really?"

"I don't see you sleeping."

Emlyn ducked to the cushions and curled up tighter.

Tylysk rubbed his eyes and doused the magelight. The red mist encircled her, low ethereal flames standing still. Patting his pocket to be sure he hadn't forgotten the vials, he left his cloak on the arm of his chair and stepped out the door.

Why on earth his master thought Tylysk made a suitable caretaker, he had no idea, aside from the fact that Vespar could trust no one else with the task. Tylysk would rather have done anything else than be saddled with Rhys's imp, even if she was who they believed her to be.

A temporary assignment, just until the council decided Rhys's fate and Master Vespar determined how to proceed. The Manor lay in mayhem, and with Lady Orrtha incapacitated, it fell to the Lord Mage to reestablish order. If he wasn't preoccupied performing the Lady's duties for her, he'd be the one tending to Emlyn.

Tylysk should have been honored to be given the task, and he was. If the Lord Mage entrusted this precious child to him—well, how could he think of anyone more highly? But the miserable task drained him.

Temporary. Tylysk could endure a few days more before they saw the plan underway. Stupid as the coincidence of Rhys's blunder was, everything was falling into place.

Tylysk cleared his head for his midnight task and crossed to the next corridor. Splinters of light found the cracks beneath the door ahead. Tylysk crept toward it. The rest of the Manor slumbered fitfully. He doubted there would be a guard surrounding Rhys's chambers, and peeking through the door, he was right. Few were bold enough to stay near him. Tylysk bore everyone's reminder of Rhys's newfound ferocity on his face.

Tylysk slinked into the antechamber, tiptoed to the bedchamber, and pressed his ear to the door before he cracked it open. A single candle illuminated the room. By the looks of it, Isabelle had coaxed the Lady into leaving Rhys in her care for the night. She huddled in the bedside chair on the far side of the room, sleeping prettily. If she was napping, so was Rhys. Once inside, Tylysk closed the door before the antechamber light sliced across the boy's face.

Isabelle hummed in her sleep. Tylysk approached her first. Touching a hand to her dark hair, he voiced the charm in his head. She fell forward. He propped her on his shoulder and raised her to the armchair, her head heavy on one arm and her legs over the other. Tylysk held his breath when she twisted onto her side, but she tucked her elbow under her head and hummed. He traced the shape of her delicate cheek with a finger.

Tylysk turned to the invalid. Chains restrained him like the beast he was, arms dangling over his head. The candlelight made his ghastly face sallower. Sweat trimmed his brow, his hair disarrayed by constant petting from one caretaker or another. The room reeked of drafts and sickness.

No amount of tonic would subdue this "disease". Nothing would banish what plagued him. Rhys was as good as dead, but even that would evade him now.

Explained a lot.

Iron rings above the headboard upheld the chains. Tylysk willed them to come undone. Rhys jumped out of his skin when his arms plummeted to his face. His bleariness sapped his strength, and Tylysk easily thrust his left arm back and secured the chain around the bedpost. The boy mumbled for Isabelle, winced when Tylysk yanked harder. He blinked his sluggish senses into place. He tensed.

Tylysk grinned. "Look out."

Rhys scowled. His bloodshot eyes followed Tylysk around to the other side of the bed. "What did you do to Isabelle?" His voice reminded Tylysk of a steel edge on gravel.

"Have I done anything to her? She's sleeping." Tylysk dropped on the edge of the bed. "How's it coming?"

Rhys glared. His glance flickered to Tylysk's left eye more than his right. Tylysk seized the front of his shirt and dragged him in for a closer look.

"Proud of your work, Master Rhys?"

The boy turned away. Tylysk let him drop to his pillow. He pointed to the gloves strapped around Rhys's hands.

"Fashionable. They seem to do the trick. I haven't heard about you slashing anyone else."

"Leave me alone."

Rhys was worse than Tylysk had anticipated. He barely had the strength to stiffen when Tylysk gripped his arm. He pulled Rhys's sleeve up and straightened his limb across the pillow. "Keep it there, would you?"

"Let go."

Holding firm to Rhys's wrist, Tylysk tugged the manacle down his arm and slid the glove halfway off his hand. He took the empty vials from his pocket and set one aside. Rhys couldn't flex his arm, let alone move it.

"I said, let go."

Tylysk drew his dagger. Rhys's eyes widened. Isabelle stretched and turned in her sleep.

"Tylysk, don't. Tylysk—"

He swiped the blade down Rhys's wrist. The boy gasped through gritted teeth. Tylysk traded the dagger for the ready vial and caught the trickle of blood oozing from the wound. Rhys squeezed his eyes shut.

"Queasy?" Tylysk asked.

Rhys made a weak fist, either in pain or to strike. The blood flowed faster. "I didn't know you fancied dark magicks, Tylysk."

"Please. What's dark about looking out for you?" Tylysk wiped his tainted dagger on the rim of the vial before setting it on the rag on the table. "Who knows what will happen to you? What a shame if we lost sight of you."

"Track me or curse me, any way you like," the boy hissed.

"Not at all. As long as you behave yourself." Tylysk held the vial up to the light, where it glowed crimson across Rhys's face. "Stay on top of things, is all."

Rhys trembled. Tylysk sat back and waited for the dribble to fill the little vial.

"They won't execute me?"

Tylysk laughed. "If you're not dead by now, nothing could kill you."

"Why?"

"Still haven't figured it out? Look at yourself. You'll come up with something. I'll tell you this," he said, patting Rhys's chest, "you won't believe it when you do."

Rhys tried to scowl, but his eyes swirled in the wrong direction. He cringed when Tylysk scooped the last drop over the rim of the vial and set the next to the wound.

"Emlyn," he said.

"I thought you'd never ask."

"You took her."

The mage shifted enough to jostle Rhys's wounded arm. "And?"

"Why?"

"Why? That's what you ask? Why?"

Rhys stared unseeing across the room. His face seeped to deathly white. "You said…"

"You are aware you're asking the entirely wrong person, aren't you?" Tylysk waved a hand in front of Rhys's glassy eyes. No response.

Tylysk checked the vial in the candlelight, his fingers sticky on the warm glass. The boy gave no reaction when Tylysk pinched his wrist for the last few drops.

Both brimming vials glowed under the candle. Tylysk smeared the stain from the blade on the nearby rag and sheathed it. He produced a third vial from his pocket and emptied its clear fluid over the gash.

Rhys yelped. Tylysk pressed the rag tight around the wound. He held firm for a moment, then let Rhys jerk away. The boy examined his unblemished arm. No scar remained.

Rhys gritted his teeth and let Tylysk clean the blood drying on his skin. Tylysk gathered the vials, took the bloody rag, willed the chains to clasp to the wall, and moved to the door. The boy watched him go, sallow and glaring once more. Tylysk held a vial between his thumb and finger and lifted it to the light.

"A lot of power here," he said. "I'll be sure it doesn't fall into unfriendly hands."

"You're the last person I'd trust it with."

"I told you, Master Rhys. Nothing could kill you now."

CHAPTER 24

Rhys

The door clicked behind Tylysk. Isabelle startled awake.

"Rhys, I'm sorry, I didn't hear…are you all right?"

I couldn't swallow.

"Here, drink. You look awful." She tipped the cup of water to my lips, then rushed to the other side of the bed. "You're dripping. Here— where's the rag?" She searched the table. "It was right here."

I hoped I looked bleary and not like I was hiding something.

"I'll get another." Isabelle gave me another drink before hurrying out.

I never told anyone about Tylysk's late night visit. I had no proof, and they'd say I dreamed it up in my haze. I didn't know how far two finger-long vials of my blood would get him, but he had the chance to steal more. I didn't dare to think what he'd try with it, either.

I had never been so afraid of anyone in my life.

I lay awake the rest of the night. Isabelle stayed up with me as long as her own exhaustion allowed. For a while, she sat beside me and propped my arms up after they'd hung and ached for three days. Blisters bubbled under the iron.

Whenever the curse took hold, Isabelle stayed at my side. She dabbed my face and cooed. "Do you remember the first time we climbed the trees in the garden? And we raced to the top, and I beat you the first time? Remember when your da would take us to the sweets shop and he'd bring those vanilla and chocolate flowers for your mother? And he'd take us out to the hills and let us play the whole day? Remember?"

I drooped for a few moments around dawn. Too soon, someone patted me awake, then unclasped the shackles. Mam begged me to eat what Aria had brought. The girl sat beside me and held the plate until it was bare, so I forced it down. Realizing why the shackles came off shooed my appetite.

Stephan and Dom helped me wash and dress. Though slow and painful, I managed to look presentable in Da's clean jerkin by the end of it. The itchy leather gloves never came off.

They waited for the summons in the antechamber while I sat on my bed and Aria took a comb to my hair. She curtsied. I found myself thinking I'd miss that, whatever happened to me. I would miss watching her play in the bailey with my dogs.

"I believe you, Master Rhys."

I looked up into Aria's eyes. They were the shade of soft grass.

"You're nice to me. You're a good person. I'll always believe you."

She didn't jitter. She didn't bolt. She smoothed a stubborn lock from my brow. I'd miss the gentle breathlessness of her voice, too.

"Thank you, Aria."

She slipped into a nervous curtsy, her shy, quiet self once more. She stood there and waited for someone to tell her what to do.

"Will you do one more favor for me?" I asked.

A curtsy.

"Do you know if they brought my satchel from the garden house?"

Aria shuffled her heels together. "I think so, sir."

"Can you find it for me?"

She drifted about my rooms without question. Though someone asked what she wanted with it, Aria retrieved my pack. I prayed I'd hidden my treasure where whoever had rummaged through it didn't find it.

I pulled out the blue waistcoat and dug through its pocket.

There it was. Flannery's letter.

Aria watched me tuck the parchments into the inside pocket of Da's jerkin. I winked and put a finger to my lips. She smiled and did the same.

Dom and Stephan helped me into the antechamber. Isabelle pecked my cheek at the door.

"Good luck. Don't be stupid."

Mam insisted the servants support me down the hall instead of the Ordinary guards waiting outside. The guards won the argument to have me shackled. She cried as they clasped the irons on. The cuffs clenched the prickly leather gloves into my wrists.

I'd expected to see the vast audience of the Gildian court in the great hall, but only the councilmen took up the long table on the dais. A green banner draped crosswise down its center, and the black eagle scowled at me. Guards stood watch at every pillar along the room. My stomach churned enough at the sight of them without the help of the stench of fresh floor polish.

The Gildian councilmen took eight of the nine seats. The four Mage Masters wore their traditional mage cloaks over green-and-black council robes, and each displayed his magic trinket where all could see. Two held jeweled talismans, one had what looked like a quill-sized scepter, and the last wore a polished brass key on a cord around his neck. An Ordinary councilman sat between each pair of mages. They murmured to one another, the nervous chatter over the fate of Caeradin's greatest realm.

Lord Mage Vespar stood in front of the dais. From a distance, his hands looked folded, but he was toying with his ring.

The guards refused to let Dom and Stephan past the door. I limped to the dais without support. Staring at the oak floor, I thought of Lizzie and Violet scrubbing away at it, Theresa carrying silver platters for the Midsummer banquet. And Flannery, her hand in mine as we sat at the table, whispering over the banquet prattle.

A fat Mage Master sat in her chair now, rolling his scepter back and forth between his chubby hands.

The guards shoved me to my knees. They stood on either side of me and faced one another, right hands crossed over to hold the hilts of their swords. Mam, who refused to join the councilmen on the dais, stood to the side and faced them. Someone else would take her place at the table, and I wouldn't be happy to see him there.

Vespar let the councilmen chatter and cast harsh glances at me. He stood there in perfect stance, heels together, face devoid of any emotion. I wanted to ask why he never came to visit me at my sickbed, but decided it wasn't the time to provoke him.

The door opened and closed far behind me. I ignored it until a hush collapsed on the councilmen. Vespar stared across the hall and stepped toward me. The tiny pad of bare feet made me turn to look.

Emlyn sprinted toward me, Tylysk hard on her heels. Vespar grasped my shoulder to stop me from rising. He stepped between us, halting Emlyn in her tracks. Tylysk snagged her arm. She stumbled the rest of the way to the dais, pleading, prying at Tylysk's fingers. Vespar blocked my reach for her. I stood. The guards crossed their swords in front of me. Once I retreated, they shoved me to the floor and took their posts.

Tylysk stood to the side across from my mother. He held Emlyn in place with his claws on her shoulders. Emlyn dried her tears on her sleeves, tucked her fists under her chin, and stared at me. She hiccupped.

Vespar didn't have to say anything about what the entire room had witnessed. He returned to stand in front of the dais. He bowed his head, and the muttering councilmen minded his signal for silence.

"Master Rhys Ioan Claytherdon, son of Lord Ioan Claytherdon, Master of the Hunt and Heir to the Lordship of Gildio."

He did it justice, I supposed, and with little contempt.

"You have been summoned before the council to answer for your crimes against the Claytherdon Household, namely the concealing of a witch, conspiring harmful plots against the Claytherdon Household and Lady Regent Orrtha, and treason."

My mouth fell open.

"Your plea?"

"Not guilty," I said. "First, what harmful plots are you suggesting?"

Mam cringed.

"You have admitted to several persons that you intend to bring down the Hunt, despite your firsthand knowledge of the dangers of witch magic."

A ruffle of Flannery's hair flashed through my mind.

The Ordinary councilmen whispered to one another. The Mage Masters flitted uneasy glances at Emlyn and shifted in their seats.

"You mistake my intent," I said. "'Bring down' implies that I mean to use violence. I have admitted to the intention to change laws and do what I can to rehabilitate these women and end mass slaughter."

"Would this not bring harm to your realm? Whatever you attempt, you will lose allies and make enemies. You put Gildio at the mercy of Caeradin's strongest lords when you have no means to defend yourself so early into your reign."

"I have considered this."

"Have you?"

I swallowed.

Vespar nodded. He paced along the dais. "Second?"

"Second, treason?"

"You have disregarded the laws of your own realm. Your title does not excuse you."

"But…treason?"

Mam shut her eyes and battled to stay where she stood.

"Let me restate: you have willfully disregarded the most vital laws set by your forebears to ensure the safety and prosperity of the realm and of Caeradin and to enable the Hunt's success. As future Lord of Gildio, you have disrupted your realm's security. You have broken the oaths you have yet to make as Lord. You have abandoned Gildio."

I stared at his feet, eyes misting. "No, I haven't."

Emlyn hid behind her hands. Tylysk rolled his eyes and stooped to hush her. The other Mage Masters grimaced and eyed her. The Ordinaries went on murmuring.

Vespar signaled for silence. "Anything else, Master Claytherdon?"

Mam braced herself. I glanced at Emlyn, but there was no point arguing that conviction.

He waited to be sure. He turned and joined the councilmen. They made a magnificent display of coming up with a verdict. Certain words echoed more than others. *Treason, witch, must, can't. His condition.*

Tylysk hovered over Emlyn, taunting me with his victory. As I watched her, Emlyn never once cowered from him, never swerved out of his reach. If anything, she retreated *to* him.

She'd already been granted the mercy Tylysk said I wouldn't find.

"Yes, my lord, I do have something."

Vespar looked up. The councilmen raised their glares, ranging from blazing to bored.

I used all my strength to stand. The guards reacted, but Vespar raised a hand to stop them.

"Before you reach a verdict," I said, "and before you sentence me, I still have rights you cannot dispute."

Vespar's brows narrowed. Mam braced herself.

"I have the right to know what you intend to do with Emlyn."

The muttering grew louder. The Mage Masters joined, though their eyes never left little Emlyn. She hid behind Tylysk's leg.

Vespar hesitated. Watching him look to the councilmen for permission to speak was as gratifying as it was awkward.

The Lady came and stood at my side. All noise silenced. If Vespar's face was capable of showing hurt or regret, I caught a glimpse of it in the way he gazed at my mother.

He came away from the dais. Tylysk drew Emlyn out from behind him. She fixed her teary eyes on me, hands folded under her chin.

"We have debated much on the subject," Vespar said. "It has come to our attention that, according to our record, this witch is the youngest ever ascertained by the Hunt. Her powers are still underdeveloped, yet undeniably remarkable."

Emlyn wrapped her arms around her head.

"In light of her age and capacities, we have toyed with the idea of an experiment." Vespar met my eye, but for the first time, it seemed difficult for him. "If her magic is so young, perhaps the danger may be suppressed. Perhaps, if guided by the proper mentor, she may overcome the inherent malignancy of her powers."

My jaw dropped. "You're joking. Who's going to teach her? You?"

Vespar raised his chin.

"Yet, you're convicting *me* of harboring a witch?"

Mam touched my back. "Rhys, mind yourself."

Vespar's eyes glinted. "Perhaps if you had brought her forward at the start, the experiment could have taken place without these tragic circumstances."

It buckled me. I dropped to the floor.

"The council has reached a verdict." The head Mage Master rose and slammed a decisive fist to the table. "Master Claytherdon is guilty."

"But—"

He pounded the table again. "The council has decided."

Vespar retreated to the dais, watching my mother over his shoulder. She fell straight to tears. She stood between me and the council.

"My lords, please. He is a boy. I beg you, be gentle with him."

The councilmen grimaced at her. Vespar stared at his twisting ring.

"Consider what you're doing," the Lady said. "Master Claytherdon is right. You cannot grant a witch this mercy while you deny him his life. If there is a greater threat to Gildio's security, I beg you, show me."

I wanted to applaud her.

After a silence, the councilmen beckoned Vespar up to the dais. He joined their hushed discussion, saying nothing himself. *Must. Cannot. His condition. Gildio, dangerous. Condition.*

Emlyn peered up at Tylysk. He crouched and whispered in her ear. She gasped and bobbed on her heels. Tylysk put a firm hand to the back of her neck and sharpened his words. Emlyn's eyes never left mine.

At length, Vespar came away from the dais and assumed his perfect stance before us. The councilmen fell silent. All their stares dropped like daggers on me. The Lord Mage glanced between my mother and me, then spoke.

Mam clutched me while I stayed on my knees, dumbfounded. Emlyn wailed. The guards seized me, disregarding my mother's pleas. Vespar drew her away.

Had I realized I wouldn't see my mother again, I would have struggled.

The household watched the guards rough me through the Manor. Isabelle screeched and battled Dom's restraint. Stephan blinked away tears. Aria vanished.

A troop of six guards met us in the bailey, lining the way to a jailor's cart. The Ordinaries shoved me down the steps. The nearest mage bound a black sash over my eyes. The guards propelled me down the line of men, and a pair of them hoisted me backward into the cage.

In a short while, a horse trotted across the flagstones toward us. Someone said, "My lord."

The gates opened. the wagon creaked and lurched forward, out and off through the city, where all could see their Lord-to-be barred in a cage. The entourage followed the short route to the eastern gate, still unable to avoid the gasps and jeers. Stones pelted the iron bars. One found its mark through the grates and bruised my chin. Too many rattled off the guards' armor, and they shooed the assailants away.

A moment of shade cut across me as the wagon passed through the city gate. Cobblestones merged with dirt road. The river gurgled to my left. After a long, straight course, the cart veered toward the sound. The iron wheels grated across a bank of pebbles before halting. The smell of wet earth and crisp river rode the breeze.

The cage door squealed open. Someone dragged me out and onward.

The river babble drew nearer. My detainers paused and held firm. The blistering sunlight on my face shaded over. Someone took my hand in both of his.

"Little boy."

My stomach roiled. I gritted my teeth.

"There is still a chance," he said. "For Gildio. For your mother, your father. If you will let me help you, you will go free." He put his hands on my face, as if he could see into my blinded eyes. "You have only to say it, and I will bring you home."

Vespar watched me crumble. I gave no answer.

His hands fell to my shoulders. I could almost see his sorry face, and almost believed it. Vespar patted my chest as he stepped around me and moved up the bank.

The guards refastened the shackles behind my back. A few steps into the water, and they turned me about, grabbed me under the arms, and raised me off my feet. I braced for a dunk, but got a wood plank in the back instead. Everything bobbed, steadied sharply. A hand gripped my shirt and hauled me upright.

"Rhys Claytherdon," an official voice recited, "this vessel has been enchanted to carry you speedily out of the borders of Gildio Province. This vessel will bear you the distance to the landing of your choice. The enchantment provides no further protection. You must defend and provide for yourself."

Easy enough with my hands shackled and empty. I wasn't sure I even had oars.

"You are no longer under the protection of the Gildian Realm and the Claytherdon Household. You are henceforth stripped of any and all titles."

The vessel teetered and drifted. The guards splashed ashore. I trembled.

"Rhys Ioan Claytherdon, you are hereby exiled from the realm of Gildio under penalty of death."

❦

Despite its role in my dismal circumstances, the drift of the river soothed me after a time. My weary body had too little strength to panic for long. I shifted and slid off the plank and into the hull, leaving nice long scrapes through my sleeves, stinging up my arms to my shoulders.

When I got my head to stop swirling, I tried to fathom what to do. I couldn't sense much, but I knew the boat was floating faster than it should have. Depending on the tributary the charmed boat decided to take, I could be in Rodhin, Itis, or Lleogren in a matter of days.

Despite what I'd been told, I doubted I had much say over where the vessel ventured. Not without oars, let alone the use of my limbs. For that matter, how was I supposed to get ashore? The swift river would sweep me under if I tried to escape. The council must have thought to execute me through incapacitation.

I watched the sun set through the leaks in the blind. I wondered how many ignorant passersby saw me and did nothing. Exhaustion overtook me despite my fears.

⁂

Darkness churned around me. Vaporous shadows prickled my chilled flesh. Then, the steady ripple with each beat of my heart.

The voice returned. The blood-red eyes opened, blinked once, and centered on me.

The being reached for me. My own hand raised with it. I willed the force to shrink to my chest and disappear, but I lost control to the crimson-eyed being.

When it lunged, I lunged. It slashed, snapped its jaws, hacked, roared. I did.

I saw nothing in the darkness but its red eyes, lambent as fire. But the horrid, sticky warmth drenched me. Between my fingers, down my chest, in my teeth. I tasted it.

The being laughed.

I jolted awake. The boat threatened to capsize until I remembered where I was and froze. The sun cast a pale glimmer through the blind's leaks. My shoulders ached from sleeping crookedly against the plank. I doubled over my lap.

My stomach gnawed on itself. My throat was dry as a mouthful of dirt. The heat intensified. Rain would have been more welcome in my miserable state.

By afternoon, the sunlight fell intermittently. The splash of the river echoed closer. A forest, I supposed, which narrowed my destination to Itis or Lleogren. The sun sank.

Whenever I came close to formulating any sort of plan, the force seized. It took my all to keep from flinging myself over the side of the boat. I thought of vanilla blossom chocolates and "The Mirror of Hilidou" and Flannery's freckles to stave it off.

The sun rose. Sunburn scorched my face around the sash. My tongue skimmed the blood dyeing my cracked lips. Nightmares haunted both my waking hours and sleep. The force pulsed in my arms, yearned for me to break out of the shackles. If I got free of them, I could save myself.

It wanted to rage. Hunt, burn, lay waste.

And eat. It was starving.

I'd gone mad by the fourth morning. If I'd had the strength, I would've thrown myself overboard hours before.

The voice returned. No hideous visions flashed across my mind. It came inside and outside my head. On my shoulder, whispering in my ear.

Kiradach sgiligh.

I shuddered. "What?"

It repeated, a wicked smile in its voice.

"I…I don't—"

It rushed me. I howled. It vanished before it impaled me.

It exposed nothing of itself. It had no form or showed its red eyes.

But I sensed every move it made, as if I were making them with my own limbs.

I huddled in the hull of the boat and wept in fear.

II

CHAPTER 25

Athrú

Athrú scraped the mud off his boots and stepped off the slimy road. Few stretches of the path had sun dried since the rainstorm the day before. He and his dog had spent the night under the partial cover of an oak when the downpour overtook them. Athrú made a habit of staying off the road, anyway. He often felt safer doing so, and he'd never confronted anything too nasty in the woods.

Irminric proved bleak this time. Athrú trekked as far as Norcrest, where merchant ships brimmed Blackacre Harbor, and Lord Palis's seaside fortress rose from the cliff, visible in splendid grandeur for miles. Midsummer had cast new life over the gray city by the time Athrú arrived. Ribbons decked the streets with fiery hues, wreaths of golden flowers adorned every door and every young girl's hair. After dusk, mages cast tremendous flames to alight in the harbor. From a distance, they were elegant candles bobbing on the water.

Bleak, in that it proved as futile as his other journeys. Norcrest was the farthest he'd wandered for his...quest, he decided, though "quest" sounded far grander than any traveling he'd done. And quests, it seemed to him, were seldom done alone. No one but his dog joined him on his fruitless excursions.

Athrú had put off the trip for several months, the longest he'd been able to withstand the surge in his veins. He strolled away from home, pretended to search about, and trudged back more frustrated. He tried to shrug it off, knowing the trip couldn't have turned out any different, but the nagging already started at his gut again.

Athrú and his dog followed the dull thrum of the river until they found its rocky banks. The sun blistered the water's surface. The dog bolted ahead and lapped up a long drink. Athrú dropped his satchel and sword and knelt at the water. His unsuspecting beast protested when Athrú sloshed a wave at him, and he ducked with his tail waving. Before Athrú sent another refreshing splash, the dog pricked up his ears and stared down the river.

"What, Chamberlain?"

Athrú caught sight of what terror stirred Chamberlain—a rowboat. A local's fishing craft, he guessed. He shaded his eyes. The little vessel drifted nearer.

He made out the figure of a person sitting askew against the planks. As still as the passenger sat, Athrú supposed he was asleep—or worse— until he wriggled and nearly capsized himself. Chamberlain toed the water and whimpered for permission to leap in the river and greet him.

Athrú frowned. From what little he saw of the passenger, the boy had to be a few years younger than he, not yet twenty. A nobleman's son, by the looks of his unkempt attire. The black sash blinding his eyes intrigued Athrú most. He waded into the water, Chamberlain paddling behind.

The boy jolted at Chamberlain's yap. Athrú guided the boat to shore. Its passenger tried to speak, but let out a ragged gasp. He collapsed.

Athrú rushed to catch him before his head smashed down on a plank. He locked his arms around the boy's chest and hefted him out of the hull. A quick fiddle with the shackles, and they fell away. When he removed the blind, Athrú expected to find the invalid unconscious, but his wide, bloodshot eyes stared up at him.

"It's all right. Rest here a moment." Athrú retrieved his water pouch and let it dribble over the boy's mouth. He dunked the dark sash in the river and laid it on the boy's blazing forehead. "You're a little young to be exiled, aren't you?"

"Where…"

"Lleogren, not far from Windborough." The short-lived relief on the boy's face vanished. Athrú patted his shoulder. "I'll help you. You're safe here."

He relaxed, though his heavy breathing strained. His consciousness slipped.

Athrú found the racing heartbeat he searched for. He shook the water pouch over the lad's face. He didn't stir. Athrú stripped the jerkin off the boy and made to unstrap his bulky gloves. The sight through the lad's white tunic stopped him.

Glassy blue tinted his skin, up his chest and to his throat. Along his back and arms, a darker sheen glinted off the ridges of dagger-sharp scales plated down his flesh.

Athrú took his hands from the glove straps, unwilling to confirm why the boy wore them. He sat back. His mind raced for what to do.

It wasn't Athrú's first encounter with this sort of thing, but one previous experience hardly made him an expert. And how had the boy been captured, let alone convicted? For as young as he appeared, Athrú wondered if he'd sustained the fearsome condition for long.

The boy was afraid—Athrú at least saw that past the eerie red ringing the blue of his eyes. His detainers had subdued him, and the thought gave Athrú a little comfort, should he have to confront the "condition" himself. The journey had left the boy frail, starved, and parched, let alone overpowered by panic. If he'd managed to maintain himself this long, enduring what he had without succumbing to the creature within him, they had some hope that he could pull through.

Athrú dragged him the few feet to where the trees shaded the water and laid him with his head on the dry banks. A touch of pain left the lad's face as the cool water swept across him. Athrú wet the sash again and draped it over the invalid's brow.

Chamberlain flopped from the water and shook himself. One look at the boy, and his ears dropped. He sniffed toward them and recoiled, rumbling low in his belly.

"Let's give him a chance, at least," Athrú said. "Come here, you old beast. Don't stray."

Chamberlain stayed in sight among the trees, where he lay in the shade with an occasional whimper.

Hours passed. Athrú watched over the boy from a distance. At times, he stirred, muttered to himself, cried out once or twice. Athrú replaced the sash when he fell to moans. He quieted when Athrú sat beside him. Nothing else calmed the most agitated moments of his unconsciousness. The times he tipped the water pouch to the lad's mouth, he managed a few swallows. Chamberlain kept vigilant guard.

The sun dropped behind the trees. As night drew close, Athrú pulled the boy from the water. He had cooled, at least, but Athrú decided the fire he made should be large enough for light alone. He kept the boy as far from its heat as the creeping shadows allowed.

Athrú tempted Chamberlain with a slice of jerky. The dog crept a wide arc around the invalid, but stayed at the fire to gnaw his food.

"What do you think, Chamberlain? Is it gone?"

The dog stuck his nose toward the boy for a long inspection. A shake of his head, and he returned to his dinner.

The boy groaned. He twisted onto his side. Athrú studied him, but the dark discoloration no longer coated his back. The lad trembled, his breathing heavy. Athrú inched to his side, ready to take up the wet sash.

He moaned, tossed, mumbled. Athrú thought he called for his mother.

"Easy, lad. Easy."

Athrú couldn't distinguish more of his muttering, except an occasional word more frantic than the rest. Names, he thought. Then the lad still had something of his own mind left, even if the body had been overpowered.

A gasp ripped through the boy, arching his back. He panted, wide eyes staring at the half moon overhead.

Athrú steadied himself and slinked closer. "Easy. You're all right."

"Where am I?"

"Lleogren, near Windborough. You came ashore some hours ago. You've been having a well-deserved rest."

The boy took in whatever the firelight illuminated—the riverbank, the contour of the ancient yews and oaks around them, the dog on his feet and intent on him.

"That's Chamberlain," Athrú said before introducing himself.

The boy gave no reaction. He searched wildly, only his eyes moving, except the sharp motions of his agonized breaths. His shaking hand crawled up to clutch at his chest.

"I'm wet," he said.

Athrú laughed. "You've been in the river a while. You needed a refreshing dip."

He blinked up at the black sky. "My head. My back."

"Wait, now." Athrú stopped him from rising, though the lad had barely lifted his head. Athrú helped him roll onto his side to face the fire. He curled into himself, twisted his fingers in his hair, and fell to tears.

"It won't stop. It won't leave me alone." He wept, mumbled something indiscernible.

Chamberlain growled. Athrú retrieved the damp sash, soaked it again, and moved to the lad's side. He snatched Athrú's wrist when the cloth brushed his brow.

"Easy. I told you I'd help you, if you'll let me."

The boy held firm until the sash dabbed his brow. He stared unseeing into the fire. His breathing eased a little, despite an occasional rasp and shiver.

"Mam? Isabelle?"

Athrú laid the cold cloth across the boy's neck. "No, lad. I'm sure they're home."

"Emlyn." The boy strove to raise himself. "Emlyn. They found her."

"Hold on, hold on."

"They're going to kill her!"

"You're in no state to help yourself, let alone anyone else."

Athrú no sooner pressed him to the ground than the boy coiled into himself, weeping. "Stop it! Leave me alone!"

Athrú grasped his wrists when the boy beat his fists against his own skull. "Listen to me, lad. Stay with me. Fight it back, and stay with me. Now listen to me."

He seemed to, though his sight glazed over.

"Tell me your name."

"R-Rhys."

"Good. Where are you from, Rhys?"

"Gildio."

"And what brings you all the way out here?"

Rhys twitched. "They took Emlyn. Emlyn…"

"Who is Emlyn?"

The boy looked across the water, where the moonlight rippled on its murky surface. "A witch. They found us. Now they'll…" Rhys's brows narrowed. "But he said…"

Rhys startled when Athrú dabbed his clammy brow. "You were exiled for hiding a witch? I'd say you got off lightly."

Again, the boy didn't seem to heed him. His eyes focused on the low flames. "Windborough," he whispered. His gaze darted to Athrú's. "You have to take me to Lord Cael."

"Not before you've seen a physician and get your strength back. In the morning, we'll get you home to see my sister. She'll set you right. Then we'll see about Lord Cael," he said when Rhys opened his mouth. "He wouldn't see you in such a state, even if you could get in."

"He'll see me. He was my father's friend."

Athrú drew the sash away, looked the pallid boy over. "Who is your father, Rhys?"

He hesitated a long while. Between shuddering breaths, he answered, "Lord Ioan."

Athrú's heart stopped. He watched the lad tremble, wracked with pain, the trim of scarlet flaring in his eyes. Master Rhys himself, cast down the river for hiding a witch?

"Please. I have to see Lord Cael."

Athrú nodded. "Yes. When you're well enough."

Rhys laid his head back and gazed at the moon, tears trickling down his temples. The river's steady flow murmured at his feet. Behind them, the forest chatter of night life hummed through the underbrush. Chamberlain settled in the firelight, chin poised on his paws, a whimper or two escaping.

"It's quiet," Rhys said, a tiny smile on his face. "It's so quiet. It stopped."

He dropped onto his back, head lolling, unconscious once more.

CHAPTER 26

Rhys

Something cold and rather foul brushed my face. I jolted awake. I opened my eyes and startled again, finding a wet nose closing in for another whiff. The dog grumbled, sat, and wagged its tail.

"Let him be, Chamberlain. He'll wake when he wakes."

I turned for a glimpse of whoever had spoken, but the jerk of my head made me dizzy. I hid my face from the early sunlight and moaned. The stranger dropped beside me.

"Sorry about that," he said. "But at least he's friendly to you now, yes? Here."

I didn't know what he put in my hand until I tasted it—dried salted meat of some kind, but it went down before I could name it. The stranger laughed and offered another piece.

"I thought you'd be hungry. You've had quite the journey, Master Rhys."

I forced myself to hesitate from taking the drinking pouch the stranger extended. "Who are you? How do you know who I am?"

"You told me. And I'm Athrú, since you don't remember." He helped me sit upright, but it took all my strength to stay that way. "Have a drink. You're parched."

I obeyed. Athrú handed me an apple, then went to stamp out his tiny campfire. I vaguely recognized his voice, though I couldn't say I'd heard it before. Little else about him stirred my memory—his short, raven-dark hair and trimmed beard and icy blue eyes, his cloudy gray traveling cloak, the sword he set to strapping to his belt. Though, odd as it seemed, his hands were familiar.

"Gildio, hm?" he said. "You've been on the river a while. Several days, at least?"

I'd forgotten how many sunsets and sunrises I'd counted. I only knew that nothing could possibly have tasted as crisp and sweet as that first bite of apple after however long it had been.

I tried to deduce where I'd landed before I looked more foolish. The thick woods around us spread for miles in every direction on both sides of the river. Birds cooed songs I'd never heard, unseen creatures skittered in the underbrush. Peaceful as the sight appeared, something about the forest hung impatient and poised.

"Itis?" I said.

"Good try. Lleogren." Athrú passed me my jerkin. "We'll see about getting you to Lord Cael. First, let's get you to a physician. We're not far."

"Lord Cael?"

"You were rather adamant about seeing him last night. You said he was your father's friend."

I paled.

"Don't worry, Master Rhys. Your crimes aren't criminal here."

I stared at the last few bites of apple, no longer hungry for it. What else had I told this stranger in my delirium?

"I thought hiding a witch had a higher penalty in Gildio. I wouldn't think your title would dismiss you. But then, I suppose your draconis would make them think twice."

I choked. The apple rolled down the riverbank and into the water. I backed away when Athrú came to help.

"What did you say?" I rasped.

Athrú blinked at me. "About…well, about your draconis. You're a draconis."

My heart stopped. I stumbled to my feet, staggered away, trembling. I collapsed on a boulder near the edge of the trees. My hands scraped down the rock, catching nothing. They still itched horrendously, I realized, and my palms blazed inside the leather gloves. I clawed at the bindings.

"Master Rhys, wait."

I tore the gloves off, stared at my deformed hands.

A glassy sheen of blue reflected off my glinting skin. Night-blue ridges plated my arms from elbow to wrist. A reptilian coarseness marred the back of my hands, along my rigid fingers, where pearl-white talons capped my fingertips.

Athrú knelt in front of me. "Master Rhys, listen to me—"

"Make it stop. I'm not a draconis. *I'm not.*"

"Easy. Listen to me."

Chamberlain howled. The dog bared his teeth and retreated toward the river.

The edges of my sight darkened. Deep in my chest, the same ripple in the shadows, the same steady beat offsetting my pulsing heart. The crimson eyes opened. I clamped my hands over my ears and hid my face.

"Stay with me." Athrú grasped my shoulders. "Stay with me. Withdraw. Put the beast away."

I shook my head. "I can't. I'm not."

"You are, Master Rhys. There is a dragon inside you. Withdraw from it."

The abysmal voice vibrated through my bones, its foreign words distinguishable for once. The same recitation, spoken more cruelly.

I curled my fingers in my hair. "It won't stop! It won't stop talking!"

"Tell me about Emlyn, Master Rhys."

I glanced up. "What?"

"The witch you found. Tell me about her."

I took my hands from my face, squeezed my eyes shut, and concentrated. "She's a little girl. She's six years old. Some tinkers brought her to Gildio. I rescued her."

Athrú grasped my shoulders, the gentleness of his voice belying the strength of his grip. "Six years? I didn't know they came so young. What is she like?"

Little Emlyn sprang to mind, hovering below the red eyes. The light on the rippling pool brightened her face in lightning sparks. She stared at me, the same horror on her face as when Tylysk stormed in the garden house.

I swallowed, a knot in my throat. "She's so little. She has soft brown hair, and her eyes are almost lavender. She has loose teeth and tiny freckles, and…no, stop—"

I stood my ground on the shadow perch in my mind, faced the beast with all the shaky strength I could summon. Emlyn dangled over the pool, rotating as if on a thread. She shrieked, tucked her legs up from the encroaching darkness below her.

"What else, Master Rhys?"

I shook my head. "She's the cleverest, most brilliant witch there has ever been. She would *never* hurt anyone. She's sweet and innocent and everything good in the world, so get back, you monster, and leave her alone!"

I lunged for her. Emlyn vanished into curling black vapor. The pool stilled.

I opened my eyes. Athrú's dog quieted. He sniffed toward me, tail wagging. I slumped against the boulder and caught my breath.

Athrú sat back. "There. Well done. You did it."

I shook my head. I was not a draconis. The idea was laughable. Mad. I was not a bedtime horror story.

But what else could it be? The inhuman eyes, the abysmal voice, its haunting vastness. Its hunger and fury. Its craving to burn and ravage.

The beast sensed magic, not me. The dragon hated and raged, not me. But I felt it, because it was me. The dragon was me.

No, the dragon was inside me. There was a difference.

Impossible. How could a dragon get, let alone fit, inside me?

Its essence, its mind. That could squeeze into a scrawny human frame. It was just magic of a different kind, as Emlyn said.

"No," I said. "This isn't…no. It's all wrong. I'm not a draconis."

Athrú grimaced.

"Then why haven't I lost my mind? How is Rhys still here?"

"I don't know, but it's excellent. Incredible you've come this far. Don't give up now."

"Don't give—skin and bones, look at me! There is a *monster* inside me!"

Athrú searched me. "I don't see it anymore."

I held up my hands. Nothing tainted my flesh. The unrelenting pain eased, and the same with my back and head. I sank against the rock.

Athrú passed me the drinking pouch. "Good. Now you know how to fight it."

"Fight it?" I said after a long drink. "I have to get rid of it. I'm not doing this."

Athrú frowned. "It isn't something you can be rid of, Master Rhys. It's what you are, simple as that." He offered another piece of jerky, took an apple for himself. "I'm sorry. Those stories weren't supposed to be real, I know."

I swallowed hard. "What do I do?"

"Keep fighting."

"How? For how long?"

Athrú shrugged. "Until it gives in. Until it learns you won't become what it wants. You won't be a beast. You said so yourself." He turned his apple on his fingertips. "You just discovered how to fight it. Now you understand what ails you, so it should be easier, I think. Perhaps it won't haunt you so much."

"But he was coming out. He—*it* almost got control."

"It got some control, but you restrained it. Him, whichever." Athrú shrugged. "For all we know, you could have been fully released when I found you, wings and all."

The idea nauseated me. That explained the pain in my back and everywhere else. My hands and feet for talons, my skin for scales, whatever else it pleased. When it claimed this fragile human mind and exchanged it for the beast's, it'd have the human frame decked in dragonhide for its destructive pleasure. No human ever overcame the dragon. None in the stories, anyway. Why should I be different?

Ash and flame, how did it get there?

Athrú stared down the bank, where his yellow mop of a dog romped in the water. "At least we know how to keep you as human as possible," he said.

Unlikely. My mind was half gone. A few days alone, and I'd stepped to the brink, and the dragon waited for me to leap.

Athrú searched me, seeming to see both inside and out. "Even if you don't remember, I said I'd help you." Something close to a tease crossed his face. "I suppose that's what I get for dragging Master Claytherdon ashore."

He rose and slung his pack over his shoulder. "Come on. We'll get you home for a decent meal and a moment out of the heat." He whistled for his dog. Chamberlain pranced from the river, shook himself, and bounded over.

Athrú took my arm across his shoulders and steadied me up the steep slope into the trees. Stones and roots gnarled the sticky ground, slowing us. A prickly aroma stagnated in the fine forest mist. Though muffled, the wildlife chatter was as busy as Gildio's streets.

"How far is it?" I grunted.

"Not far. Windborough's a few miles that way," Athrú said, nodding southeast. "My sister and I live outside town a ways. How quick was your journey?"

"Took quick." A few week's journey on foot, and I'd made it in a matter of days in a pitiful rowboat with no oars.

"I wouldn't imagine banishment being the preferred punishment for your crimes," said Athrú. "I would've thought they'd do you in or do nothing."

I brushed a willow branch out of our path. "They had to do something. Lord Mage Vespar's tried to 'set me right' my whole life. He gave up."

"And execution?"

My heart strained to beat. "My mother did what she could." Athrú neither said nor showed anything, but I said, "Whatever anyone thinks of my mother the Lady being as vicious as the Hunters, it isn't true. She's not what people think."

"Nor are you." Athrú eyed me. "What came over you?"

I relayed what I'd told Flannery before she ran from the gardens, rectified his view of Da before he asked how I'd escaped such barbarous ideals.

Athrú resituated my arm across his shoulders. "Then Master Vespar keeps hold of this witch and throws you away."

"Why would he turn now? After all this time, all this heartache. I don't believe him."

"But he made it known at your trial—he made it public, if only to you, so why wouldn't he do as he claims?" Athrú whistled for Chamberlain when he skittered into the trees out of sight. "But, yes, strange to change sides now and punish you for the same."

We rested to let Athrú stretch his cramped limbs. Chamberlain plopped at my feet and waited for me to tousle his golden-red ears. As we moved on, he stayed at my side awhile before scampering into a fallen spread of brittle leaves.

Athrú turned us south, farther on until the rumble of the river became a memory. Breaking the silence, he said, "Emlyn must be extraordinary to win their mercy. If only we knew the real intention behind Vespar's plan."

"It won't fail," I muttered. "Emlyn doesn't have a wicked bone in her body."

"And he knows it. Perhaps he thinks the same as you but fears the repercussions."

I'd suspected that before. Vespar claimed to be as unhappy about the Hunt as anyone. Time and again, he fretted how a hasty decision would spark the other lords' contempt, but how did he fear it enough to turn his head and let hundreds of women and children die year after year? What made him think enfolding Emlyn into his schemes wouldn't incur the same rage as stopping the Hunt altogether? And why Emlyn?

"This won't stay in Gildio long," I said. "Whether or not he intends to end the Hunt, he'll have to do something to keep Emlyn out of its clutches, and I can't imagine he'd overstep the Caeradin Council to do it."

"Especially when news about you spreads," said Athrú. "Why send you away when he claims to seek the same as you? What does he gain now that you're gone?"

Whatever Athrú sought to unravel, it wasn't coming undone. Nor did I believe this stranger could deduce more than I about my tutor, nor could I imagine why it mattered to him.

"What will you do?" Athrú asked. My glance answered enough. He nodded. "I might have guessed. As long as that is what's best. And perhaps you should see what Lord Cael has to say before you break your exile."

Chamberlain whined as my knees gave way. Despite the dog's anxieties, the dragon stayed hidden. The past hour had been the longest I'd gone without a nightmare in days.

Soon, the crooked tree line of the woods spliced with a vast green clearing halved by the dirt highway running east to west. A cottage near the road soaked in the gentle rays of country sun. The charming wood structure guarded the glen, a minute castle complete with a turret on one side. Chamberlain bounded ahead.

"Almost there. Steep here." Athrú hefted me down the slope and across the meadow to the back of the house. He gave the locked door three short raps.

"Oedolyn!"

A quiet bustle from inside, and the door opened. The girl's sparkling smile vanished at the sight of me.

"Hullo," Athrú said.

Oedolyn grasped my arm and helped me through the doorway. "Sun and stars," she said, voice feather soft. "Here, sit down."

I stumbled into the chair she pulled from the kitchen table. Oedolyn examined me with a physician's intensity. Based on the assortment of herbs drying upside down between shelves of colored bottles and tins on the walls, she was something of the sort.

"What happened?" She fingered my face, winced with me at the sting of my sunburn. "Sorry. Here." She rushed across the kitchen and rummaged through a cupboard, standing on her toes, barefoot on the earth floor. Athrú came to the table and waited for her to notice him.

At a glance, I wouldn't have guessed the two were related. However similar the shapes of their faces, the lines of Oedolyn's were softer than Athrú's. His black hair offset his sister's long honey curls, the way the dark storm blue of her eyes contrasted the cold ice of his. Something about their expressions matched too, except Oedolyn's seemed exaggerated compared to Athrú's subtlety. I guessed Athrú was a few years shy of thirty, and I doubted Oedolyn was much older than I.

Athrú looked me over. "Nightveil, I think, sister mine. And tyliac, if you haven't run out."

Oedolyn hopped to reach the top shelf of the cupboard. "Get him that rag." She pointed to where there was no rag.

Athrú obeyed anyway. He wetted the cloth with the bottle she handed him and brought it to me. "On your face. Might sting a little."

It hardly compared to the relief the chill left on my face. The scent reminded me of a frozen winter morning in the Manor gardens.

Oedolyn returned to the table with a blue bottle in one hand and a tin in the other. She smiled pityingly. "Sorry, but you look awful."

I smiled back, but it stretched my cheeks and hurt.

Athrú stepped to his sister's side, pecked her cheek, and gestured to me. "Oedolyn, this is Master Rhys Claytherdon."

Her jaw dropped. The freezing rag should've steamed from the heat surging to my face.

"You're—" Oedolyn stumbled backward into her brother. She fumbled through what I guessed was a curtsy. "I'm sorry, milord, what I said—"

"It's all right," said Athrú. "Master Rhys got himself into trouble. I found him floating up the river."

I dropped my gaze. Oedolyn's eyes sparked with real fear.

"Why?" she said.

Athrú pulled a chair out across from me and urged Oedolyn toward it. She flashed me another glance, as if it were disgraceful to sit in my presence. He pressed her down by her shoulders. "I'd rather you were sitting when he tells you."

Oedolyn sat straight backed, pale as cream, her huge blue eyes growing wider. We both panicked when Athrú left us to see what bubbled over the fire. He waved for me to speak. Oedolyn went pink to her ears.

"Athrú," she hissed. "I'm sorry, milord, we—"

"It's fine. And Rhys is fine. I'm…just Rhys."

She took no comfort in it. She stiffened under my gaze like a peasant under a king.

"Oedolyn, what's left?" Athrú stirred the pot on the fire.

"The…uh, the…"

"These?" He pointed to the carrots on the counter.

"I'll do it."

"I've got it. Go on, I'm listening."

For a moment, the sound of a knife going through carrots overpowered the room. I looked away from Oedolyn's terror and related what had happened, from rescuing Emlyn from the tinkers to the morning Tylysk raided the garden house. What Vespar had done, that I had to end the Hunt.

But not Flannery. The wound was too bloody to expose.

By the time I finished, Oedolyn had calmed herself and refilled my bowl of cheese and vegetable soup twice. Athrú stirred his helping with a crust of bread and stared at the empty chair across from him.

Oedolyn planted her elbows on the table, hid her mouth in her fists. "That poor girl. And you. I'm so sorry."

I stared at my food.

"But going back…" Oedolyn glanced at her brother. "Are you sure that's best? If Master Vespar says she won't be touched—"

"And if he's lying?" I said. "I wouldn't trust him with Emlyn to win Gildio back, and I wouldn't leave that to him, either."

Athrú counted on his fingers. "Emlyn, the Hunt, Vespar. Quite a bit for an exile. If Vespar's plan is as unsavory as you believe, let's hope some other lords will listen, too."

Those who would were the least influential powers in the country. Rivariar, Itis, Lleogren. Corandul had some sway over the others, but they kept to themselves. Everyone else either stood with Vespar or remained so fickle no one bothered to lure them one way or the other.

Oedolyn twisted a lock of her hair around her finger. Her eyes flickered between her brother and the table. "Did you find what you were looking for this time?"

Athrú peeked up at her, studied me. "I don't know. I found something, for certain, but not what I expected."

"Then you'll be going too."

"I've taken on some fair responsibilities. Which, mind you, will not be yours once he's on his feet."

"Nor yours," I said. "You've risked enough pulling me off the river and into your home. I won't ask more of you. This is my battle, not yours."

Athrú finished the last of his bread. "I'm afraid it will be everyone's battle before long."

Oedolyn gathered our dishes, frowning. "Everyone's battle but the likes of me."

"You know what I meant, Oedolyn."

"I do, and I don't like it. Roping yourself into this, marching headlong into a disaster better left to lords and mages," she said, a scold as gentle as I'd ever heard.

When Athrú stood, the top of Oedolyn's head came no higher than his shoulder. With a motion that might have been an embrace, he gathered her hair in a fist and wagged it in her face. Oedolyn shoved him, battling a smile.

"I know," Athrú said. "That's why I tell you no."

Oedolyn bit her lip. "Well, the state he's in, you won't get anywhere fast. We'll get you some fresh clothes, and then you should rest. You can have the loft."

My heart jumped to my throat. If I closed my eyes again, the dragon would pounce. Athrú said nothing if he noticed my uneasiness. He stepped into the next room, returned with a bundle of clothes, and beckoned me to the staircase. Oedolyn blushed when I thanked her.

The low, slanted ceiling forced us to duck into the loft. A few mattresses decked with woolen blankets rimmed the square space, the rest of the floor open to sleeping pallets. Dimmed lanterns dangled from hooks on the ceiling. The afternoon sun peeked through the shutters of the low window.

"You get many visitors?" I asked.

"The crossroads aren't far from here," Athrú said, dropping the clothes on a mattress. "Oedolyn's the closest physician. We get a few wanderers now and again."

I sank down on the nearest bed when my legs gave out. Athrú stayed at the stairs, grimacing and waiting for me to say what was bothering me. I didn't, though the thought of sleep and being alone paralyzed me.

"You don't have to face that beast alone," he said.

"Why would you do this? You let a monster into your house."

Athrú shook his head. "No. We'll see to that."

"A criminal, then. You saved my life. I can't ask you for more."

His kind smile slipped. He looked away. "There are things I'd like to see set right too, Master Rhys. As far as I can tell, helping you would accomplish that."

CHAPTER 27

Vespar

"**O**rrtha." Vespar extended his hand. "Come with me. Staying here so long will not help."

She sat at the foot of her son's bed, turned away from the mirror across from her. Her eyes lifted to meet Vespar's, but she remained unmoved by the shift from a professional tone to one more endearing. Orrtha gripped a parchment in one hand and clutched the Gildian pendant to her heart in the other, the silver concealed in her rumpled handkerchief.

Vespar knelt beside her. She let him gather her hands in his, soft, delicate feathers on the work-roughed stone of his palms.

"Orrtha, I assure you, Rhys is all right. He would have come ashore some time ago."

"How can he be?" Her voice bore no strength. "Look at him—"

"He is a strong, clever lad. He will manage."

Orrtha shook her head. "Couldn't he write to me? One word, so I know he's alive?"

Vespar doubted Rhys would risk it, but he said, "I'm sure he's trying, my lady."

"And if that awful beast—"

"Orrtha." Vespar tightened his grip on her fingers. She matched her eyes to his, the beautiful hazel-brown misting. "He is alive, be certain of that. But of anything else—there is no use drawing conclusions until you have more answers."

Vespar studied her pale features. The tired lines of her face were fair, and the disheveled waves of her auburn hair framed her beauty. He took her handkerchief and dabbed her cheeks.

Orrtha crumpled. She doubled over and dropped her head on his shoulder.

Vespar's heart quickened, but he cradled his arms around her. His cloak smothered her words, except the broken names of her son and husband.

He held her, as much shielding himself from his vacillating remorse as comforting her.

Rhys had made his choice. He had concealed a witch. He was no more above the law than any of his subjects, and he had chosen banishment over liberation when he refused to relinquish her. Vespar stood by his word—had Rhys brought the girl forward, he would have his place in the Claytherdon Household, his right to lordship, and much else he desired.

This child was the rarest gem. So long Vespar had waited, allowing the Hunt to drag on, enduring the insurgence Ioan and Rhys poured upon him day after day, withstanding the Lady's doubts when she grew too weak to fulfill her duties alone, all for this one child. Had Rhys slipped through his fingers with the girl, Vespar would still be awaiting what the Hunters would never bring him.

Fool boy. He had only to understand the girl to know Vespar's mind. Rhys blinded himself from her gifts, not just as an Ordinary himself, but with his unabashed devotion. The boy knew nothing of her, yet he hoarded her as a dragon guarded its egg.

That was Ioan's stubbornness. Ioan's rashness, his ferocity, his resolve.

The resemblance between father and son struck Vespar with further guilt. He never denied how he and Ioan were as good as brothers, odd as the match appeared. The two met when Vespar accepted his appointment of Lord Mage not two days after his graduation from the Academy at twenty. Excitable, lighthearted Ioan was eighteen. At first, Ioan overwhelmed Vespar with his loudness and, at worst, lack of discipline, but the Lord Mage's quiet studiousness soon tamed him. Ioan was compassionate and generous to a fault, as obstinate as his son. Vespar appealed to Ioan's spirit the way the Gildian Lord drew on Vespar's reserve. Intellectually, Ioan held his own against the Lord Mage as few others could.

His memory, and his near exactness in Rhys's face and mind, still haunted Vespar. He wished no harm on Ioan's son, the little boy he himself had carried on his shoulders and dueled with wooden swords. Now, Rhys's crooked grin had soured, the spark in his blue eyes dulled, and his playful laughs silenced.

Vespar cast the boy from his mind. He had work to do. Gildio staggered under the pressure of Lady Orrtha's loss. Some barons were already murmuring about the lack of a Gildian heir should something befall the Lady Regent. They knew the fearful depths of her grief, and some wondered aloud after her stamina.

Vespar grasped Orrtha by the shoulders and raised her up. She stared at the floor. He cupped a hand to her cheek. Pink bloomed there, the shy, bashful hue of a young girl unsure of the affection presented to her.

Orrtha had changed, as well. Vespar expected nothing less, so long withstanding the lonely role of a widowed mother. Yet he still saw the young woman who had come to the Manor at fifteen to become Lady Claytherdon. She'd been bolder then, more playful with her wit, but her gentleness hadn't faded in the least.

Several months after Ioan's death, after Vespar swore to care for his widow and son, he truly recognized her loveliness, delicate and tender, and how no one had ever needed him so much as she.

For all Vespar tried, the boy kept her from him too.

"Let me help you," he said, claiming her beautiful gaze. "I will. I always have."

She revealed her broken, grateful smile. Vespar thumbed the corner of it.

He touched the fingers holding her parchment. "What's this?"

Orrtha folded the page. "It's from Annalyn. She heard the news. She asked if I wished for her to come and stay awhile."

Vespar smiled, though torn. A visit from Ioan's sister would do Orrtha good, while at the same time set him a step aside. Her presence might allow him more time to see to other pressing matters he had assumed, but Annalyn presented potential danger. Vespar needed, wanted, Orrtha's loyalty. Dearest Annalyn had followed after her brother and become a wayward Claytherdon herself, and her innocent, unintended persuasiveness was nothing to scoff at. She could convince the most skeptical that the sky was in fact green without an inkling of what she'd done.

Vespar had time. He could ground Orrtha before Annalyn arrived.

"It will be good to see her," he said. He raised Orrtha to her feet. "Isabelle and little Aria have worried for you, my lady. Perhaps you would go relieve their anxieties?"

Orrtha looked on the room, the remade bed where shackles no longer hung, the chair where she had slept while her son agonized and grappled his newest infirmity. She stared at the empty hearth, where she and her husband had sat and watched their son play with knight figurines, where Ioan had sung the boy to sleep. Vespar drew her away.

The Lady let him guide her down the hall, her arm hooked through his. "How…" Orrtha hesitated until Vespar's soft gaze prompted her further. "Where is Emlyn now?"

"She is in Master Tylysk's care for the time being. We've had much to see to, and I haven't decided how to proceed."

"But she will remain in your charge?"

Vespar glanced at her. Orrtha's tone was strangely empty.

"Will you find her family?" she asked. "Her poor mother."

Orrtha's concern came as a pleasant reprieve from her everlasting contempt for the girl. After witnessing Rhys's battle to defend Emlyn at his trial, she had attempted to be indifferent rather than bitter. Acknowledging that Emlyn's mother must have felt the same as she had softened her.

"We will, yes," he said.

"I...I intend to do my part while she is here." Orrtha sought his approval with a glance. "I won't turn her away, should she need me."

Vespar's smile relieved her. "I will tell her, my lady. That is most kind."

They parted ways at the staircase, where nervous Aria stood at the top. Though fidgeting, she awaited her Lady, glancing between her and Vespar with a lamb's meekness. For all her uncontrollable mannerisms and plaguing, unhappy condition, Aria's tender diligence could be a comfort to Emlyn. Vespar suspected Tylysk would soon tire of his duty unless Emlyn softened him more than he exposed. Vespar wondered at times, the way he handled the child, if Tylysk forced a gentleness to please his master, or if he battled to uphold his willpower under Emlyn's adorability.

Vespar reassured Orrtha once more, then watched her follow Aria before making his way to Master Tylysk's chambers.

A weary-eyed Tylysk answered the door, his fresh scar inflamed. "Milord," he said. He moved aside to let his master in, but Vespar stayed in the doorway.

"Has she been difficult?" Vespar asked, smiling.

Tylysk returned his master's jest with a slight roll of his eyes. "No, sir, not terribly," he said, heaving a deep breath. "She's resting, but I—"

"No, leave her." Vespar spotted her tiny form nestled on the sofa in the next room. Her exhaustion outweighed that of anyone's, lingering under the mages' eyes in constant dread. Vespar would mend it, and he trusted Tylysk would adapt to doing the same. Emlyn had nothing and no one else. She had no choice but to turn to Vespar.

"I'll see her when she wakes," he said. "Now that things have calmed, we can proceed."

"Yes, my lord."

Vespar looked down at his ring. "I presume you've recently done some outside work?"

"A few nights ago, sir."

"Then you have further work to do. Have it done. You've always excelled at pentacles."

"Thank you, sir."

"Don't forget to report."

"Never."

Vespar laid a bolstering hand on his second's shoulder. "We're on the move, Master Tylysk. At last."

"At last, sir," Tylysk answered with a smile. "I'll follow you on."

"I have never doubted," he said, and Tylysk swelled. "As always, you've done excellent work. Emlyn knows she must depend on you. You've eased her through the door." Vespar matched Tylysk's gaze. "Despite her being so conflicted, she will turn to you for her protection. Are you willing to give it, Tylysk?"

"Absolutely." Tylysk's stiffness belied his hesitancy. He caught himself. "There's no greater honor than for you to ask it of me, my lord," he said. "There can be no greater assertion of your trust. Emlyn is most precious to you, and I will always do as you ask."

"Then I ask this, and it will ensure our victory. It will take both of us to earn her trust. If we can accomplish that…" Vespar couldn't speak the next words, but Tylysk understood.

"Yes, my lord. It will obey you now."

CHAPTER 28

Rhys

Ystach vychwn

Suspended above the shadows, ash and smoke gyrated into a gale around me. Stinging soot breezed into my eyes. The dust in my lungs forbade me to breathe. The whirlwind amplified his voice.

Kiradachn sgiligh.

My heart wasn't beating. The pool of shadows below me lay still as an obsidian slab. An empty vastness opened behind me, beyond an edge that wasn't there. His massive presence towered an arm's length away.

Ystach vor taigh.

His words meant something to me now, a language I once knew, but no longer understood.

Kiradach pyr vaych.

"Leave me alone!"

The eyes blinked open.

"Go away! Get out!"

The gale dispersed, dropping me on solid darkness. A thread of blinding blue light rose from the lifeless pool. It encircled his form, spiraled up to his crimson eyes. Plates of midnight blue scales surfaced in its wake, hovering in midair to craft his gigantic face. They shone with the wavering glow of light on water. I turned away before the light moved to shape his dagger teeth.

Trych maeligh.

He roared. So did I.

The force of it tore my flesh. Scales knifed through my skin. A pair of monstrous wings lanced from my back. The release left me face down in the shadows. He waited.

I sat up, crouching low. The wings expanded, set to shoot into the air. I stared up at him and awaited his command.

Oedolyn yelped when I bolted upright. She lost her balance, and her wet rag landed in my lap. Half my face was cool and damp, the other ablaze.

Oedolyn regained herself and inched to my side. "Are you all right?" Her brows narrowed as I battled to slow my breathing. "I'll get Athrú."

"I'm all right." I smeared the cloth down my burning face. "Sorry."

She folded her hands in her lap. "What can I do?"

"I'll be fine."

Oedolyn wrung her fingers. If Athrú had told her anything of my condition, or if she guessed it herself, she revealed nothing of it, nor could I tell how many signs I gave away to prove it to her. I looked at my hands, expecting to find them riddled with scales. Oedolyn exchanged my gaze easily, so I assumed my eyes no longer bore the eerie red Athrú had mentioned before.

"Whatever I can do." Her smiles made her sparkling eyes half their normal size. Sunlight through the low window streaked her hair with the soft yellow-white of morning. As short as the dream seemed, I thought it was early evening.

Oedolyn gathered her supplies. "Sorry to wake you. I'll let you rest."

"It's all right. I…don't think I can sleep more."

She grimaced understandingly. "Your clothes are washed." She motioned to the bed across from mine. Neatly folded, Da's jerkin lay beside the fresh tunic and trousers, the leather crisp and gleaming. I swallowed—the rumpled parchments of Flannery's letter rested on the jerkin buckles.

"Breakfast is almost ready," Oedolyn said, summoning a warm smile. "Hurry down."

I waited until she padded down the stairs and out of sight, then swiped Flannery's letter off the bundle of clean laundry. At least Oedolyn had spared them from a sound scrubbing, and otherwise, they appeared untouched since I last handled them. I stowed the parchments in the inner pocket of the jerkin.

Chamberlain sat at attention in the middle of the cramped kitchen, watching Oedolyn busy herself with breakfast. He abandoned his futile plea for food and came for a pat on the head.

"I'll have your breakfast in a moment," Oedolyn said. "Sorry to say, it'll be more meager than you're used to, Master Rhys."

"Er, not at all. You and Athrú have already done more than I could ask for."

Oedolyn brought a wooden platter of toast with tart jam, sided with a chunk of cheese and a handful of blackberries. She went to the door to call Athrú inside before sitting at the table. "You look better today. Still red, but that will take time. Terrible, what you've been through." She shuddered. "But you're alive, thanks to your dragon."

We exchanged a long look. Oedolyn spoke as if she'd seen my case a thousand times.

"Athrú told me," she admitted. "I had to be sure I was caring for what I could. Your dragon will do the rest."

"Apparently, I'm missing a great deal I should know about draconi," I muttered.

"Athrú and I met one once. That's how we know anything."

"How did you escape?"

Oedolyn tucked a curl behind her ear. "Not all draconi are as monstrous as the stories say. The one we met was like you. He hadn't lost himself, either." She shook her head, plucked up a blackberry with another rosy smile. "You're good at hiding it, you know. If your nightmares are as bad as I'd imagine, I'd think you'd be mad by now. The dragon must have to fight you as much as you do him."

It gave me some strange courage. Tales of draconi described the human succumbing to the dragon, not the beast overpowering the human. Humans would fight, I supposed, however slim their chances of withstanding the dragon. All the stories asserted there was no chance. Humans were weak, dragons were not.

Athrú came in the door as I asked, "Why am I different? Why does the dragon struggle with me?"

He shrugged and sat at the table. "Who knows? Perhaps you're a stronger human than other draconi have been." Athrú bit into a slice of toast and thumbed the jam from his lip. "Perhaps the dragon's cause isn't as powerful as yours. Your fight for everything else may overpower his will to subdue you."

The dragon rustled through my chest—the same sensation as the roiling force. I shoved him away.

"What happened to him?" I asked. "That draconis?"

Oedolyn stared at her hands, ignored her brother's glance. "Who knows?" she said. "That was years ago."

Athrú motioned between her and her nibbled breakfast. "Eat. We have to be off to meet Eoin soon."

"Who's Eoin?" I asked.

"Our way in to see Lord Cael."

Oedolyn brightened, took another blackberry. "Don't worry. You'll be in good hands."

Athrú led us east down the road to Windborough. Oedolyn and I strode beside the small creaking cart while Athrú guided his black steed, whom Oedolyn called Starbolt. Lazy Chamberlain grew bored of walking the weathered trail and sprawled in the cart. The road sliced through the trees, where pale light found the crevices of the forest canopy and dotted the thick woods on either side.

With the dragon quiet in another person's presence, I thought of home without him jarring me. Mam, for certain, was unwell. What would come of her without me? Was my banishment enough to provoke her to embolden herself against Vespar, or would she fall apart? Vespar would redouble his efforts to claim her affections without my diverting her from his advances. Where did that leave the household and Gildio?

And Emlyn—I still couldn't believe Vespar's plot. Tylysk claimed to have her in his care, but their deplorable relationship couldn't have been better than a jailor and his prisoner. Yet the liberties they granted her the moment they stripped me of mine made me doubt myself. By the looks of it, Tylysk went from being Vespar's work dog to Emlyn's guard dog, and by the time I saw Emlyn for the last time, she'd grown used to it. Used to him.

And Flannery. Always to Flannery.

"What? Sorry, I was…thinking."

Athrú took his hand from my shoulder. "As long as it was only that."

"No, he's quiet at the moment." The dragon rolled over in my chest. I put a hand to where I felt the stomach-churning toss. Chamberlain snorted.

I swerved for something else to think about. With my last thought hinging on Flannery, I asked, "How often do Hunters pass through here?"

Oedolyn shuddered. "Too often. They pass by the house every few weeks."

"There aren't enough witches for Hunting that often, are there? Not in Lleogren, anyway?"

"No," said Athrú. "The highway runs through Rivariar and Jeiosach. They come down from Priodas and Ethelfled, too." He motioned toward the house with a sweep of his arm. "You can always tell where they've been by how many prisoners they carry."

I grimaced. Jeiosach's and Priodas's victims were often as many as Gildio's. In friendlier lands, Hunters scoured out fewer witches when people strove to hide them.

"How often do they stop here?" I asked.

"Twice a year, at most," Athrú answered. "They don't find many witches here."

"How…what do they…what happens when they're here?"

The siblings sent me a look. "You don't know?" said Oedolyn.

"Vespar didn't think it was terribly important to my side of the job."

As we reached the end of the forest tunnel, Athrú guided Starbolt onto the road that broke from the highway and curved south, though the horse needed no prompting. He scanned the distant patchwork of rolling green and farmlands.

"I suppose it isn't what you'd expect," he said. "It isn't so much a raid as a pickup. They expect witches to be handed over. It's never used, but there's a jail in town to hold witches until the Hunters come."

"That doesn't suit the Ethelfledian warrior image," I remarked.

"Until they're unhappy with what they find." Oedolyn hugged herself, shaking her head. "Some Hunters, and not just the mages, can smell out a witch. They know when someone's hiding. And that isn't to say they don't use force anyway."

"Then they resort to kidnapping."

Athrú frowned. "There's no such thing as kidnapping in the Hunt."

I imagined Flannery against the massive brute who'd snagged her without a thought as to who witnessed or cared. How her whole village watched as they tossed her into a wagon. How they'd been powerless to save her and Abigail.

I blinked. Then my face, my nose, throbbed nauseatingly. My vision flashed white. Athrú hoisted me to my knees. I spluttered dirt from my lips.

"What happened?"

Oedolyn thumbed my watering eyes and said, "You fainted."

Athrú brought a water pouch from his saddlebag. I took a sip, spying Chamberlain in the cart. His tail wagged, but he stood and watched with drooping ears.

The dragon turned over. The shift shuddered through every bone in my body. The skin on my arms prickled. I squeezed my eyes shut.

Athrú drew Oedolyn away before he knelt and grasped my shoulders. "Concentrate. Withdraw, like before."

A violent tremor ripped through my limbs. Chamberlain growled. Oedolyn hushed Starbolt's frantic whinnying.

"Come on, Rhys, just like before."

"He won't stop—"

"Fight back. You're the master, not him." He waved me away when I looked at him. "Go on. He's in there, not out here."

I ducked my head and clamped my hands over my ears. Athrú stood back.

As I turned inward, an image of the dragon's lair appeared in my mind, though I couldn't tell if I imagined it or not. A long tunnel of arching stone walls, its craggy surface charred black, snaked onward. A vast cavern lay ahead, flaring with vibrant yellow-gold, pocked with shadowed cavities. Jagged lines of broken amber pillars speared from the ground here and there. I inched toward the mouth of the cave.

His gigantic head dropped into the doorway.

I yelped and jumped back. The side of his face leveled with me, its dark surface steeled with gleaming scales. His blood-red eye hovered close enough to see my petrified reflection in it. He laughed, a low rumble in his throat. He lifted his head from the ground. The sound of chains followed his movements, louder as he shook the kinks from his long, lithe neck. The links spilled from an iron collar clamped around his throat. He peered over his shoulder, smoke rising from his nostrils, teeth bared.

I made a mindless run for it. The blaze from his jaws launched over my head and down the tunnel. I surged past his downward swipes. The claws slammed the yellow earth and rattled the ground. The rise of his talons sprayed rubble into my back. I bobbed under his ruthless claws, twisted him about. One last swing, and I tripped backward from the downward strike and ducked under his arm. I lunged for the chain.

His head lurched forward. He writhed against the unyielding iron. I scrabbled to keep my feet on the ground, dug my heels in, and yanked.

He trundled out of the shadows. His massive body towered above me, tall as the Manor walls, jagged with glassy scales and plates of silver down his throat. A crown of spikes sprouted from the back of his head, ridged his face to his steaming nostrils. His wings unfurled to immense sails, their span as wide as he was long. He switched his barbed tail.

I planted my feet and braced myself. The dragon thrust his talons into the cavern floor and strained against my grasp. He whipped his neck about, jerking me from side to side. My fingers clambered up the chain link by link. We stood locked, neither able to uproot the other.

I let him raise me to my toes. The sudden slack surprised him, and I wrenched the chain backward. His head jutted forward, craning his neck, throwing his balance. I stomped on the chain before he raised his head.

The dragon met my gaze full on. His face, those wicked crimson eyes, lingered mere inches from mine. He bared his teeth.

Don't. Don't say a word.

Trych—

I stomped on the chain once more, shortening the slack. The beast's head dropped.

Don't.

He glared, tail switching.

He wrenched his head up and thrust me aside. He roared, caustic smoke curling from his massive jaws. The force of it pinned me to the ground. The dragon slinked into a crevice in the cavern wall. His eyes glittered in the dark.

I opened my eyes. I steeled myself for some retaliation. Nothing came.

Athrú and Oedolyn relaxed. "You did it," she said, grinning. "Better?"

I nodded. Chamberlain tiptoed from the cart to sniff my clammy face. Athrú clapped me on the shoulder. "Come on. Can you walk?"

I rose to shaking legs but managed on my own. The dragon rumbled. I massaged my aching eyes, sensing a headache.

"Skin and bones, why?" I groaned. "*How* is it here? And how long has it been here?"

Athrú clucked Starbolt into motion down the road. "Who can say? Why would a dragon sacrifice its form for a human's? But nothing said it couldn't claim a child, if it liked."

Oedolyn stared at her fidgeting fingers. "Some stories say a dragon can claim a child before they're born."

The thought sickened me, however tragic. Then the beast had only to wait for the prime opportunity to manifest itself. Like a mage or witch's magic, it occurred to me.

My stomach churned. The sight of the red scar down Tylysk's face haunted me. The recollection of it, and of the night he visited me at my sickbed, drove a shiver up my spine.

The dragon savored the memory of the wound.

CHAPTER 29

Emlyn

Emlyn woke when hands gripped her shoulders and forced her upright. Cold tears dried on her cheeks, and her head hurt from pulling her hair in her sleep. She blinked up at Tylysk and whimpered.

"What's the matter?" he demanded. "Why are you crying?"

She ducked her head and wiped her eyes on her sleeve. "I'm sorry."

Tylysk released her, biting his lip. He took the seat on the sofa beside her. He tapped his fingertips together. "Why were you crying?" he asked, voice soft this time. "Did you have a nightmare?"

Emlyn shuddered. Her kitty, Plink, had to have been there, rubbing his fluffy brown coat on her legs, meowing so loud the whole house heard him. When she first woke, she thought she was in her brother's room, curled up in his armchair with a spellbook on her lap. Tylysk's study reminded her of her brother's, with the same books on the shelves and the writing desk covered in parchments and quills, except her brother kept his tidier than Tylysk did.

Emlyn hugged her knees. If Plink had just stopped mewling so loudly, they wouldn't have found her huddled in her brother's study.

They grabbed her, slapped a hand across her mouth so hard it stung her cheeks. One carried her down the stairs while the other led the way and hissed at Emlyn to shut up. She tried to wriggle out of her captor's bruising grasp. She couldn't see their faces, but she knew their raspy whispers.

They dragged Emlyn outside. Coming up the wet road, a tinker wagon sloshed through the rain and puddles. In her terror, a spell slipped from her shaking fingers. Her captor dropped her with a cry, and Emlyn's bare feet and knees sank in the fresh mud. She tore down the sticky path toward the house. Her kidnapper's accomplice picked up her skirts and chased her up the steps to the door. Emlyn's dripping hands slipped from the locked handle. She jumped away from the woman's grab and tripped down the steps, landed hands first in the mud and gravel.

Before she picked herself up, Emlyn was dangling off the ground by the back of her soiled dress, the way the servants picked up Plink by the scruff of his neck. Emlyn clung to the wrist over her head and cried.

The huge, disgusted tinker held her away from him like a drowned kitten. His dark eyes swept over her. Emlyn saw in them the same hatred everyone else showed witches.

The tinker tossed a money pouch at her kidnapper. He snatched it, and the woman swiped it from his greedy fingers. The tinker dumped Emlyn inside his wagon door, mud and all, and slammed it in her face.

Emlyn never thought she'd be glad to see Tylysk, but at least he sent away the memory of those horrible tinkers.

"Well, you're fine now, whatever it was," he said.

Emlyn hid her face and massaged the knots out of her hair.

"All right, sleepyhead? You've slept the morning away."

A deep breath, and Emlyn nodded.

"Good. Master Vespar wants to see you."

Emlyn's heart jumped to her throat.

"But"—Tylysk raised a finger—"I have something for you, if you're a good girl and go talk with him."

If he didn't have Rhys, then she didn't care. She wouldn't talk to Master Vespar, or even look at him. It was his fault she'd never see Rhys again. Now she was trapped here, probably forever, stuck in Tylysk's study while he put magic circles around her so she wouldn't run away. She wanted Rhys more than anything in the world.

But she wanted her kitty and ribbons and home. She wanted her brother. She wanted Mama.

"Do you want it or not?"

Emlyn stared at him. What was she supposed to say?

Tylysk moved to the door. "I'll show you, then you tell me."

She sank into the sofa cushions. Tylysk was just being mean again. He didn't really have anything for her. Rhys was right when he said Tylysk was the worst person she'd ever meet. He said that about Master Vespar, too. But then, she was still alive, and no one had hurt her. Yet.

Tylysk came to the doorway. "I…found this for you."

Emlyn's breath got stuck. He held up a dress—a long pink dress with puffs and ribbons all down the sleeves. Flowers embroidered the white underneath the pink skirt. It was a twirling gown, where the big skirt would whirl when she spun.

Tylysk licked his lips. "Well?"

Emlyn felt herself smile. Tylysk cracked a grin.

"Go put it on."

She dressed when Tylysk stepped into the antechamber. She wished she had a mirror so she could see how wide the skirt went when she twirled. Emlyn had never been this beautiful before, like a princess in the old stories her brother used to tell her.

Tylysk smiled when she tiptoed out of the study. It warmed her a little.

"These too." He dropped the soft brown slippers at her feet. "You're not going barefoot."

Emlyn stepped away. "We have to go now?"

"Yes, right now. He's waiting."

Emlyn blushed and felt stupid. The dress made her forget what he got it for in the first place. "But, Master Tylysk—"

"Ah, we made a deal. If you want to keep that dress, you're going to see him."

She tried to glare, the way Rhys would have, but she couldn't get her eyes to do it.

Tylysk pretended to pat down the knots in her hair. "All right, you're very pretty. Come on."

Emlyn had counted five days since Rhys's trial, the last time Tylysk took her out of his chambers. Emlyn had never seen a real castle before, but she hadn't imagined them being this big. The arched ceiling went so high, it scared her to look up at it. Gildio's flags and fancy tapestries lined the cold gray walls. Shiny black and green tiles decked the floor. Giant windows let in the sunshine, some near the floor and some higher up. Tall candlesticks stood in the long spaces between them on either side of the hall.

Unsteady beats of magic pounded around them. Emlyn sensed each thread vibrating through the Manor, all buzzing and weaving together. Tylysk didn't seem to notice. He must've been used to it. But she sensed hundreds of threads, all working at different things, though Emlyn couldn't tell what. She recognized the guards' spells—Emlyn used to watch them from her garden house window while they marched around the wall. It spooked her, how she could sense them, but they never noticed her. Not until Tylysk broke through her Concealment charms.

Emlyn remembered the double staircase across from the garden door. Each stairwell curved toward the other, both up to the same corridor. She remembered the first door up there, the one Tylysk took her to before.

Emlyn backed away. "Are we going up there?"

"We're not seeing Lady Orrtha, if that's what you're asking."

She tried to hide her relief. She didn't like being around Lady Orrtha. She was always so sad, and she always looked at Emlyn like she couldn't bear the sight of her. After all, it was Emlyn's fault Rhys got in so much trouble.

Tylysk tugged Emlyn up the stairs. They turned left at the top and stopped at the door with a shiny eagle knocker. Tylysk knocked. Master Vespar's voice came from inside, dull through the door, but it chilled Emlyn all the same. Tylysk led her in.

Master Vespar sat in a high-backed chair, busy at work over the parchments on his desk. He glanced up, smiled at her. "Look at you, little one," he said. He left his quill in the inkwell and came around to them.

Tylysk took her by the shoulders and steered her in front of him when she ducked behind his leg. Emlyn clung to her skirt.

"You look lovely," Vespar said. "Did Master Tylysk find that for you?"

Emlyn nodded.

"How kind of him." The mages exchanged a glance Emlyn couldn't read. "Has he been good to you?"

"Yes, Master Vespar," she recited.

"Very good. I knew he would be."

When she peeked up at Tylysk, he had that mean smile that made her feel cold inside. Vespar dismissed him. Tylysk stooped, whispered in her ear to behave herself, and left her alone with Master Vespar.

He went to his desk to wipe his quill. "I'm sorry it has taken me so long to see you again. I've been quite busy. Now that things have settled, you have my full attention."

Emlyn shuffled her feet. Tylysk didn't tell her she was supposed to say something. That's what it seemed Master Vespar wanted. But he just smiled, like he'd known Emlyn her entire life, and he was just a relative she'd been too little to remember meeting.

Vespar held out his hand. "Let's go for a walk. It's beautiful out, and you could do with a bit of sun."

Emlyn fought the urge to step away. She grasped his fingers, careful not to touch his magic ring. His hand was surprisingly soft.

The bright sunshine in the garden took some getting used to after being trapped for so long in Tylysk's study. The breeze kept it from getting too hot, and it smelled sweet with the flowers and Melys trees.

Emlyn wished Vespar would let go of her hand so she could run. Not away, but just to sprint down the lawn. Her bones were still stiff from being pent up in the garden house too. She wanted to run, and keep running and never stop.

Vespar brushed his thumb over her fingers. "I'm astounded that Master Rhys hid you out here, and for as long as he did," he said. "How long had he been planning to take you away, my girl?"

Emlyn tried not to shudder when he called her that. "A few days, I think."

"Ah," he said. "I might have guessed."

The sad way he said it made Emlyn think of Flannery. She walked up the path where Flannery and Rhys had wandered before they climbed the trees far away in the grass. She'd watch them, and when Rhys looked at Flannery, he had a silly grin that made Emlyn giggle. She'd been Vespar's fault too. Poor Rhys.

Vespar guided her through the hedges, going nowhere, the way Rhys used to. Questions scratched at her throat, but she swallowed them. Vespar wouldn't tell her what he wanted with her, or why she was special enough to keep. Rhys hadn't believed his explanation, so she didn't either. Besides, he'd just tell her she was too little to understand.

"Tell me again how this happened," he said. "The tinkers brought you here?"

Emlyn stared at her slippers.

"How did they find you?"

She shook the nightmare from her head before she saw her kidnappers pulling her hair and the tinker grabbing her. In real life, it'd gone too fast for her to remember it clearly, but the dream terrified her enough.

"The tinker bought me from the servants," she said.

Vespar frowned. "Where were your parents?"

Emlyn turned away. She missed Mama and Papa so bad, magic welled up in every bone in her body, and it took everything she had to keep it from escaping.

"They got sick last year. They died."

Vespar squeezed her hand. Maybe he sensed all the magic building up inside, and he was forcing her to keep it there.

"Who was your father?" he asked.

"Papa was an earl. He worked for Count Brandling."

"A nobleman. That explains your schooling. I can tell you've had some, haven't you?"

Emlyn's cheeks warmed. She had a governess and tutors, yes, but Magic had always been the best teacher. She wouldn't be so clever without it.

"Who is your guardian?"

"My brother." Emlyn hesitated, heart thumping. "He's a mage, but he doesn't know I'm a witch. *Please* don't get him in trouble."

"Hush, my girl, I believe you." He looked over the spread of red and violet flowers. "Count Brandling. You must be from Babondodd. I have a few mages there who work for me. One of them wrote me some months ago to tell me his sister had died in a terrible accident. His name is Master Heldran."

Emlyn tripped.

Master Vespar stood in front of her, holding her hand, his face sad. "You're the girl who drowned, aren't you?"

That was why Heldran never came for her. He thought she died. After all this, she wanted him more than anything, but now, he was working for *Master Vespar*?

Vespar crouched beside her. "Poor girl. And poor Heldran, all this time, thinking you were drowned. And Master Rhys has been hiding you from him."

Emlyn hid her face on her shoulder. She hated when he and Tylysk said those things. Rhys wasn't bad. He loved her. He promised.

But Heldran was supposed to love her too, wasn't he? And Emlyn loved him the way she loved Rhys. But it made her sick to think of Heldran not wanting her anymore when he learned about her magic.

It made her head hurt. She couldn't tell what was good or bad anymore.

"I'll send for him," Vespar said. "I'm sure you want to see him."

"Yes, Master Vespar," she said, and a sob broke it in two.

He smoothed her tears away. "Dry your eyes, my girl. You have nothing to fear. I can promise you this, Emlyn: you are far safter here than anywhere in Caeradin. I'll see to that."

She didn't care. She didn't believe him.

Vespar led her on. They looped though the garden hedges and started toward the castle. Emlyn struggled to answer his questions about her magic. She didn't know how long she'd been able to use it. She thought it'd always been part of her, not that it chose her. No one taught her to use it; she just read Heldran's books. She didn't want to say that, but it impressed Master Vespar rather than bothered him.

Tylysk met them at the end of the path. As they got closer, Emlyn smelled incense and candles on him. His magic's essence pulsed from whatever he'd been doing. He had that unpleasant smile on his face.

"Success?" asked Vespar.

"Yes, milord." A glance at Emlyn, and Tylysk said nothing more.

Emlyn ducked her head and tried not to listen while Vespar told Tylysk what she'd said. She felt Tylysk's stare on her before he rustled her hair. She peeked up to watch a grin split his face.

"You're Heldran's sister? What are the chances?" He pinched Emlyn's cheek, as if Heldran made everything fine between them. "I'll write him, milord."

Emlyn tried not to listen to most of Master Vespar's request, but she heard enough to understand she'd still be stuck with Tylysk. Emlyn shook inside. She wanted to stomp and scream at the mages, rip her hand out of Vespar's, and run to her garden house. She cringed away from Vespar's reach to pat her head.

"I-I don't want to stay here. I want to go home with Heldran. Please, Master Vespar?"

He pursed his lips, stooped to look in her eyes. "We'll wait for Heldran. I'll explain everything then. But I will tell you, if you can be patient a little longer."

"Please?"

Vespar's eyes were bright and hard, like light on a green jewel. "Stay with Tylysk. He will keep you safe."

Before Emlyn opened her mouth again, the castle door behind them burst open and swung against the wall. Tylysk whisked Emlyn behind him, then eased his grip when Isabelle came running.

He reached for her. "Isabelle, what's wrong?"

She swerved away from him and went to Master Vespar. "My lord, the Lady's fainted."

CHAPTER 30

Vespar

Vespar hurried after Isabelle to the Lady's chambers. What could have happened? Mere hours before, he'd drawn Orrtha around the first corner of recovery. What could have buckled her so soon?

"She and Aria were working on their embroidery, and she collapsed," Isabelle said. The girl's face flushed with more than the immediate worry. The pink in her eyes told Vespar the women's discussion had drawn too close to Rhys, though he'd advised Isabelle to avoid the topic. That, or the three of them had silently brooded together in the way women did, knowing one another's unspoken thoughts.

Thinking on it, Vespar realized Orrtha hadn't come to the dining hall since the disaster had struck. The platters of food brought to her chambers went untouched. Vespar had no doubt she lay awake in heartsickness through the night. Physically and otherwise, Orrtha had borne all she could withstand.

Two physicians were tending to the Lady when Vespar arrived. Aria huddled in the corner away from them, compulsively tucking her hair from her face. She scurried under Vespar's arm and into Isabelle's embrace.

Orrtha lay in her bed, yet unconscious. One physician examined an injury beading her hair red around her right temple. The other met Vespar at the door.

"She fell before the girls could catch her," he reported. "She caught the corner of the window seat."

Vespar looked to where the unfinished embroidery lay abandoned near the window, spools half unraveled across the floor.

"It's nothing too terrible, my lord. It would be less distressing if not for her greater pains." The physician pursed his lips, watching his colleague dab Orrtha's temple. "It is her grief, my lord. A broken heart."

Vespar didn't appreciate the sentiment. "She will overcome. She did before."

"I don't think she did, sir."

Vespar cast Ioan from his mind, though he always lingered like an eavesdropper. "It is the recent sting that ails her now."

The physician frowned. "Her son was much of her strength the first time. Now…"

Orrtha stirred, clutching her aching head between her hands. The physician let Vespar pass into the room. He refused to hear the rest of his sentimental concerns.

Orrtha's eyes fluttered. The second physician forbade her from rising, and she dropped to the pillows. A wild search about the room, and her glassy eyes fell on Vespar.

"Be still, my lady."

"I'm all right."

"No, milady, you are not." Vespar sat on the edge of her bed to keep her from rising.

Orrtha lay back. The physician daubed a salve on her wound and placed a bandage over her temple before retreating. Orrtha pressed it in place. She shifted her humiliated gaze away from Vespar. He swept a stray strand of hair from her face.

"It will pass," he said. "It is a dagger now, but it will dull with time."

Orrtha faced the windows. The gardens whispered under the warm breeze below them, but the angle showed the great knolls divided by the city's north wall, looking ankle-high in the distance. "It has never dulled, my lord," she said. "If anything, it's been whetted."

"Think no more on it now." Vespar folded her hand in both of his. Taking the risk, he said, "Neither Ioan nor Rhys would see you grieve yourself into such a state."

Vespar saw her heart break in her eyes. He pressed a kiss to her slender fingers. One fingertip skimmed his lip. Orrtha let her hand fall, remembering the physicians in the room. They stepped out with stiff bows.

Orrtha gazed over the hills, as if she might see her son hiding there, a small boy prancing over the green. A line of afternoon sun ribboned the soft edges of her profile and illuminated her skin with amber light.

"Did I not do enough?" she asked. "What happened to my son?"

Vespar said nothing. By now, his comforts sounded hollow, even to him.

Orrtha returned her gaze to his. Gold spliced with shadow halfway across her lovely face. "It would be different if I had agreed, wouldn't it? Rhys might have heeded a father."

It both warmed and chilled him. She regretted her rejection of his proposal, which he could easily interpret as a reconfirmation of her own affection. Despite her refusal, Vespar suspected her perpetual dependence on him stemmed from something more. And he had never suggested it was too late to change her mind.

But Rhys would have retaliated more. The boy's battle had deprived Vespar of Orrtha's hand in the first place. Vespar had thought it petulant, but Orrtha couldn't withstand her son's fuss, even for her own good, for her family's welfare, for her kingdom's security.

"If I had the courage, I would have listened," Orrtha said, turning to the light. "My husband took my strength with him."

Vespar cupped a hand to her cheek. "You are strong, Orrtha. I have never known a more courageous soul."

"Then why did I not fight? Why is my son gone?"

He smoothed her hair from her face and touched his lips to her brow. Orrtha clung to his hand on her cheek, the one anchor keeping her from falling from the precipice.

"I will help you. I have made my oaths to the Claytherdon House and to the realm. I swore to Ioan I would care for you. I leave you to decide by what means I do so, but I will fulfill whatever duty you ask of me."

Orrtha's face lingered inches from his, delicate and sweet as a winter lily in his hands. Her supple mouth waited, tempting him. Luring him closer, Orrtha traced a finger along his jaw, across his neck and up to his hair. He obeyed. He hovered a breath above her enticement. He held the shape of her pale, tender throat.

"I have a request, milord."

Her lips skimmed his as she spoke, chilling and delightful. Her fingers stilled in his hair. Vespar stooped to meet her.

"It is clear to me, and everyone else, that I have always been unfit for my duties."

Vespar looked from her delicate mouth to her eyes. She avoided his gaze. "Orrtha, you give yourself too little credit," he said.

"The council has always questioned my capabilities, and perhaps now they will voice their concerns rather than whisper them behind their hands." Orrtha's fingers slipped down his shoulder, falling away from him. "They have sought your guidance and authority where mine has failed them."

"My lady—"

"I relinquish my duties as Lady Regent to you."

Vespar gritted his teeth. He took his hands from her face, inching away. "Milady, please consider what you're doing. I strongly advise against it."

"I have considered it." Tears glossed Orrtha's relieved smile. "For years, I have considered it. If it is my duty to ensure Gildio's security, I can only do so by giving her to one more capable. In any case, we both know the council and nobles are debating my capacities."

Orrtha eased up from her pillows. "Isabelle," she called. The girl hurried to the door, and Orrtha said, "Bring the physicians with you."

"Orrtha, please, I cannot allow you to do this."

She paid Vespar no heed. The physicians entered and bowed. The Lady beckoned them and Mistress Isabelle forward. "You will be our witnesses. Stand here."

The men crept nearer despite Vespar's deterring glance. For one who thought she had no strength, Orrtha resisted his discouragement better than a stone wall. It couldn't be this way, not with his other, more demanding achievements finally underway. The idea of the Gildian Lordship might have appealed to him in the past, but if Emlyn was who he believed her to be, and his plans continued unhindered, lordship meant nothing to him.

"I had hoped you would consent to a different means to share your burden," Vespar said, attempting to ignore the physicians and Isabelle standing by.

The young Mistress glanced between them. "Milady?" she said, then sought an answer from Vespar. The girl read his dissatisfaction well enough. "But, my lady—"

Orrtha silenced her with a raised hand. She stood, despite the physician's objections. Weak fingers trembling, she removed the Gildian pendant from around her throat. The chain spilled her auburn hair about her shoulders. Isabelle took the jewel and held it in both hands.

"My lady," Vespar tried.

"Kneel, please."

Vespar lowered to the floor.

"Lord Mage Vespar," the Lady recited, meeting his gaze, "will you swear to protect the realm of Gildio, and lead her by the laws and statutes laid down by your predecessors, and take your place as Master of the Hunt and Lord of Gildio?"

For a moment, Vespar could only think she'd made a very untraditional abridgment of the oaths. A substantial enough excuse to decline his advancement, but he doubted Orrtha would think the same. She never wavered.

How could he accept? He would assist the Lady Regent in whatever capacity she required, but solely shouldering the duties of lordship would divert him from his set task. For years, he'd awaited this child, endured a lifetime of doubt and despair for this chance, and Orrtha disrupted it with the offer of Caeradin's most powerful realm and title.

Most powerful realm, perhaps. Title was another matter entirely.

The pendant weighed on Isabelle's palms like a slab of lead.

There was the Gildian council, he supposed, though he dreaded to think how they would take this breach of convention. Master Tylysk stood faithful beside him, as would Master Heldran when he arrived. And while the encumbering obligations of lordship proved less than ideal, Vespar couldn't deny the title's advantages.

With such a backing, It could not deny the Lord Mage now.

Vespar matched his gaze to Orrtha's. "I will."

Isabelle passed the pendant to her Mistress with shaking hands. Orrtha looped the chain over Vespar's head. She set the pendant to his chest, smoothed a finger across its gleaming surface. Three specks of green mirrored from the emeralds and glowed on her throat. Vespar's heart pounded beneath the silver.

"Let Mistress Isabelle and these gentlemen witness your oath," she said, "and may you forever keep it. Rise, Lord Vespar, Master of the Hunt, Lord of Gildio."

He rose. The dumbfounded physicians knelt. Isabelle amended her gape with a deferential dip of her head. Orrtha kept hers bowed.

"Will you dismiss the Lady Regent from her duties?"

Vespar forced himself to recite, "You are dismissed."

Orrtha raised her face, and the feeble ceremony ended.

She suddenly became timid as a young girl, unsure what to do. Vespar shot a glance at the physicians, and they escaped the chamber. Isabelle, pink faced and wide eyed, took her dismissal in kind.

Orrtha folded her hands and lowered her eyes. "I will do as you bid me, my lord. The household and Manor are yours."

Vespar bit back a stroke of anger. Had his confession not been clear? Did she think his fondness for her would change with this motion?

"I won't send you away, if that is your concern," he said, sharper than he intended. "The Manor is your home. You are still Lady Claytherdon."

"Thank you, my lord."

Vespar stepped away, unsure what to do himself. Orrtha curtsied to him for the first time, and moved to gather her unraveling tapestry from the floor.

"And Mistress Isabelle, my lord?" she said. "It would be customary for her to be in your charge now."

Vespar rubbed his eyes.

"I suppose you might have pondered other plans for her. Her previous betrothal will not be reinstated."

Vespar hadn't thought to think on it. He watched Orrtha twine the green thread around its spool. A part of him urged him to leave, and he started for the door. But, seeing her delicate, weary beauty, her utter resignation to his advancement, Vespar went and raised her up.

"Orrtha, please, I wish for things to be no different. Just moments ago, you led me to believe..."

How dare she.

Vespar stood away from her. Orrtha stared at her feet.

"An excellent trick," he said. "Is this my reward coming around? Did you think to snare me the way your son was?"

Orrtha put a hand to her mouth and wept. Vespar made for the door, for the first time not bowing in her presence. She called after him and ran to catch his sleeve.

"Please. That wasn't my intent."

"Was it not?"

She stammered. "Give me time. If that is what you wish, I only ask for time to heal."

"You've made it clear you will neither recover nor consent."

"I have just consented."

"When you believed your well-being depended on it." He removed her hand from his arm. "I won't have you if I am to be your lifeline before anything else."

Lord Vespar left Orrtha to weep, neither able nor wanting to look at her.

CHAPTER 31

Rhys

Lleogren's capital spread as far as one of Gildio's streets coiled into a haphazard spiral with its minute castle at its center. A few roads straggled away from the main street, dotted with tiny shops and houses. At its busiest, the city still bore no resemblance to Gildio's quieter hours.

Despite their humbler circumstances, the people exuded more cheer than Gildio's bustling impatience. Many waved to Athrú and Oedolyn, and she veered aside once or twice to ask after someone's ailments. Children chased one another and playful dogs down the road. Some tugged Athrú's sleeves and begged for the story of where he'd traveled recently.

"Irminric again," he replied. The children pouted, but paid too little attention to pester him long. Athrú answered my curious glance with a tight smile. "The adventures they hear about are much more thrilling than the ones I have."

Athrú passed Starbolt's reins to Oedolyn, and she went on to tend to her errands. "This way," he said, turning his back to the castle. "Eoin's shop is down here. And besides, you can't go back to Gildio emptyhanded."

The dragon snorted, protesting his suggested uselessness. I glanced up at the pewter sign swinging over the entry ahead, its black image the silhouette of a hammer and anvil.

The heavy clang of hammer and tongs and the hiss of dunked glowing iron met us down the street. The blackened roof extending from the shop's sooty walls darkened the open, sweltering smithy, except the searing orange radiance from the forge. One smith pumped the bellows while another poured molten iron into a cast. Athrú nodded to them and passed through the door at the back.

A dirt courtyard spread behind the shop, edged by a long row of stable stalls. Perhaps a dozen horses took shelter there, noses deep in oat bags and hay. A wooden enclosure ringed the courtyard from one edge of the stable to the other. Athrú made for the gate.

A russet-brown mare blinked her dewy eyes at us as we approached, swung her head to look at her master. The short, elderly man brushed her shining coat with his back to us. All I saw of his features were hunched shoulders, weathered hands, and a shock of bristly white hair. He crooned to the horse as he worked.

"Isn't she new, Eoin?" Athrú patted the mare's neck. "She's lovely."

Eoin beamed at her. "My new beauty. Came up all the way from Itis, would you believe? Worth every silver, aren't you, m'love?" He smoothed a knobbed hand down her nose. Of a sudden, he grinned up at Athrú. He dusted his hands on his leather apron and shook Athrú's hand. "My, lad, what are you doing here? You said you'd not be home till next week. You can't think to dazzle me with tales of such a short journey."

"I might just. I rescued this one off the river."

When he turned, Eoin startled me with how his spectacles magnified his crinkling eyes. The old man searched me. "Aha, on the river. Where from, then?"

"Gildio, sir."

"Ah ha ha." Eoin tilted his chin up. "You're not Master Rhys, are you?"

My heart stopped.

Eoin chuckled. "Word is fast, young man. Heard it from Lord Cael's own mouth. He was intrigued by the news of your banishment. Can't say I'm not too, honest." He waited, his huge eyes fixed on me.

"Haven't you heard?" Athrú said. "A witch child and a few misunderstandings, and I end up hauling Master Rhys off the exile's boat."

"Gracious," Eoin laughed. "A Claytherdon and a witch, what a pair."

I bit back my annoyance.

"They're holding the witch in Gildio," Athrú went on. "Rhys means to retrieve her."

Eoin's grin faded. "Oh, indeed? Very odd. You think it best?" He nodded at my silent determination. He set aside his brush and took up his cane. "Suppose that's why you came to see me. Need something to stave off the hangman?"

I swallowed, but Athrú said, "If you have something to do the trick."

"Ah, I can never be sure." Eoin winked and bumped Athrú with his cane, then poked me in the ribs with it. "But my, look at him. Better get some muscle on this one quick, 'fore a stiff breeze makes off with him. Did your masters ever let you hold a blade, lad?"

Sounding pettier than I meant, I said, "I trained with Swordsmaster Perreth himself, sir."

"Did you now, did you? Ha. I would've expected more from him and more on you. My, what a green lad he was. Brawny, but nimble as a whip. His rather small brain might account for his inhuman courage, however. Last I saw Perreth, he'd just passed his evaluations to join our ranks."

My face burned with embarrassment. "You're a Swordsmaster?"

"Was." He waved the accomplishment away. "Long before either of you crawled out of your cradles. I served in the wars when Lord Cael was green as a willow shoot." The old Swordsmaster hobbled toward the stables, mare in tow, his thin, crooked frame creaking. "In fact, Lord Cael's grandfather was my first patron, if you can believe. You wouldn't have guessed I was so young, would you? Ha!"

Eoin led us to the shop, rambling to Athrú about techniques I should learn and methods he'd taught as a Swordsmaster, some of which I'd heard. Athrú pretended to listen.

The shop was as much an armory as the one I expected to find in Lord Cael's castle. Some blades exhibited along the walls were chipped and dull while other glistened. An assemblage of swords, daggers, double-bladed axes, halberds, pikes, and even a war hammer decorated every available inch of whited-washed wall.

"In case you feel creative," Eoin said, spotting my study of the hammer. His boney fingers gave my upper arm a squeeze. "Don't know that you could lift it," he muttered under his breath. "Now, what were you thinking?"

Athrú joined Eoin to look me over like a slab of meat. "Heavier, I think, and with good reach," he said.

"So something like yours." Eoin examined the wall for a sample, brows drawing together. "Or heavier?"

"He could manage it."

"Could he?" Eoin scrutinized me, finding little to impress him.

Athrú waited for me to say it. Irked, I glared at my feet. "I'm a draconis," I mumbled.

Eoin's eyes lit up. "Ah! Yes, that makes a difference. You could take that hammer, if you wanted, Master Rhys. You might look right well with it." He went on about the few draconi he'd encountered on his journeys, but interrupted himself halfway through saying how civil I was. "Aha, try that one."

He pointed to a sword and listed its features, but reconsidered and moved to another. Athrú took a few down for me to hold. I felt little difference between them except the weight. Nothing convinced Eoin.

"Aha!" he spouted. "There's the devil. Grab that one there." Athrú obeyed, standing on his toes to reach the narrow blade. Eoin inspected it. "Long tempered steel and silver, steel hilt, silver pommel. About as heavy as that short sword we looked at there, but thinner. The silver adds a touch of the weight."

I held it point upward, let it fall in my hand to feel its weight in motion. As far as I could tell, even fastidious Captain Perreth would have approved.

Athrú tested the sword himself. "Moves well. Firm. Good reach, good balance."

Eoin agreed. "And the longer handle will make a good grip should you need, ah, a bit more extension than just the blade." He winked. I couldn't for the life of me grasp why he thought I'd consider using my draconis. "Well?" he said.

I grinned up at the blade's tip catching the forge light.

Eoin laughed. "It needs a touchup. We'll hand it off to the lads. Two of Caeradin's finest, you know." He cradled the sword to his chest and puttered to the smiths.

"He was really a Swordsmaster?" I whispered to Athrú, watching the elderly warrior struggle with a blade almost the same height as he.

"My father fought in his ranks. He still works with Lord Cael now and again. Better he take the news to the council before we stride in unannounced." He leaned around me to peer out to the street. "I'll speak with him. See if Oedolyn's about yet."

I thanked Eoin and stepped out of the blazing smithy. With Oedolyn nowhere to be seen, I leaned against the wall and waited.

Market-goers and busy folk meandered past me, many bidding me good afternoon. Some recognized I wasn't from Windborough and made sure I had a place to stay. The Lleogrian kindness might not have been as warm if they knew to whom they spoke.

Down the road, a girl a few years older than Emlyn entertained some children with colorful smoke animals romping through the air. The girl spotted me watching. She pranced to my side. She rubbed her palms together, focusing hard, and thrust her hands into the air. A smoky falcon spiraled about us before soaring upward to glide down on my shoulder. The girl's eyes twinkled at my gasp. The cloudy bird screeched at me, the sound muffled and distant. It cocked its head at the girl as she stroked the misty feathers down its chest. The falcon launched into the air to be lost to the sunlight. The girl giggled and skipped away to take her mother's hand.

I swallowed my astonishment. The girl's mother let her use magic in public, where witnesses to her "crime" abounded. Better yet, she'd performed her trick for the once Master of the Hunt. The girl had training if she could create those charming figures so well. I knew Lleogren condemned the Hunt, but I hadn't imagined they'd take such risks.

Reminding me of its place here too, a mage's spell stung the back of my head. I searched around for the source. Nearby, something gave off a faint, hot, herbal scent. My right wrist itched.

The dragon forced me around to the right. I blinked away the dizziness and put a hand to the wall as my feet moved on their own. The beast shoved, a jolt against my ribs. I reeled forward before regaining myself.

"Stop it," I muttered.

He rammed into my chest. I stumbled.

"All right, stop!" I beat a fist to my chest, where the dragon lurked. He grumbled.

I tiptoed on. The spell surged. That alone brought on a friendly headache, but the acrid scent worsened it. Sidling the shop wall, I peeked around the corner into the alley.

A dirt spiral settled to the ground in the shade. I inched closer. The breeze smoothed the disturbed dust across the lifeless backstreet, brushed away the faintest remains of a perfect four-foot circle. A bitter tang tainted the air. I crouched, fingered the fading line. The dirt burned to the touch.

"Rhys?"

I jumped out of my skin.

Athrú stopped beyond the alley, hands raised. "What?"

I swallowed. "You startled me, is all."

His face was unreadable. He didn't press.

Vaporous shadows formed a black column in the center of the amber cave. Its base flickered with murky flames, and its smoke bubbled and roiled straight up in a pillar. The dragon lazily reclined in full view. He'd shrunken since the last nightmare he brewed, stood at fifteen feet rather than thirty or more. His plated tail curled around the shadow column. I felt limbless and limp, except something heavy hung about me.

The beast's foul words rumbled through my head.

"Stop it," I commanded, but my voice echoed far away. The dragon pressed on with his recitation.

Wake up, *I told myself.* Just wake up.

The dragon released a breath across the darkness. A knot of shadows unraveled and scattered. Flannery hung suspended in the black gale, her eyes shut tight, her face empty, her hair whipping in the wind.

I ran for her, but the weight trapped me down. I sprawled toward the yellow earth. Cold metal broke my fall—the dragon's chains constricted around me, hung off my arms and legs and shoulders. I arched against them to free myself, to shove from the iron mound under me. I called, screamed for Flannery, anything. She didn't hear.

Wake up. Now. Wake. Up.

The dragon stretched a fist into the black flames. He uncurled his claws. Flannery plummeted to his palm, listless as a rag doll. His talons closed around her.

"No, don't!"

He spread his claws. Red-tainted daisy petals drifted from his palm into the dark gale before smoldering to ash.

CHAPTER 32

Tylysk

Tylysk bowed to his master and watched him march down the corridor, though it was all he could do to keep his jaw from slackening. Not that he wouldn't follow the unusually brusque orders, and not that he wasn't honored by the faith his master had in him. He'd never have Vespar question his loyalty, so he affected his enthusiasm and said, "Of course, milord." But for all the task would prove his fidelity, Tylysk would rather have done anything else.

Emlyn would remain under his protective eye until his master spoke otherwise. Regardless of Heldran's arrival or other duties of his own. Despite the fact that he'd never handled a child before Emlyn, and he saw himself as fit for the task as a beast at a banquet. His master attempted to garnish the idea by labeling him her guardian. Her nanny, more like.

Vespar's terseness startled Tylysk, but he said nothing of it. Emlyn's presence calmed him, and a few pats of her head eased his disquiet. But when he turned to leave, Tylysk finally saw that what vexed his master hung around his neck.

The Gildian pendant. Something had gone very wrong.

Tylysk looked down at the girl at his side, lips pursed. By her exhausted discontent, the news cheered Emlyn as much as himself. Once, she used to shrink under his eye and try to disappear. Now, she peered up through her lashes, saying nothing, a miserable quirk on her lips.

"Come on," he said. "I have work to do."

The girl tagged behind him the rest of the afternoon as he finished his tasks. At least he'd completed his pentacle work. Emlyn wouldn't disrupt that, nor would he have let her witness it. An intricate chalk circle, an unsavory incense, and a few drops of blood were more than a child needed to see.

As they traversed the mage quarters of the castle, they both endured stares from his colleagues, a few thoughtless jests from the most ignorant, and more disapproving frowns than anything else. Emlyn ducked inside his cloak. Tylysk gritted his teeth and let her.

As soon as he could, Tylysk returned Emlyn to his chambers. He requested their dinner be brought to them instead of meeting Master Vespar and Lady—or rather, Mistress Orrtha now—in the dining hall. Emlyn rarely nibbled what he brought her in the past, though by the sound of it, her stomach often gnawed on itself. Tylysk doubted he'd get the skittish girl from her sanctuary in his study again today if he dragged her by a lead.

There she stayed on the sofa, watching him work at his desk, too small for her feet to touch the floor. Whenever he caught her staring, she traced patterns in the cushions, fiddled with her hair, pet the soft ribbons on her new gown. It surprised Tylysk how she adored that dress. When she thought he paid her no mind, she'd spread the skirt and twist back and forth or toy with its long ribbons. It diminished her gloom a little, even if the poutiness never left her lips. Otherwise, Tylysk had reached the extent of what he knew to do with her.

He would never have gone to Isabelle, though it might have eased his mind. She always excelled at this sort of thing. Not that Tylysk wasn't capable. Of course he was.

It had been days since Tylysk had seen Isabelle until she came bounding through the garden in search of Master Vespar. She was pretty when worried, pink in the cheeks and a few stray locks framing her face. A tiny ringlet caressed her pale neck, too short to stay in her jeweled pins.

He hardly knew what she'd say if he asked for her help. If she knew he, well, wanted her help. It was extraordinary enough for a Mage Master to care for a witch, but to do it alone, without…

Well, Heldran had done it, and Rhys, the witless oaf. If they could, Tylysk could.

Still, the thought of her companionship lessened his doubts. Tender Isabelle couldn't tell him no, could she?

Emlyn darted out of view of the antechamber when a knock came at the door. Tylysk rolled his eyes and answered it.

"You're la—" He closed his mouth.

Her lovely red lips twisted like the braids crowning her hair. With her head high, she brandished a teardrop emerald at her soft throat, and a matching ring adorned one of the fingers drumming the tray she carried. Tylysk thought her winter-green gown and gold girdle made her appear more a lady of Gildio than Orrtha had ever been. The idea suited her, just as the dress suited her dark hair and pearl-smooth skin.

"Well?" Isabelle hoisted the tray for him to see. Tylysk counted three plates stacked on the corner. "Are you going to let me in?"

Tylysk glanced over his shoulder. A twist of Emlyn's pink dress whipped around the corner. He licked his lips, thinking fast. He forced himself to say, "I don't think that would be wise at the moment."

"This isn't getting any lighter." Isabelle stepped out of Tylysk's reach. "I'll drop it if you try to take it."

"On the floor or on me?"

"If you move, we won't find out."

Tylysk sensed Emlyn peeking at him. He lowered his voice. "Master Vespar hasn't allowed her any visitors yet. We still have yet to secure her immunity."

"I thought that was implicit in the fact that she's locked in your chambers instead of a cell. Unless you have some spare chains lying around, perhaps a rack." Isabelle searched over his shoulder.

He stepped in the way of her view. "Paperwork," he said, only partially fibbing. "We hold nothing against you, milady, but her safety must come first."

She raised a brow, lips tight. "Are you asking for raspberry sauce down your tunic?"

"Only to what we owe the pleasure of your company. I would've imagined you'd be at Mistress Orrtha's side at a time like this."

"She's more than content with Aria. Now, if you don't want to wear your pork and potatoes, I suggest you let me through."

Tylysk peered back once more. Emlyn ducked out of view for a breath, then peeked with one eye around the door frame. Tylysk pressed a thumb and finger to his eyes and stepped aside. "Come get your supper, Emlyn."

Isabelle set the table while Emlyn cowered, watching from the next room. With Tylysk's coaxing, she inched through the door, flat to the wall, and sidled into the room.

"Sun and stars!" Isabelle's gasp made Emlyn jump. "Master Tylysk didn't tell me he was hiding a princess in here."

Emlyn blushed. "Master Tylysk got this dress for me."

"Did he?" Isabelle eyed him. "I never knew you had a taste for fashion, Tylysk."

His taste for pork was quickly evading him.

"I brought you a surprise." Isabelle lured the girl with a bend of her finger. She tapped the polished cover poised on one corner of the tray. "You'll have to eat your supper first, but Rhys told me you like a particular treat." She ignored Tylysk's stiffening and took her seat.

Emlyn climbed into the chair next to Tylysk and across from Isabelle, blushing to her ears. Tylysk slapped a slice of pork on her plate, a few seasoned potatoes, a hunk of bread and some raspberry sauce to dunk it in. Isabelle brimmed a wooden cup with cider from the decanter and passed it to Emlyn, then filled Tylysk's goblet. He'd rather have had something stronger.

Emlyn watched him slice a potato and take a bite. He gestured with his fork. "Eat."

The girl shifted her nervous gaze to Isabelle before taking up her fork. The Mistress's encouraging smile brightened her brown eyes.

Tylysk observed the girls' lopsided conversation. Isabelle spoke enough for them both while Emlyn nodded or shook her head. Their discussion held nothing of interest to him, except Emlyn wished she had a hairbrush and some ribbons, and she couldn't wait to see Heldran. The more she nibbled, the more color returned through her pallor, besides the raspberry jell accumulating in the corners of her mouth.

"Now tell me about Master Tylysk." Isabelle watched him over the rim of her goblet. "Has he been good to you?"

Emlyn nodded.

"Be honest. I'm not afraid to put him in his place, if I must."

Tylysk pursed his lips. Isabelle wrinkled her nose at him, but a lethal glint in her eyes overrode her tease.

Emlyn tore a bite of bread and nibbled at it without looking up.

"I can't imagine he's done something to you, has he?"

Another shake of her head, easier this time.

"No. He's just a mage and he spooks you, doesn't he?"

Emlyn bowed her head. Tylysk rolled his eyes to meet Isabelle's sharp scorn.

"I don't blame you," she told the girl, but aimed her glower at Tylysk. "The world has flipped on its head, and you're caught in the middle of it. I'd be afraid too."

The little witch finished her bread, sinking in her chair.

"I can tell you this." Isabelle claimed Emlyn's gaze. "Aside from Master Vespar, there's not a soul in Gildio who can protect you half as well as Tylysk." Isabelle put a hand to the side of her mouth and whispered, "He's just a little rough around the edges, isn't he?"

Tylysk swelled at her frank commendation, though her observation pricked it. He forced a smile, and Emlyn didn't cringe when he tousled her hair.

"Not at all," he said. "We're better friends day by day, aren't we?"

"Yes, Master Tylysk."

Isabelle shot him another look, but dismissed it before Emlyn noticed. "I don't suppose you've had too much supper for your treat?" she said. She unveiled a cup of plump scarlet strawberries. Emlyn's tiny smile crept to her face.

Tylysk passed the girl the cup and a napkin and nodded toward the study. Emlyn slid out of her chair. "Thank you, Mistress Isabelle."

Isabelle beamed warm as sunshine. "Good night, Emlyn."

Whatever the girl did, it wasn't the curtsy she attempted. Isabelle giggled, either at her or the surprise on Tylysk's face. Embarrassed by her clumsiness, but grinning all the same, Emlyn padded to the next room.

"How precious is she?" Isabelle laughed. "Better and better friends, are you?"

"We're getting used to each other."

"Sounds about right." She raised her goblet to her lips. "When will Heldran be here?"

"We hope no later than tomorrow evening. Not that it will matter." Tylysk answered Isabelle's questioning look with the news of Master Vespar's most recent request.

"Why wouldn't he put her in Heldran's charge?" she asked. "We all know both you and Emlyn would prefer it."

"Heldran's guardianship over his witch sister is a conflict of interest. Since Master Vespar is further engaged as lord, the duty falls to me."

"Then you're not her protector. You're the warden who keeps the witch on her best behavior while she's on probation."

Tylysk drummed his fingers on the stem of his cup. "The council demanded that she never go nor be left anywhere without a capable Mage Master." He omitted the request for detaining pentacles when needed, as Isabelle would categorize that under "having done something" to Emlyn.

"Do you really think her capable of some assault?" Isabelle asked dissuasively.

"They do."

She softened when he said nothing more. "When do you present her again?"

"In two months, at the latest. We're confident she'll convince them."

Isabelle's lips tightened. She gathered the empty plates onto the tray. "You won't tell me why he cares, if I ask, will you? Innocence never stopped him before."

"No witch has been as innocent before."

"Rhys would disagree with you."

"And that's why he's not here."

A sadness tinged her glower and made Tylysk almost regret his words. Almost.

"Don't let Emlyn hear you," she warned. "You won't lure her into your snare that way."

Tylysk snorted. "Snare?" He followed her to the door. "Is sparing her life a snare?"

"Sparing her life, no. Whatever you intend to do with it is another matter."

"What more do we intend?"

"Please. Neither of you would go out of your way to rehabilitate a witch unless you could profit by it. What makes Emlyn more profitable than any other witch who's fallen at your feet?"

"She is not a slave, my lady, and that you would think us so low—"

"Then why where you so low as to be rid of her rescuer? Of the one joy in her life?"

Tylysk grasped Isabelle by the elbow before she stepped through the door. He glanced back to be sure Emlyn wasn't eavesdropping. He lowered his voice. "Rhys broke the law before Emlyn's abilities were realized. He refused to expose her and would have run off with her had we not discovered them. He chose to neglect his realm, his people, rather than let Emlyn go."

Isabelle's arm tautened in his hand. She stared him down, glaring. Tylysk dared a step closer, dared to loosen his grip. He opened his mouth.

"Don't say it," she hissed. "He did *not* leave me."

Tylysk slid his hand down her arm, let his fingertips taste her wrist before claiming her hand. "You still love him."

Isabelle burned a tender pink.

"And here I thought you'd given up that pursuit long ago."

"And you will never abandon yours, will you?" Isabelle ripped from his grasp and stalked down the hall. Tylysk followed a step, called for her. She never turned.

He trudged to his chambers, kicking himself for his stupidity. He leaned against the door after it closed, rubbed the headache from his eyes. After all these years, Tylysk believed he'd steeled himself against Isabelle's censures, but this struck more fiercely than ever. Taking a deep breath, he steadied himself so Emlyn wouldn't see it.

In his study, sitting cross-legged on the sofa, Emlyn sucked the strawberry juice from her red fingertips one by one. Tylysk watched her from the doorway until she peeked up.

"Did you actually eat any of them? They're all over your face."

Emlyn smeared the napkin across her stained chin. Tylysk sent her to clean up in the washroom. She flitted through the door, light as a butterfly.

Tylysk dropped in his desk chair, determined to distract himself from Isabelle's coldness. He searched the spread of parchments, locating the correct page when a note scribbled itself across it. Tylysk reorganized the messaging parchments and readied his quill.

He hadn't realized the hour until Emlyn returned, mouth gaping in a yawn. She blushed at his raised brow, scrubbed her drooping eyes.

"Lie down, Emlyn. Go to sleep."

She crawled onto her makeshift bed and tugged the blanket to her chin.

Tylysk dipped his quill and scratched along the parchment. A reply faded through in Heldran's brisk scrawl. Good, he'd be at the Manor tomorrow evening.

Emlyn flopped over and snuggled into her pillow. Tylysk rubbed his eyes. For a moment, in his lingering heartsickness, he wondered if he'd slipped somewhere, made a foolish mistake that had forced Master Vespar to assign him to something…inconsistent, he decided, with everything else he performed for his master.

Tylysk had remained in the Lord Mage's good graces since he entered he Academy as a raw boy of ten, stayed there until he graduated at twenty-two. He was a rarity at the Academy, a nobleman's son whose father could afford to send him to secondary and mastery schools. Most of his peers completed their education at fourteen, when they moved on to apprenticeships. Ethelfledian boys left for the Hunt unless they showed particular promise. Those who stayed until eighteen tended to serve under Mage Masters.

Tylysk completed his twelve years and earned the status of Mage Master. Top of his class, no less, tied only, by the most absurd coincidence, with Heldran.

Master Vespar sometimes reminded his second of his own resemblance to Tylysk. He'd swept through the Academy with ease, highest marks in his year, renowned as the finest mage of his generation. Before he graduated, and graduated early, his remarkable potential promised him the position of Lord Mage in the Claytherdon House, while most Mage Masters never attained the higher rank. By the time Tylysk entered the Academy, Caeradin considered Vespar the nation's finest mage.

It must have been their academic similarities that caught his master's eye. Tylysk stayed at Vespar's side from the first and was appointed his second on graduation day. He served the Claytherdon Household, doing whatever was asked of him and preparing himself for all his master had trained him.

Two years later, he was playing nanny.

Tylysk bit his lip. He imagined Isabelle's sour expression as he bemoaned his task, the disgust firm on her frown. Her easy way with Emlyn hadn't gone undetected, nor had he failed to notice Emlyn make her first stretch from her cocoon, albeit sheepishly. But the little butter-fly retreated to her refuge and shielded herself from Tylysk's rough edges.

Emlyn nestled deeper. He caught her peeking to see if he was watching her. Those sleepy blue-violet eyes blinked at him. Tylysk beckoned her with a bend of his finger.

She crept out of her blankets, but came no closer. She clung to the collar of her dress, her bare feet turned in toward each other. Tylysk held out his hand. Emlyn tiptoed nearer. A reply splayed across the parchment, and he scribbled a few words to avoid Emlyn's anxious gaze. Her pink lips quirked.

"You know you're going to be here for a long time, don't you, Emlyn?"

Her lips flickered downward.

"Heldran will be here tomorrow, and he'll do his part, but Master Vespar thinks it best that I keep an eye on you."

Emlyn hid in her hair.

"I was thinking on what Isabelle said," he continued, taking quill to parchment. "How hard this is for you, and for everyone else. So to see things move smoother, you and I are going to make a few deals." He let his pen rest in the inkwell and planted his elbows on his knees, stooping face to face with the girl. "First, if I promise not to be so rough, you have to promise no more tears. Deal?"

Emlyn blinked, surprised. She nodded. Good enough.

"Second, if you promise to listen to Master Vespar and me, I'll see if we can't find you a better room. Deal?"

Another, more eager nod.

"Third…" Tylysk faltered. He drummed his fingers on the desk. "I know you're afraid, Emlyn. Isabelle was right about everything, wasn't she?"

The girl bowed her head.

"But you have a special gift, a special strength." Tylysk tapped a finger to her heart. "Master Vespar and I believe you can use it for good, while the rest of Caeradin doubts. But," he said, looking in her eyes, "you can prove them wrong. Master Vespar will teach you how. You will be the first free witch, Emlyn."

Her jaw dropped. He ignored her silent questions. "So if you can promise to do as he asks, whatever he asks, I…" He took a deep breath. "I'll see if I can't take you riding sometimes, or let you play with Aria and the dogs, or something."

Emlyn stared, her dismay and dejection softening. Her head cocked like a little bird's.

"All right?" Tylysk extended a hand. "Promise?"

She raised her shoulders to her ears. "Yes, Master Tylysk."

He licked his lips. "You—don't have to call me *Master* Tylysk. That's… whatever you like, all right?"

Emlyn wasn't thrown by his briskness. His stumble lifted the corners of her mouth. She grasped his fingers, her hand no bigger than his palm.

Tylysk released their handshake, turned Emlyn about, and nudged her toward the sofa. "Go on. I'm almost done here."

She stepped away, sending him a gaze he couldn't interpret. She nuzzled beneath the blanket. Soon, a gentle hum in her sleep tugged Tylysk around to look at her again.

He hadn't expected all that to spill from his mouth. Who was he to say what Master Vespar would or wouldn't let him do with Emlyn?

Was it enough to startle her into reconsidering her situation? At least enough to jerk her into neutrality? As long as Rhys wasn't her hero and Tylysk wasn't her villain, he could draw her to his side. As long as she wavered, Tylysk could win her over.

For his master. For their cause. For what should have been, and had always been, Lord Mage Vespar's.

Tylysk cleaned his quill and put away his work. Emlyn hummed, tossed onto her side, her thumb halfway out of her mouth. Tylysk rubbed his eyes.

For good measure, he pulled the drooping blanket over her shoulder before dousing the magelight on his way out.

CHAPTER 33

Rhys

I spent half the night upright. Every moment I lay down, my back prickled and ached with the threat of scales and wings. His amber cave brightened my head. The dragon said nothing, never looked at me. He craved to run and rampage, to blaze and ravage, then circle back to some craggy mountain hideout.

He recoiled when Oedolyn woke me. He eyed her with the same heat as he always regarded Athrú and turned his back to her gentle smile.

"You're running late," she said. "Hurry down, or you'll have to eat your breakfast on the road." Oedolyn padded to the staircase, hesitated when I lay still. Her sparkling smile scrunched to one side. "You're not nervous, are you, Master Rhys?"

I didn't answer. This tiny, humble cottage was infinitely more inviting than the halls of a foreign lord I'd never met, and the cramped bed too snug to abandon for apprehensive councils.

"Eoin said Lord Cael is anxious to meet you," Oedolyn said. "And if you won Eoin over so easily, you'll have no trouble with the council." She hurried down to the kitchen.

Chamberlain refused to follow the three of us down the road. He howled at me until he lost sight of us. We moved onto Windborough's streets before the dragon slithered into a cavern pocket and watched, crimson eyes on me.

High atop the spires of Windborough's ancient castle, the Lleogrian red lion on blue banners hung limp with no breeze. Stained-glass windows displayed armed warriors and distinguished mages in spreads of ravishing color. Farawl Silverblade raised his sword with a six-pointed crown dangling from its tip. Tenbur, cloaked in his famous scarlet mantle, faced half a dozen dragons too small to be believable—the beast in my head snorted at them.

Waiting for us outside the council chamber, Eoin squatted on a bench, his cane planted between his feet. His large eyes glittered behind his spectacles.

"There you are." Eoin waved us over. He looked even smaller in his dark-green doublet and thin boots instead of his dusty stableman's clothes. He'd combed down his shock of white hair, except a spiral at the back of his head stood straight up. He turned his grin to me. "You're a bit green, Master Rhys."

Oedolyn unhooked her arm from mine and urged me to sit beside Eoin. The old man patted my knee.

"I told you, you have nothing to worry about," said Oedolyn. All the same, she fiddled with my collar more than once before she fussed with Athrú. He tickled his sister's face with her feather-duster hair.

Eoin rose from time to time to peek through the door. He prattled on about his new mare, who'd come all the way from Itis, if we could believe, and was far cleverer and more a beauty than that half-witted gobermouch's old brute that was so hefty and dismally colored, Eoin once mistook it for a cow.

One last peek inside the council chamber, and Eoin nodded. Oedolyn plucked something off my sleeve and ushered us away. Athrú followed me in.

The great hall doubled as the council chamber and was half the size of the Gildian Manor's. A scarlet carpet ran from the door up to the small dais. The stained-glass windows dappled the red and blue tiles with iridescent light. Lion banners draped down the walls. Crackling live torches, not magelights, banished what few shadows the vast windows couldn't reach.

The councilmen occupied thirteen chairs at the long table. Lleogren's Mage Masters wore their distinguishing blue robes trimmed with red, but their uniform attire gave no clue as to which was Lord Mage.

Lord Cael moved from his place at the head of the table to greet us, smiling through his silvering brown beard. His rank granted him a fur-trimmed mantle with a gold clasp, but the rest of his assemblage was at least as humble as those of his counselors. The Lleogrian pendant of the lion and rubies gleamed on his chest.

"Master Claytherdon," he said. I made to bow, but Lord Cael grasped my hand. "You are most welcome."

"Thank you, my lord." I dipped my head. "I'm not accustomed to hearing that."

He laughed. "That will soon change, I wager. Please, sit."

The men shifted down a seat to make the two chairs on either side of Lord Cael's available for us. Once seated, he said, "The Lords and Ladies are all a-chatter about your 'misdeeds', Master Rhys. Rest assured you are safe within Lleogren's borders, and many other lords, and Lady Meliud, have expressed the same."

"Thank you, sir." It hardly conveyed my relief.

"No doubt the truth has warped since it left Gildio. Perhaps you would revise the news with your side of the tale."

All eyes fell on me. I straightened in my seat. "I'm afraid there's little to warp, sir. I attempted to save a witch child from the Hunt and hid her from my household." For once, I could face their polite astonishment as I relayed Da's ambitions to end the Hunt. No outrage accompanied their shock.

"I never knew that of your father," Cael said, "but I'm not surprised. He was a great young man, and always of the highest respect."

"Thank you, my lord."

"And you also mean to see the Hunt ended."

"It will be difficult now, sir, but I intend to do all I can to continue my father's ambitions."

One of the councilmen started an applause.

"I ask for your counsel, my lords. There is more I'm sure that has not crossed Gildio's borders." I swallowed hard, the dragon constricting my throat. Athrú offered the steady support of his gaze from across the table. "One would assume this witch would fall to the Hunt upon our discovery. However, Lord Mage Vespar, with consent from the Gildian council, has retained the girl for himself."

"On what grounds, and for what purpose?" I assumed the gaunt mage with a hook nose beside Athrú was the Lleogrian Lord Mage, based on how near he sat to Lord Cael.

I related my standoff with my tutor at the trial, of his certainty of Emlyn's capacities, of the experiment of her innocence. "Master Vespar believes that through proper mentoring, she may prove herself guiltless and possibly lead to the freedoms of other witches."

All eyes widened with surprise, a few jaws gaped. Most brows narrowed. The councilmen exchanged puzzled frowns.

One round man down the table asked, "Is it a concern, then? Have we not hoped for something to lead to the Hunt's end? Perhaps Master Rhys's banishment was a matter of due process."

"We don't believe Master Vespar's motives are so sincere, my lord," said Athrú. "If it were so simple, perhaps Master Rhys would not have been convicted. We believe Master Vespar has an ulterior purpose for the child."

Cael drummed his fingers on the tabletop. "Do you believe this purpose to be malicious?"

I had no doubt, but I bit my tongue. "If it were not," I said, "he wouldn't conceal her as he does. Protocol would bid him to bring such a move before the Caeradin Council, and all of Caeradin knows of his strict enforcement of protocol."

"I believe even Master Vespar would neglect protocol to circumvent Lord Calibor's displeasure," said the Lord Mage, frowning.

"Indeed, Master Corrick." Cael gestured to the mage. "But Calibor hasn't intimidated Master Vespar as he has others. Master Vespar and Lady Orrtha would not face Calibor without the backing of several allies, either. If he did not fear his actions being known, he would make them known."

The round gentleman down the table spread his hands, shrugging. "What could he plan to do with the child? If he means to prove witches guiltless, power to him. Why should we complain if he takes a stand to save our daughters?"

"Why has he not attempted this with another witch?" a spectacled mage asked. "Why was the tanner's wife not spared, or the mason's little one last spring?"

The gravity of his words weighed on every face in the room. A heavy silence dangled in it for a long moment, before another, younger mage spoke up.

"Their powers must not have been as developed as Master Vespar believes of this child's. As Master Rhys said, he is fascinated by her gift. He is caught not by her innocence, but her strength."

"How old is the girl?" Master Corrick asked.

"Six years, sir."

Brows went up, but the mages frowned at the implications of Emlyn's youth. Her extraordinary strength would grow alongside her, invigorated with experience and age. Emlyn's potential set her on the same path as the most renowned mage in Caeradin.

Master Corrick shook his head. "Even with evidence, such accusations would set Caeradin on the path to war. Vespar would retaliate, with Fydar and Eldra at his flank."

The spectacled mage tapped his fingers together. "And—forgive me, Master Rhys—won't Master Rhys's refuge in Lleogren draw attention? Our allies will think little of it, but the other lords will be suspicious of the timeliness between his arrival and our allegation."

My fingers fumbled under the table. I'd forgotten how much influence I still had over Caeradin, all because I no longer had any real power. Lorhurst, Ethelfled, Priodas, and some others would think I was brewing trouble to send their way. Nothing could ruffle Gildio without her allies pricking up their ears.

"But if Master Vespar plans to use the girl's powers for himself, and to malicious ends, we can't stand by and let him," the young mage blurted.

"And if we are wrong about Master Vespar?" asserted another councilman. "If we have read an inordinate amount into his deeds, what then? We can't withstand him, and who would come to our aid?"

"If we are right and do nothing, what then?"

"It is my experience," the rough, weathered man to my left interrupted for the first time, "that you don't wait till the knife is in your back 'fore you take measures to prevent it." He drummed his fingers on the table, as he'd done in silence the entire discussion. He scanned a hard eye across his colleagues. "Isn't the solution simple, gentlemen?" When no one spoke, he leaned forward, elbow on the table. "If he hasn't got the girl, he hasn't got the power."

The unavoidable murmur arose. I glanced across the table to Athrú. He leaned back in his chair, fingers steepled in quiet contemplation.

Lord Cael raised a hand for silence. "Before we read an inordinate amount into Sir Dair's remark," he said evenly. "What are you suggesting, Dair?"

Dair shrugged. "I don't suggest anything, except if you don't want him to have power, you'd better make him powerless."

"Have you suggestions on how to do so?"

Dair gave a throaty laugh. "How else, my lord?"

"We cannot resort to kidnapping." Master Corrick frowned across the table to his colleague. "That *will* incur Master Vespar's swift hand. We will not stoop so low."

"Nothing we do will make him bless us, either, sir. Either way, his hand will fall. You'll have to decide with how much force."

I looked down to hide my reddening face as the councilmen debated around me. I hadn't considered Emlyn's rescue to be kidnapping, though the repercussions had always been clear. Retrieving her was defending her from her inescapable fate, nothing more or less. But with Emlyn secure under Vespar's protection, legally granted by the Gildian council, any action against her was a crime.

Sir Dair's point was clear. If Vespar thought to use Emlyn's strength for himself, his strike would be swifter and more lethal. Precious Emlyn had no defense against his guile. She would fall into his snare, and Caeradin would be at the mercy of Vespar's redoubled power. If Emlyn's "kidnapping" was Caeradin's only chance…

"Unless you have any other ideas," Dair called over the extended tumult, reclining in his seat. "If the other lords find out about the girl, they'll come to the same answer. Would you rather Lady Eldra or, ash and flame, Calibor get his hands on her? If we don't make this move, the child will die or fall into more unsavory hands. I wager you don't want her blood on your conscience, sirs," he said, eyeing Master Corrick.

A disconcerted hush fell over the chamber. Lord Cael studied me, smoothing a hand over his beard. His glance wavered to Dair, then to Athrú, before plummeting on me again.

"Master Claytherdon?"

My heart thudded. "I will do as you think best, sir, but I agree with Sir Dair."

He nodded, but said, "Do you speak from your head or your heart, Master Rhys?"

I swallowed. "I know the danger is real and near, my lord, and we cannot be idle while Ve—while Master Vespar sets his plans into motion. But in my heart, I fear what he or anyone else will do to her. She's precious to me."

Cael looked me over, smiling. "Why do I get the impression that whether or not the council approves, you would attempt this course of action?"

I showed a half smile. "Because you would be right, sir."

"Indeed." He laughed. "You have admirable tenacity, Master Rhys."

"Vote," Dair said, to which Master Corrick pursed his lips. The younger mage councilman seconded the motion.

Cael raised a hand for silence. "Those who wish to proceed with this course?"

His hand stayed up. Dair brought his fingers off the table. The stiffness of the young mage's arm revealed his conviction. Three more tentative hands, then, pursing his lips, another relented. Cael called for the second vote, but by the way Master Corrick's frown tightened, there was no need. The dragon in my chest grumbled.

"So be it," said Cael. "We will bring the child to safety. Meanwhile, we will ready ourselves in defense for whatever reprisal may come."

The councilmen nodded and muttered their consent.

With that, Lord Cael called for a short dismissal. Athrú left to share the news with Oedolyn and Eoin. The dragon snarled, eager to leave, but Cael beckoned me to stay behind. We stood away from the table, under the light between the murals of Silverblade and Tenbur.

"I will send word to our allies and warn them," he said. "I will do what I can in that respect while you are engaged elsewhere. But I believe you know whom to avoid," he added. "Lorhurst and Rodhin, and stay clear of the northeast."

"Yes, my lord."

A twinkle came to his eye. "You catch one by surprise, Master Rhys. Gildio and Caeradin are both in need of something like you."

"I won't abandon them, sir."

"You have my confidence." He paused. "By the by, you're almost of age, aren't you?"

"Not until the Welding, sir."

"Indeed? How coincidental. It will come faster than you think. All the better it does. You have some wisdom beyond your years, but it is the years, not the wisdom, that soothes the wary." Cael folded his hands, stepped farther from the table. "How has your mother been, lad? We've had no word concerning her yet."

I stumbled for an answer. After this blow, Mam could be in any possible state of despair.

"She's…well, milord. Thank you."

Cael grimaced. "Shall I write her for you? Direct word from you may be unsafe, for the both of you."

Something constricting my chest unraveled. "If you would, sir. I worry for her."

I couldn't think what more to say, but Lord Cael saw it in my face. "Well, we can't forget her place, can we? Whatever Master Vespar attempts must have her consent. Our hopes should be greater, thanks to her."

To my shame, I doubted.

The Lleogrian Lord peered up at the colored portraits around us. "Your father reminded me of many of those men, Master Rhys. And you of one…where is he?" Cael turned a circle and glanced at each warrior, then motioned to one behind us.

A dark-haired man with a bright teal cloak stared across the room. The divided background showed both snowy winter and green summer. The tree behind the warrior bloomed half spring and aged half autumn. His blade struck into what looked to be a sapphire the size of a steppingstone between his feet. He gripped a wooden staff in his right hand. Its gnarled top was cleaved in two, haloed in reverent light. Suspended over his outstretched left hand, tendrils of white vapors formed the crescent moon.

"That is Haylad," said Cael. "He was a few generations after Silverblade. His misadventures started young when he stumbled across a magic staff believed to have belonged to Lord Praed himself. And it proved true."

"But the staff was destroyed," I said, looking at the hewn rod in Haylad's hand.

"It was damaged during his battle with Blodica, but never destroyed." Cael stepped closer to the portrait, dabbled in flecks of colored light. "He spent his life guarding the staff against all forces of Magic, mage and witch and otherwise."

"He was a mage?"

"No, indeed, as Ordinary as you and I. Haylad spent his days on the run. Many sought his life, sought the power of the first Wizard's staff. You can imagine the adventures." Cael motioned to the moon, the flames, the sapphire. "An Ordinary boy swept into the affairs of Magic." He stepped out of the reach of the light, as though he were unworthy to be touched by its colors. "I believe you have a mark to make, Master Rhys, as Haylad did. You have work to do."

Lord Cael frowned. He took the Lleogrian pendant into his hand, peered long at it. "I know Master Vespar little, but he has never struck me as the deceitful sort. But if you say his intentions are not as he and his council claim, I believe you. I can imagine what strides he will take now that Lord Ioan's heir is no longer eligible for the inheritance, and what more he might try from there. I fear Master Athrú is right. If Lord Mage Vespar's true intention was to end the Hunt, I doubt the council would have exiled you."

No. And Flannery would never have been hunted. Those despicable tinkers would never have abducted Emlyn. The Hunt would have ended while Da lived, if Vespar had cared about it in the least. He didn't then, he didn't now. Only Emlyn mattered to him. Had I not been banished, I would still stand between him and the helpless child whose powers he meant to exploit for himself.

Cael pressed the lion pendant to his heart, brows narrowing. "If you mean to take on this task and retrieve the child, I cannot think to send you without an escort. Perhaps Captain Rodd can spare a few of his rangers. Ah, of course, you've heard of them, haven't you?"

I shut my slackened jaw. Lleogren's Ranger Elite, Caeradin's finest marksmen, renowned trackers and woodsmen, said to be so stealthy even Hunters couldn't sniff them out.

"I would be more than grateful, sir."

"Consider it done." Lord Cael laid a hand on my shoulder. "Take heart, Master Rhys. You have friends beside you."

CHAPTER 34

Heldran

As the late afternoon sun lowered in the west, Heldran blew the ink across his parchment dry. He was certain he'd forgotten something on his list for Alric, but his oncoming travel nerves chased them from his mind. Long after he stowed his quill, he sat in the chair and strove to remember.

Heldran drew the ribbon from his pocket. He traced a thumb across its sleek surface. Four months ago to the day, it'd been ripped from Emlyn's hair as the rushing water dragged her under. Heldran pressed it to his lips.

Not caring what was missing from the list, Heldran locked his study door and crossed the foyer to Alric's desk. New boxes of fresh chalk rested atop a pentacle guidebook on the corner, alongside paper parcels of candlesticks and herbs. Alric rose, straightened his spectacles. Heldran handed him the list.

"If you'll have the circle ready for me when I return. I won't be long."

"Yes, sir."

Heldran forgot the ribbon still lay in his hand until Alric respectfully lowered his gaze. He tucked it in his pocket. "I don't know when I'll be back from the Manor, but I'll leave you in charge until you hear otherwise."

"Of course." Alric gathered his supplies and marched to the pentacle room. Heldran fetched his horse and rode out of the city streets.

Stretches of green rolled in low mounds far behind his father's house. Heldran followed the uneven trail to veer from the road and cut across the heather-laden meadow. Along the way, he paused for a handful of wildflowers.

Beyond sight of the house, where the hill curved down into the glen, stones stood upright or lay flat in the vast green. Rows of them, wind beaten and battered with age, fenced in with unfeeling stone walls. Heldran tied his horse to the gate and followed the pathways around the markers. Time had worn many engraved names to illegibility, some overrun with moss and weeds. Fresh flowers and free blossoms adorned a few others.

Heldran slowed at the two large, yet unblemished upright stones. Six smaller markers, almost as untouched, lay in two rows below the large stones, woefully close together. One last space awaited his own turn to rest.

Heldran laid a few flowers on each grave. The bright-faced poppies for his brothers, the sweet, inelegant stalks of heather for his sisters. The pale blue rainveil, with its teardrop petals under its drooping white face, rested between the greater stones of his parents. He knelt at Emlyn's empty grave and propped the bundle of daisies on her headstone. He caressed its petals.

He'd barely known Emlyn, or any of his siblings. One stillborn sister, three claimed by fever in childhood, the twelve-year-old brother just after Heldran taken by an accident. Then Emlyn, not two weeks after her sixth birthday.

Heldran had been trapped at the Academy for most of her life. When he came home for the summer, he had to reintroduce himself until she was finally old enough to remember him. Emlyn was four when he graduated, five when they lost their parents. Heldran did all he could for her, worked night and day to guarantee her security and care. She was all he had.

He pinched his eyes. Couldn't he ever sit here with them and not cry?

Heldran envied them. When he was young, his mother told him of faraway meadows dusted with fragrant flowers and willows to climb, stretching on until the horizon spread into a delicate sea. Sunlight faded to fairy starlight, never a cloud unless someone wished for rain. At first, Heldran imagined such a place would be dull, until Mama explained his stillborn sister lived there, and his little brother would join her soon. They all would, in the end.

They all dwelt in that meadow without him. He wanted one moment with them, one glimpse, and to not feel alone. So crushingly alone.

Father had said everyone takes turns going. Heldran hadn't understood how grim that was until he was older. Mother would wonder aloud who had come to take the children away, leading Heldran to believe one couldn't cross unless someone came to guide them. Had the other children come for Emlyn? Had Mama and Father? Who would come for Heldran, and when?

His horse pawed and snorted. Heldran gripped the ribbon in his pocket.

"I have to go away," he said. "Tylysk wrote me. Do you remember Tylysk? He said Master Vespar has an urgent assignment for me. I don't know how long I'll be, but I'll come visit whenever I can. Yes, Father, someone's looking after the house. Yes, Mama, I'll be careful."

Heldran uncurled his fingers from the ribbon. It brushed the stone of his baby sister's grave. He clutched it again and stuffed it in his pocket.

Alric had the circle ready for him. The seamless, interlacing lines encompassed the five precise runes. Burgundy candles rested atop each, awaiting their flames. A wooden stand with two thin arms cradled a marble bowl of crushed leithl leaves in its holder. Simple measures, but enough to see Heldran didn't get lost in the magical void halfway to the capital of Gildio.

Alric passed him a lighting stick. "Happy journey, sir."

Heldran numbered his steps to the center ring of the circle, touching toe to heel—about two and a half down the middle line. Good, Alric had measured well. He stooped and touched the lighting wand to each candle. Magic stirred with the flames around him, like dust aroused by a heavy footfall. Heldran faced the stand beyond the circle. The leithl leaves smoldered, and a thread of white smoke coiled from the embers. Its bitter scent itched Heldran's nose.

A glance at Alric, who nodded. Heldran placed the doused lighting stick across the arms of the stand. Resetting his feet, loosening his knees and shoulders, he clutched one hand to his silver cloak pin. He extended his other palm above the rune in front of his feet. A deep breath, and Heldran enunciated the enchantment.

An amber glow emitted from the circle. A furious draft rushed upward from the chalk lines around him. The void swallowed him.

Heldran hated this part.

It was a few seconds, but it seemed he spent hours drifting outside his body, watching himself dissolve and reform through the suffocating darkness. If there were such things as ghosts, that must have been how it felt to be one. Airy, weightless, frail. Locked outside himself, unable to breathe, the constant sensation of drowning.

He tried not to think about that.

With a sun-bright flare, a snap ripped through the void. Heldran reformed.

He opened his dizzy eyes, intact, if a bit ruffled, standing firm in another pentacle seventy miles north of the first, in a study identical to the one he'd left.

A secondary mage welcomed him to Gildio. He checked his ledgers. "Master Heldran, yes? Your luggage arrived before you," he said, as if Heldran's one small chest had terribly inconvenienced him. "You're to report to Master Vespar straightaway. Follow me, sir."

Heldran pinched the wicks of the candles alighted by his arrival, dismissing the circle, and followed the other mage.

It had been nearly two years since he last visited the Manor, but nothing had changed since his school days. The upstairs mage quarters, still pristine and sterile as ever, lay quiet but for the low thrum of magic beating the air. Its musty scent of parchments and ink hadn't dulled, either.

They passed the classroom where he and Tylysk had taken private lessons with Master Vespar years ago, he a scrawny, nervous boy of ten. Tylysk had been as pompous and unruffled then as the day he graduated. Heldran never resented Tylysk's speedy ascension through the ranks, as his own had been no slower, but Tylysk's good looks probably got him as far as his wit did. Though his academic intellect matched, or even surpassed Tylysk's, Heldran thought he'd had to slave for his position more than the other.

They reached the familiar door with the brass eagle knocker grasping the handle in its talons. The other mage departed. Heldran straightened his cloak, knocked, and entered.

Master Vespar stood over his desk, running a finger along the scrawl on a parchment and thumbing the stem of his goblet. He'd changed little as well, except a tinge of gray touched his temples, and the lines of his face were wearier. After the recent calamity at the Manor, it hardly surprised Heldran to find his master so tired.

"My lord," Heldran said, bowing.

As he glanced up, Master Vespar smiled and regarded him as he had when Heldran was a schoolboy—kind, proud as a father, and, to Heldran's surprise, with profound relief. He came around the desk to greet him. "Heldran. Look at you, my lad. Not a hair on your head has changed."

Heldran made to speak, but spotted the pendant resting over his master's heart. Vespar noticed Heldran's widening eyes and lifted the jewel into his hand.

"The Lady?" Heldran asked.

Vespar eyed the pendant as though it were leaden. "She has abdicated. We haven't yet spread the news, should she reconsider. The circumstances were quite informal."

His master appeared less than pleased and as doubtful the Lady would change her mind, but Heldran bowed anyway. "My lord," he said.

"Come, Heldran, no need for that. Sit. We have much to discuss."

Vespar brimmed a second goblet with a red wine as Heldran said, "Tylysk mentioned you would need me for an extended stay, sir?"

"Yes, and I thank you for coming so quickly. You can imagine how matters have complicated since Master Rhys's banishment."

"Indeed, sir. I was sorry to hear of it. He always seemed a decent lad, when I knew him."

"You've heard the story, then?" Vespar nodded when Heldran did. "Quite unfortunate. But he made his choice, and we must all bear the consequences." He returned to his desk. "There is a pressing matter I've summoned you to assist me in, Heldran."

Heldran braced himself. He'd debated the reason for his summons since he'd received Tylysk's message. The household's representatives in Babondodd, including Heldran's mage division, were yet unshaken by recent events. However, if and when the news of Lady Orrtha's abdication spread, unrest would follow, with confusion and shifts in duties, counts and earls making way to pay homage to their new liege lord. And who would replace Lord Vespar as Lord Mage?

But the look on his master's face made Heldran reconsider. "Has it something to do with Master Rhys, sir?"

"To an extent." Vespar set down his cup. "Let me begin by offering my deepest condolences. The news of your sister grieved me."

Heldran took the goblet from his lips, biting back a frown. "Thank you, my lord."

"Forgive my seeming insensitivity—how did you learn of the incident?"

"She was playing with her friends. They came to me straightaway."

"Was there proof?"

Heldran stuttered. He remembered those months ago, standing at the water's edge, where the mound of pebbles waited on the bridge for the children to cast them into the river. Where his sullen servants watched him search the rushing foam. The memory of it hung on him as chilled as the rainfall that day.

Heldran drew the ribbon from his pocket and showed his master. "She was wearing this in her hair. It was all our servants could find of her."

"Is that what they told you?"

Heldran was taken aback. "Yes, sir."

"Yet you found no other proof that your sister had been there?"

Heldran stopped his mouth from flapping. Vespar nodded toward the door. Heldran looked. His goblet fell from his hand.

There was Emlyn.

There she was. Breathing. Alive. Emlyn.

His Emmy, wearing a new pink gown, rosy face beaming. The same precious sparkle in her eyes, her curls longer than he remembered, and she a little taller. His beautiful sister, standing with her feet turned in, the way they always did.

Heldran buckled. An eternity passed before Tylysk let go of her hand, and Emlyn bounded into his arms. He held her, clinging to a ghost that might disintegrate in his hold. He cupped her face in his hands. He traced every line of her unblemished features, her brows, her light freckles, the shape of her mouth. His fingertips alone gave him the proof his eyes could not believe.

Emlyn let him, grasping his wrists until she broke the distance between them. He cradled her, kissed her face until a mangled sob tore from him. He buried his face in her hair and wept, not caring that his master and Tylysk were watching.

Too soon, his master disrupted their reunion with a hand on Heldran's shoulder. "Your servants sold her to a tinker, Master Heldran."

His head shot up. He blinked at Tylysk, who grimaced. Vespar spoke more gravely.

"The same tinker Master Rhys confronted."

The words passed through Heldran before striking him with a dagger's force. He propped his sister upright by her shoulders.

"You're a witch?"

Emlyn smothered her face in her lap, arms curled around her head. She scuttled out of reach, though Heldran begged her not to go. Frowning, Tylysk gathered Emlyn away. It stung him—why would she run to Tylysk and cringe under her brother's eye?

"Emmy girl," he said.

She looked. He read her longing to run to him, but her teary glances at the other mages locked her to Tylysk's side. The weight of the hand on Heldran's shoulder became a claw.

He wheeled around on his knees and clutched the hem of the Lord Mage's cloak. "Please, master, she's a child. I beg you—"

"No harm has come to her yet, Heldran, and so long as I see to it, none ever will."

The bewilderment closed off Heldran's throat. He sat on his heels.

Vespar offered a hand to raise him up, but Heldran stared at the floor. Vespar bolstered him with a squeeze to his shoulder as he crossed the room. Emlyn cowered, but he laid a gentle hand on her head.

"Tylysk and I have taken the liberty to investigate her powers," he said. "Emlyn is profoundly gifted, and despite her age, I have never encountered strength akin to hers. Her powers exceed that of anyone's in this room."

Heldran's eyes locked to Emlyn's, she more confounded than he, and so small. He almost laughed. She could not, in a thousand years, compare to Lord Mage Vespar. No one could. Certainly not a child who shouldn't possess magic at all. How could she have room for so much power in her tiny, innocent being?

The realization clutched Heldran's chest.

"The Enchantress?"

Vespar beamed down on the girl. Emlyn looked as if she wanted to melt between the mortar seams in the floor.

"Impossible. She can't be."

"Magic chooses whomever It wills," said Vespar. He slid a finger down Emlyn's cheek the way he would the feathers of a hunting falcon. "As one Enchantress falls, another must take her place. Magic has Its own will and mind, and we cannot determine who will replace what It has lost."

His master spoke less than he concealed; Heldran heard it in his voice. By the looks of it, Tylysk knew Vespar's mind. Fury burned in Heldran's chest, a redoubled need to snatch his sister away.

But he hobbled to his feet. How could he question them when they had spared Emlyn's life?

"You are reassigned to the Manor, Master Heldran." Vespar caught his mage's desperate gaze. "More pressing tasks demand your talents here."

Emlyn squeaked something at Tylysk. He crouched and whispered in her ear.

Vespar put his back to them, drew nearer so the others couldn't hear. "There is no question of how precious she is to you," he said.

Tears stung Heldran's eyes. "More than anything, sir."

"Yet your servants peddled her to a tinker."

Heldran's chin hit his chest.

"The task I have for you will amend that. There are few greater deeds you could do for your sister." Vespar grasped Heldran's shoulder. "Find her Wizard."

CHAPTER 35

Heldran

Heldran felt his bones had crumbled. Find the Wizard? Impossible. His master had dabbled in the search himself years ago and knew how meager his chances were. The Wizard would go undetected as long as he liked. How could Heldran, a study-bound mage as powerless as an Ordinary where the Wizard was concerned, hope for the smallest hint of his whereabouts?

Heldran stared at his trembling sister. Emlyn needed her Wizard. They had a shared duty together, Wizard and Enchantress. Aid each other, protect each other. Little Emlyn couldn't find him herself.

Heldran couldn't refuse, not after abandoning her for months, believing she was dead, leaving her to a tinker to be retrieved by Master Rhys himself. Heldran's gullibility had led to the Claytherdon Household's downfall. He'd left Emlyn in the hands of the mages whose duty was to exterminate her kind.

Heldran would do anything for her. He wouldn't lose her again.

Vespar patted an encouraging hand over Heldran's heart, then beckoned Emlyn and Tylysk with an outstretched hand. Heldran lifted Emlyn up when she came.

"What will happen now?" she whispered. Heldran hushed her with a kiss to her temple.

Vespar regarded her for a long while. Heldran knew his master's mind set to calculating a thousand decisions and consequences in the length of a breath. His hand crept to the pendant around his neck.

"I have thoroughly considered the circumstances at hand. We have subdued the council's apprehensions, but there is still the matter of the law." Vespar met Heldran's eye. "The council has made a generous exception in Emlyn's case, but with the understanding that she would remain in my custody."

Heldran swallowed.

"I have no doubts in your capacities as her guardian, Master Heldran, but we must appease the council's doubts. Where the law is concerned, there is no other who can ensure her immunity. For the time being, Emlyn must be placed under my guardianship."

Heldran squeezed Emlyn tighter. Give her up? His parents had left her to him. Not even Lord Vespar had the right to take that from him.

The council wouldn't care. Heldran had no power to save his witch sister from what would have befallen her if his master hadn't interceded. Lord Vespar had saved her. Heldran owed him his life.

Why did he doubt? As long as Emlyn lived, what did it matter how they made it so?

Heldran licked his lips. "For how long, sir?"

"As long as it takes to convince the council of her innocence."

"Heldran, I want to be with you," Emlyn pleaded. "I don't want to stay here. *Please.*"

Heldran glanced at Tylysk. For once in his life, the other mage looked sorry for him. Even so, he urged Heldran to speak with a nod in their master's direction.

Heldran dried his sister's tears and said, "I understand, sir."

Vespar hesitated to be sure, then nodded. He looked to Tylysk. "If you will send for Theresa, have her prepare a room for them."

When Tylysk left, Vespar motioned for Heldran to take the seat in front of his desk. Heldran held Emlyn on his lap. His master took his place across from them, smiling on Emlyn.

"You have nothing to fear, little one. No one can hurt you now."

Emlyn stayed silent.

"You and Heldran will stay at the Manor. You'll be living like a princess."

Heldran tried not to frown at his wordplay. The Enchantress, Magic's Princess. Nothing else mattered to Vespar and Tylysk but Emlyn's place as magical "royalty". Why? Lord Mage Vespar couldn't possibly have lagged too far behind Emlyn in strength. Why did he need her? Why did he need both of Magic's Authorities?

Emlyn nestled against her brother's chest.

"I'll teach you of your magic," Vespar said.

She fingered the lines of Heldran's palm, eyes low.

"There's much for you to learn before you can fulfill your role as Enchantress."

"Why?" she said.

Vespar rotated his ring, fell quiet for a time.

"So I can be a good witch?"

The glint in Vespar's eyes faded. "So you can be the greatest witch of your generation."

Even if Heldran had the nerve to beg for more answers, it was too late. Tylysk returned, objecting as the doe-eyed girl Heldran recognized as Mistress Isabelle marched through the door. She was prettier than he remembered, and grown more, but she remained disdainfully under Tylysk's romantic attentions, as always. Heldran rose and bowed to her.

Isabelle dipped a brief curtsy. "My lord, Theresa is preoccupied in the kitchen. If I may, I will take Emlyn. I wish to do my part while she and Master Heldran are here."

Vespar spotted Emlyn's sudden earnestness. At his motion, Heldran set her on her feet. She tiptoed around to the Lord Mage. Heldran strained to hear what Vespar whispered to her, searched for an interpretation in Emlyn's eyes. When Vespar looked to her for an answer, Emlyn nodded.

Heldran caught her hand as she moved past him.

"I'll be there soon, Emmy. I'm here now. Don't be afraid."

She nodded. Tylysk patted her head. Isabelle grasped Emlyn's hand and broke into gentle conversation with her on the way out the door.

Tylysk took the seat beside Heldran. For the first time, Heldran noticed the fresh scar snaking down his face. Tylysk caught his questioning stare and smoothed a thumb over the gash.

Vespar lifted his goblet. "Any reports, Master Tylysk?"

The Mage Masters exchanged a glance, and Tylysk broke the silence with a smirk. "Rhys hasn't moved yet, sir, but he met with Lord Cael and his council yesterday."

"Master Rhys is in Lleogren?" Heldran asked.

Vespar spun his ring. "Tylysk was able to dowse for him, and he found Rhys taking refuge in Windborough."

"Lord Cael knows about Emlyn," Tylysk said, eyes darkening. "His council believes we have some 'plan.'"

"They believe we might strike," Vespar said.

Tylysk nodded. "Rhys told them what little he knows of Emlyn and spooked them into thinking a war is coming. It won't be long before Lord Cael spreads the word."

Vespar regarded his ring. "And Rhys?"

"No less than expected, except Lord Cael means to aid his endeavors."

"We have time. He will be stopped."

"Or face the gallows when he arrives," said Tylysk, a persuasiveness beneath his gravity.

Heldran's breath shortened. "He's coming back? He's breaking his exile?"

"He claims to have cared a great deal for your sister," answered Vespar.

Heldran's throat closed off.

"He will be stopped, and we will deal with Lord Cael. This won't set us off our plans." Vespar thumbed the Gildian pendant with his right hand. The silver and gold clashed, and Heldran thought he held more power in those trinkets together than Emlyn could ever have.

"We have eight weeks to prepare Emlyn for the council's summons."
Vespar eyed his men. "We begin tomorrow. You're dismissed, gentlemen."

Tylysk moved to the door, but Heldran hesitated. He stammered, and
all that came was a pathetic, unsatisfactory, "Thank you, my lord."

Vespar smiled. Heldran followed the other mage into the corridor.

As soon as the door closed, Tylysk punched Heldran hard in the arm.
"Gah! What was that for?"

Tylysk grinned. "Were you really too busy for a visit? All the lads
agree, it's not the same without you."

There was the Tylysk he remembered from their school days. Heldran
couldn't bring himself to be glad to see him.

Tylysk watched him as they strode down the hall, waiting for him
to crack. "What are you so glum about? Your sister's alive. She's the
Enchantress, skin and bones, and has the protection of the most influential man in Caeradin. Everything's lined up for you both."

Heldran flashed him a sour glance. "I'd be happier if you'd tell us why.
You know everything, don't you? And speak of, what were you doing
with Emlyn?"

Tylysk's smirk slipped. "I've been assigned to look after her while
you're both busy," he said, gripping the hilt of his dagger. "Don't misun-
derstand; Emlyn's a sweet girl, but for both your sakes, I'd rather have
your miserable job."

Heldran was stricken. "Take it. Why aren't you looking for the Wizard?"

"The council would be suspicious if you were left to tend to her. Your
relationship would compromise the 'experiment.'" He marked the word
with a bend of his fingers.

"What 'experiment?'"

"If Emlyn, as the Enchantress, can prove her innocence, perhaps the
innocence of other witches can be proven too."

Heldran tripped over his own tongue. That was it? That was all they
needed Emlyn for? By all means, if she could save potentially guiltless
lives, Heldran was glad to help.

But why the Wizard?

"That's all this is?" Heldran searched Tylysk's scarred profile as they moved down the stairs. "There's more. That's all the council knows about, this 'experiment.' What's the real plan? I have a right to know, if it involves my sister."

"It isn't my place to say anything. Master Vespar will tell you when it's time. You and Emlyn will have to earn it."

"Like you earned your way to being his lackey, and now he lets you in on everything?"

"That's a bold word—*lackey*. Are you jealous?"

"Not at all. You just tend to forget you weren't the only one our master thought well of."

"Then it's a wonder he sent you away."

"And a wonder he kept you."

Tylysk's heated glance turned his scar blood red. Heldran withstood for a moment, but looked away first. He rubbed his eyes.

"I just got her back, and you're trying to steal her from me."

"That isn't his intent. You have to trust him."

Heldran didn't press further. It infuriated him anyway, being less than helpful and robbing him of what should have been his own duty. And he didn't care for Tylysk's reluctance to do it. Heldran ran his hands through his hair, head pounding.

As they passed the giant doors of the library, Heldran caught sight of his rippling scar again. "What happened, Tylysk?"

He ran his fingers along the crimson thread. "I witnessed the initial release of a draconis."

"*What*? What draconis?"

"Master Rhys."

Heldran startled to a halt. "My sister got hidden away by a *draconis*?"

"Almost." Tylysk cinched up his sleeves to show off the rest of his scars, healed to a lattice of white threads. "The beast released itself when we found him and Emlyn."

"Was she hurt?"

"Of course not. As far as we know, Rhys never did anything to her."

Heldran breathed again, relieved, though he hadn't expected Rhys to have hurt her. Except, now…

They strode the rest of the way in silence. Tylysk turned left at the second corridor and opened a door on the right. Heldran left him in the antechamber and rushed to the next room.

Emlyn sat on one of the two beds, eyes closed and lulled to sleep. Isabelle ran a brush through Emlyn's hair and cooed to her. She beckoned Heldran in, glowered when Tylysk came to the door. Rescuing them, Isabelle dragged Tylysk out with a brutal yank on his sleeve.

Emlyn took no notice of Tylysk and Isabelle's scuffle. Heldran moved to the bed across from hers. He wanted to gather her up, reassure himself that this wasn't an illusion flipping between dream and nightmare. She looked peaceful despite the pinch of her brows.

She tottered. Heldran dove to catch her, but Emlyn woke herself. She moaned and scrubbed her eyes before she saw Heldran kneeling beside her.

"It's all right, Emmy," he said, caressing her face. "Don't cry."

She wound her arms around his neck, nestled her cheek on the rough folds of his cloak. Heldran sat against the headboard and cradled her close. He expected to break the surface of consciousness at any moment, for his sister to have been nothing but a memory.

Heldran reached into his pocket. "I have something for you."

Emlyn fingered the silk ribbon across his palm. "Rufus ripped it out when he pulled my hair."

"How did they know?"

She hugged her knees, hid her face as she confessed to sneaking into his rooms to read his spellbooks. Her cat followed her, and his incessant yowling drew the servants' attention.

His master's words haunted Heldran again. Tinkers, servants, evidence. What an expertly devised sham. Heldran had fallen for a pair of despicable children's feigned tears. Rufus and Hilda, who'd served his father's household longer than Heldran could remember, grieved alongside everyone else, when all those months, they'd fondled a few extra gold pieces behind their backs.

Heldran struggled to imagine Emlyn reading his collection of tomes. At first, he suspected she'd skimmed through the pages and enjoyed the colored illustrations of spells and pentacles at work. No, she strove to understand them. She told him of the potion she crafted and how it had all the right *properties*—she stumbled through the word—just as the book described.

Heldran believed her. The tale of Master Rhys's banishment hardly lacked for rumors, one being that the witch said to have cursed him used one potion or another. Harmless as her intentions were, Emlyn confirmed them.

He was sore and stupid. Duped from every side. Even Emlyn had fooled him. Was he really so blind?

Heldran raised Emlyn's chin. "Why didn't you tell me?"

She went red up to her ears. "I—I was scared."

"Did you think I'd give you up? That I wouldn't love you anymore?"

Emlyn couldn't look at him.

Heldran stroked her hair. "I would have helped you. I would've done everything I could. You're my Emmy. How could I give you up?"

Her voice was so small. "I didn't want you to get in trouble, either."

Her softness broke through Heldran's rage and befuddlement. For the first time in months, he no longer felt so alone.

Heldran cradled her as she drifted, her head heavy on his chest, her ear pressed to his heart. Refusing to let her go, he rocked her until his own exhaustion claimed him.

CHAPTER 36

Rhys

I sprawled in the dirt, flat on my back outside our training circle behind the house. My stick flew somewhere out of my hands. My ribs had to be an ugly purple.

Athrú stood over me. "I thought you said you trained with Swordsmaster Perreth."

"I thought I had."

He pulled me up. "Both hands on the hilt. Don't let this one slip." He jostled my arm.

I caught my breath and slumped for my "sword." My attempts to parry Athrú's strikes most often landed me on the ground with a mouthful of dirt and a fresh bruise. He reminded me that whoever might have gone easy on me in training at home would not do the same when I returned.

We crossed swords in the center of the dirt circle. Athrú almost gave me another lesson on not meeting the foe's eye before a duel, but I matched his gaze in time to avoid a thump on the shoulder. He counted from three.

He slid his stick down toward my shoulder. I twisted my hilt up to block at an angle. He scraped down my blade and swung for my legs.

I hacked the opposite way and whacked his rod upward to smack into my shoulder. I flinched backward as the end of his stick skidded across my chest. A step back, but Athrú stabbed.

He batted his weapon between my boots. "Your feet that time."

I glared at them. Captain Perreth always complained they'd been carved from lead.

"And this one." Athrú put his sword to my knee, raised it in the direction I parried. "I could've gone for your neck, and the enemy would."

I nodded and clutched my aching side. Sweat dribbled into my eyes. The sun worsened it, blinding me and searing with a drier heat than I was used to. But the training circle was the same as Captain Perreth's, and the surrounding spread of forest resembled a gentler perimeter of castle walls. Chamberlain bounded off, and for a moment, I searched for Aria chasing him.

"Slower." Athrú beckoned me to the circle. "Concentrate on footing."

He attacked, one sluggish hack at a time, correcting my position when he didn't think a friendly swat was necessary. Athrú's lessons baffled me—the Swordsmaster taught with patterns and order, every lesson the same as the last. Athrú's tactics exposed nothing discernibly methodical, yet he won every duel.

Satisfied with the progress my leaden feet were making, Athrú let me attack. At least I went more than three swings without taking a spill. Athrú blocked whatever I tried.

The dragon stirred. I lurched away and dropped the stick for the…I'd lost count how many times. The beast was bored. He knew how to batter Athrú down without this nonsense. Athrú never took more than a cautious step away.

Once the dragon slinked to his cavern, I kept attacking. Athrú made an untraceable move to throw me down and somersault me backward.

"You didn't block," he said, laughing. He hauled me up.

"There's no point in looking pretty about it," the gruff voice said.

Athrú and I looked toward the house. Judging by his garb, I guessed the stranger waiting at the door was the ranger Lord Cael had promised to send—dark cloak, rugged leathers, and a dark scarf about his neck, ready to cover his scruffy face. His silvered hair fell to his shoulders, and white scars marked his weathered features. A broadsword and dagger hung from his hip, a longbow strapped over his shoulder, and he wielded a walking staff as tall as he. He trundled over to us.

"Sir Dair," I said.

The councilman grunted. "Looking pretty doesn't keep you alive. You do what you must to save yourself."

I glanced at Athrú. "What about cheating?"

"Is it cheating to keep yourself alive?"

"Then what about honor?"

The old ranger muttered something like a laugh. "There's nothing very honorable about killing a man."

Dair traded his staff for my stick and went to the circle. Athrú followed, flashing a helpless glance at me.

A few thwacks, each pressing the other. The ranger stepped so Athrú's dodge got him the ranger's shoulder in the chest. Athrú stumbled. Dair snagged his foot behind Athrú's ankle. He tumbled, and the ranger struck the stick from his weakened grip. As Athrú made to rise, Dair pressed him to lie flat on the ground with the stick to his chest.

Dair tossed the stick aside. He sent me a significant look before he helped Athrú to his feet. Athrú put a hand to the ache in his chest.

"I'm to escort you to Waymere," Dair said. "Captain Rodd is there with his rangers."

Athrú, Oedolyn, and I followed him down the southern route to Windborough's scattered villages. Three miles to Waymere, most of it through meadows and farmlands, and we came to the hamlet before midday. The few straggling earth roads of thatch-roofed cottages and cattle were encompassed by grain and barley fields to the south and a vast orchard to the north. Women gathered the low fruits while children clambered up for the highest pears and plums.

At the edge of the orchard, a dozen children crowded under an ash tree, peering up at another dark-cloaked ranger perched on the lowest branch. His whisper lured the children nearer, each captivated with mouth agape. Dair rolled his eyes and led us on.

"I ducked under the rubble," the younger ranger said. The children startled. "I could hear the beast smashing through the rock with his bare fists, throwing around boulders as big as houses, searching through the ruins for me. I kept quiet, not a breath.

"He stomped!" The ranger leaped from the tree and slammed to the ground on his feet. The children jumped, squealing. "Almost smashed me flat, his huge, hairy, warty feet this close to my face." He held his palm a finger's width from his nose. "He could smell me right there, right where he couldn't see me. He waited, listened.

"He swept the rubble away. I ran, but he stayed after me, roaring and howling and crushing everything in his path." The ranger pounced. The children shrieked and laughed, scattered as he chased them as a stalking troll.

"He nabbed me!" He scooped a boy over his shoulder, tickled him until his face went scarlet. "And next I knew, he had me in his fist, dangling from his putrid fingers." The ranger scuttled up the tree to hang upside down from the limb. The children gathered. "He lifted me up, right over his mouth, all yellow teeth and horrid breath, and—"

"I don't remember it that way," Dair called.

The other ranger spotted us and grinned. "And who should save the day but Sir Dair! See that walking stick, children? That is the same walking stick that took the beast down. Bashed its head clean in. You can still see the marks on the stick. See?"

The children ventured nearer. Dair shooed them away to sprint into the orchard. The ranger in the tree watched them go, pouting.

"That wasn't nice. They were just curious."

"And still reining you in like a tender nursemaid," Dair returned.

The ranger shrugged, grinning. "Braidac," he said. He stuck his hand out upside down, flipped it around for me to shake, then let his arms hang. "You're Master Rhys?"

"Just Rhys is fine."

"Oh, good. I don't like formalities. You can call me Brai, if you like."

Dair whacked him in the back with his staff. "Down, pup. You've had your fun."

Brai grasped the branch and flipped backward to land on his feet, cloak over his head. He swept it back with a gallant flourish. Spotting Oedolyn, he glanced over my shoulder to wag his fingers at her. She rolled her eyes, either at his acrobatics or his short golden-brown hair in a ridiculous disarray he didn't bother to fix.

Dair frowned at him while Braidac resettled his bow over his shoulder. "Did you make it to the village 'fore they caught you?"

"Yes," Brai said defensively. "Just waiting for you. Rodd and the lads are at the tavern." He bumped me with his elbow. "Come on."

Still the largest structure in the village, the tavern compared to a sizeable barn. Men from the field gathered for their midday meal, lounging around rickety tables, chattering while a red-lipped barmaid passed out drinks and bread and cheese. The scent of cinnamon cider surrendered to the smell of dirt and toil overwhelming the common room.

"Bit snug," Brai said, squeezing out of the barmaid's way. "That's why Rodd likes it. There's never an eye or ear he can't see."

He motioned to the corner near a window, where three more rangers waited. Another robed figure sat among them. Dair tromped over at the sight of him.

"You have business with the captain too, Master Corrick?" he grunted, tight lipped. "Or don't I represent the council well enough?"

The Lleogrian Lord Mage regarded his colleague in kind. "Well indeed, Sir Dair. If other pressing matters did not call Lord Cael elsewhere, he would be seated here instead."

Dair grumbled something untoward under his breath. He dropped into the chair across from Master Corrick, nodded to the ranger seated in the middle. "Cap'n. Master Rhys."

Captain Rodd stood and extended a broad hand to shake mine. His dark eyes made his brown hair and beard seem lighter than they were. I'd expected someone more akin to Dair, but the not-yet-middle-aged captain showed no signs of age. A small scar nicked his right jaw, and his slender nose was slightly crooked. His grip betrayed the strength of his wiry frame.

"I've heard much about you, Master Rhys," he said. "You bear your fate with admirable fortitude."

"Thank you, sir," I replied as awkwardly as a child praised by Tenbur himself.

The captain greeted Athrú likewise. He placed a polite kiss on Oedolyn's fingers, and a smiling rosiness bloomed up to her ears. Braidac saluted him, grinning.

Rodd waited until I sat across from him before taking his place again. "We're told you need an escort across the border, Master Rhys."

Before I could open my mouth, Dair and Corrick spoke at once. Rodd looked between them until Dair took the upper hand in relaying the council's decision to retrieve Emlyn. The captain disregarded Corrick's disapproving grimace.

Dair reached into his cloak pocket and produced a scroll in the same moment Corrick did. The ranger scowled, but relented. The mage passed the message to Rodd.

"You'll find a more detailed proposal here," he said, failing to keep a triumphant glance from Dair.

Rodd skimmed the page as though it bore nothing more burdensome than a prediction of next week's weather. He traced the lines of his jaw with a thumb and finger. "You'll take the task despite the risks?" he asked me, no judgment in his tone or expression.

"It is my task to take, sir. I won't ask another to go in my stead."

Rodd nodded. "Again, admirable, but the risks are many. I cannot protect you from your exile should we be overtaken."

Braidac snorted. "As if we would be."

The captain tilted his head and smiled at the silent ranger to his left. "The chances are slim, but never enough to discard."

"It is foolhardy, Captain," Corrick said. He scanned the noisy common room, lowered his voice so the clamor deterred any eavesdropping. "We cannot think to abduct this child on mere suspicion. Master Rhys would forfeit his life on a meager conjecture."

"The vote is cast, and it is what it is." Dair drummed his fingers on the table. "The boy will go it alone if he must, and he will be overtaken if he does."

"But *abduction*, Sir Dair…" Master Corrick's fingers fumbled over the gold trinket hanging around his neck—his magic trinket, I guessed. "Shall we be no better than the brutish mercenaries who raid our countryside, or as unfeeling as the Hunters? We accuse Master Vespar of such deceit when our endeavor is no more honorable."

"You could go knock on Vespar's door and ask, if that soothes your sensibilities."

Corrick's brow wrinkled, but he licked his lips. "It is reckless and callous of us to consider. Besides, surely Master Vespar anticipates this and means to draw the boy back. Master Rhys would face the conviction of both his exile and kidnap—"

"It is *not* kidnapping," I blurted, slamming my hand down on the table between the dueling councilmen. "This is a rescue. Emlyn is the balance between Master Vespar's power and our downfall. If we save her, we save your people and mine alike."

Rodd smiled. "If my sensibilities needed soothing, they would be soothed, Master Rhys." He rolled the scroll and laid it on the table. "Whichever way we were to be persuaded, we have our orders."

Dair tossed an arm over the back of his chair and all but smirked across the table. Master Corrick traced a fingernail down the embossed pattern on his trinket and bit his tongue.

The discussion lulled long enough to let the barmaid lay out a platter of cheese and bread and a pitcher of cider. When no one else moved, Brai pounced for a share, which he divvied up between himself and Oedolyn.

Rodd folded his bow-roughed hands over the parchment. "If I may ask, where will you take…Emlyn, did you say? I fear Master Vespar will track us here to reclaim her. Should we expect to escort you further on?"

My heart pounded faster. "I'll take her as far from Gildio as I can. But I can't ask your help farther than our return here. Lord Cael will need you when Master Vespar retaliates."

"Lord Cael would not see you abandoned, and neither would I," Rodd said. "We'll know better when the time comes, but I won't deny you one or two of my men to see you to safety elsewhere.

"Corandul, maybe," Dair muttered. "Lord Landorin—"

"Yes, Lord Landorin would grant you refuge," said Master Corrick. "He will best know what further steps should be taken."

"And it'll be right lovely come winter," said Braidac, slicing the rising tension. He clapped a hand to my shoulder. "If you need a guide that way, take me with you. I miss the sea."

"I wouldn't count on it." Dair eyed Master Corrick as he spoke, but said, "Sir Braidac navigates as well as a blind pup."

"I don't, either," Brai retorted, "but I could smell my way to Corandul if I had to."

"Lucky for us, you won't have to smell our way to the border." The old ranger watched the barmaid bustle past and returned to staring the Lord Mage down. "If you've nothing further to discuss with the captain, you should leave us to plan our abduction."

Master Corrick quelled his irritation with a deep breath. His fingers went on tinkering with his trinket. "If it's all the same to you, Sir Dair, I believe Lord Cael would appreciate a briefing on your plans, which I shall relate to him upon my return."

Dair glowered. The mage went on fumbling with his gold. Athrú and I exchanged side glances. Rodd noticed and looked between the warring men, lingering a second longer on Corrick. He raised a single finger from the table. Behind me, Braidac shifted his weight enough to face the mage head on, his mouth swollen with cheese.

"Of course," the captain said. He ignored Dair's hardening expression, looked to me, and said, "Is a departure one week from now suitable, Master Rhys? My men will need time to prepare."

"I—yes, of course, sir."

"Very well. We'll plan on that." Rodd stood, stole a square of cheese from the plate, and moved from the table. "Thank you, gentlemen. Milady," he said, nodding to Oedolyn.

Master Corrick's fingers froze. "Is…is that all, Captain? Haven't you more to discuss? How will you cross the border? How will you get into the city? How will you go unseen?"

Rodd dusted the cheese crumbs from his fingertips. "Crossing the border is the easy part, sir, but my men and I can't devise further strategy until we see the city ourselves."

The mage gawked. Dair leaned back, at last flaunting his triumph. Corrick covered his humiliation with a laugh. "Surely the lad can assist you with the details."

"I have no doubt, milord, but with so much at stake, I must depend on my own eyes for those particulars."

"You don't mean to charge in so blindly?"

"Only to the border, sir. I'm certain we can find our way."

The two silent rangers followed Rodd to the door. Braidac saluted me, waggled his fingers at Oedolyn, and took off after them.

Dair heaved himself from his chair with his walking stick. "Don't let us keep you, Master Corrick. I'm sure Lord Cael is expecting you."

The mage set his jaw and rose. Saying nothing, he marched to the door, stopping the barmaid in her tracks with his determined passing.

Athrú and I beat each other with sticks every morning, taking advantage of the cool dawn before the heat swept in. He retraced the training circle behind the house each time, restated that if either of us set foot outside the ring, we were considered dead.

We trained for hours, hunched against bruises and tender muscles. Athrú broke my stick once and had to hunt around the woods for something suitable he could whittle smooth. When we finished, Oedolyn locked the back door on us until we scrubbed down at the well.

Chamberlain kept silent vigil nearby. The more I focused on the duel, the less I sensed the dragon's approach. Whenever Chamberlain so much as whimpered, Athrú and I swerved away from each other. The dragon paced and grumbled and watched.

The weather shifted. Dusty winds buffeted us. Athrú withstood the gusts, though the breeze kicked dirt into our eyes. Every time I raised my stick to parry Athrú's blows, I sneezed.

The windswept clouds broke all night and well into the next morning, reducing our circle to a mud pit. Again, Athrú endured the terrain. I slipped in the muck, rain plastered my hair over my eyes, dripped cold under my tunic.

After another useless plunge in the mud, Athrú called for a rest. I threw my stick in the dirt and plopped in the grass. He dropped beside me. Rain pummeled us. Distant thunder rumbled long after lightning cracked the faraway sky.

Athrú swept his damp black hair from his brow. If he said something, I heard nothing. He looked over and spoke again. His voice made no sound.

Chamberlain's howl jolted us. He pinned his ears down, back arched, teeth bared, wild eyes on me.

You are supposed to be improving, not reverting to the weakling you were.

I jumped at the dragon's voice. His same harsh, abysmal tone reverberated through my head. He spoke my language, but the words echoed in his gnarled tongue.

All I could think to say was, "Sorry?"

When will you accept what you have proven? You are nothing without me.

"I know what you want, and you're not getting it," I answered, eyes on Athrú.

His brows narrowed understandingly. Chamberlain yowled. Oedolyn stepped out the door to quiet him, but heeded Athrú's warning to keep her distance.

We are two parts of a whole, the dragon rumbled. *One can do nothing without the other. You are a feeble, useless whelp without me. You will not save that child if you do not release me. The enemy is too great.*

I let out a laugh. "Oh, you're tempting, but—"

You will not reach the walls of the city without my aid. Had you released me before, we could have retaken the child and avoided your banishment altogether.

"And left everything to burn and my people to die."

You cannot say that for certain, nor can you say I would make such an attempt in the future. Release me—you will find your proper strength.

I collapsed with a thrust to my chest. My feet and hands shook, my skin bristled. The dragon blocked my mental image of restraining him and showed flashes of his huge face, as rapid and indeterminable as lightning. I ground my teeth, dug my fingers into the grass. Rainwater choked me. Athrú stayed near.

If you would not resist, it would not hurt so.

"You're not coming out!"

My fingers tensed to claws, piercing into the dirt. Dark, gleaming blue stained my skin. It prickled and rose as the dim outlines of scales lanced through. I panicked.

"Call him back, Rhys," Athrú commanded. "Withdraw."

He is a fool, the beast hissed. *How can he know the ways of a draconis? What can he know of a dragon's mind?*

My mental image swirled out of control—the chains constricted to suffocate me, and the dragon whipped me through the air, slammed me into the crags of the cavern walls.

"Rhys, listen to me."

Her voice startled me, how it sounded like Isabelle's. I opened my eyes to find Oedolyn, drenched and mud splattered, kneeling at my side. She ignored her brother's warnings and drew closer.

The dragon snapped its jaws at her, forcing my head off the ground. He surged stronger. Oedolyn gripped my rigid fingers and stroked my hand. The beast flinched away from her touch.

"Easy," she cooed. "Easy."

"Oedolyn," Athrú said.

The dragon lunged in his direction. I jerked onto my side. Chamberlain snarled.

Oedolyn resisted her brother's efforts to shield her. "No, Rhys, listen to me," she whispered. "We're here. You're not alone." Her palm smoothed along my tingling arm. "Start here. Put these away."

Letting her voice uphold me, I focused on my limbs, forced the scales to recede. The sensation of withdrawal broke through my fingertips and ripped up my arms. I cried out. The pain warped Oedolyn's words.

It is inevitable.

I shifted my focus to keeping my feet from splitting through my boots. My eyes were gritty with soot. My mouth tasted like I'd licked a fireplace clean.

I will have you. It cannot be undone.

"Easy, easy."

The pain moved between my shoulder blades—daggers drawn out of my flesh and into my spine. The strain pressed a howl from my scalded throat.

Resist as you will, but I have already won.

I collapsed.

Chamberlain fell silent. He wandered by the house and whined.

Oedolyn kept hold of my trembling hand. Her smile warmed the cloudy glade. She swept my dripping hair from my eyes. "You did it. It's gone. Just rest."

Athrú whispered to her. She hurried to the house. Turning me off my back, Athrú tore open my tunic and examined my dripping wounds. The chilled rain soothed my blazing skin.

I whisked in and out of consciousness with the rhythm of Oedolyn's soft hands bandaging my back. She tucked a blanket around me, though the deluge found its way through. Chamberlain approached, shaggy and sopping. Lucidity escaped my grasp as his cold nose snuffled my face.

CHAPTER 37

Emlyn

"There." Isabelle straightened the necklace she let Emlyn borrow. "Ready."

Emlyn never had so many dresses to pick from, all different colors and designs kept in a big wardrobe. She chose the sapphire one with the jewel on the waist. While the soft folds hung wide and long, it was too heavy to twirl in. The gold trimming itched her neck, but she said nothing about it. She'd rather have worn her pink dress, but Isabelle sent it for washing.

Aria dressed Emlyn's hair with twists and curls. Emlyn handed her the ribbon Heldran had given her, and she threaded it through a pin and tied a pretty bow.

"You're beautiful," she said, sounding breathless. "You're a princess."

Emlyn didn't feel like one. "I don't want to go."

Isabelle fiddled with the jewel at Emlyn's waist. "You at least have to show Heldran how gorgeous you are." She grasped Emlyn's hands, her mouth scrunched to the side into a rosebud. "It won't be as bad as you think. Master Vespar is an excellent teacher, and Tylysk will be right there too. But that's not much of a comfort, is it?"

A knock at the door made Aria jump, but she answered it. She ducked under Tylysk's arm and bolted. He didn't bother to watch her go, just beamed at Emlyn from the doorway.

"She's lovely, isn't she, Tylysk?" Isabelle said sharply.

"Indeed." He squatted down to face Emlyn. "Ready? Ah ah ah, you promised." He raised a finger an inch from her nose. "No sad faces, you promised."

Isabelle waved Tylysk aside. "She's nervous, that's all. Slippers, Emlyn."

Tylysk held Emlyn's hand while she stepped into the shoes. She tried stretching her cramped toes, but the stiff slippers squeezed more. Tylysk gripped her hand tighter and pulled her through the door. Isabelle stayed a step behind.

Midday sunshine brightened the long hallway, made the green banners and tapestries gray with the glare. Emlyn wanted to run in the gardens, no matter how hot it looked outside. The heat wouldn't have bothered her after being trapped in this stuffy old castle, always pinned to Tylysk's side.

But he promised, too. If she was good, he'd take her horseback riding. He'd let her go play. And she had to work hard for Heldran too.

"What do you think of all this, Emlyn?" Tylysk swept a broad gesture with his arm. "Living at the Manor, lessons from Caeradin's greatest mage. You have it all, don't you?"

She looked away. None of it mattered. It wasn't home. Rhys was gone. No one bothered to explain anything or ask what would make her happy.

Emlyn sank. No one cared.

With a glance at Isabelle, Tylysk swung Emlyn onto his side to carry her. She turned her face away. His red scar glared at her a breath away.

"Tell me something you'd like, sleepyhead." Tylysk ducked his head to meet her eye. "You've been very good, and you deserve a reward."

Emlyn searched his face. Tylysk had at least stopped being mean to her, as he promised, but she could tell he was working hard to be nice. He'd stopped shoving her around, stopped saying horrible things about Rhys, and he didn't frown as much. But Emlyn thought it was another trap to get her to do something, like her pink dress had been.

She gripped the hood of Tylysk's cloak. "Nobody will give me what I want."

"Oh, come now, there has to be something."

Emlyn thought. A window they passed showed the garden, its hedges hiding the tiny cottage tucked in the corner. She thought she'd been a hundred times happier in her garden house than she could ever be in the castle.

Tylysk looked out the window too. "Something out there?" His breath tickled her cheek.

She gave in. "My dolly? And my storybook?"

"Done." Tylysk bounced her a little, then looked at Isabelle. "And Isabelle's been good to help you, hasn't she?"

Emlyn nodded. She'd liked Isabelle even before they met. Rhys told her she was his best friend, and she was the nicest person in the Manor, except maybe Aria. At least, she was nice to most people.

"You've been good enough to let me," Isabelle said. "I'd thought you and Master Vespar would've welcomed my help sooner, since you've both made it clear Lady Orrtha no longer needs me."

Tylysk rolled his eyes. "I never said your help was unwanted—"

"No, indeed."

"And I never said *Mistress* Orrtha doesn't need you. Just that, under the circumstances, you are in Lord Vespar's charge as *his* ward."

"She will always be my lady," she said. "She is more a mother to me than my own."

Tylysk resituated Emlyn on his side and looked at her as he said, "Lord Vespar was never far away all those years."

Isabelle pursed her lips, and Tylysk grinned at her. Emlyn saw what Isabelle wouldn't. He liked her. She saw a touch of hurt in his eyes, but as often as Isabelle barked at him, he must've been used to her not liking him.

She didn't want them to fight anymore, so she said, "Tylysk, why did Lady Orrtha stop being Lady?"

Tylysk's surprise stopped him at the foot of the stairs. He looked to Isabelle, who fumbled for an answer. "She's…ill, Emlyn. She's worried she can't tend to her duties."

"Is she going to get better?"

"Yes, of course. She needs time, that's all."

They both smiled that stupid grown-up smile that told her she was too little to understand, and everything was fine even though it wasn't. Her servants at home smiled that way when Mama and Papa got sick.

Heldran never made that smile. Emlyn liked Heldran's smile, since he didn't show it too often. It was soft and real. He didn't use up his real smiles. He wasn't afraid to tell her she had to be ready in case Mama and Papa didn't get better. He knew about sickness. He told her all about their other brothers and sisters. If he knew what would happen to Lady Orrtha, he'd tell her.

As they reached Master Vespar's door, Tylysk sent Isabelle a pointed look.

"I know I'm not invited." Isabelle's glower faded when her eyes shifted to Emlyn. "You'll be fine, darling. I want to hear all about it when you're done."

Isabelle took the opposite hallway. Emlyn watched her disappear until Tylysk set her on her feet. He nodded toward the door. Her bones quivered too much for her to knock.

Tylysk crouched and met her face to face. "It won't be so bad," he said, as soft as Isabelle had. "You're a lucky girl, Emlyn. This is the last opportunity you want to walk away from."

She didn't know what that meant, but he sounded sure. She bowed her head.

"If you do well today, I'll take you to see the dogs."

Emlyn peeked at him. He twitched his eyebrows up. He motioned to the door. Emlyn forced herself to knock.

When Tylysk opened the door, Emlyn darted to where Heldran sat in front of Master Vespar's desk. He got his quill down in time before she bounded at him. He held her tight, but pulled away sooner than she wanted. But he had one of his real smiles, and it warmed her through. He touched the ribbon in her hair, planted a kiss on her cheek.

Though Emlyn hugged his arm, Heldran turned her around to face Master Vespar. She bowed her head. Vespar beamed at her.

"You're more a princess than there has ever been, my girl," he said.

Emlyn looked herself over, though his approval calmed some of her nerves. Rhys said Master Vespar was too picky about how people dressed and walked and spoke. He got mad if Rhys just put his hands in his pockets. Remembering that, Emlyn pulled her shoulders back, the way her governess always told her. Eyes up, stand straight, chin up. But she could never get her feet right. They turned in when she wanted them out.

Vespar smiled more warmly. Tylysk gave a small laugh through his nose. Heldran squeezed her hand.

"We're almost finished." Vespar gestured to the chair next to Heldran's. Emlyn crawled into it, and Tylysk stood by her. Heldran sent him an unhappy look, but he didn't care.

The mages discussed something she didn't understand. She remembered Heldran talking about some of those things when he came home from work. Sometimes they mentioned province names, but Emlyn didn't know where they were, and she didn't remember their names until she heard them. She stopped listening to much more than their different voices.

Heldran wiped his quill and straightened his parchments. Emlyn's heart thudded. Tylysk patted her back, and she slid out of her chair. Heldran stooped beside her.

"Remember what I said last night?"

Emlyn nodded. Be brave.

"I'll see you after lessons. Be good." Heldran kissed the top of her head and left.

Tylysk gripped her hand as Vespar led them out of his chambers and down the hall. Magic prickled behind each door they passed. Anxious, she stepped into Tylysk's leg by accident. She wondered if even Master Vespar could keep those terrifying mages away.

Vespar guided them to a room at the end of the passage. A few windows and mageglow lamps lit the cold, stuffy chamber. Tall bookcases stood in a line against one wall, and slate boards hung on the other. Tables and shelves held shiny magic trinkets and instruments. A smaller table in the far corner was set with lighting sticks and chalk and incense. A glass case bore bottles of herbs and colorful juices. Ahead, a green banner with Gildio's eagle, its wings and long tail spread and its claws open downward, pointy beak facing up, covered most of the wall.

Master Vespar put a hand to her back and steered her to the middle of the room. Tylysk stayed by the door, leaning against the wall, and watched.

Emlyn stopped on the spot where Vespar motioned. He stood in front of her, a few steps out of reach, perfectly between the eagle's wings. He folded his hands and studied her. Emlyn's shoulders inched up. Magic bloomed in her chest.

"Are you nervous, Emlyn?"

She nodded.

Master Vespar did too. "I'm pleased by how well you've maintained your magic. After all you've endured, I would have expected you to slip. Did you know magic is influenced by emotion?"

Emlyn shook her head.

"Magic has a strong bond with emotion. That is why, when a mage or witch is terribly afraid, or angry, or happy, they may use a spell they don't intend. Many discover their powers this way. Perhaps…you discovered yours after your parents' deaths?"

That was exactly when it happened. The first time she used a spell, and not on purpose. She just pretended, and it worked.

Vespar nodded. "In order to use your gifts, you must pay close attention to your feelings. Everyone does this in their own way. Tylysk and Heldran express how they feel in different ways, don't they?"

When Emlyn peered back at him, Tylysk arched a brow. Heldran was so quiet compared to him. Then, she noticed, maybe that was why Master Vespar showed little himself. He had so much power, he couldn't risk feeling too much, or it would escape.

"We have many years of practice at this," said Vespar. "It's a rare thing if we slip. You are young, and it will take time. Yet you've proven your capabilities already."

Emlyn nodded. She didn't want to say Magic helped with most everything. It helped her be clever. It did whatever she said without spells and charms. Thinking of that, and what Master Vespar said last night, about how strong she was…

Nothing made sense anymore. She peered up at her teacher.

"Yes, my girl?"

Emlyn steadied her breath. "Master Vespar, what's an Enchantress?"

It surprised him, but he smiled. He beckoned her to the table, where he leaned against its edge. "Do you know what Magic is, Emlyn? Or rather, what It's made of?"

She shook her head.

"Magic is energy. Sheer energy and power. This energy must have some place to live. That's why there are mages and witches, and certain animals and plants with magic. We are Magic's homes. It has chosen to live within us. And, just as we use the strength from our bodies, we can use the power Magic houses within us."

Vespar watched Emlyn try to understand, then went on. "But there are many mages and witches. Some are stronger than others. Some are better at certain magicks than others. Some are given more of Magic's energy than others."

Vespar took Emlyn's hands. He turned her palms upward, caressed them with his thumbs. He spoke without taking his eyes off them.

"The Enchantress is the strongest of all witches. She is given more power than any other witch. She is sometimes known as Magic's 'Authority.' Some call her Magic's Chosen, or Magic's Princess. You could say the Enchantress is a palace, rather than a house."

He turned her hands over to rest on his palms. His gold ring pressed warm on her wrist.

"The Wizard is the same. He is Magic's Authority, Magic's Prince. The Wizard and Enchantress work hand in hand. They protect and aid each other. In the past, they were the overseers of all mages and witches, as a king and queen oversee their kingdom. Then what happened, Emlyn?"

She swallowed. "Lady Blodica."

"That's right." Vespar noticed her fear. "You will not be like her, Emlyn. I'll see to that."

She hoped not. It was Lady Blodica's fault all this had happened, that the Hunt had started, that Flannery died and Rhys got banished.

Emlyn drew her hands away. "How do you know I'm the Enchantress?"

"Your powers are especially strong for someone so young, and they will grow as you do. Only an Enchantress could have the strength and skill you possess at your age."

The idea of that much magic living inside her, that she was a palace, made Emlyn's heart pound. She felt so small. "I don't want to be the Enchantress."

Vespar frowned. "Magic gives Itself to whomever It wills. We can't decide for ourselves."

"How can I be stronger than you? You're stronger than everyone. Everybody knows that."

His eyes darkened. "But not stronger than you, my girl."

Magic tingled across Emlyn's skin, made the hair on her neck stand on end. Then she understood. "That's why you want me here? Because I can do things you can't?"

Master Vespar didn't answer. He looked down at his ring.

Emlyn stepped away, finding Tylysk had abandoned his post by the door when she bumped into him. Magic jolted her. She jittered, but another thought crossed her mind.

"Is that why you sent Rhys away? You thought he'd stop you?"

Master Vespar raised his chin. Tylysk's hand slipped onto Emlyn's shoulder.

"But he didn't do anything wrong," she said. "He was just worried about me." Another jolt made her gasp. "But…are you going to hurt him?"

Tylysk's grip tightened. "That's enough, Emlyn."

She ached. She got Rhys in trouble because of her stupidness and her horrible magic, and Vespar and Tylysk wanted her to betray him even more, after all he'd done for her. He saved her life. He would make everything better. He loved her. He promised.

Summoning all her courage, Emlyn ripped from Tylysk's grasp. "I won't," she said, then the anger and sadness and everything else compacted to a scream. "I won't help you!"

Emlyn dodged Tylysk's swipe and bolted through the door. His clunking steps followed her, faster than she was. Fear strapped around her, and her sobs slowed her down. At the top of the stairs, Tylysk snagged her by the elbow. He thrust her aside, held her arm over her head so she couldn't struggle.

Before he could open his mouth, Tylysk spiraled through the air. He heaped onto his side, clutching his stomach with a strangled breath. The force of it jostled Emlyn straight down to the floor, where she sat in horror and watched. Her skin tingled, her breath hot with magic.

Tylysk wobbled to his feet. He extended a stiff hand, his face glaring red.

"I'm sorry!" Emlyn shrieked. "I didn't mean to!"

"Come. Here."

Terror swallowed her whole, made her want to fall on the cold floor and cry herself empty. She hurt Tylysk. Now she really was the evil witch everyone believed she was.

Emlyn trudged toward him, arms wrapped tight around her head. Tylysk let his hand fall. Emlyn cringed, thinking he would hit her, but he crouched and tugged her arm from her head. His scar glowed red.

"I'm sorry," she whimpered.

"You told me so. You have someone else to tell."

"I don't want to help him."

"You must not understand." Tylysk grabbed her chin, his thumb digging into her jaw, fingers pressed too close to her throat. "You are in Lord Vespar's charge. Were it not for him, you would be gone. If he is going to persuade the council to let you live, you will do as he says. You have no choice."

Emlyn stared at him, too stunned to make a sound. Tylysk turned away from her tears, sighed, and scrubbed his face. He tried to hold Emlyn's hand.

She stepped away. "I want to see Heldran."

"He's working."

"Please?"

Tylysk's lips tightened. "Not until you apologize to Master Vespar."

Emlyn crumpled. She couldn't win.

Tylysk grasped her wrist and yanked her down the passage. Mages peered through open doors, searching for the commotion, but Tylysk waved them away. They glared at Emlyn before locking themselves up again.

Emlyn hid her face in Tylysk's wrist. She didn't understand how she could've hurt him. She hadn't used magic herself. It felt different from when she told Magic to do things, even if she didn't mean to. This time, it hadn't flowed through her, filling her up and coursing through her bones. Magic had worked Itself out of her. It attacked Tylysk on Its own.

Magic was so big, and she was so small. She couldn't be Its princess.

Master Vespar stood in the same spot near the table, inspecting his ring. Emlyn was sure he was furious under that blank face. Tylysk let go of her hand, closed the door, and blocked it. Emlyn crept to her tutor. Tears dribbled on her dress.

"I'm sorry, Master Vespar."

His gentle smile worried her. "That, little one, is what I've been expecting. I wondered if you were taking all this too well." He held out his hands. Emlyn nervously placed hers on them. When she peered up at him, he asked, "Do you believe I would ask you to hurt Master Rhys?"

"You and Tylysk hate him," she blurted.

He didn't react. "Do you believe he will come for you?"

She said nothing.

"You hope he will?"

"Rhys loves me," she said. "He promised."

"Despite Heldran being here?"

Emlyn blushed.

Vespar looked at Emlyn's hands, the faintest sadness to his mouth. "Do you understand that if Rhys comes back, he will be in worse trouble than when he left?"

When Emlyn understood, her heart choked her. "You can't do that," she squeaked.

"It is the law. If Rhys tries to come home…" He frowned. "I won't deny that I am angry with him, Emlyn. But I would never ask you to hurt him."

"Then what do you want me for?"

She watched his steady lips quirk. He stammered for words without making a sound. She sensed Tylysk tense behind her.

Master Vespar knelt down and looked in her eyes. "I want to protect you, little Enchantress. Few others can see it, but you are precious. All I wish from you is your trust."

Vespar folded her hands in his. Emlyn let him, unsure if she believed him. But his eyes dimmed, and Emlyn saw sadness there. For one tiny moment, Emlyn felt bad for him.

"I'm sorry there is so little else for you, my girl. I am all you have."

She believed him.

Emlyn did her best in lessons.

Every afternoon, after Master Vespar finished his work and Emlyn would rather play outside, she found herself in that chilly classroom instead. Tylysk joined them most of the time, but he was always *Master*

Tylysk during lessons. He stood by the door, looking bored, but his attention stayed on her like a hawk circling the sky.

Lessons went on for weeks.

The first day, Master Vespar gave her a heavy purple book with gold letters on the front. She recognized it—Heldran had the same book at home. He'd studied from it all twelve years at the Academy, he said. Heldran helped her read three pages every night before bed while Isabelle brushed her hair.

Vespar began her studies with simple spells she picked up easily. She knew lots of others, and with Magic doing what she told it to, she could do whatever he asked. She didn't tell him that, though. She didn't know what he'd say, and if it was bad that Magic did that.

But sometimes, she couldn't tell if Master Vespar was good or bad, either. He was patient with her, praised her, was gentle when he corrected her few mistakes.

Tylysk was the same way. After that first horrible day, Tylysk never spoke crossly to her again. He kept his promises and let her play with Aria and the puppies. He took her riding through the hills behind the Manor and into town for strawberry candies.

Once he stopped being so awkward about it, she liked going places with him. Especially riding—she'd sit in front of him on a beautiful gray horse, and they'd shoot through the bailey, dart up the road, and wind around the hills so fast it stole her breath. Sometimes he let the horse wander, and Emlyn leaned against him, sheltered close with his arm tucked around her. She felt safe there.

Around it all, Emlyn couldn't tell what was good or bad anymore. Rhys would tell her it was bad. He'd say Tylysk and Vespar were tricking her, and sometimes she thought about it. Sometimes she believed it.

But she went on with lessons and being Enchantress, not knowing if she was doing good or bad herself.

Soon, Master Vespar stopped teaching her spells. Emlyn wondered if he suspected what Magic did for her.

Midafternoon, after the time she used to study charms, Vespar trained her on potions and elixirs. Heldran helped her study lists of ingredients and their functions in different formulas. Sometimes, she and Master Vespar made simple concoctions, smaller than the one she made in the garden house.

At the end of the day, Master Vespar let Emlyn draw easy circles and pentacles on parchment with an array of bright colors he set out on the worktable. She memorized each rune and incense, learned their patterns and purposes. He wouldn't let her make real ones, though. It was one of the most dangerous magicks, and Emlyn's hand wasn't steady enough to draw them cleanly yet.

One afternoon, some weeks into it, she overheard the mages whispering while she sketched. She kept her head down, but listened.

"She's a quick study, thanks to her gift," said Vespar.

"I didn't learn those circles until my eighth year," Tylysk remarked. "Has she already tested out of her spells?"

"She doesn't need them. Magic bends to her will without so much as a breath."

"Could that be…problematic, sir?"

Vespar's cloak rustled when he shifted. "She wouldn't have the heart to turn on us. She's learning where her loyalties must lie." His voice darkened. "Master Rhys never broke; that was my mistake. But Emlyn does not worry me. She will succumb."

She wasn't sure what that meant, but the words made her shudder. She dipped her quill, heartbroken. Vespar was winning, and Emlyn only cared about riding with Tylysk and playing with Aria. She did everything he said without thinking about it anymore.

Drawing the last line of a rune into place, she wondered what Rhys would think of her now. How disappointed he'd be that she wasn't brave.

"Come show me your work, Emlyn," said Vespar.

She wiped her eyes before her tears dripped on the parchment. She dried the ink with a shaky breath, cleaned and stowed her quill and inks in their cupboard, and presented her work.

"Excellent, my girl. Much tidier today. Your lines are getting straighter, and you corrected the Bel rune from yesterday," he said, pointing with his little finger.

Normally, his praise would've warmed her up, but Emlyn just said, "Yes, Master Vespar."

Tylysk inspected the drawing over his master's shoulder. "I have a question for you, Emlyn," he said. His smile was more playful than mean anymore. "What does a Blaze Spell do?"

"What kind of Blaze Spell, sir?"

He exchanged Vespar's impressed look. "Fourth-Level Expel."

"It's a defense charm. It puts a fire circle around you and keeps everything out."

"Good. What kind of metal would you use to make a bane's chest?"

"Iron and copper."

"Why?"

"Because only the person who closes a bane's chest can open it. Iron can make magic not work right, but copper makes magic work better. If you put copper inside, it holds the spell that keeps it closed. If you use iron on the outside, other magic won't work on it, so nobody can use a spell to open it."

"What are the runes in the Kevrry Circle?"

"Hir, Rol, and Aer."

"Why would you not put ashenclove for duskwing in what kind of elixirs?"

"You use duskwing in Mrinthir elixirs to heal wounds that won't stop bleeding. Ashenclove stops infections. If you put ashenclove instead of duskwing, you would bleed more. And it would taste disgusting."

They laughed. Emlyn blushed.

"Very good. You've studied hard."

"Yes, Master Tylysk."

He glanced at Vespar, then bent down. "I think you've earned this."

He reached into his cloak pocket. Emlyn's heart skipped.

It was Laela, her golden-haired princess doll with the lavender dress and a crown of rosebuds. Emlyn squeezed her close.

Tylysk pressed a finger to her nose. "If you keep it up, I'll find your storybook."

CHAPTER 38

Rhys

Oedolyn examined my wounds as we sat down to breakfast. She set out an array of ointments on the table, prepped another roll of linen, and peeled the bandages away. I winced when she touched my back.

She cringed. "Sorry. I'm sure it hurts."

"No, your hands are freezing." I peered over my shoulder. "Honest, I feel like nothing happened."

Oedolyn turned me toward the cloudy morning light through the window. "It looks like nothing happened. Not a scratch, not a scar." She brushed a fingertip between my shoulder blades, where the pain had been the worst the night before.

I inspected my hands. Bruises tinged my fingertips from clawing at the ground, but no talons showed. No scales, Oedolyn assured me the red in my eyes had cleared. Nothing, except the dragon went on storming around his cave, and his footsteps offset the beat of my heart. When I barked at him, he glared, slithered to a higher pocket of his cavern, and lodged himself somewhere uncomfortable, wedged like something I swallowed got stuck halfway down.

Of course, he hadn't succeeded. Recovery was brief now, a night's rest, but how easy would it be when he released in full?

I tried to think "if" instead of "when," but the dragon flashed the hideous memory of Tylysk's bloodied face.

You will need me, he rumbled. *You will see.*

"That's encouraging," Athrú said, not knowing he'd spoken right after the dragon. He set a plate of bacon and bread in front of me. "Maybe you're on the far side of besting him."

The dragon glared at him, as if being denied some credit. As if he let me overpower him this time.

The beast swung his heat around to me. *Why would I let you win? You are but a jailor.*

You're the one who weaseled your way into my head in the first place.

You will need me.

No, I don't think that's it. You're not the generous sort.

You will see. The dragon crawled down the amber crags headfirst, lithe as a forest cat. He lounged in his sleeping pocket and left me alone.

Despite our busyness in training and preparations for the journey, the anticipation stretched the last few days into sluggish weeks. By dawn the next morning, we would be on the road to Gildio, where the headsman awaited my return. Still a few weeks more before I saw Emlyn again, but at least we'd be moving.

Athrú and I returned to Eoin's smithy. The forge burned low this time, bright enough to light the worktable the smiths shared. One tweaked a few links on a hauberk while the other finished some silver tooling on a scabbard. Eoin stood behind them, standing on his toes to watch their work. He glanced up at us.

"Finishing touches. Be but a moment."

The smith smoothed a polish down the leather scabbard, then showed Eoin.

"Ah, good. Very good. Here, lad." Eoin brought me the black sheath. Shining silver capped its tip and embellished the long side in a sharp, elegant lattice.

"Yes, good, but here." Eoin waved the same smith over. The craftsman passed me the cloth-bound sword.

The thin blade glinted fiery orange in the furnace light. The narrow cross guard widened at the blade, where three silver talons fastened a polished sapphire. At the end of the hilt, the silver pommel had been tooled into a dragon's scaled head.

"Seemed fitting," Eoin said. "Legends say the ancient Dragon Lords had these sorts of blades. I hear there's one on display in Elfryth. You'll have to go see if the rumors are true." The old man winked.

I smiled. I couldn't fathom why my draconis intrigued him, but the sword was magnificent all the same.

Athrú bowed and sought permission to take it. He weighed the blade between his hands, tested its grip and balance, ran its length between his thumb and fingers. "Excellent, as always, sir." He passed me the sword. It gave a gratifying ring as it slid into the sheath.

"Twelve gold is all I ask," said Eoin.

Athrú and I exchanged glances. "So little?" he said.

"Our contribution to your cause. Just be sure to use it well and wise, mind. Oh, and this." Eoin tottered to the table, where the second smith finished binding the last of the metal rings on the chain mail. Eoin nodded. "And you checked the back? Oh, this is the back, oh yes. And look at that. Here, lad, see." I went to his side. "I found this, thought it might be useful. We've made a few alterations to suit your, ah, more robust needs." Eoin patted my back, right where the wings would sprout.

"This, look here." He pointed to a few clasps holding together two narrow slits. "They shouldn't break, but they'll come undone when you need. You don't want to be on the battlefield wriggling out of your armor to make room, do you?" He laughed, and halfway through said, "Oh, this too." Eoin tossed me a padded flannel tunic to fit under the mail. He pointed to the oversized buttonholes in the back.

The dragon's tail flicked. *He can foresee what lies ahead.*

Hush up.

"Might be a tad big," Eoin unknowingly interrupted, "but you'll grow into it." He bit back a grin at his joke.

"Thank you," I said. "How much for this?"

"Oh, not much. Just a promise." Eoin stepped up to me, planted his cane between his feet, and raised a gnarled finger. "Pick your battles carefully, and win them. You've picked a battle all wish to fight but none has yet dared to declare. I want your word that you will win it."

I licked my lips. "I'll do all I can, sir."

"Ah, see? That is a good promise. Not too proud, just humble enough to prove your honesty." Eoin lowered his nose and peered over the rim of his spectacles. His eyes shrank to beads without the lenses.

"You have a wise man's head and a warrior's heart. Too few men in the world have either, and fewer have proper courage. The men who do— ah, they are the men who become heroes."

Eoin inched his spectacles up and grinned. "Settled. But I expect to hear plenty of news about the both of you while you're gone."

Athrú laid an array of tine and silver equal to twelve gold on the table. "We'll see if we can't smuggle you that relic from Elfryth, if we get that far this time."

Eoin laughed. "Yes, I'm still waiting, Master Athrú."

We thanked him and the smiths and stepped out. Eoin watched us wander down the road and waved when we looked back.

"I'll pay you back," I said to Athrú.

"With what, Master Rhys? Think nothing of it."

"I do. Everything you and Oedolyn have done, and nothing I can give for it. And I won't ask you to go to Gildio with me, either."

Athrú stopped in the middle of the road, gave the folk around us a long study. Market-goers roved from one stall to the next, following the calls of merchants along the street. A woman drove her chickens through her gate before they strutted after a man towing along a stubborn goat. On the stoop outside a sweets shop, a teenage mage helped a younger boy perfect a trick spell to impress a little girl who watched on with her arms folded and her toe tapping.

"How many witches do you think are out there?" Athrú asked.

I looked around with him. He didn't expect an answer I couldn't give.

"Too few," he said. "How many of them do you think dread every morning they might wake to find Magic has claimed their daughters?"

I frowned. "Too many."

Athrú nodded. "My parents dreaded the same of my sister. It never claimed her, but even so." He scanned a somber eye across the sunny road. "I can remember my mother comforting the inconsolable each time the Hunters made a successful round."

I looked away from the busy street, drawn to the thought of Flannery and her sister, imagining her family's anguish.

"You can't do it alone, Master Rhys," Athrú said, "nor should those who wish to fight for your cause, our cause, be denied."

He smiled, though a gravity still tinged his icy eyes. He clapped me on the shoulder. "Come on. Oedolyn has a few errands for us. We'll stop at the tailor's first."

As we followed the curve of the road, the smell of buttery pastries spilled from the bakery across the street, sweeter than it had ever been at home. A fiddler led a ring of children through a dancing game. A florist's stall stood near the tailor's, tinkling with chimes and bells. Athrú and I moved up the steps to the shop.

"Buy a flower, sir?"

I turned. The girl offering a scarlet rose bore a startling resemblance to Aria, down to the way she tucked her hair behind her ear. Except, despite the summer warmth, her skin was porcelain pale and cold, and she dropped into a steadier curtsy than Aria's. The girl raised a smile and steel gray eyes.

"Forgive me." The girl curtsied again. "I didn't mean to startle you, sir."

"Not at all. You…remind me of someone." I cleared my throat. "Your flowers are beautiful. Some of these I've only seen in books before."

"You must come from far away. All but a few I grew from those I found wild in the woods." The girl returned the rose to the basket at her heel. "Perhaps there's something else you would prefer."

She tiptoed around the stall, running her fingers along a spread of tinkling crystal chimes. A set of frosty prisms reminded me of magelights, if the lights could be frozen. The gentle, eerie ting echoed on nothing, reverberations deepening with each rebound. I thought it must have been the sound Magic made, if It had a sound.

"No, not Magic," the girl said, startling me again. "They say the echoes are the sounds of souls. I might imagine so. It's very mournful, very lonely, don't you think?"

It was. "Where did you find them?" I asked.

She caressed the crystals. "You would never believe me. Some days, I don't believe it myself."

The girl let the echoes die away and studied me a moment. "If I may, sir, I believe I have something you might like." A quick search of her wares, and she returned to me. "Perhaps this will also remind you of someone."

My heart dropped. A single, perfect daisy.

The girl stroked its petals with her fingertip. "Yes," she said, passing it to me. "I believe that is the sound of our souls, now and beyond."

I hesitantly took the flower. The girl's chilled fingers brushed mine.

"You must be brave, sir, for all you face."

I glanced up into her eyes. They glistened true silver. Aria's likeness diminished the longer I looked at her. Something in her voice resembled those crystals.

I handed the daisy back. "Er, thank you miss. I think my friend—"

"Long roads. Sleepless nights under heavy skies. Miles of despair. The beast within."

I swallowed.

A chill came to her gaze, sharp as an icicle. A wicked smile bloomed on her face. The dragon growled.

"You are a terrible thing, sweet boy. Your courage will fail you, and soon."

It already wavered under her gaze. She watched it in my eyes. She reached a hand to me.

The girl recoiled. For a moment, I thought the dragon had ringed my eyes with red, but she stared past me. Athrú stepped out of the shop, a parcel under his arm, squinting at our exchange through the glare of afternoon sun.

I turned back. The girl was gone.

Athrú came to my side. "What are you looking for?"

"She was right here."

"Who, Maggie?" He nodded toward the far end of the stall. The seller down the row, a middle-aged woman with bushy yellow curls, passed a bouquet of lilies to a customer.

"No, not her. You didn't see her?"

Before Athrú could answer, Maggie passed him a bundle of lavender and a pair of jars. "Much as it pleases me to see your handsome face, I'd like to see Oedolyn from time to time," she said. "Tell her to fetch her own order next time, hm? Unless your friend here would be gentleman enough to make the trip for her." A wink, and the woman bustled back to work.

I took a share of Athrú's armload before he dropped something, though the way my hands shook, I could have dropped something myself.

A sullen silence hung over the kitchen at supper. Chamberlain contented himself with a helping of unseasoned pork and huddled by the hearth instead of snuffling for scraps at the table. Oedolyn pretended to eat by tearing her slice of bread into crumbs to dunk in her honey. Athrú said nothing of her poor appetite and pretended to be hungry himself. I ate my food and stayed out of their unspoken quarrel.

"Eoin said he would look in on you," Athrú said, peering across the table to his sister. "And you're not to hesitate to call on him should you need him."

Oedolyn squashed a bite of bread between her finger and thumb.

"Chamberlain will stay home this time," he went on. The dog grumbled at the sound of his name. "I'd rather he were here with you than lost in the woods with us."

She didn't answer. The hearth light cast warm orange across her empty face.

I took a drink of cider to avoid Athrú's glance. Frowning, he returned to his food and said nothing more.

With the awkwardness about to burst, Oedolyn whisked our empty plates away and sent us to bed. The rangers would be waiting for us before light, she said, and we were in poor shape anyway. Athrú pecked his sister's brow and did as he was told.

"Rhys," Oedolyn said.

I stayed behind as Athrú rounded the corner out of the kitchen, Chamberlain at his heels. Oedolyn offered me the parcel we'd brought her from the tailor.

"This is yours, for the journey."

"What else are the pair of you going to give me?"

She blushed. "Go on."

She took the wrappings when I undid them. Dark-green folds of wool unrolled from my hands. The hooded cloak spread wide enough to bundle myself in it twice over. It was plain and practical, except a silver double-clasp pin with a knotted eagle.

Oedolyn's ears went red. "The way you talk about Gildio...I know you miss it. I thought you might like something to take with you."

I swelled. Gildio's green. Gildio's eagle.

Oedolyn returned my gratitude with a sparkling smile. I folded the cloak so the pin lay on top. She straightened it, biting her lip.

"There's one thing I'd ask you," she said.

"Anything."

She peeked toward the next room, where we heard Athrú washing at the basin. "I know he said he'd look after you, but...if you'd do the same for him?"

"Of course." Spying her frown, I said, "He'll be home sooner than you think."

"He usually is." Oedolyn traced a finger along the eagle's head. "But it's different this time, isn't it? Everything's changing. And here I am, watching you and my brother get stirred into this mess, unable to do anything."

The softness of her scold made me smile. "He just wants to keep you safe."

"I know. That's why I worry." Oedolyn shook her head, eyes on Athrú's shadow in the next room. "He's too busy thinking of others to think of himself."

I stepped in the way of her view, caught her eye. "He'll come back. I'll make sure of it."

Oedolyn showed the tiniest smile. She stood on her toes and pecked my cheek. My face burned.

"For luck," she said, unable to meet my eye. She turned me toward the staircase. "Go. Get your sleep."

⁂

Slumped in bed against aching muscles and restlessness, I lay awake, thinking of Flannery. It had been four weeks and three days since her murder.

Her rosebud lips brushed mine, left the sweet-berried taste of her mouth. The violet perfume of her hair overtook me. Her laugh breathed so real on my ear, I turned to look.

I fumbled in the dark for Da's jerkin, half spilling off the bed. I shoved myself back up and dug through the inside pocket. Tucked away, where I stowed it every night, was her letter. I couldn't bring myself to unfold it this time. I held it to my lips.

Flannery urged me on, as she swore she would. I could feel it.

Emlyn was waiting for me. She knew I would come. I wouldn't lose her to Vespar, too.

CHAPTER 39

Emlyn

Emlyn hesitated from going outside, but Aria promised that running with the puppies was just as fun in the rain. The dogs scampered across the bailey as fast as always. One found a puddle on the flagstones to splash in. Aria showed her how to slide across the slick grass, but Emlyn fell in a heap before she got far. She shivered with her hair dripping in her eyes and her soaked sleeves sticking to her skin, but she hadn't had this much fun since…well, since the tinkers got her.

Emlyn had stopped counting how many days she'd been at the Manor. She'd lost track around twenty-seven, she thought. She was used to living there and doing the sorts of things Isabelle said mistresses and ladies at other manors had to do, too.

After a few weeks of lessons, Master Vespar added more subjects to study. Tylysk helped her with letters and numbers, and Heldran told her history stories. She liked listening to them, except the ones about the Great War and Praed and Blodica. Since she was Enchantress, she felt she *was* Lady Blodica, and she'd end up doing all the same horrid things the first Enchantress did.

Master Vespar promised he wouldn't let that happen. She would never be a bad Enchantress.

Emlyn felt a little better, but at the same time, hearing it from him made her uneasy. The way Rhys had said it warmed her up, but when Vespar said it, it always made her feel cold and like everyone was staring at her.

Heldran reminded her all the time how she had no reason to be afraid of Master Vespar. He said Master Vespar was his second father. He took care of Heldran and Tylysk while they were at school the way he'd care for Emlyn. She wasn't afraid of him anymore, but she never wanted him to be another father. She missed Papa too much for that.

But then, sometimes, she thought Rhys would be something like that, or like Heldran, when she could leave the garden house.

Emlyn tried not to think about Rhys so much. It made her sad, and Heldran said she shouldn't dwell on him. She didn't know what that meant, but she tried not to.

She hadn't seen Lady Orrtha much since she arrived. Remembering how upset Lady Orrtha had been, what she'd said when they found Emlyn, she stayed as far away from her as possible. Besides, whenever the Lady came into a room, someone whisked Emlyn out of it.

No one said if Lady Orrtha was feeling better. She didn't look sick, just tired. She wore her hair down now instead of pinned up, and she'd stopped wearing as many jewels as before, but she was still beautiful. Isabelle said nothing about it, and Heldran never brought it up, so Emlyn thought she at least wasn't getting worse. She still didn't understand why she'd given up being Lady and why she'd made Vespar lord. Why wouldn't she make Isabelle the new Lady instead?

Aria grasped Emlyn's hand before she darted across the lawn again. She pointed to the stable gate, where Tylysk and Isabelle stood out in the rain to watch them play. He waved the girls over. Emlyn ran, puppies at her heels, until she realized it wasn't Isabelle with him.

Aria slid to a halt beside her. "What's the matter, Emlyn?"

Emlyn clutched the collar of her dress and stepped away.

"Haven't you met Lady Orrtha?"

Emlyn shook her head. Tylysk beckoned them again. Lady Orrtha turned aside, but whatever Tylysk said stopped her.

Aria took Emlyn's hand. "It's all right. She's very nice."

Emlyn trudged beside her, feeling silly in her soaked clothes and her messy hair in her face. When they reached the stable, Aria curtsied to both Lady Orrtha and Tylysk. Emlyn did too, but hers was too fast. She clung to Aria's hand.

Lady Orrtha smiled. Despite how tired she looked, she was as beautiful as a queen. "Sun and stars, girls, have you been out here through the whole storm? You're quite lovely messes, I must say."

Emlyn blinked and looked to Tylysk. He made a little nod toward the Lady.

"Run inside before you're frozen through."

"Yes, milady," Aria said with a curtsy. Emlyn did the same, and Aria led her to the door. Stalks of hay and straw dust stuck to her shoes and wet legs, and Emlyn felt even sillier. She hurried ahead of Aria.

"Emlyn?"

She stopped short in the ankle-deep straw and turned.

"I've been told the cook made fresh cake today. Perhaps you'd like to share some with me once you've cleaned up?"

Emlyn blinked. She glanced to where Tylysk stood behind the Lady. He gave a tiny bow and motioned for her to do the same. Emlyn curtsied. "Thank you, La—Mistress Orrtha." She bolted into the castle.

Aria helped her dry and dress in her favorite pink gown and braided Emlyn's hair. Emlyn trembled with nerves.

"Lady Orrtha is the nicest person in the world," Aria said. But she hadn't been there when Lady Orrtha told Master Vespar to get rid of Emlyn.

Tylysk was waiting for them in the hall. As soon as Aria managed a shaky curtsy at the sight of him, she ran away. Tylysk grasped Emlyn's hand and led her on. She expected to go to Lady Orrtha's chambers, but they passed the stairs and made for the dining hall.

"Believe me, Emlyn, you have nothing to be afraid of. Mistress Orrtha isn't the least bit scary." Tylysk said it the way he used to talk about Rhys, as if he were nobody at all.

"What about lessons?" Emlyn asked.

"You have time to spare. Master Vespar would be glad to hear you spent a moment with her. It will do her good."

"But you've never let me see Lady Orrtha before."

"Mistress Orrtha, Emlyn." Tylysk opened the door for her. "Go on. I'll wait for you."

Emlyn crept into the dining hall, where the rain outside the high windows made the room dark. The fireplace at the far end was glowing, and the room had a warm scent from the rushes on the floor. Emlyn tiptoed past the empty table to the hearth, where Mistress Orrtha sat on the wood floor with some pillows. The servant waiting nearby left out the side door.

Emlyn jumped at the sudden prickle of magic—a spell from a mage upstairs, she guessed. It still took some getting used to so many magicks in one place, always buzzing and thrumming.

She waited for Mistress Orrtha to look up from her needlework. She set her embroidery aside and patted the pillow beside her. "There you are, Emlyn. Come, sit with me."

Emlyn dropped to the floor opposite her, close to the warm fire.

"I'm glad to finally meet you. I'm feeling some better, and I thought we might visit for a while. Have some cider. You must be freezing."

Emlyn took the cup Mistress Orrtha filled from the pitcher by the fire. The hot cinnamon tickled her nose.

"How have you liked the Manor? Has everyone treated you well? And your lessons? Master Tylysk tells me you've studied hard. Have you enjoyed your lessons?"

Emlyn nodded at each, but hesitated at the last.

"It's all right if you haven't. Master Vespar—"

"It's not—" Emlyn went pink and ducked her head. "Sorry, milady."

The Mistress urged her to speak. "I—I like lessons. I like learning about Magic."

"Do you like having Master Vespar for a teacher?"

Part of her did. Lessons weren't as boring as the ones with her tutors at home. And Master Vespar knew what to say when she grew frustrated and how to make it better.

But if she liked Master Vespar, what would Rhys think?

"Has he been kind to you?"

"Yes, my lady."

Mistress Orrtha refilled Emlyn's cup. "I didn't imagine otherwise. He has no intention to be hard or cruel." She frowned. "But he makes mistakes, like everyone else. Sometimes his ideas are more…extreme than he can foresee, I think. If he could find any other way to do something, he would take it."

Emlyn said nothing. Whatever that meant, it didn't make her feel better about everything he'd done to Rhys.

Mistress Orrtha peered into Emlyn's eyes. "I've felt the same way you have. Then I thought how, despite what we think, he must miss Rhys, too."

Something about that made Emlyn feel strange.

"However, I've noticed he's been a little more cheerful since you arrived, in spite of everything." She smiled, and it was one of Rhys's side smiles. "Even he can feel, Emlyn, and he can even feel happy."

Emlyn sipped her cider to look away.

"At any rate, it's good to hear you've done well. I'm sure it's better with your brother here." Something about Emlyn's nod made Mistress Orrtha say, "What is it, dearest?"

Emlyn hugged her knees, warmed by what she'd called her. "Heldran works a lot. He's gone before I wake up in the morning, and he goes back after I go to bed."

"He must be determined to finish his work." When Emlyn didn't answer, she added, "But he should be careful not to wear himself too thin."

As Mistress Orrtha shifted, Emlyn couldn't help admiring her beautiful dress. That dark blue and red was pretty on her, and Emlyn had always wanted pearls like the ones she wore. She had a simple gold band on her right ring finger. Her hair hung long in perfect waves, just like a princess's hair.

"Isabelle enjoys your company," she said, drawing Emlyn's attention again. "I have no doubt she's been good to you too."

"Yes, my lady. I like Isabelle. She helps me with everything."

"I'm glad. I think Isabelle knows how you feel, being away from home. Her parents live far away in Atlarand, and she came here when she was your age."

"How come?"

"Well, a long time ago, her parents and my husband and I had an agreement that Isabelle and Rhys would be married."

Emlyn's eyes widened. "Really? Why didn't they?"

Mistress Orrtha shook her head. "Their fathers had too many disputes they never resolved. Isabelle's father didn't care for what Rhys and his father believed."

Emlyn hesitated. "About witches? Then why didn't Isabelle go home?"

"We hoped they would reach an agreement. But the way things are, Master Vespar may have other plans in mind for her."

Emlyn didn't like the sound of that. "Is he going to send her away?"

"No, I don't believe so, dearest. But I wouldn't be surprised if he and her father arranged another proposal." She brimmed Emlyn's cup once more. "Are you getting warmer, Emlyn?"

"Yes, my lady."

Mistress Orrtha looked Emlyn over for a long moment, but Emlyn didn't mind anymore. "You're becoming something of a Mistress here too, aren't you?"

Emlyn went cold again.

"It would do you good to learn to be a lady. It would serve you greatly when the council summons you."

Emlyn tried to ignore that. It rattled her bones to think about it. "My governess taught me about that."

"Very good. Isabelle could teach you. I would be glad to, should Master Vespar approve."

"He won't let you?"

The Mistress looked into the fire. "He worries for my health, as we all do. If he believes it would be too much wear on me, he would see someone else take my place."

Emlyn didn't press, but despite the gentleness of her voice, the words sounded like something grown-ups said to make her stop asking questions.

The servant girl returned, carrying a tray with a platter of small cake squares and a bowl of strawberries and cream each. Mistress Orrtha laid it on the floor between them. The servant curtsied and disappeared.

"Aria tells me you're fond of strawberries. Help yourself."

Emlyn scooted closer and picked a strawberry after Mistress Orrtha dunked hers. The bite melted on her tongue, as sweet as her candies.

Mistress Orrtha smiled brighter when Emlyn did. "Good, aren't they? Aria likes to dab the cream onto her cake and put the strawberry on top."

Emlyn tried, but the Mistress had to spread the cream for her. The soft cake crumbled in her mouth.

She'd forgotten the prickle of magic until it moved. She glanced around. It was too close to be someone upstairs.

"Speaking of Aria," the Mistress said, making herself a tiny strawberry cake, "I wanted to thank you for being so kind to her. She's never had someone to play with before."

Emlyn's heart sank. "She doesn't have any friends?"

"Seeing how she is, she hasn't been able to make friends her age. They haven't been kind to her."

"How come?"

Mistress Orrtha beamed. "Because they can't see in her what we can. She is our precious Aria, and we love all she is."

Emlyn still didn't understand. Was there something wrong with Aria? Emlyn didn't think so, except sometimes she ran away from Master Vespar and Tylysk, but Emlyn had wanted to do that for a long time herself.

"She showed me her marble collection once," Emlyn said. "They're really special."

The Mistress took another strawberry. "Rhys brought her some for her first birthday she spent with us. That's all she's asked for every year since. Rhys always brought her some."

Emlyn blushed. She hadn't meant to make her so sad.

"Rhys has always been good that way—eager to leave people better than he found them."

Emlyn curled her arms around her knees, careful to keep her sticky fingers off her dress. She turned her face from the hot fire.

"What do you think of him?"

Her heart jolted. She stammered.

Mistress Orrtha reached across to her. "You have cream on your chin, little one." She wiped it away, waited for an answer.

"Well…he's my best friend. He saved me."

The Mistress wiped her hands on her napkin. "I know you're dear to him, Emlyn. He told me how precious you are to him, and he risked his life to prove it."

Emlyn hid her face, but Mistress Orrtha grasped her hands and guided Emlyn to her side. "Knowing what he sacrificed, and knowing he did it for someone he loved…I wish with all my being that he were here, but I'm proud of his courage to make such a choice. I'm proud of his good, strong heart."

Emlyn peered up into her soft eyes. "Really?"

Mistress Orrtha cupped a gentle hand to Emlyn's cheek. "And if you are so precious to him, you shall be precious to me."

Emlyn's heart skipped. Before she could stop herself, she stooped into Mistress Orrtha's embrace. She was sweet with flowery perfume, how Mama used to be. The Mistress held her tighter, the way Rhys would.

For the first time, Emlyn thought she had a mama again.

Mistress Orrtha gave a tiny laugh and pecked Emlyn's cheek. "Come now, sit with me and finish your strawberries."

As Emlyn dropped to the pillow beside the Mistress, she caught herself from toppling when the prickle of magic ripped from around her. She tried not to let Mistress Orrtha see.

"Did you enjoy yourself?" Master Vespar asked Emlyn, straightening his parchments.

"Yes."

He almost laughed at how wide she grinned. "Yes, you did. You have strawberry all around your mouth."

Emlyn wiped her face with the back of her hand and followed him across his office as he put his books away. "She wants to teach me how to be a lady."

"Indeed?"

"She says it would be good for me."

"Yes, it would, my girl."

"Can she, Master Vespar?"

"It's certainly possible, Emlyn, but you'll have a better chance if you recite your runes."

She did, all forty-four of them, only stumbling once.

"And have you practiced your pentacle drawing today?"

Emlyn opened her mouth before she stopped herself. She hurried to the door, where Tylysk stood waiting, and turned back. "Then can she?"

"My, silly girl, I've never known a child so eager to improve her etiquette."

She didn't know what that meant, but she said, "I like Mistress Orrtha. She said I'm becoming a Mistress like her and Isabelle, and I want to be like them."

Master Vespar and Tylysk glanced at each other. "Do you, indeed?"

"Please, Master Vespar?"

He stood over his desk, looking into her eyes. Emlyn folded her hands under her chin. He smiled and shook his head.

"Take Master Tylysk and practice your circles. I'll speak with Mistress Orrtha while you're gone."

After supper, Heldran and Isabelle took Emlyn to her room to read before bed. She sat in Heldran's lap this time, the book propped on her knees, while he read the words in her ear. Isabelle watched from the vanity bench while she mended Laela's ragged dress.

Emlyn leaned into Heldran's chest, and his heartbeat almost lulled her to sleep. He stopped midsentence, brushed a kiss to her hair, and laid her on the pillow. Emlyn didn't want him to go, but pretended to sleep, hoping he wouldn't leave too soon. Isabelle tucked Laela under the blanket next to her.

Heldran stayed, kneeling at Emlyn's bedside and smoothing her hair. It made her warm just to be with him, to feel nothing mattered in the world. For that one moment every night, she was home.

Too soon, Heldran sat back, groaning behind his hands. "I'm sure she's fine, Isabelle. You don't have to sit with her."

"You're tearing yourself apart working so late. Those potions aren't doing you any good."

He tried to argue, but yawned instead.

"You weren't asked to break your back," Isabelle said.

Heldran stroked Emlyn's arm. "There's nothing. I can't find anything. Lord Vespar says no one has seen or heard from any Wizard in the past decade."

"Will you have to go out?" Isabelle's question made Emlyn's stomach hurt.

"Not yet." Emlyn breathed again. "I'm gathering whatever clues I can first. But there's nothing. I can't…"

The bed sagged when Isabelle sat beside them. "If it's been that long, what if he's not the same Wizard? What if there's been a new one since?"

"We would have felt it—that much magic shifting from one mage to another."

"Well, then…" Isabelle brushed her hands together. "You have to have narrowed something down. You can't be expected to search the whole country."

Heldran gave a feeble laugh. Emlyn turned onto her stomach before she sank too deep into sleep. Heldran rubbed her back, lulling her more.

"What about the Academy?" asked Isabelle. "They might have something. Anything."

No answer.

"And he can't hide forever. He has to find his Enchantress too, doesn't he?"

Then Emlyn wondered how hard Heldran was trying. If the Wizard came, would he take Emlyn away? Someone she didn't know, maybe someone old and mean, coming to steal her from everyone she loved?

Why did everyone want to take her away?

Emlyn didn't know she'd moaned until Heldran whispered, "Shh, Emmy girl," and stroked her hair. "Yes, that's the Wizard's duty, just as it's hers to find him."

"That's why he asked you to do it." A silence settled in, until Isabelle said, "You don't think it's all strange? All this with Lord Vespar and—"

"Incredibly," he said, "but I can't afford to think on it, if it will keep Emlyn safe. We only have a few more weeks before the council summons her, then…"

Heldran cupped a hand to Emlyn's cheek. "I have to find him. It doesn't matter to me what he does beyond Emlyn. If finding the Wizard will keep her alive, I'll do it. Let Lord Vespar do whatever else he pleases."

Isabelle shifted. "Did you know Master Rhys?"

"Not well. I remember Tylysk tormented him to no end, and once I tried to make amends for it when he wasn't looking."

Emlyn tried not to smile too wide.

"Rhys has been my dearest friends since I came here," Isabelle said. "I know he cares for Emlyn, and he would do everything he could for her."

Heldran said nothing.

"Sometimes it's difficult to choose a side. Some days, I choose the Manor and try to keep things calm here. Other days, I miss Rhys so much I could scream. I'd imagine she feels rather the same."

Heldran stayed silent. Emlyn peeked with one eye until he spoke. "How is Mistress Orrtha?"

Isabelle hesitated. "Little better, but I think Emlyn did her some good today. And now that Master Vespar will let them—"

"But there's no sign that she will reclaim her title?"

"She's of no mind to."

Heldran took a deep breath. "How could it be that just as Master Vespar discovers the Enchantress, the Master of the Manor is banished and Lady Orrtha steps down? Lordship fell in his lap."

"He didn't want it," Isabelle said, somewhat crossly. "He tried to stop her."

"And if he draws the Wizard in, what kind of power would he have?"

The hush between them blistered Emlyn's stomach, but they said nothing more. Heldran pulled the blankets over Emlyn's shoulder before he followed Isabelle out of the room.

Emlyn lay awake, too befuddled to sleep. She thought of Rhys far away, and Heldran, and how she loved them both. She realized they'd hate each other now. They stood on different sides. Emlyn didn't know if loving them both was good or bad.

CHAPTER 40

Rhys

Sometime before dawn, when it was pointless to lie awake in bed any longer, I rose and dressed. Da's jerkin fit over the flannel shirt and chainmail. I swung the Gildian green cloak about my shoulders, and the silver eagle pin gleamed on my chest. My new blade secure on my belt, I padded down the stairs.

Nothing but the low embers in the hearth stirred in the kitchen. No one in the next room, either. I stepped out the door into the chilly predawn. A lantern illuminated the back of the house, where Chamberlain kept sleepy guard. I went to stroke his ears.

"It isn't that simple."

Oedolyn's plea froze me. I glimpsed around the corner of the stable, where she and Athrú stood at Starbolt's stall. She wore a simple riding gown and boots, and the lingering moonlight cast a white sheen down her long braid. Athrú was set with his own traveling cloak, swallowed in the dark beyond the lantern's reach. He swung his pack onto his shoulder, but Oedolyn blocked his escape.

"I can't sit here and watch you get wrapped up in this again."

"Then why would I see you do the same?" Athrú's firm tone was as patient as ever. "Why would you leave everything you've built up here?

Your patients, your work—"

"I think you know why," she said gently.

Athrú frowned. "You can't change this, Oedolyn."

"You never gave me a chance. You wouldn't listen to me. I could help you, if you'd let me. Stop laughing at me!"

He'd only smiled on her. He stroked Starbolt's nose. "You have so little confidence in me."

Oedolyn sighed, rubbed her eyes. She stopped him from turning aside, stuttering for another excuse. "Then what will happen to me while you're gone? You were there. You heard what the council thinks will happen."

"You're far enough away from town. They can't find you here. They never have."

Oedolyn searched the stable for the keenest argument. "What about Emlyn?" she said. "That poor girl…she'll need me."

Athrú had no response. I bounced back when they moved. Chamberlain whined and ignored my silent motions to stay put and keep quiet.

"Rhys?"

"What?" I blurted. "'Morning."

Oedolyn stormed to my side. "You tell him."

"Tell him what?"

She sagged. "Maybe you don't need my help, Master Rhys, but Emlyn will. She'll have the lot of you gentlemen," she said, shoving my shoulder. "But she'll need me, too."

The set of Athrú's narrowed brows warned me not to agree.

"It's not my choice," I said.

"It is. It's your task."

"I'm not—"

"Would I help Emlyn or not?"

I sank, avoiding Athrú's eye. "Of course you would."

Oedolyn turned to her brother. "And what will you warriors do with her while you're out warring and scheming?"

I looked away, but Athrú held her gaze. She tiptoed nearer, her features pale in the lantern light. Fear shone in her wide eyes. Not the fear of being left behind, but of being alone, that her one safe haven in the world was wherever her brother went.

If I read it, Athrú did. He sighed and removed the sheathed knife fastened to his belt. He held it level with his sister's eyes. "This does not leave your person."

Oedolyn nodded.

He kissed her brow. "Get your things."

She sprinted to the house. Athrú frowned at me, as if he'd forgotten I was there.

"Sorry," I said. "I shouldn't have…"

He raised a hand to stop me. "She's right about Emlyn; I'll grant her that." Athrú stared at the door a moment, a similar anxiety in his own eyes. He shook his head and tossed his hands up.

A shroud of indigo haloed the trees to the east. A scuff of moon lit the murky sky, and stars shrank from the imminent dawn. Sparkling dew sharpened the dark meadow. The black wall of forest encircled us, alive with early birdsongs.

I looked toward the road. A horde of shadows followed the path and would have been lost to the dark if their movements hadn't exposed them.

I nudged Athrú. He spared them a glance and called Chamberlain away before he barked.

I counted thirty rangers as they neared the lantern light, each garbed the same as their captain—night-blue cloaks and dark leathers, scarves at their throats to cover their faces, bows and full quivers on their backs. Most wielded at least a sword and knife at his hip; a few had a set of daggers. Captain Rodd met us first, with scowling Dair and grinning Braidac at his flank.

"I'm more than grateful for your company," I said, shaking Rodd's hand.

Rodd held his head high with a humble smile. "Lleogren won't abandon this cause so long as we have breath, Master Rhys."

Oedolyn locked the door and turned to startle at the sight of so many rangers. She all but disregarded Braidac's wave and padded to my side, double-checking her medicine satchel.

"Are you sure?" I asked.

"Of course. It would haunt me all my life if I stayed behind."

"You'll be missed."

"Hardly," she snorted, but a sadness followed it. "There are plenty of physicians around who do better work than I."

"What about Starbolt?"

"Eoin will be to fetch him this afternoon." Oedolyn ignored Athrú's look.

Once the troops gathered, Rodd pointed to the south. "We'll follow the river into Gildio and cut south into the city from there. With all the causeways beyond the border guarded, we'll have to find a suitable ford to cross. The forest will conceal us most of the distance."

With that, we broke into the trees and marched toward the river. It serpentined southwest, the tree line hemming its rocky banks. Beech and yew covered us, an occasional giant oak gnarled the leaf-strewn way with its ancient, jutting roots. Braidac strolled beside me, chattering most of the way, unless he managed to steal Oedolyn's attention.

By midday, when we took a brief rest, I was sweltering under my cloak and chain mail. The relief of getting off my feet proved as painful as staying on them. A ranger swatted me in the chest and jested about my miserable city-lad state. If the heat discomfited the rangers in their full garb, it showed only in the glaze of sweat on their brows.

The troops kept conversation subdued on our winding journey, though we were safe within Lleogren's borders. Some of the rangers asked about Gildio's capital. As the Ranger Elite, and oftentimes Lord Cael's delegates, most lords allowed them passage into their lands, but they avoided crowds whenever possible. The idea of leaving the comforts of the wild forest for Gildio's tamed flagstones and overpopulation must have been dismal.

Oedolyn fell into step with me, ducking under a low willow branch. Travel and heat coated her cheeks with red. "Rhys, what about your mother?" she asked. "Now that you can't be lord, she'll still be Lady. What do you think…"

I couldn't answer. Lord Cael was right—Vespar couldn't act without Mam's consent. She'd stand in his way as much as I had, or would, if she could withstand his guile. How long before Vespar tired of playing puppeteer? If something happened to Mam, Gildio was his.

"She'll do what she thinks is right. Won't she?" Oedolyn looked for my assent, but I didn't give it.

We stopped when the horizon halved the sun. The clearing we came upon spread just wide enough for all of us to make camp. Moss-trimmed stones crowded the old autumn leaves. Tree limbs wove into a canopy overhead. A slight breeze kicked up the scent of earth and aged trees, while the thick woods stifled the wildlife chatter.

Chamberlain tagged behind a few rangers who notched their arrows and ventured into the trees again. A few more masked their faces and scattered for a scout ahead. Braidac followed Oedolyn around in search of tubers to add to her satchel. A mage ranger got a fire going. Once the rest of the company settled down to rest, I no longer felt useless doing the same. I flopped in a spread of leaves and guessed at which rangers were mages.

I couldn't watch the rangers skin and butcher the rabbits they retrieved. Chamberlain giddily dropped a fluffy, lifeless mass at my feet. He nosed it closer, begging me to share in his excitement. The same ranger laughed and called me a poor city-lad, and again when I nibbled the tasteless, meager meal.

"It's fresh, anyway," Brai said, shoveling a bite into his mouth.

"I doubt Master Rhys has seen as much travel as you," Rodd said, standing over us. "And something tells me he has a better taste in cooking than most of us."

Brai eyed his next bite with a nauseated pinch to his face. "The things I've had to taste. This is a pastry."

"I won't ask," I said.

Rodd shook his head, smiling. "We'll be kind to you tonight. You two, fourth watch."

When the captain set off to divvy more assignments, Brai bumped me with his elbow. "We got off lucky. Third watch is the killer."

Once supper was eaten, the camp grew busy. Rangers joked to one another, some whetting or oiling their blades and bows. Oedolyn laid out her sleeping roll, which Chamberlain claimed for himself. Dair squatted on a fallen tree and whittled his walking staff, his hard eye coursing back and forth across the camp. Braidac scooted over to make room in the tree-root bunk he was lounging in. I bundled my cloak around myself against the knotted discomfort and flopped down next to him.

Across the clearing, Athrú spoke low to Rodd. The captain listened with a small frown and an occasional glance around, often to Oedolyn or me. He ruminated a while before answering. Athrú's expression exposed less of the discussion than Rodd's.

"What's that?" Braidac pointed with the tip of his bow.

I looked at my hands, not knowing I'd taken Flannery's letter from my pocket. I stowed the parchments away. "It's nothing. It's...not important."

Brai raised a brow. "Sure. What's her name?"

"What?"

"It's from a girl, isn't it? Maybe someone an exile left behind?"

I tightened my cloak around me. "It's not like that, exactly."

"Uh huh. Then what's it like, exactly?"

I glimpsed around, finding no one taking particular notice of our conversation. Athrú returned to Oedolyn's side, I supposed to relay whatever Rodd had told him. They paid us no mind.

I heaved a deep breath. "She's, er...her name is Isabelle," I said, cringing. "She's a friend. We were engaged, but her parents decided they didn't like my da's politics."

"Ah. Because I could've sworn you were pining, the way you were holding those papers, and how you keep looking at Oedolyn."

My face flushed. "I don't keep looking at Oedolyn," I whispered. "Even if I did, how would you notice, as much as you stare at her yourself?"

Brai shoved me, grinning. "I don't stare, I *admire*. And I rather admire the way her hair straggles out of her braid."

I didn't look. I'd been thinking most of the day how Flannery's hair had looked like that after she'd climbed a tree.

Brai nodded toward Athrú. "He's a quiet one. He's the one who found you, right? Seeing you through to the end, hm?"

His grin faded when I shared what Athrú told me the day before, standing amid Windborough's streets. Brai ran a hand along his bow. A sad smile quirked his mouth.

"I sometimes think I should take some of the lads, and we'd hunt down the Hunters, so to speak," he said, motioning to his comrades. "Silent raids, rescue whoever we can, get them home." Brai scowled. "They sicken me. It's a game to them. And what they possibly think they can gain from it, who knows, but something has to keep them at it for this long. Sheer depravity, if nothing else." Brai shook his head, stretched, and sank into his tree-root cradle.

Staying at Oedolyn's side, Athrú propped himself against a boulder. Chamberlain sprawled on his lap. He stared into the low embers of the fire, his weary face empty.

"Do you know the story about Tenbur and the Ice Peak dragons?" Brai asked.

I blinked. "I think—"

"Not the way I've told it." Brai raised a finger. "Humor me."

The next few days were little different. The river took a wide swoop northward and wandered away from the trees. Rodd opted against straying from the cover of forest to follow it. It would course its way back, and we'd follow it again if we didn't stray too far south.

The dragon kept low, except the occasional grumble or shift to be sure I acknowledged his presence. Every so often, he turned his face to me, stared a moment, and looked away. If he was searching for pity, I gave him none.

Athrú arranged practice scrimmages with the rangers in the evenings when we made camp. Though I thought I'd improved under Athrú's tutelage, the rangers proved impossible to force out of the circle. But I stayed on my feet longer; I doubted the rangers put a fraction of their usual training effort into it.

The fifth night, I spotted Dair watching us practice. He kept to the back of the line and to himself. He hadn't said a sentence to me since we'd set out.

Braidac caught me staring at the old ranger as we finished a scrimmage. We dropped on a fallen tree and took our share of supper from Rodd.

"You know about Dair, don't you?" Brai said. He kept his back to the comrade in question. "He's a hero, you know. He's done unbelievable things, including saving Lord Cael's father from a cavalier and taking a javelin in the leg for it, when he was in the army."

My brows went up. "And he could still be a ranger?"

"Ah, just took a few good healers to get him up again. Besides, that was years ago, before he joined the Elite." Brai leaned closer. "Don't be fooled by the whole walking stick thing. My story about the troll wasn't that far off."

I risked another glimpse at Dair. The gruff ranger sat on a boulder, smoothing his knife along his staff. "He sat next to me at the council meeting," I said.

"He's in there sometimes," Brai answered around a bite of cheese. "Lord Cael likes to keep him around. He's clever with war matters and such."

Brai waved cheerfully when Dair caught him staring. "He likes his space. Puts a word in every now and then, but for the most part, we let him be. He's not so bad. Seems all rock and shade, but he has a decent sense of humor if you catch him in the right mood."

I looked at my food in time to avoid Dair's shifting gaze. He sheathed his knife, leaned on his staff, and moved on.

"The right mood, mind." Brai grinned.

I took a drink from my water pouch. "He and Master Corrick are dear friends," I said.

Brai snorted. "Dair says Master Corrick makes things difficult just because he can."

"Are all Lord Mages that way, then?"

Brai crooked a smile, but lowered his voice. "They've been at each other's throats since Master Corrick got here, back when Cael became lord. He won't say what, but Dair has something against mages, I think. Even gets grumbly with ours here sometimes." He nodded to a few other rangers milling about camp. "But I hear Master Corrick isn't exactly faultless, either."

"What makes you say that?" Athrú's voice came from overhead.

Brai jumped. "The things I hear, of course," he said, watching Athrú settle against the log beside us.

"How many of them are true?" he asked.

Brai shrugged. "Some. Some say the Academy rubbed off on him too much, and he's for the Hunt. Rodd said he made a fuss about it at a council meeting once, so that's at least true," he answered Athrú's skeptical look. "And who knows but that he and Vespar are on decent terms."

I grimaced. "He was rather interested in our plans."

"Well, we are supposed to tell the council what we're doing in case things wriggle out of our hands, which they never do."

Athrú massaged the scrimmage ache from his shoulder, the firelight glowing on the sharp line of his mouth. "That doesn't put him in league with Vespar. But he was a little beside himself when we met with Rodd."

Dair cut our discussion short by trundling past close enough to hear. Brai shrugged, mashed the rest of his cheese into his mouth, and lounged in a tree-root bed. Athrú left to chase his dog from Oedolyn's sleeping place.

The next evening, I might as well not have entered the training circle. Bout after bout, I sprawled in the dirt or dropped my sword, or a ranger pinned me back with a blade across my chest or neck. The rangers were well at home in the tangled sanctuary of the trees and made light work of navigating the inhibiting terrain. The thick forest squashed me into submission as much as my dueling partners did.

Taking a drink from my pouch, I glanced around to see Dair perched on another boulder seat, whittling his staff. He waved me over.

"You've tried that same move four times now," he said, "and three of the four, it's landed you on your backside. Don't you think they'd have caught on?"

"Which move?"

Dair's expression made it clear that my ignorance was imbecilic at best. "Upward strike, down to the right with a sidestep into your opponent's foot while trying to get behind him."

I thought through my last duel. "I hadn't noticed," I muttered.

"Then you must not notice all the other blunders you're making. None of them are improving, either." Dair eyed me, motioned for me to bend down. "These lads are going easy on you, and they're still better than you in every way. What d'you have that they don't?"

Nothing I could think of. They were stealthier, cleverer, always knew what to expect. Brutally quick and strong. Compared to them, I was as threatening as a wet rag.

Dair touched the tip of his knife to my heart. "Nothing wrong with a little help, aye?"

The dragon cocked his head.

I swallowed my astonishment. If nothing else was cheating, that was, and I told him so.

The ranger darkened. "Battle's not about being fair. It's about making it out alive."

He scraped his knife off Da's jerkin, leaving a crease in the leather. When I stood grimacing at him, he waved for me to get on with training.

What was I supposed to think? I wouldn't risk the lives of my comrades, my friends, just to beat them in training. I'd rather swallow both my pride and a mouthful of dirt before I let the dragon slip. Besides, how did Dair know about my draconis?

The dragon thought nothing of it. He rather liked Dair now. No one else ever invited him to play.

I glanced around the rangers, dreading another bone-rattling spill. I could expect them to go easy on me, but what would I do when I confronted someone determined to kill me? How could I save myself, without…

Stop that, I hissed. *I hate it when you do that.*

You must think on it sooner or later. I only prompted.

Do you have to take over my head when you do it?

The dragon held his regal head high.

I looked to Dair. The war-hardened ranger had to have confronted a draconis before. If everyone else insisted I was different from my fellow monstrosities, perhaps he saw what made me different. He thought I could handle myself at the hands of the beast outside my head too.

"You're sure?" I asked.

Dair waved me away.

Heaving a deep breath, I strode to the training circle. The dragon slinked to the center of my chest to shove me along.

The sooner you overcome your pride, the better for the both of us and your companions, he said. *Have it done.*

I glared at him, but said nothing to counter. I stepped into the dirt ring, shook the nervous shudder from my hand, and grasped the hilt of my blade.

To my dismay, Captain Rodd crossed swords with me. I met his steady eye and concentrated. The hair on the back of my neck prickled.

Nothing funny, I said.

The dragon waited and watched.

I wasn't sure what to do. I imagined the dragon's strength—the sword went feather light in my hand. I withdrew, but the beast offered enough muscle to withstand my opponent. His senses extended.

The din of forest life thrummed, riding the sound of stretching leathers, rustling cloaks, creaking trees. The slightest breeze kicked up the scent of sweat and earth, the smoking tinder in the fire, the herbs Oedolyn rearranged in her satchel.

The dragon centered in on my opponent. The sound of Rodd's heartbeat distracted me, made my own speed up. I caught the scent of leftover jerky grease on his fingers tight on his hilt, the oil he'd cleaned the blade with the night before, the trickle of sweat down his temple into his beard. The dragon ignored it all. He took stance and stared the captain down.

Athrú counted from three.

My blade hurled toward Rodd's wrist. He ripped his sword up against mine, knocking me away, but the dragon planted my feet before I lost balance. The beast parried every blow until Rodd sidestepped and swung down at my leg. I bounced out of range. I made to hack downward from overhead, but the dragon redirected my sword to hook under Rodd's. He staggered back to avoid the upward slice to his chest. I ducked under his arm, drove my shoulder into his side, and sent him barreling across my back.

Rodd slid to the ground, swept his leg at my ankles. The dragon twisted me around to somersault to my feet in time to block the captain's downward swing on the way up. I drove his blade to the side, circled down, and stabbed.

Rodd went rigid with the blunt side of my blade poised against his ribs. He showed no surprise, but his rangers gawked around us. The captain smiled, bowed, and surrendered.

"Unconventional, I suppose," he said, shaking my hand, "but effective. Sir Dair had some good advice for you."

When I looked around for the old ranger, he'd moved off somewhere else.

I turned to meet Brai's stunned chatter and commendation, Athrú silent at his side. I couldn't read his expression, but the shame arose within me all the same.

The dragon withdrew when I ordered him to. He fixed his crimson gaze on me.

Do you see?

I refused to answer. He receded.

Athrú woke me late into the night for my watch. I took the spot beside drooping Braidac. I shifted my sword onto my lap and scrubbed the sleep from my eyes. Brai sucked a deep breath and tossed his head up, stayed awake by clapping his face.

"Is first watch any better?" I groaned.

Brai yawned. "Dunno. Depends."

"You've done it a lot."

"Most nights, going on four years." Brai shrugged. "I'm the newest recruit, if you haven't noticed. And all the others have at least ten years on me."

"You must be good. You're an Elite."

Brai's grin glinted white in the moonlight. "As a matter of fact, I happen to be a fairly excellent marksman. Two hundred yards. In the dark, if need be. And no exaggerating."

I cocked a brow.

"Rodd can tell you. And he'll tell you how I broke through a man's armor, leather, *and* mail, at that distance, and still caught him in the heart."

"Really? At two hundred yards? Was it in the dark?"

Brai glowered. "I'll admit, it wasn't. But it happened, whatever you think. Bet you've never touched a bow in your life."

I let him have the victory.

He fingered the longbow in his lap, a caress down the polished surface. Intricate carvings wove down either side of the grip. I couldn't recall seeing it anywhere but his hand, except the few times he strapped it to his back.

"My dad made me a bow before I could even say his name," he said. "Had me training on it soon as I could pull the string. I was winning tournaments against grown men when I was ten."

That, somehow, was easier to believe. "Was he a ranger, too?"

"No, but he could've been. He was in the army. They put him on the wall and let him loose. Till the enemy broke through once, stormed the keep and cost him his leg." Brai made a clean severing motion below his right knee. "That's why he wasn't a ranger. Well, besides Mum. Sad, but lucky, I s'pose." Brai made an odd smile. "If he had been, I might not be here."

"So you're the ranger instead."

He shrugged. His grin diminished. "A rather roundabout way of explaining it, I suppose."

The glint in his eye spoke of a story on his lips, but the fact that he didn't leap at the chance to relate it told me he wasn't of a mind to. I didn't pry.

"Lord Cael told me I was like Haylad," I said before the silence settled. Brai perked up. "I don't know anything about him, except he found Praed's staff."

"Then you don't know he dueled Lyrus Nightstride."

My brows went up. Nightstride, as infamous as Silverblade and Tenbur were celebrated; Tenbur's apprentice who turned to dark magicks.

Brai smirked, knowing he'd snared me. He leaned against his tree. "Nightstride wanted the staff, so he followed Haylad until he cornered him in the mountains in Priodas. And Nightstride defeated him."

"What?"

"He did. At least, that's what he'd like you to think."

Brai waited for me to break his dramatic silence. "And?"

He grinned.

At the end of the second week, Rodd told us we had crossed the border.

His men kept their bows in hand. I followed their example when they pulled their hoods down over their eyes. No one dared speak. Everyone hushed their movements, though Athrú's, Oedolyn's, and mine whispered over the forest noise. Athrú kept his sister near while Braidac stood guard over me. They both undoubtedly shared my thoughts.

As of that moment, Vespar had every right to kill me.

CHAPTER 41

Tylysk

Isabelle stood in the doorway across the room, peeking into the bedchamber, candlelight swathing her face in gold. Beyond the door, Heldran laughed as Emlyn related her silly adventures with Aria. Emlyn yawned, and Heldran whispered through a lullaby. Isabelle smiled.

Tylysk tried to remember the last time she'd smiled at him. He could recall once, when they first met. He was thirteen, and she a scrawny girl of eight, clumsy with her curtsies and bedecked in an inordinate number of ribbons in her hair. She had three gaping holes in her teeth and said his name with such a lisp, he cringed.

He hadn't cared for her then, except her feisty retorts were laughable, and it mortified Rhys when she came to his rescue. But, as Isabelle grew out of her scrawniness, and she bloomed to loveliness, and her wit sharpened, Tylysk found himself liking her ferocity. She'd grown bored of dealing with him, despite the sincerity in his kindness toward her. When he hoped he'd made it known that he…well, he couldn't stand to be away from her. That he liked her. Loved her.

It stung—for all his efforts, Isabelle seldom acknowledged him with more than a scowl. He understood he wasn't exactly blameless in some respects, but he was trying. Didn't that account for something? Anything?

Tylysk cherished her averted smile, knowing it would vanish when she turned to see him standing there. When she did, he looked away. He'd rather stare at his feet than see her beautiful smile twist and have his heart plummet for the thousandth time.

Isabelle closed the bedchamber door and stalked to him, head high as a swan's. "Did you need something?"

Tylysk looked from the floor to her eyes, both the same hue of warm, dark mahogany. A wisp of hair caressed her cheek. And pale red lips, lightly pursed, tender and waiting.

"No." He straightened from the doorframe. "Unless you were leaving. I'll walk you to your chambers."

His dejectedness must have shown through his own smile. Isabelle's sternness softened, though she eyed him. She stepped out to the hall ahead of him. Silence barreled down on them. From the corner of his eye, Tylysk watched her delicate fingers knot together. She broke the quiet with a sigh.

"I suppose I should tell you how impressed I am. When Emlyn first told me you promised to take her riding, I laughed. But look at you."

That was uplifting—as close to a compliment as she ever offered him.

In truth, Tylysk hadn't expected to take Emlyn as many places as often as he did. At least he had the girl in the palm of his hand, and she worked hard for her rewards. Little could impress Tylysk, but Emlyn's progress over these past weeks stunned him. She molded more and more into an Enchantress every day.

"She says she enjoys your outings," said Isabelle. "You?"

Tylysk glanced at her, finding sharp expectancy. "I suppose."

"You're only doing your job."

"It is my job."

"Then you don't enjoy it."

"I didn't say—"

"But you won't admit it." Isabelle glared at the passing tapestries. "Poor thing."

Tylysk made a face. "Poor thing?"

"Can't you imagine what she's thinking? Rhys saved her life, and you ship him away for it and do the same yourselves. A month ago, she believed she was dead. Now, after your silly games, she doesn't know whether to hold onto Rhys or submit to you."

"Submit to living in a palace where no one can touch her? How awful," Tylysk said. "I'd much rather wander the country with a convict, never knowing when I'm going to eat or where I'll lie down at night."

"That's not fair—"

"It is. Had Rhys smuggled her out, they wouldn't have lasted long."

"I'm just saying, she's conflicted," Isabelle snapped. "Between you and Heldran on one side and the man who rescued her on the other, she doesn't know her head from her foot."

"Man," Tylysk scoffed.

"Yes. He's braver than most and certainly better."

Isabelle held her head high and defiant. The magelights gleamed on her dark hair, cast her lithe shadow across the cold walls. Tylysk traced the hilt of his dagger with a finger.

"Are you conflicted?" he asked.

"No. I am loyal to my lady."

Tylysk grimaced. Who was Orrtha now? Lord Vespar had been more than gracious in letting her stay at the Manor, after what she'd done to him. How she tried to snare him, determined to punish him for her frailties. Isabelle toed a precarious line.

"Say, perchance, Mistress Orrtha doesn't recover," he said.

"She will. Emlyn has worked miracles with her."

"Yet, say she doesn't. What would you do then?"

"I don't know. Perhaps I'd go home to my mother."

Tylysk swallowed his annoyance. "If Lord Vespar allowed it. You still forget you are in his charge. Would you not be loyal to him?"

Isabelle looked at the passing magelights rather than at him.

Tylysk spread his arms. "What are we doing that's so terrible?"

She rolled her eyes.

"So you don't want me to take Emlyn riding?"

"No, you…" Isabelle huffed. "Never mind. You're so wrapped up in your schemes. Go on, then. Do as you please."

Tylysk's face burned when she slashed him with a lethal glance. He reached for her hand. "Isabelle," he tried. She quickened her pace. "If I don't understand, help me to."

"Why? So you can be a more obedient dog?"

He fought not to be stung. "So I can help Emlyn."

"Ha."

Tylysk sped ahead of her and sidled in front of her chamber door. "This is my duty, yes, but Emlyn trusts me too," he said. "If there's something to be taken care of, help me do it."

Isabelle curled and uncurled her fists, face scarlet. He'd shaken her, at least. She didn't know whether to rage at him or forgive his blunder. She let Tylysk grasp her hand, met his eye. Hers glistened with her beautiful ferocity.

"No." Isabelle stood away from him. "You've done your damage. You've put her on the front lines, and she will stay there until either you or Rhys takes the final blow."

"Let's not be dramatic—"

"Please. Stubborn Rhys won't let this rest, and even you don't think he's stupid enough to go at it alone. If I were Lord Vespar, I'd be terrified to have him out of my sight."

"Lord Vespar would fight back."

Isabelle's lips quirked. "Let's not be dramatic, Tylysk."

She slammed the door behind her.

Tylysk leaned against the wall, rubbed his weary eyes. Feeling ridiculous, outwitted, and furious for somehow erring so atrociously, he trudged to his chambers. Thinking, for the first time, for as much as he loved her, no one could make him feel as poorly as Isabelle did.

Late into the night, the brewing clouds burst. A thunderclap woke Tylysk, though he hadn't quite been asleep. Isabelle's reprimand kept him tossing. He thought to open the window and air out the stuffy, sweltering room, but hail pelted the glass, and gusts whistled down the fireplace chimney. He stared at the canopy while thunder drummed overhead. In a few moments, another lightning strike followed, white through the cracks of his bedcurtains.

Could it really have been six weeks since Emlyn came? The days eluded him, once Emlyn started behaving herself. Tylysk no longer thought about taking her riding, or out to play with Aria, or to the sweets shop at the end of the week. Outings had become as routine as lessons.

Once she'd grown used to Tylysk, Emlyn became an absolute babbler. She was always at one question or another, sometimes asking before he finished answering the previous one. He watched her play her pretend games, and on rare occasions, Emlyn invited him to join. After Aria displayed her modest array of marbles, Emlyn begged Tylysk to teach her to play.

He couldn't help thinking she smiled at him more than Isabelle ever had.

Tylysk scrubbed his face—the cut through his chin stung as it stretched. He forgot the wound sometimes, and he couldn't decide whether it was because it was new, or because it was so wholly a part of him now. Remembering that horrific day made the scars on his arms itch.

As he thought of the brief moments before the attack, a sickening hollowness churned Tylysk's stomach. Emlyn's face, her terror, her stream of tears. How she cowered from him, pleading for her life in the tiniest, trembling voice. Tylysk shook the memory away, but it persisted, vibrant and violent as the lightning beyond his bedcurtains.

Whatever Isabelle thought, Tylysk had enough sense to know Emlyn was conflicted. He'd been there from the start, the moment of her discovery, and she'd seldom been anywhere but at his side since. Tylysk couldn't be sure of what Isabelle accused him, ignorance or callousness, or both. But Emlyn was happy—what did it matter if he enjoyed their outings together as long as she did?

Tylysk froze with his hands on his face. He shot up, focused, and extended the slightest thread of magic. The sound beyond his bedchamber silenced. He withdrew, thinking perhaps Heldran or Emlyn was awake in the next room.

It came again. The merciless squeal of the ancient hinges on his antechamber door stopped, then moaned as the intruder inched it open. Tylysk slid to his feet, groping for his dagger on the nightstand. He left the sheath behind and slinked for the door. Lightning glinted white-hot on the blade. Tylysk pressed his ear to the door, but heard nothing else.

In the same moment as a thunderclap, something thudded beyond the door. The table, he thought—it scraped across the floor. Perhaps the intruder was searching for something. He didn't dare extend his senses. If whoever lurked there was a mage, he'd detect Tylysk's spell.

Then, for a dreadful moment…Emlyn.

Thunder roared, simultaneous with a crack of lightning. The hair on the back of his neck stood on end. Emlyn screamed.

Tylysk raised his dagger and flung the door wide.

Emlyn squealed. Her eyes glowed white in the dark, wide as gold pieces.

Tylysk lowered his dagger, breathing again. He waved the magelights on. "Skin and bones, Emlyn. What are you doing in here?"

Her arms constricted around her doll's neck. Another shatter of lightning, and Emlyn shrieked and smothered her face in its hair. She scuttled into Tylysk's leg.

He set the dagger on the table and knelt down. "It's just noise. It can't hurt you."

She blushed, but when another thunderbolt lit the room, she ducked into his chest.

"Emlyn, what are you doing in here?"

"The storm."

"Where's Heldran?"

"Working."

"This late?"

"He always works this late."

Tylysk rolled his eyes. That explained Heldran's potions, if he was working to all hours of the morning.

Emlyn clamped her hands over her ears and squeezed her eyes shut.

"All right, all right. Just till the storm passes."

She hugged him around the neck, her doll dangling down his back. Tylysk flopped into his armchair and cradled the girl on his lap. Emlyn nuzzled her face on his shoulder.

Another pelting hailstorm roused Emlyn more. She cowered from the unyielding downpour and every flash and rumble. Tylysk laid his head back. If Isabelle could see him now, she might not have been so brusque with him.

Some while later, as the storm ebbed, Emlyn peeked up with her head heavy on his shoulder. "Does your scar still hurt?"

Tylysk fingered the crevice through his lip. "Not usually."

"Did it hurt really bad?"

Tylysk remembered little else of the attack. His memory clouded around how it happened. The worst pain came from his eye, then his cheek—those drowned the rest. One eye saw red blood, the other glints of flailing blue. After the slash to his face, he couldn't feel the claws hacking down his arms. He was too confounded, too numb with agony.

Emlyn sat up, flinching at distant thunder. She studied his wound from his jaw to where it broke his left brow in two. "I'm sorry he did that to you."

Tylysk said nothing, but she interpreted his silent seething well enough. "Why did he do it? Rhys wouldn't hurt anyone."

"No? Not what you thought of him, is he?"

Emlyn lowered her sleepy eyes. "But what happened to him?"

Tylysk frowned, trying to appear sympathetic, for her sake. "He… became a monster, Emlyn. He has a real monster inside him."

Her brows narrowed, a skepticism to the sad set of her mouth, despite the evidence vivid on Tylysk's face. "Inside?" she asked.

"It lives inside him. Sometimes it comes out, and he hurts people. You're lucky he didn't hurt you."

Tylysk expected the same reply as usual. Rhys loved her, and on and on. It didn't come, but something like it tried to cross her face. She couldn't muster it.

"He can't hurt you anymore. You're safe here." He grimaced. "Would I ever hurt you, Emlyn?"

"Never."

A grin crept up on his face. Emlyn showed him a rosy smile, interrupted by a yawn. She made to settle down, but laid a gentle hand on his chest, propped herself up, and kissed the slice through his cheek.

Tylysk let her nestle down. One last rumble of thunder, and Emlyn fell asleep.

It came soft as the lips on his cheek. Bafflingly too, after brooding over Isabelle. Emlyn loved him. And no one had ever loved him the way she did. No one had ever needed him the way she did.

He'd never recognized how small she was. This Enchantress of incomprehensible power, the answer to his master's injustice, the hinge on which Caeradin turned, was a lonely little girl frightened by a summer storm.

Tylysk cradled Emlyn nearer and rested his scarred cheek on her brow. She hummed in her sleep.

CHAPTER 42

Rhys

Rhys.

I shot up. Brai jerked in his sleep next to me, but returned to his lopsided slumber. No one else stirred. My head pounded. Irritated, I waited for the dragon to say more. Nothing.

Moonlight severed the chilly glade, illuminating half in pale gray. Night creatures chittered in the shaded forest. Athrú's shadowed form huddled against a tree across the clearing, but the polished tip of his scabbard caught the light and cast a diagonal stripe under his eye. Oedolyn nestled safe nearby, Chamberlain curled up at her back. As I dropped down beside Athrú, I spotted Rodd leaning against an oak across the clearing.

"Not your watch yet," Athrú whispered.

"Can't sleep."

"Something bothering you?"

"A little."

He understood. Oedolyn twisted in her sleep, a pinch to her brows. Her disquiet reminded me of their dispute the morning we set out. It wasn't the first time they'd hinted at previous misadventures. I didn't want to ask, but the question simmered in my chest.

"Oedolyn's brave to come along," I said. "Emlyn will adore her."

Athrú said nothing. The reflected light cut across his frown.

"She worries about you. She doesn't like it when you're gone too long. I don't blame her." I leaned against the rough tree. "I suppose that's how Emlyn feels, waiting for us."

"Oedolyn never had anything to fear for me."

"She did this time." I twiddled a dry twig between my fingers. "Have you been as many places as Brai claims he has?"

"Hardly. Nor have my travels been as…extraordinary, shall we say."

I snorted. "That's one word for it." I looked across the glade, where the rangers slumbered tight in their cloaks and sleeping rolls, some cradled in the lowest branches of the surrounding oaks. Athrú hushed Chamberlain when he grumbled and wriggled onto his back for the most uncomfortable sleeping position.

Rhys.

His voice came from the right. I looked, expecting to see something of him on my shoulder. Chamberlain raised his head, ears pricked.

Athrú sat forward, scanning the trees. In the same moment, Rodd straightened from his tree, eyes fixed on the grass. He crept to one of his rangers and tapped him twice on the knee with his foot. The ranger lay still. The captain returned to his post. All sense of quiet lifted from camp.

A spell tingled at the back of my head. It dulled to a low pulse thrumming upward from the forest floor. I searched around, hoping it was coming from one of our mage comrades. Chamberlain cocked his head, sniffed the air, and bared his teeth.

Rhys!

The arrow hissed past me, so close its breeze stung my eyes.

We launched to our feet, swords raised. Oedolyn bolted up and stumbled to her brother's protection with his longknife in both hands. Arrows and curses darted from the darkness on all sides. Athrú knocked Oedolyn down in his scramble to shield her. Someone yanked my cloak and jerked me to the ground. Braidac bounced in front of me, bow bent.

"Stay down," he ordered.

I rolled onto my stomach and ducked my head. The troop closed ranks around us. Mage rangers cast misty white shields between us and the trees. Darts struck the impenetrable barriers and hung stagnant in the air. A flick of his arm, and a mage volleyed the arsenal through the dark. Screams splintered the woods. Below me, the vibrations drummed stronger.

The oncoming barrage shifted from darts to curses alone. The mages braced themselves. A final, fiery impact shattered the shield to my right, thrusting its wielder to the ground.

"Back!" Rodd commanded.

I scrabbled across the clearing on my stomach, Oedolyn at my side. When the volleys ceased, Athrú drew her up, and I scrambled to my feet next to Brai. Moonlight glistened on the sweat trickling down his temple. My hands trembled on the hilt of my sword.

Brai bolted.

"Where are you going?" I shouted.

The enemy emerged from nowhere. Some sixty men, huge, hooded, and masked, funneled into the clearing yards beyond the tree line, smashing through their own invisible barrier, their savage blades glinting. Too many hands sparked with readied spells. Behind me, the clash of steel made my blood run cold. Braidac, the coward—where did he go?

Oedolyn's knife barely missed my gut when Athrú thrust her in my direction. "Get out of here," he said. He jabbed a finger at me. "Don't you leave her."

The dragon silenced my protest. I gripped Oedolyn's wrist and ran. Acrid curses burst around us. Oedolyn dodged the swipes of our enemies, her knife slicing into a pursuer's arm, stunning herself more than him. The foe charged us, disregarding the rangers unless one got in his way.

"They know it's you," Oedolyn said. "They know who you are."

She whipped aside with a shriek. The axman behind us coiled her braid around his fist and wrenched her backward. The pain weakened her hold on my wrist. Before I could raise my sword to him, a chink through chain mail and a thud of pierced flesh halted the foe. He grasped at his throat. Oedolyn collapsed on top of him. An arrow protruded from the muscle between his shoulder and neck at such an angle, it had to have come from above.

I glanced at the branches overhead. Braidac's shadow balanced on the thin limbs, raining arsenal on the enemy.

Chamberlain bellowed over the fray. Choked screams and the stench of smoke overpowered the tiny battlefield. As we crossed the moonlight into shadow, Dair barreled out of the woods and slammed his staff into an enemy's back.

"Off with you, 'fore I let them have your hide!"

I redirected Oedolyn through a breach between battlers. My grip on her wrist weakened as my hands flared with heat.

Not yet, I said. *Not now.*

They will follow you. You cannot overcome them alone.

A little strength. That's all I need.

His huge face glared. *You are wrong.*

He summoned enough power to swat our assailants out of our way and into their comrades. Their scuffle opened a breach in the skirmish. Oedolyn slipped into the trees and grabbed my hand.

I jarred backward, and my cloak and pin jerked into my throat. I choked. My legs went liquid. The foe parried my flails, flung me to the ground. My foot sank into his gut and sent him sprawling. Answering Oedolyn's screams, Chamberlain pounced and chomped into his leg, teeth sinking into his flesh. The attacker howled and kicked him away. Chamberlain hobbled after us into the woods.

The enemy captain's command roared over the din, ordering our pursuit. Arrows and spells whistled around us and cracked into the trees. The night-veiled forest strangled the earth with roots and foliage. The tree canopy blocked every trace of moonlight.

Useless in the crowded woods, the arsenal stopped flying. Three glowing magelights brightened the enemies' paths, suspended above mages' clawed fingers. The ache in my head spiked. The dragon growled in pain.

Oedolyn pulled up short. Ahead, four more magelights glared through the trees. We swerved to the right and sped on.

We faltered into another glade. Thinking fast, or not at all, I released Oedolyn's hand and turned back. She and Chamberlain staggered to a halt.

"Rhys, you can't fight them," she said, panting. "There are too many. We have to keep going."

"They'll overrun us. Besides, I'd like to see who's after us."

"What does it matter who? You know why they're here."

I exchanged her terrified glance. The moonlight quivered on her knife.

Magelights simmered from all sides and merged together to come straight toward us. Smoke curled from between the dragon's jaws. I swallowed.

"Take Chamberlain and go. They won't follow you. They want me."

Oedolyn stood her ground.

"I can't stop them alone. I don't want to hurt you."

She stepped away. "You wouldn't…"

A crack ripped through the glade, and a burst of evaporating scarlet fire seared between the trees. Chamberlain bolted. Another explosion flared nearer to us. I doubled over, agonized by the mage curse. The dragon writhed.

The third sulfuric eruption knocked us off our feet. By the time Oedolyn and I recovered, the enemy trampled out of the trees, jagged weapons raised. Two seized Oedolyn and disarmed her of her knife. I sheathed my sword and lifted my hands before two more piled on me. A dagger edged my spine. Archers and mages stood by with darts and spells notched.

Where were the rangers? Where was Athrú?

The men stood aside to let their dark-cloaked captain pass. He laid his hood back, exposing a pale, rugged face and near-black eyes. A white scar cut across his throat, as if he'd survived someone slitting it. The moon glowed crimson on his tainted longsword. The one time I might have welcomed the dragon's aid, and he hesitated. He eyed the enemy commander, poised for attack.

Oedolyn staggered. She gaped behind the hand clapped over her mouth. Her detainer swore at her last attempt to wrench free.

The captain froze where he stood. He stared at Oedolyn, face empty of all but subtle, wide-eyed shock. He paid me no mind and crept forward, sword hanging at his side. He looked her over, the way someone would look over a child he hadn't seen since she'd grown.

Oedolyn lost all her strength to her terror. The captain glowered when her captor thrust her up again. She cried into the hand across her face.

The dragon stayed still, watching.

The commander sharpened his glare, and the hand dropped from Oedolyn's mouth. Tears dribbled down her ashen cheeks. She took the courage to meet the captain's gaze. He smiled.

"My lovely." He broke the distance between them, lurking as though she were a doe about to bolt. She faced him, resigned, but dreading.

He scooped the tears off her throat and lifted her face. "Look at you," he said. "Look at you, my lovely." He brushed a thumb over her wrinkled chin, stooped down.

"Excuse me. I'm over here."

Nothing else I'd done had drawn his attention in the least. He eyed me, bored and inconvenienced. A sob squeezed from Oedolyn's throat around his fingers.

"She's done nothing wrong," I said. "You won't get any reward for her."

He arched his brows, perhaps impressed with my simplemindedness. He let his hand fall from Oedolyn's face.

"What is this, my sweet?" He gestured to me with a lazy motion of his blade. "I wouldn't have imagined you stirring yourself into this boy's affairs. Or, perhaps, it's rather telling to find you here." The captain eyed me again. "The rumors are true, then. But what I find curious…" He grasped Oedolyn by the chin. "You let him near you."

Oedolyn trembled. "It's not what you think," she said.

"Then what is it, pretty one?"

"Your employer doesn't want to be kept waiting," I spat. "Let her alone and do your job."

The captain pursed his lips, swept a strand of hair from Oedolyn's eyes. "Give me a moment." He turned to me.

"No, Righnách, please."

He frowned at her. Oedolyn cowered from the slightest heat of it. Righnách smiled his approval and came face to face with me. The dagger slid down my back.

"Eager to face your judgment, Master Rhys, and to send your friends to the same? Even she helped a criminal break his exile." Righnách shook his head. "But I would never do that to you, would I, my queen?"

Oedolyn shuddered, face scarlet.

Righnách returned to me. "Pity. Not a day within the border and you've met the hangman. You should have stayed away, Master Rhys. I hear your witch brat is better off now than you've ever been."

I refused to be thrown.

Righnách shrugged, glancing me over like an old horse he might buy. His eye caught on my sword's dragon pommel. He struck his plain blade in the dead grass and stole mine from its sheath. The dagger moved to my neck when I struggled. Righnách tested the blade for himself, ran it between his fingers, studied its ornaments.

Why aren't you doing anything? I demanded.

Wait.

Oh, now you'll be patient?

Righnách narrowed his eyes at me, returned to studying my sword. "Much has changed since you left Gildio, Master Rhys. You wouldn't recognize it."

"I didn't leave Gildio."

"Right. They threw you out. Tells you what your people think of you."

The dragon snarled at him for me.

"Please," Oedolyn tried, voice trembling, "let Rhys go. If—if you—"

"You know better than to play that game with me," Righnách said, laughing.

"Then make your move," I said. "Wait much longer, the Ranger Elite will be on you."

"That will be something to see if they make it out of there alive."

I glared, fuming.

Righnách slithered to me, smiling as if on a child. "You're so well behaved, hatchling. Believe me, you'll wish you hadn't restrained the beast," he said. "Now I know why your master sent me to hunt you down. I know what it takes to slay a draconis."

He shook his head at Oedolyn. "But what a terrible waste, my lovely. He's so young. I doubt he's met his companion properly, has he?"

He tipped the point of my sword to my stomach. Oedolyn cried for him to stop. Her captor stifled her with a bloodstained hand.

What are you waiting for?

The dragon did nothing. He crept backward. I was alone.

Righnách opened his mouth to speak.

The smallest thrust.

I didn't feel the blade go in. I felt the warmth, my tunic sticking to it, felt it rising up my throat and spilling sickly heat into my mouth. My body rippling, my lungs shriveling, the waves of Oedolyn's shriek.

Righnách stood over me. He patted my face. "Come out and play, little beast."

The nightmarish shadows consumed the starless glade, Oedolyn, the army. I moved, flailed. Steaming wet seeped through my teeth, between my fingers, down the backs of my hands. The darkness muted and warped any sound outside stretching muscles. With every breath, I tasted and inhaled smoke.

And the freedom. The escape.

"Rhys, stop!"

The shrill cry cut through the muffled tumult. A blade skidded off the scales on my neck. I couldn't stop moving. The raging energy, the crushed vitality, was limitless.

"*Rhys!*"

I froze. The shadows lifted. The dragon receded.

I straddled one of the men, my claws hot with the red of the wounds across his open chest. It leaked down my chin. Panicked, I scrambled away, backing into another corpse. I looked around.

Nine mangled bodies, some skewered with weapons, lay strewn across the glade.

I fumbled to my feet. I staggered, clutched the fiery pain in my side. Oedolyn cowered in the trees, the eerie glow of forsaken magelights glazing her bespattered figure. Chamberlain poised between us, snarling with bared teeth.

The pain in my side spiked. I fell to my knees. Convulsions wracked my entire being, jarring everything around me. My stomach emptied itself. I landed face down in the grass.

CHAPTER 43

Athrú

Athrú endured the distraction of Rhys towing his sister through the fray, but jerked around at her scream. An orange flare to his chest sent a shock through his limbs and buckled his knees. He fell, white cracking across his vision as his head bounced off the ground. A blade hurled down on him. Athrú parried, forced the sword up, rolled under it and onto his feet, and swiped. The enemy slumped.

Athrú's vision bubbled. The clash of blades and howls throbbed through his blinding headache, worsened by the scent of blood and caustic magic. Spells illuminated the dark with bursts of color, making the air simmer. He forged on, battered by too many foes. Their thirty against at least sixty battle-hardened mercenaries—they stood no chance.

Above him, Braidac scuttled across tree branches with his bow at work. He clambered over tangled boughs from one tree to the next before the enemy discovered his hideaway. Mercenaries dropped at random. The wiry rangers held their ground, though Athrú doubted any would go unscathed. Bodies congested the tiny clearing.

As he twisted around to meet another foe, Athrú saw him.

And Righnách saw Athrú.

The enemy's snarl melted to shock. Athrú's heart pounded more agonizingly than his head.

Righnách directed his blade at Athrú and ordered the advance. The rangers were forgotten. The mercenaries careened around and charged.

Athrú rushed him, but Righnách retreated to the cover of his men. He bellowed another command, and half the troop scattered into the woods. Athrú charged against the curses constricting around him. Righnách disappeared into the dark.

Rangers broke through the lines. Braidac leaped from his perch and slammed onto a pair of mercenaries. Rodd ordered a defense around Athrú. Those who still stood encircled him with readied weapons. Braidac notched an arrow. Dair raised his staff in one hand and prepped a throwing knife in the other. Their eight mage comrades' free hands glowed.

Athrú was trapped. He had to get out, to save Oedolyn. Rhys couldn't stop Righnách. They'd never make it. He had to save them.

The enemy swarmed, swords and axes and spears directed at the rangers, spells aimed at Athrú. They constricted him, pulling him down, crushing him.

But not to kill him. Never to kill him.

A blaze of light collided with dark. Power pulsed in the air, making the hair on the back of his neck stand. The light and dark narrowed and shot back into a crackling speck, humming as the brightness intensified. The charged collision erupted.

Blinding white seared the glade. The force splintered and felled the innermost ring of trees. No man standing withstood the blast, ranger and mercenary alike.

Athrú moved first, despite his stinging welts and swirling head. He choked, hacked for air. He got his knees under him.

All thirty rangers stirred. No mercenaries moved. Silence overwhelmed the clearing.

A few rangers lay down again, swallowing moans. Others moved to help them. Small blazes belched the stench of smoke through the forest, and rangers hurried to stamp them out or roll corpses over them. Braidac slumped to Athrú's side.

"What just happened?" he panted, face white.

Athrú shook his head. He staggered into the trees, Braidac a step behind. They ignored Rodd's calls, and several more rangers followed them.

Athrú ran, though every muscle screamed at him. He had to stop Righnách. Get Oedolyn back. Save Rhys.

Of course Vespar had set Righnách to the task. There couldn't be a better tracker, a more ruthless bounty hunter. Vespar knew Righnách wouldn't fail him. He never did.

"This way." Braidac steered Athrú to the right. "Look, they turned."

Athrú didn't have a ranger's tracking eye, but he veered on, blade in hand. After an endless stretch of darkness, a hazy white glow spilled from another clearing. Athrú quickened, Braidac at his heels. They braced themselves for another clash, but stumbled into silence. They halted at the edge of an empty glade.

Empty, except for disfigured carcasses strewn across the red grass, so mangled, it was difficult to recognize they had once been human bodies.

Braidac clamped a hand over his mouth. He looked to Athrú.

His stomach clenched his teeth together, but he said, "Rhys."

The ranger's brows narrowed before his eyes widened. "You're joking," he breathed.

"Athrú!"

His sister's cry jolted him into the clearing. Rhys lay on his back, blood spattered on his ashen face, dyeing a ring around his cracked mouth. No scales remained, but patches of blue shone beneath the crimson stains. Oedolyn stooped beside him, swabbing his hands clean, while Chamberlain whined and tiptoed the perimeter. Athrú reached to comfort her, but she screamed for him to let her be.

"Oedolyn—"

"I'm trying," she wept. "I'm trying. I'm trying."

Athrú pressed his ear to Rhys's burning chest. "He's alive, sister mine, we have time."

"He's not listening to me. I've done everything I know to do. I'm trying."

Braidac knelt beside her. For once, his mouth wasn't flapping.

Oedolyn breathlessly related the incident—most of the mercenaries had fled at Rhys's release, the rest at the sight of his victims. But before that, with Rhys's own blade…

The cloth fell from her quivering hands. Oedolyn threw herself at Athrú, too overcome to sob. Braidac took her place to watch over Rhys and scrub the gore away. His careful fingers fumbled.

Oedolyn snapped upright. "He found us. He knows where we are. He'll—"

Athrú cupped his hands to her face, looked into her misting eyes. "Never, Oedolyn."

She clutched his arm. "Did Righnách see you? Athrú—"

Chamberlain snarled. Braidac grabbed Oedolyn's hand. She turned to Rhys and startled back. Athrú raised a hand to quiet them.

Rhys gazed upward, unseeing, pallid face as expressionless as a corpse. Scarlet rimmed the blue of his wide eyes. He didn't move, not even the rising of his breaths. Athrú wasn't sure he was breathing at all.

He reached a hand to find Rhys's heartbeat. A spread of scales speared through his chest under Athrú's hovering palm. He drew away. The scales receded, deadly gems sinking into flesh. Athrú looked into Rhys's empty face.

"I know you can hear me, dragon."

A sheen of glassy blue bled across Rhys's skin.

"You've made your point. Let him go."

Rhys's fingers curled.

"No. You've done enough to him. Release him."

The claw swung up. Athrú lurched aside. Oedolyn shrieked into her bloodstained fists. Braidac drew her away, then pounced on one of Rhys's flailing arms.

"Now you listen to me," the ranger hissed. "You're not putting this on us. You get back here." Braidac wrestled Rhys's claw to the ground again. "You going to leave us to do your job? You going to let Vespar win? Are you going to leave Emlyn? No, so get back here, you…rot you, come back!"

Rhys arched with a tremendous gasp. Braidac and Athrú jerked backward. Rhys choked up blood, slumped onto his side, and dislodged it into the grass. His bare muscles tautened with agony.

Braidac retreated to shelter Oedolyn. Athrú crept closer.

"Rhys?"

His petrified eyes flicked to Athrú's.

"Easy. Where's the dragon?"

Rhys stared up at the murky sky, unblinking with horror, face an eerie gray and crimson under the moon. "What have I done?" he gasped.

Athrú put a hand to the boy's heaving chest. "Listen to me. Where is the dragon?"

Rhys's sight glazed with momentary focus. His brows pinched. More fluid spurted from his mouth. He cringed, shuddered.

"Is the dragon away?"

Rhys nodded.

"What's wrong with his wound?" Braidac pointed.

Athrú pressed on Rhys's shoulder to keep him down and looked for himself. The flesh around the gut thread rippled, too faintly to tell at first glance. He brushed a finger along it, though Rhys sucked a sharp breath. The spread of shining blue was tough with dragonhide.

Oedolyn examined it. "It looks better than just a moment ago," she said, brows narrow.

Athrú rubbed his eyes, as swallowed by irritation as by relief. "If the dragon had released himself sooner, there'd be no wound at all. This would be a nick to a dragon's hide. He saved your life."

Rhys glowered. He turned from the carnage around him and faced the trees.

Behind them, the last of the troops limped into the glade. Rangers set to piling corpses, readying a pyre secure in a mage's barrier. The wounded sank to the bare ground before their companions could prepare suitable resting places for them.

"Some others need your attention too, sister mine." Athrú gathered her satchel together, but kept a roll of linen and a vial of rainveil oil.

Braidac stood, flourished a hand to Oedolyn, and raised her up. Before stepping away, he stooped over Rhys's head.

"By the way, you look gorgeous."

"You're lovely as ever, Brai."

The ranger grinned. "Oh, guess what?" He steered back. "You missed it—Dair took out some fifteen men on your tail with that walking stick of his, just like I said he could, and you *missed* it."

"Did he?" Rhys slurred. "How did you keep track?"

Braidac faked a scowl, but crouched and grasped Rhys's hand. "Don't you ever pull that again, hear? I'm not doing that pretty talk again."

He led Oedolyn to her next patient. Athrú watched his sister droop, as much in need of his comfort as the others needed her tonics. She grasped Braidac's hand in both of hers.

Rhys choked. He tipped onto his side, and the force of the cough curled his knees up. Chamberlain snuffled his face and made to clean off the gore until Rhys waved him away.

Athrú couldn't say he approved of what had happened, but Rhys had had no other choice. He'd driven Righnách and his men off, saved Oedolyn's life, and survived. Yet, what would the dragon think? He'd snagged a taste of what he craved, and Rhys had let him have it. Clever beast, letting Rhys sustain such a wound to prove himself the one defense between his human and death.

Athrú felt he'd swallowed a stone. If not for the dragon, Rhys would be dead, Oedolyn swept away by their childhood terror. And Athrú…

Well, that couldn't be helped. Righnách had seen him. After years of painstaking efforts to stay low and safe, it'd taken a matter of weeks of exposure to be found. Who was Righnách to keep his knowledge quiet?

"Who was that?" Rhys asked.

Athrú gritted his teeth. He dabbed the rainveil oil along Rhys's stitches.

Rhys awaited the answer he wouldn't give, then relented. He sat up with Athrú's help, clutching his side, head lolling. "He'll come back, won't he?"

Again, Athrú didn't answer.

"But I scared him off. That's comforting, isn't it?"

Athrú doubted. Impressed him, perhaps, but never scared.

He wound the bandage around the boy as Rhys asked, "How did you make it out?"

In truth, Athrú wanted to forget what had happened. "The enemy split up when they went after you. We overtook the rest." He changed the subject, shaking his head. "How did they find us so quickly? They were waiting for us."

It drained him to think too hard, but Rhys considered, biting his lip. "What if...Master Corrick..."

Athrú's brows narrowed. "You think he would expose us?"

"What if Brai's right? What if he's in league with Vespar? That would explain why he tried to stop us from going in the first place."

Athrú didn't deny it, though he doubted that Master Corrick would so blatantly betray Lord Cael and his council. Unless, perhaps, he sought to appease Vespar and protect Lleogren from his wrath with willing cooperation, which still seemed a stretch to Athrú.

"He knew nothing of our plans. There's no way he could have known we'd crossed the border by now," said Athrú.

Rhys brushed a thumb down his right wrist, an anxious compulsion Athrú doubted the boy realized he ever succumbed to. "It's all I can think," Rhys said. "He hasn't since..."

"Who hasn't what?"

Rhys licked his lips. "Before they banished me, Tylysk took some of my blood to use in pentacles. I could've sworn he used it the first time we saw Eoin, and again when we met with Rodd. I felt it. But I don't think he's touched me since." Rhys turned to watch the dark trees. "If Tylysk didn't find out for himself, someone had to tell him where we were and how to find us. All I can think is…"

"Master Corrick."

Rhys nodded, pressed the heel of his hand to his eye when the motion pounded through his skull.

Athrú watched the rangers milling about the clearing, frowning. Captain Rodd tended to the wounded and dealt quiet orders. Athrú caught Dair's hard eye, and the old ranger stalked over to them, beckoning the captain along. Dair dropped on the nearest boulder with a groan.

"Alive, is he?" he gruffed. "So's everyone else, though some wish they weren't."

Athrú looked over the settling camp. The few mages with any remaining strength saw to the worst injured. Braidac held Oedolyn's satchel as she wound a sling around a ranger's arm, the man gagging on a tonic, burbletack or wickling for the pain.

Rodd crouched beside them. Of all the rangers, he'd walked away from the scrimmage the most unscathed, more ruffled than battle weary. All except Braidac, who'd spent most of the conflict scuttling across tree branches.

Once certain that Rhys would recover, Rodd said, "Clearly, we have to keep a sharper eye out. I trust my scouts when they say they found nothing amiss last night. This force was too well hidden, and their numbers tell us Master Vespar knows you haven't returned alone, Master Rhys." Rodd scanned a keen eye across the black trees. "We have a few hours to rest. We'll have to move before sunup. Some of the men will have to be carried."

"What about you, boy?" asked Dair.

"I'll manage," Rhys said.

"Hm. I won't hold my breath." Dair hauled himself up. "Get your strength back proper. We'll not have this ruddy journey be for nothing."

Once Oedolyn finished her rounds, and those with an appetite had something to revive them, camp settled to quiet. Some muttered and grumbled how they'd stumbled into the enemy's snare, unappeased by their mage comrades' reminders of the magic barrier that shielded the horde from detection.

After a time, Braidac took Athrú's place beside Rhys so he could rest. Oedolyn saw to her brother's bruises and welts before she wilted beside him, Chamberlain on sleepy guard at her feet. Rhys and Braidac nodded off, as did most of the rangers. The others made use of their restlessness and strung together litters for the wounded. A reeking pyre smoldered near the edge of the trees.

Oedolyn unraveled her braid and massaged her scalp, let the disheveled honey tresses spill across her trembling shoulders. She stared into the flames, eyes glazed. Athrú had never liked the way she looked in firelight. It reminded him of torches and smoke, terror-ridden nights, Righnách's wolfish smile. He draped his cloak about her shoulders to shield her from it.

"You've tended to everyone else," Athrú said. "Were you hurt?"

She shook her head.

He studied her pallid face anyway. Save for her unrelenting tears, she gave no sign that she'd been touched.

"He left you," he said.

Oedolyn peeked in Rhys's direction, he far out of earshot. Rhys twisted onto his good side and coiled tighter in his cloak. Oedolyn hid her face.

"Rhys wouldn't let him near me," she whispered.

Athrú drew her out of the firelight dancing on her hair. He dabbed the tears from her cheeks, and Oedolyn crumpled.

"He wanted to see what Rhys would do," she said. "He knew it wouldn't kill him. He did it so his dragon would…" Oedolyn stared long at Rhys, where the orange glow of the pyre wavered across his clammy face. "But Rhys came between us. Righnách thought he would be too consumed to recognize me, let alone protect me." She hugged her knees, shaking her head. "What does it matter? He won't stay away, now that he knows."

Athrú tucked her hair behind her ear. "He won't touch you again, Oedolyn."

She looked away. "He will always come."

Athrú drew his sister to his side, safe under his arm. Oedolyn smothered her face in his sleeve. For all he tried, he thought of no words to comfort her.

She silently wept herself to exhaustion, as she had each night during their first long march to Gildio.

CHAPTER 44

Emlyn

Tylysk dismounted and lifted Emlyn down. "You're awfully quiet today."

Emlyn tiptoed around to stroke the horse's nose and looked over the valley. Everything was green, the few trees whispering in the wind, the fields spreading farther than she could see, the hills cradling the castle. Emlyn noticed the days weren't as hot anymore, though summer hadn't ended yet. She wondered how long it was until autumn, and if she and Aria could play outside when it snowed in the winter. She didn't feel like playing now, though, even if the warm sun sent away the clouds.

"Something wrong?" Tylysk asked.

"No." Emlyn stepped away.

"How did you do with Lady Orrtha today?"

"Uh huh."

"What did you talk about?"

"Fine." Emlyn plopped down in the grass. Tylysk sat beside her.

"Excellent. Sounds like you had a rather yes morning."

"What?"

"My thoughts exactly."

Emlyn rubbed her eyes. Tylysk nudged her with an elbow.

"I brought you all the way out here, and you're nodding off."

"I didn't sleep good."

"Why is that?"

Emlyn didn't answer until he bumped her. Heldran's words from a few nights ago had kept her awake every night since—Master Vespar was Lord Vespar, and he wanted both the Enchantress and the Wizard. Emlyn didn't understand why that was important, but she knew it was, and it worried Heldran.

Without thinking, Emlyn stood. "Tylysk, you and Master Vespar have promised and promised to tell me why you want me here. You're never going to say, are you?"

"You know why. So Lord Vespar can keep you safe, and he can teach you to be a good Enchantress."

"That's not the only reason." Emlyn put her fists to her hips. "Master Vespar needs me to do something he can't. Well, how am I supposed to do it if I don't even know what he needs me for?"

Tylysk shook his head, smiling. "You're a silly girl."

"Am not. I know that's what he wants."

His smile disappeared. "That's for Master Vespar to tell."

"I don't care."

"Would you like it if I demanded you tell me a secret Heldran entrusted to you?"

Emlyn frowned and didn't answer that. "It's not fair," she said.

"What happened to Master Vespar wasn't fair either, little girl, nor is it fair that he's had to wait most of his life to do anything about it."

Emlyn ducked her head at Tylysk's tone. He sighed and squeezed her hand.

"He has everything in place. He'll tell you when it's time. You have to trust him."

"I'm trying," she whimpered.

"And you've done wonderfully. You've excelled in your lessons, you've done everything we've asked. You meet with the council next week—you can't stop now, can you?"

Emlyn shook her head, trying to be brave. "Then what happened to Master Vespar?"

Tylysk pursed his lips. "He waited a long time for something important, then he was told he couldn't get it."

That was a little silly—Emlyn had been told she couldn't have lots of things too. "How come?" she asked.

"If he knew, he would have set it right." Tylysk patted her cheek. "No more of this. We'll keep our promise. Just be patient."

Emlyn believed she'd been as patient as she would ever be, but she nodded.

"Go on. We have to be home soon."

She waited, hoping he'd say more if she stayed, but gave in. She plodded down the hill, keeping to where Tylysk could see her. It still made her angry, but at the same time, she felt bad for Master Vespar too. If it made *him* upset not to get something he wanted, it must have been more special than she could imagine. How could she possibly help with that?

Emlyn darted about the field, trying not to think about it anymore. She wished Aria wasn't afraid to leave the Manor, and then they could play out here, where they didn't have to stop when Swordsmaster Perreth trained his knights, and they had the entire meadow to run in.

She watched the faraway river sparkle under the sun. A long road rolled down the knolls into the city. On a hill near the Manor, a dog chased some sheep across the green. When she looked over the city, she spotted where the tinkers had stopped and where Rhys had found her. The thought made her shiver.

She'd given up not thinking about Rhys. She dreamed about him sometimes—he'd help her climb the trees in the garden or sit with her in her tiny cottage and sings songs to her. Other times, he was the terrifying monster Tylysk warned her about.

Emlyn dropped in the grass to catch her breath. She sort of remembered what had happened in the garden house, but she'd closed her eyes for most of it. Emlyn thought Rhys had turned blue, but that sounded ridiculous. But…he did have claws, like a monster.

Rhys hadn't meant to hurt Tylysk. It was an accident. It had to be. Was that what got him into trouble? If Vespar didn't get in trouble for helping a witch, why did Rhys? Where was he? What did someone who was banished even do? She wanted to ask Mistress Orrtha, but Emlyn wouldn't dare make her sad and sick again.

But she missed Rhys so much, she thought it might crush her.

"Come along, Emlyn."

She trudged up the hill, watching the city, the long river winding into the distant hills. She stopped when she noticed something down the road. She squinted for a better look. Inching along the hillside, she tiptoed toward the highway.

Emlyn recognized the horrible sounds of carts and squeaky wheels, but no tinker wagons moved down the road. Five or six travelers followed the highway, their clothes dark, muddy colors. Some had fur around their collars or shoulders despite the summer warmth. They had only one wagon with them.

Emlyn's heart raced. It was a cage.

"Emlyn?"

Her legs moved on their own. She crawled nearer on her knees. There were giants around the cage, with huge swords and axes and spears. The one in front had to be a Mage Master—a silver four-pointed star gleamed on his chest.

One man grasped a chain around his fist, wrestling against the anxious black dog on the other end. On all fours, the animal came to the man's waist. Emlyn had never seen anything that dark before. The sun left no shine on its deep black fur, and the darkness looked like it would suck the world up into it.

Emlyn looked away from the cage without counting how many girls were inside.

She yelped at the hand on her shoulder. Tylysk hushed her.

"Come on. We have to get home."

"Tylysk, look."

He yanked her up and turned her away from the road. "Hurry up."

Emlyn tried to follow, but her feet planted to the ground. Her heart pulsed. Magic quivered around her. "You have to do something."

"We have to go. If they see us—"

"I have to help them."

Emlyn didn't know why she said it—she strained to go with Tylysk, to dart to the Manor and hide. But Magic prickled across her skin, seized her bones. Her arm tugged from Tylysk's grasp on its own.

He gripped her wrist tighter. "No, Emlyn. We're going home."

"I have to save them."

"Do you see those Hunters, Emlyn? If they spot you—"

"They're going to die, Tylysk!"

"If you go down there, you'll die too!"

His voice was just a whisper, but it shook Emlyn to her bones. She battled the magic clutching her. Only Master Vespar could save her.

Her feet refused to budge. Her hand raised on its own.

Tylysk snagged her wrist before the spell came out. He dragged her up the hill. Magic swung her arms to hit him, dug her heels into the ground, shrieked at him. Clapping a hand over her mouth, Tylysk scooped her up and ran.

A piercing cry echoed across the hills, a spooky sound of both a howl and a shriek. Emlyn covered her ears and looked back. The black dog steered its master up the hill, shredding the grass under its paws. Five more giants followed them.

Their horse skittered. Tylysk hoisted Emlyn into the saddle, but a curse exploded near them, knocking him off his feet. The horse bolted. Emlyn fell on her back, her head thudding the ground. She lost her breath.

Tylysk rolled on top of her to shield her from another curse. He shot a spell at the Hunters with his dagger. He yanked Emlyn up, then faced the enemy with his sword and knife ready. Emlyn clung to his cloak. She tried to summon a shield, but her headache left her too dizzy to concentrate.

She shrieked when she heard swords clash. Tylysk clamped Emlyn to his side and swung, but the Hunters came too strong. One struck Tylysk's sword from his hand, and the blade cracked as it flew.

The huge black beast charged. Tylysk swung her out of its reach, but a Hunter jabbed him in the stomach with the stick of his spear. Tylysk crumpled, knocking Emlyn down. The Hunters pounced on him.

Emlyn scuttled backward from the dark monster. Shadows, both misty and flaming, flickered around its massive body. It pinned its pointy ears down and centered its empty yellow eyes on her, stalking nearer. Spit dribbled from between its bared teeth. It rumbled, arched its back. It lunged. Emlyn screamed.

The chain jarred the dog, and it tumbled. Emlyn cowered with her face to the grass as the creature sprang at her, snarling and chomping its jaws inches away.

A deep voice barked a command. The beast fell silent. A hand gripped the back of Emlyn's dress and hoisted her off the ground.

The dog stayed poised and intent on her, the chain taut in its master's fist. Two of the other Hunters pinned Tylysk's arms behind him. Another, a woman, to Emlyn's horror, kept his head up by twisting her fingers in his hair. The fourth rested a heavy sword on Tylysk's neck. Tylysk glared at the Mage Master dangling Emlyn from his grasp, blood dripping from his lip and a bruise swelling under his eye.

The mage drew Emlyn against his chest, where the star pendant burned into her spine. His horrid breath brushed her cheek.

"There is a penalty for hiding witches in Gildio," he rumbled. "Shall we watch?"

The Hunter raised his sword high from Tylysk's neck. Emlyn shrieked.

"If you do either of us harm, you will have Lord Mage Vespar and

Gildio's army to deal with," Tylysk said.

The Hunter held his sword over his head. Tylysk glared, his white face scarier with his red scar.

The mage's laugh jostled Emlyn. "Boy, who are you to tell me what Gildio's army will do?"

"I am Mage Master Tylysk. Lord Mage Vespar is my master. You will release us."

"Are you? What would Vespar and his man want with you, *drágam*?" the Hunter growled in Emlyn's ear.

"That's none of your concern. His business is his own."

"And of all the excuses we have heard, yours is the most lamentable. Peasants have groveled to me with better tales."

The mage held Emlyn away. The black dog snapped its jaws at her toes. Emlyn curled her legs up and clung to the Hunter's arm. The mage looked her over, growling with a laugh.

"She's your whelp, isn't she, boy? Is her mother scrubbing floors in the Manor kitchens, Master Tylysk?"

He wasn't thrown. "She is under Master Vespar's protection. You will release us."

"Enough." The mage motioned to the other Hunter by waving Emlyn at him. He lifted the sword higher.

"Tylysk!" Emlyn squealed.

The mage raised his hand, and the Hunter left his sword in the air. He drew Emlyn closer, pressed his knife to her cheek, and turned her face. His scarred features were rough and bristled, his eyes cold. "And you? Have you an excuse of your own, hm?"

She glanced at Tylysk from the corner of her eye. "P-please don't kill him."

"What shall I do with him, then? Someone must answer for the crime. You, *drágam*?" He dangled Emlyn over the dog's mouth. It jerked against its chain for a taste of her feet. Emlyn wailed.

"Then prove me wrong," Tylysk said. "If you take us to Vespar and you are right, you will have my head. If you don't and you're wrong, he will be at the front of his men to hunt you down."

The mage frowned at Tylysk, twiddling his knife between his fingers. "Father is sure of himself, *drágam*. Perhaps you shall announce us to Vespar and the Lady yourself."

The mage barked at his followers in a different language. They thrust Tylysk to his feet and forced him down the hill. The mage hauled Emlyn under his arm and followed, the dog a leap behind. Emlyn hid her face until they came to the castle.

By the time they reached the bailey, the cage had passed through the gate. Guards dragged screaming witches away. Emlyn couldn't look at them.

The Mage Master stalked up the steps. Swordsmaster Perreth halted him, warned him to let Tylysk and Emlyn go and leave, but Tylysk stopped him. Captain Perreth ignored him and raised his sword at the Hunters. The mage lifted Emlyn over the dog's chomping jaws, and the captain stood down. He stepped aside, glowering, sword still in hand.

The Mage Master started down the corridor to the right.

"You'll find Master Vespar in the council chamber that way," Tylysk said.

One of the other Hunters hit him.

The mage dumped Emlyn on the floor. He clawed a hand around her neck, his fingers so long and broad, they almost met around her throat. The flat side of his blade pressed tight under Emlyn's chin. She trudged the way on tiptoe, head tilted back. A spell throbbed under the fingertips on her neck. Tylysk's steady footsteps followed her, and the sound of them eased her own jittery steps.

Once they reached the council chamber, the Mage Master smashed the door open with his foot and lugged Emlyn inside.

"Emlyn!" she heard Heldran cry.

In the middle of the room, the Hunters shoved Tylysk to his knees and hovered with the sword over his neck. The chained beast never broke its empty-eyed stare from Emlyn. It snapped its jaws once more before its master jerked him out of her reach. The Mage Master fixed Emlyn in front of him, showing her off.

Heldran made to run for her, but Master Vespar put a hand in front of him. He stepped away from the table where he and Heldran stood over scattered parchments. Master Vespar approached, his face empty, but what Emlyn saw in his eyes terrified her.

The mage bowed the way tinkers pretended to bow, doubling Emlyn over too. She choked against the blade. "My lord, this boy claims he and this witch are in your charge."

"He is correct in saying so."

The Hunter blinked. "That is impossible. The girl—"

"Is no concern of yours. The Gildian Council will soon decide her fate. We have no need of your services where this child is concerned. Release them."

Emlyn could hear the seething in Vespar's voice. The Hunters looked to their leader. He scraped the knife along her throat, his fingers tightening around her neck. "My lord—"

"Release them!"

The Hunters stood away from Tylysk so fast, he fell on his stomach on the floor.

The mage kept hold of Emlyn, snarling. "You can't—"

Magic erupted, thrusting the mage to the floor. Emlyn escaped to Heldran's outstretched arms. Threads of magic crackled around Vespar in white sparks, live and raw, his cloak spreading in the gusts, his hand and ring extended.

"You will not touch her. You will tell your comrades this child is under the protection of the Gildian Council. She will not be touched."

The Hunters backed away, shielding their eyes. The black dog whimpered and cowered. Parchments swept across the room, caught high in the cruel wind. Banners billowed straight outward, flat on the gusts. Magelights smoked and sparked. The air pulsed with magic, hot and suffocating. Heldran hid Emlyn against his chest.

The mage Hunter stumbled to his feet. "Lord Calibor will not be pleased."

"Lord Calibor will know of your insubordination, and he will be certain of this child's immunity. Go!"

The Hunters retreated for the door, but waited for their leader before abandoning the chamber. The hand around his knife whitened with his grip. The Mage Master stalked out, never taking his burning eyes from Emlyn.

Master Vespar withdrew his spell, heaving for breath. Parchments rustled to the floor from one end of the room to the other. Banners rumpled to the ground. The magelights died, casting a darkness across the council chamber.

Tylysk stayed on his knees, head bowed. Master Vespar finally looked at him, and that look made Emlyn want to run. Her heart sank to her feet.

"My...my lord," Tylysk tried. "I—"

Emlyn wriggled out of Heldran's embrace. "Master Vespar!"

He slowly looked at her, jaw tight. Emlyn hesitated, but left Heldran's side.

"It's my fault, Master Vespar."

He blinked, the sharp line of his mouth flickering downward.

"I wanted to help those witches. Tylysk tried to stop me, but...I couldn't. It was Magic. Magic made me do it."

Heldran grasped her hand. "Emmy—"

She pulled away. "It was! I wanted to come home with Tylysk. I tried. I knew I couldn't save those witches, but Magic still made me. It didn't want to go with Tylysk."

Tylysk remained huddled on his knees, staring at the ground.

"Please don't be angry with him, Master Vespar."

He watched Tylysk for a long moment, breathing heavily. At last, he said, "Tylysk."

He kept his head bowed. "Forgive me, my lord."

"Is it as she says?"

Tylysk swallowed. "She was not herself, my lord."

Master Vespar glanced between them all. His jaw tightened as his fists did, his hands shaking. Lingering on Emlyn, his fingers softened. He held out his hand.

Emlyn ran to him. He dropped to his knee to catch her. She buried her face on his shoulder and cried.

Vespar kissed her brow. He touched a finger down her left cheek, and it stung. When she noticed the blood left on his hand, Emlyn panicked.

"No, my girl, hush." He pulled her close. "Are you hurt elsewhere?"

Emlyn shook her head. He lifted her chin for a look at her throat. The memory of the knife chilled her skin, but he didn't seem to find anything. Master Vespar dried her tears.

"Heldran will take you and Master Tylysk to see the physicians. I'll be with you soon."

Heldran helped Tylysk to his feet before lifting Emlyn into his arms. Master Vespar was slow to let her go. When she peeked back over Heldran's shoulder, Master Vespar hadn't moved from the floor.

CHAPTER 45

Vespar

Vespar stood when his knees couldn't bear the hard wood floor any longer. His shock got the best of him, and he staggered to the dais to sit on the step, disregarding the parchment crumpled under his foot.

He was too bewildered to consider what could have happened. Tylysk had gone to great lengths to have Emlyn elsewhere the few times any Hunters came. He had known this troop was due today—what had led him to steer Emlyn near them?

His gold ring glittered more brilliantly. He loosened it off his finger before it burned him.

If Emlyn spoke true, Magic had Its own hand in the near tragedy. Vespar had never heard of Magic constraining Its wielders to do anything against the user's will, let alone forcing Its Authority to do so. Had Magic truly influenced the incident and their potential fate?

Vespar fisted his ring so he wouldn't cast it across the room.

Why had Magic turned against him? What had he done to incur Its contempt? It was a fickle tease, tempting him with favor so long, only to recant Its offering when the time came for Vespar to claim it. They said Magic had a mind but no heart, yet Vespar thought Magic took great pleasuring in torturing him.

In his youth, Magic found more favor in Vespar than any other. It took him too early in life for him to remember. The Academy accepted him at the early age of nine, and Headmaster Alkirk himself raised him to the next class higher. Year after year, Vespar advanced to the top of his class with little effort. Some professors joked that he took Magic for himself before Magic could claim him.

Within a few years, not one mind doubted what lay ahead in Vespar's future. Headmaster Alkirk made certain the boy knew it, he a fledgling of thirteen, with seven more years of school to come. A magnificent inheritance awaited him.

Vespar was nothing more than a green-eyed son of a silversmith, short for his age, with a ready smile and an eagerness to please. Eight years of his tuition came from the Headmaster's pocket when Vespar's father couldn't afford his secondary and mastery schools. Vespar clung to the Academy's promises as he would his breath. He would not fail the Headmaster, nor his father, nor Magic Itself.

Before he graduated as a Mage Master, his headmaster promised Vespar to the Claytherdon Household as the next Lord Mage. His guaranteed potential, and most certainly the key to his position, still lay ahead. A few days after graduation, the silversmith's son moved to Gildio Castle to serve under Lord Defyd, side by side with his eighteen-year-old heir, Ioan.

The next six and a half years had been the most grueling of his life while Vespar awaited summons from the Academy. He and Ioan were in town when he received word, huddled in the falconry during a sudden downpour. Vespar sprinted through the rain, nearly plummeting into a pool of mud on the school grounds before bounding up the front steps. He remembered not caring that his cloak hung askew and the wet plastered his hair down. He slicked the damp locks from his forehead before the Headmaster's door opened to him.

A servant took his sodden cloak and hung it by the hearth. As always, the Headmaster displayed a tin of Rodhinian dates on the corner of his desk, which seemed to be all that got him through the tremendous stack of parchments to sift through. Decades later, Vespar would be reminded of this study by the bitter scent of the grayhold leaves the Headmaster would smoke in the pipe resting on the mantle.

As ever, Headmaster Alkirk welcomed him with a warm, wrinkled smile. He seemed cheered by his former pupil's arrival, despite a rainy-day dreariness about him. Seated before the Headmaster's desk, Vespar awaited the news with his typical deference.

Alkirk dismissed the servant and said, "I won't keep you long, my Lord Mage. I know you have many duties to attend to. Date?" He took one for himself when Vespar declined. He seated himself across from Vespar and folded his hands on top of the desk. His eyes remained on his fingers. "You might have noticed a recent displacement, so to speak, within Magic, did you not?"

"Yes, sir," Vespar said. Every mage—and every witch, for that matter—must have sensed Magic's vigorous shift, how it had rocked like a ship on the sea, jostling Its wielders before settling into Its normal pace. The displacement had alerted Vespar that his Headmaster would soon call on him.

Alkirk nodded. "We received word today, confirming the Wizard's passing."

In the first breath, Vespar was elated, triumphant. But, watching the Headmaster's passive features, doubt clutched his rushing heart.

"Sir?"

Alkirk raised a remorseful gaze.

It clubbed Vespar to the chest. He sat back in his chair, a hand over his mouth. "How do we know I'm not the next Wizard, sir?" he asked.

The penitence in Alkirk's expression offered him no comfort. "If you were, you would not ask me how I knew."

Vespar sank in his chair.

Alkirk mirrored his despondency. "It seems Magic has turned on us," he said, "but your efforts and potential were not in vain. To be named

Lord Mage under Caeradin's most influential lord before you were named a Mage Master—that is nothing to scorn."

"Lord Ioan and his father were promised a Wizard, Headmaster, not the second best."

"It should make little difference. You've proven your capabilities during your years of service. Your position and his impression of you are in no danger for what is beyond anyone's control. Lord Ioan would be foolish to think ill of a most talented mage."

"Most talented," Vespar repeated. "Someone has surpassed me, sir." He studied the Headmaster. "Do you know who?"

Alkirk had dreaded the question. He wrung his hands, searching for the most tactful answer. "We have some insight, but our investigation is young."

"Enough insight to be certain, sir."

Alkirk sighed. "Professors Darkspur and Bedarak have been in contact with our colleagues in each province. So far, they are drawn to the neighboring corners of Rivariar and Lleogren."

"Forgive me, sir, but that is not 'who'."

"I will not be discourteous and give you a false report, Master Vespar," Alkirk said. "I prefer to be definite in the matter before anything is revealed."

Vespar's cheek twitched. He looked away. "Will he be brought to the Academy, sir?"

"We would prefer it, but those provinces are not in our jurisdiction. He is not compelled by law to attend, as Gildian mages are. He must come of his own accord."

Vespar scoffed to himself. Both provinces balked from the Academy's politics as much as its tuition. The one Lleogrian in Vespar's class was destined to become Lleogren's next Lord Mage, with no one else qualified for the position.

Lord Vespar had forgotten what the Headmaster said next as he ventured stalwartly on one of his infamous tangents. He hadn't listened anyway, instead staring into the low-burning hearth. He understood his Headmaster couldn't have foreseen Magic's duplicity better than anyone else, but it stung Vespar with betrayal. If Magic was as unpredictable as his professors always warned, and such great care had to be taken in Its wielding, how could anyone presume Vespar's fate would be so glorious? Why did they not wait it out in silence, when no harm or despair would have befallen them when the time came for their hopes to be dashed?

For all their studies, they could never predict Magic's next move. They could no more direct Magic to Its next Wizard than they could divert It from claiming a witch.

"And I was telling Prof—ah, look!" Alkirk reclaimed Vespar's attention. "Another note from Professor Bedarak." He took the receiving parchment from the top of the pile, hooked his spectacles on his nose, and traced a finger along its message. The color leaked from his face.

"Sir?"

The Headmaster set the page on the desk, message downward. Vespar sat forward, once again disregarding his poor manners.

His instructor eyed him. "They saw him," he said, "but there are no specifics listed. No name."

Vespar's jaw tightened.

Alkirk picked up the page and ran a finger along the scrawl. "A village boy," he quoted, "no more than eight or nine."

Vespar sat back. "I was bested by a child? A lowly, ragged peasant child?"

"Magic has Its own mind and will," Alkirk said. "I suppose we cannot determine who will replace what It has lost."

His words provoked Vespar more than reassured him. He had lost his incomparable, most coveted inheritance to a bratling who wouldn't learn so much as his letters. Nothing could be more insulting. Humiliating. Heartbreaking.

Vespar had been Magic's lamb fatted for slaughter.

Lord Vespar took his hands from his face. That was all he wanted—the inheritance, the legacy and line of Lord Praed himself it seemed he was bound never to attain.

In years past, before Ioan's death, at times Vespar wished Magic would disown him. Misfortune stalked him wherever It did. It paved his path with gold, then led him over a precipice before he could step back.

But Emlyn—Magic awaited her every will. If there was no one It could torment, it was the Enchantress. Magic offered Itself to her, a precious child swallowed in the affairs of mages and lords, of Caeradin and war. Yet now, she bore a chain around her neck.

Vespar regained himself and gathered the parchments strewn across the room.

Emlyn could not have been more perfect: young, meek, eager to please, a bud learning to bloom. Vespar had long imagined the Enchantress as a spirited, headstrong woman, a warrior queen he would have to break. Someone like Flannery, he supposed. Praises be that she hadn't been the Enchantress, weak, impulsive, uneducated. Yet, if she had, perhaps they might have avoided banishments and abdications.

But he had a joy in Emlyn he would otherwise never have found. Vespar imagined her bubbly, playful character might have been Rhys's had he not fallen to brooding and contempt after Ioan's death. Once she'd grown accustomed to her new life, Emlyn freed herself of her bashfulness and chattered sweetly to him, sought his approval on everything from her newest gown to her latest pentacle sketch. She was a happy little girl while the world darkened around her.

Rhys had abandoned his tutor. Where Emlyn beamed, he glared. He sulked, and she glowed and longed for Vespar's attention. Rhys had once been the drop of sunshine she was, and that was the boy Vespar missed.

Vespar seldom imagined himself being a father, but with Emlyn ever under his protective arm, he'd grown to think of her as his own.

It had been long since he let his rage—and fear, admittedly—escape him. The sight of Emlyn's terror had ignited his spell, and while he scrabbled to contain it, it broke from his grasp. But it provided a defense against the Hunters when diplomacy would have gone over their uncivilized heads. One wrong word, and Emlyn's throat would have been slit and Tylysk beheaded.

Vespar forsook the parchments on the table and made his way to the infirmary.

"Milord!"

Her voice chilled him, though it bore such tenderness as it always had. He glanced back and kept walking. Orrtha caught up with him.

"I just heard," she said. "Are they all right?"

"Emlyn and Master Tylysk have gone to the healers, but I don't believe either is in too dire need of attention."

"Sun and stars." Orrtha clutched at her throat, where the Gildian pendant no longer hung, and hid it by tucking her hair behind her ear. "And you, my lord?"

His heart had yet to slow, but he said, "Yes, thank you, milady."

They walked on in silence. Orrtha's red mouth quirked, the way her son's would when he had something he was not in the mind to share. "I presume you haven't informed the other lords of Emlyn," she said.

"I hadn't thought it necessary until the council made their decision."

"I believe your position is clear. At any rate, presenting her to the council seems…unnecessary?"

"It is the order of things."

"Yes. It has also been the order of things for them to adhere to your guidance." She bobbed her head. "I mean to alleviate Emlyn's distress in the matter, and the complications that will arise with the other lords."

Vespar knew well enough the other lord's potential aggravation. It was his most convincing argument to prevent Ioan from ending the Hunt as spontaneously as he wished. The lords had to be eased into Ioan's ideas, not forced. In any case, Ioan had no singular authority to discontinue the Hunt.

Had he found the Enchantress sooner, Vespar might have plotted the revolution alongside Ioan. He needed the power Emlyn and the Wizard would grant him before the stauncher lords would heed him. Once he had it, they would attend him, and they would know Magic's way.

Yet, for now, Caeradin's nobles had to settle for Gildio's Lord Mage and the pretense of a radical undertaking against convention.

Orrtha smiled, the light from the garden pale on her face. "I would hate to see what Eldra would say. She squawks if Calibor and Jaccius don't let her complain first."

Vespar returned her smile, for Orrtha's sake, but Priodas's elderly Lady Eldra was the least of their concerns. Calibor would prove the most lethal, bad-tempered, brusque, and distrustful. It had taken years of struggle for Vespar to secure his respect. After this incident, Calibor might be of a mind to declare war on this breach of law.

Vespar rubbed his eyes. The news should never have left the Manor. No one beyond the household knew of Emlyn's immunity. Caeradin believed she fell to the Hunt after Master Rhys's banishment. Now, word would advance to Ethelfled and back.

Of course, Rhys had carried it as far as Lleogren.

They had no time. Where was the Wizard?

"At least they're unharmed," Orrtha said, regaining Vespar's attention. "You saved her, my lord. I would not have had your courage."

"I must disagree, my lady. I believe Emlyn has shown you a strength you did not know you had."

She bit back a frown. "Strength of the body is not strength of the heart, but Emlyn's company has been rejuvenating."

"I'm pleased to hear you have both benefited."

Orrtha fell silent until they reached the infirmary. Stopping Vespar at the door, she said, "I know Emlyn is as precious as a daughter to you. I know you've long needed her, whatever it is you've sought all these years. If I had to guess, since before Ioan left us." She curtsied, fixing her gaze to the floor. "I hope you find it, my lord, and I hope you gain all you have desired."

Vespar stared at his feet. He dipped his head. Orrtha dismissed her-self. He watched how her supple hair fell to the middle of her back and concealed her slender figure, how her graceful footfalls made no sound. Vespar swallowed, his chest too hollow to breathe at the sight of her. She faltered at the corner, met his eye, and was gone.

In the infirmary, Vespar passed through the heavy scent of tonics and poultices thickening the stifled room. Heldran waited on a bench with Emlyn on his knee. While inflamed, her left cheek bore no sign of injury but a thread of white scar. Tylysk sat beside them, holding a compress to the welt above his temple. He pointed between Emlyn's scar and his own.

He noticed Vespar first and rushed to his feet. He bowed, but clutched his side when he bent too far.

"They mended a broken rib or two under his bruises, sir," Heldran said.

"The Hunters hit him, Master Vespar. They were going to cut off his head!"

"Shh, Emmy. Look here at me." Heldran dabbed a cloth to her red cheek.

Tylysk resigned to bowing his head instead. "I have no excuse, my lord." Emlyn objected, but Heldran hushed her. "I can only ask your forgiveness for my unbearable mistake."

"You used your strength and wit in bringing her home to us, Master Tylysk. There's no need to consume the rest of it now."

Thrown, Tylysk backed down and dropped beside Heldran.

At Vespar's gesture, Emlyn slipped off her brother's lap. She let Vespar lift her up and curled her arms around his neck.

"I'm sorry, Master Vespar. I won't ever do it again."

Vespar sat beside Heldran and held Emlyn on his knee. The lads were silent.

"Magic is treacherous," Vespar said. "For all our study and practice, we will never fully understand it. It does what we can't explain. When we think we have tamed it, It turns from us. It thinks It can manipulate us." He glanced between his men. "We cannot let It control us. It surrendered

Itself to us. We are not Its slaves. I used to think so," he said, brushing Emlyn's hair from her eyes. "No, we are not Its slaves. We are Its masters. It will do *our* bidding. It will not defeat us. Nothing will."

Vespar set Emlyn on her feet, folded her tiny hands in his, and looked in her eyes. "You are not Its servant. You are more than a princess. You are a queen. Magic gave Itself to you. It did not take you captive."

Emlyn stared at her feet. "I didn't mean to let it do that to me."

"I believe you, my girl." He raised her chin. "You overcame, and thankfully Master Tylysk was there to help you."

Tylysk bowed his head.

"And you will continue to overcome. Magic will obey you, precious Enchantress. You are Its queen. You will put Magic in Its place."

Emlyn fingered her healed cheek. "That sounds scary."

"That is why I teach you. You are not alone. Heldran, Tylysk, and I will always be here."

Heldran squeezed his sister's hand.

"Think of what you will do when you take your place, little one," Vespar said. "Think how you could prove your innocence and show Caeradin the truth about your kind. All the good that will come. You are not Lady Blodica. You are queen Emlyn."

She peeked back at the lads. "I could stop the Hunt?" she asked.

"You could change the whole of Caeradin. You could rebuild her anew."

Her lip quivered. "But, what about…"

Vespar rested a gentle hand under her chin. "We can't dwell on Rhys any longer. He made his choice."

"But he can help us. He promised to make everything better."

He shook his head. "Rhys is far gone, my girl. It is too late."

Emlyn smeared her tears away herself. She considered, sought Heldran's opinion, then Tylysk's. A deep breath, and Emlyn faced her tutor. "Yes, Master Vespar."

He grasped her hand. "All will be well, my precious girl. You can trust me a little longer, can't you?"

"Yes, Master Vespar."

He pressed a kiss to her brow. "Go and see that Mistress Orrtha knows you're all right. Take Tylysk with you. Perhaps you'll find Isabelle along the way."

Emlyn's mischievous grin made her teary eyes twinkle. She pulled Tylysk to his feet. Vespar patted his second's arm as they went to the door.

Heldran stayed on the bench and watched his sister leave, frowning. His brown eyes were lifeless still, but less so than when he arrived some weeks ago. Before he knew the truth behind Emlyn's disappearance, he'd been a shell, soulless, nothing in his eyes at all. At least a spark had returned to him, despite his exhaustion. Vespar never blamed him. To be forced to relinquish guardianship over his sister to his master, not moments after their reunion, could have made any other man lose faith.

Vespar followed Heldran's gaze toward the door. "Where did she get her eyes, Master Heldran?"

He was taken back, but smiled. "She is our mother through and through, sir. Her eyes were so gray-blue, some days they looked lavender, like Emlyn's."

"You must take after your father, then." Vespar nodded when Heldran did. "There's no doubt he did well by his children, for Emlyn to be so learned, and you also, when you came to the Academy. You were a right little scholar at ten, lad."

"Thank you, sir."

Vespar waited until Heldran looked up. "I would never question your loyalty, Heldran. You have always made your position clear, however blindly you've had to follow."

Heldran showed an unconvincing smile.

"It is for Emlyn's sake, and yours, that I chose Tylysk as her protector. Tylysk and I needed to gain her trust, and that you allowed him to watch over her shows Emlyn your own confidence in us. Tylysk has had to adapt to his new role, and in doing so, he has helped Emlyn ease into hers. For your sake, so you would continue to trust us."

Heldran folded his hands tight together.

"However much Tylysk likes to complain," Vespar said, and Heldran strove not to concur, "he would have struggled with your task more than you. He would be halfway to Elfryth to search for the Wizard. But you are cautious. I don't believe the Wizard would run from you as he would from Tylysk or me."

Heldran sat back with a deep breath. "I've tried everything, sir. He's evaded me before he knows I'm looking for him."

Vespar twisted his ring. "He has always known we've been looking for him. Since we first met, he has known."

Heldran stared. "You've met him?"

"Years ago. He was as ghostlike then as he is now. He soon disappeared."

"Why? What is he hiding from?"

Vespar held his ring to the magelight, where it glittered silver on gold. "The Wizard has what I need, Master Heldran, and he was not of a mind to give it."

"Then what of Emlyn?"

"I believe she can convince him otherwise. But do not let this seeming insensitivity sway your opinion of my fondness for her. Truly, that is all I need from her yet. Though afterward, it would be best for you to remain here. It may be unavoidable." Vespar replaced his ring and met Heldran's eye. "We would not wish to separate her from her Wizard, would we?"

CHAPTER 46

Rhys

We broke camp before dawn. As the day drew on, the thick woods grew too close together, and little sun leaked through the web of leaves overhead, but at least the shade provided some well-deserved relief from the heat.

Four of the wounded had to be strapped to litters, and those who carried them plodded through the knotted forest. I managed to stay on my feet but still needed my arm across Brai's or Athrú's shoulders to hobble along. Oedolyn kept steady vigil over the weary troops, her medicine satchel at her hip.

Around midday, when we stopped to rest, Oedolyn finally spoke to me. She and Athrú had avoided my subtle inquiries all morning, but when it became clear that he would say nothing, Oedolyn relented. She lowered her voice when her brother turned his back.

"We don't know who Righnách is, exactly," she said as she plastered a salve onto my wound. "We think he's a bounty hunter of sorts."

I shifted on my bristly cushion of leaves. "And...you?"

Oedolyn blanched. She shook her head, whisking a lock of hair from her face. "He led a Hunting raid on our village when we were young."

I avoided her eye as she wound a fresh bandage around me. Saying nothing more, she moved on to help the injured rangers.

I could no longer chase away what little I recalled of the night before. I'd come away from my first battle, most of which I had no memory, with a wound that should have killed me. Vespar was so eager to see me dead, he didn't wait for me to show my face to prove I'd broken my exile. Yet, thanks to a gruesome draconis release, his assassin failed.

I glanced in Oedolyn's direction. I didn't wish to pry into that, nor did I want to think how she could distract Righnách from his duties enough that I had to remind him to kill me. But with Oedolyn in his sights, I was certain we'd see him again.

The siblings said as much as either of them would, so when Athrú dropped next to me, I simply asked, "How far do we have left?"

"Hard to say. We're off course, and the way everyone is, it could be another two weeks."

I rubbed my exhausted eyes.

"Rodd will get us back to the river. That will speed things up."

Oedolyn hewed into our conversation by ordering Athrú to leave me alone and threatening to pour enough moonjoy tonic down my throat, we'd be in the city before I woke again. Chamberlain flopped beside me and forbade me to move.

I never slept. The wound ached—I should've taken Rodd's offer for an earlier rest. I was frustrated with our crawling pace, furious for letting the dragon take control, cross with him for everything else.

That wasn't necessary, I snapped.

No reply.

How was that necessary?

How else would you have escaped? You cannot overcome one ranger without my aid, let alone an army. You would not have survived without my forcing such unnecessary *tactics.*

As degrading as it sounded, I didn't deny it. *You took your time. He could have killed us.*

Now you know you need me. He turned to meet my glare, a sharp glint to his blue scales. *You forget I am part of you. Did you think I would not also sustain a wound? A minor one, but a wound nonetheless. Thanks to me, you will be well again in a matter of days.* He turned away, head tilted haughtily.

I'm not happy with you.

Why should that matter to me?

Why would I ever let you out again after what you did?

I told you. You need me. I am all that stands between you and death. He shifted away to gape his monstrous jaws in a yawn. He limped to his amber sleeping pocket, coiled into himself, and nestled down. *You had best get used to it. We are bound together for the next dragon's age.*

Too soon, though some hours later, the others set to breaking camp. I choked on a dose of mold-flavored burbletack juice for the pain and chased it down with a heel of stale bread. Braidac loomed over Oedolyn, watching as she peeled the bandages away. He cocked his head.

"Is it supposed to look like that?" he asked.

The pestering collar of my shirt blocked my view of the wound. "What's wrong with it?"

"Nothing." Oedolyn brushed a finger along the stitches. "It looks better than it should. How does it feel?"

I shrugged. "Better than this morning. I can probably walk the rest of the day."

"Night, you mean." Brai grinned. "No sun to warm our merry way this time. It'll be nice. Not so hot. Glittering stars and moonlight to guide the way." He made a face at Oedolyn to produce an eyeroll and a satisfactory blush. I arched a brow at him and got a fist in the arm.

We moved off when the sun dropped beneath the horizon. I trusted Rodd's judgment, but the darkness unnerved me. The waning moon offered little light, cracked and averted by spidering tree limbs. We found the river by the scent of its muddy banks; its babbling seemed stifled by our presence, when I'd hoped it would drown out our own hushed sounds.

Come morning, talk was limited as we arranged camp. Athrú held a quiet discussion with Rodd. Braidac stayed beside Oedolyn more and more, drawn in by shy smiles and, more often, soft fear in her eyes. Athrú pretended not to notice, but sent them sidelong glances. Brai wasn't deterred by her brother and held Oedolyn's hand when she'd let him.

They knelt together in the middle of camp, digging through packs for dried fruit and jerky. Braidac paid no mind to what he was doing, and Oedolyn wouldn't look away from her own busy hands. He must've said something ridiculous—she doubled over, shoulders quaking with laughter. I'd never seen her grin so wide, her blue eyes so small.

For the umpteenth time, I saw something of Flannery in her. Perhaps in the way her honey-gold hair moved, the one strand falling in her face, the warmth of her voice. I turned away.

I jolted. Dair stood a step away, his expression condescending.

"Your guard is low." He bumped his staff to my chest. "What did I tell you? To fight is to make it out alive. And no shame to get help."

I stammered for a moment. "I heard you bested fifteen men before they could catch Oedolyn and me."

Dair didn't acknowledge. "You're still off your guard. I could skewer you right now if I had half the mind, and you'd be so unprepared, you wouldn't scream."

I startled back. I glanced down, expecting to see his calloused fingers curled around the hilt of a dagger.

"I'm rather new to this," I said, "and I trust my companions here."

"So said every fool who had his throat slit." Dair drew away. "Should I have come from behind? Should that assassin creep on you in the dark? Your draconis can't protect you unless you're fast enough to heed him."

Dair turned aside, but I said, "And if I'm unprepared? What—"

The dragon raised my hand in time to catch the staff as Dair swung it toward my head. I stared, mouth ajar. Dair's gaze met mine, dark as ever.

"Don't be unprepared."

He jerked the staff away. He wandered off, not caring that everyone was staring after him.

⁂

Four nights later, we found the stark tree line gating the forest from the empty fields. Outward, lazy knolls and meadows of night-shaded green spread farther than we could see. The river split them, shrinking toward the western horizon.

Braidac pointed to where tiny flecks of light blinked not too far away. "Ostburn, I think," he said. He traced the horizon toward a further square of lights a touch north of west. "Then there's the capital."

"We'll have to cross soon." Rodd gauged the river. It wasn't wide here; I could throw a stone halfway across. As for depth and swiftness, it was impossible to tell with the murky water reflecting a meager trace of moon on its glassy surface. A squat, cavernous cliff ran alongside it a short distance from the bank.

"We'll wait for light. These cliffs go down a ways." Rodd motioned the length of the precipice with a sweep of his arm. "We'll find shelter in the caves when we find a ford."

We went on through the remaining hours of darkness. Chamberlain trotted alongside me. He took no notice of the dragon near the surface, watching the outside through his window, senses pricked.

By the time the sun rose at our backs, Ostburn lay directly south of us. Rodd frowned at the ford we found—while shallower and traversable, the current had widened by several yards. It would have to do.

Oedolyn took Rodd's arm at Athrú's request, and he led her across the water. One by one, the rangers raised their gear over their heads and stepped into the shallows.

Brai elbowed me. "Come on. You could use a bath."

"You're fresh as roses too, Brai."

Athrú and I followed him into the water. Dair, as ever, brought up the rear. Chamberlain paddled to the other shore and clambered onto the high banks ahead of us. He barked, skittered along the banks, snuffling the water.

The river came as high as my stomach. The gentle current swept away weeks of grime. Its chill stung the wound, but the coolness after long days of heat made up for it. A few rangers bobbed their heads under.

Brai yelped and jumped, ramming into me. "What was that?"

"A bit of weed, boy. Don't let it frighten you," Dair muttered.

"No, something moved. It grabbed my ankle."

"A fish?" I said. "They could bite."

Brai splashed me. "Look, it was right here."

I peered through the crystalline flow, seeing nothing but my boots on pebbly riverbed. I shoved him. "Don't wait for it to grab you again. Go."

Brai moved, watching his exaggerated steps. I strode around the questionable spot. Nothing. Athrú shrugged when I glanced back.

"There! I saw it!"

"Enough of your games, boy," Dair barked.

"I'm not playing games!"

"Then what was it?" I looked where Brai pointed.

"I don't know. It moved too fast. And no, it wasn't a rotting—"

Brai went straight under, sucked into the water. Before I could reach for his flailing arms, it constricted around my ankles and hauled me down.

The shock of it froze me, and for a moment, I forgot not to breathe. I kicked against whatever had me, propelling myself through the water. It gripped tighter. It pulled me down, back flat against the riverbed. My lungs and wound screamed. The dragon clamped my jaws shut and growled at me to hold my breath.

I swiped at Athrú's cloak. The hem ripped from my fingers. He and Dair were lost to sight as the thing dragged me on, too fast to tell in which direction.

I scrambled for my sword, clutched at the hilt in both hands to keep the current from sweeping it from my grasp. I hacked outward, catching nothing but water. An icy chill spread up my leg from my captor's tightening grasp. White flashed across my vision. My lungs shriveled. The dragon squirmed.

I came ashore, dragged foot first onto the banks. I hacked for air. Somewhere to my left, Brai choked up water. The unyielding hold pinned me down and out of his reach. I blindly swung my sword. The grip lurched upward to clutch the front of my tunic, the chill of it stealing my breath. I opened my burning eyes.

It was a child. A girl with long, bushy curls the color of sun-glistened snow hovered a cold breath above my face, her silvery eyes fixed to mine. A sheen of starlight radiated from her, shrouded a blinding cloak around her. She was barely existent, her marble-white being fragile as frost.

The girl frowned and searched me. The water on my face and hair frosted under the chill she exuded. The dragon writhed to escape, but my limbs stiffened.

The girl released me and bounced backward into the air. I scrambled away to find Brai in a juddering heap behind me. The creature on him hissed in my face. I lurched to my feet, sword ready, and glimpsed around.

More creatures, men and women alike, came crawling from the river and its muddy banks as if from their graves, hovering in the shade of the cliffside. Their pale-yellow eyes were empty, glowing orbs, their beings less solid than the girl's. She was untouchable flesh and bone, while the creatures resembled humanoid wisps. An occasional moan or whimper rode the sound of an exhaling breath. The haunting noise echoed on itself.

Brai yelped and scrambled out of his abductor's grasp. He readied his bow, though the river had claimed most of his arsenal, and I doubted it would have done more than my blade had. Brai put his back to mine, directing his last arrow around the horde of creatures.

I kept my eyes on the girl. She hovered in midair, standing on solid nothing. She cocked her head, unsure what to make of me, I thought.

Brai turned his head enough to whisper in my ear. "Where's the sun?"

"What?"

"Is there sunlight that way?"

I glanced past the girl. The cliffside shaded the riverbanks as far as I could see. I knew the creatures had dragged us to the other side of the river, but whether upstream or down, I was too disoriented to tell. The nearest sunlight shone halfway across the river.

"If we get in the sun, they'll let us go," Brai hissed. "They can't go in the sun."

"How do you know?"

"That's a pretty sword."

I turned to find the girl walking two gossamer fingers along the edge of my blade. She tiptoed the length of it, light on the air, level with me. She brushed the sapphire on the hilt.

"Pretty. You must like dragons. Your dragon is this color, isn't he?"

Brai went stock still. I stuttered. The girl studied me closer, glancing from one of my eyes to the other. The dragon poised low. Smoke curled from his nostrils.

"No, I guess not." She shrugged. "He's darker than this. Who's that with you?" The girl glided around to Brai and giggled. "Uh-oh, silly ranger. What happened to all your arrows?"

Brai paled.

"Doesn't matter anyway." The girl tapped the arrowhead with a finger, then drove her hand down on its tip. The shaft passed through her palm. Brai dropped the arrow and whipped the bow out of her reach. She giggled.

"Silly boys. My mistress would like you, little ranger." The girl skipped to me. "She'd like you too, but she doesn't want to keep you."

Brai, unnaturally lost for words, gaped, face almost as pallid as the girl. I tried to laugh, for his sake.

"Oh?" I said. "What's he got that I don't?"

The girl giggled behind her hands. "Silly, it's not what he has. It's what you have."

The dragon bared his teeth.

"But, then again…" The girl paced the air, hands folded behind her back. "She might can take it away. Maybe, if you really want her to."

Brai jabbed an elbow into my back. "We have to get to the water. Swim for it."

"Wouldn't you like that?" She loomed a step away, beaming with a wry smile. "You never liked your dragon before. He hurts you. Why would you want to keep him?"

The dragon whisked his snarl to me. *Do not be tempted.*

That's tempting enough, no matter who it comes from, I retorted. *Little help you are again. What are you stalling for this time?*

"Come on." The girl reached a hand to me. "The ranger can come too. We'll go see my mistress."

Brai clutched the back of my shirt. "This way. When we're past the horde, we'll jump."

"I don't think they'd like that, little ranger." The girl glided over my head to dangle nose to nose with Brai upside down. Frost crystallized on his hair and scruff. "They'd just catch you, anyway. You're not fast enough."

Brai trembled, whether from chill or sheer terror, I couldn't tell.

"Shouldn't you tell us who your mistress is if we're supposed to meet her?" I asked, voice cracking.

The girl shook her head, swept her curls from her face. "No, silly. It's a surprise."

"Never mind," Brai whispered. "Go your way. The others are that way."

"But they're not invited." The girl whipped around to him again. Her horde drifted toward our escape routes, some swarming overhead. "My mistress doesn't care about them. Only you."

"We don't care who your mistress likes," I spat. "We don't care what she wants. Let us go."

"Even if we did, we'd just come for you again." The girl dropped down to tiptoe along the ground, balancing on an invisible ring around us. Our sodden footprints iced over beneath her feet. "My mistress always gets what she wants. She knows how to get it. She knows lots of things. She knows what will make you come." The girl stopped in front of Brai, a wicked smile twisting on her face. "That might be fun."

The dragon urged me to attack somehow, but even if it would have worked, I couldn't raise my sword to a girl little bigger than Emlyn, whose spooky, dimpled grin was crooked with baby teeth. Her clashing appearance and demeanor deterred Brai as much.

"My mistress knows how to find lots of people too," the girl cooed. "You have lots of people to find, don't you, little ranger?"

Brai trembled. He shook his head.

She extended a hand to him. "Come home with me. My mistress can help you find them."

Braidac drew away, staring into her face. "No. Leave them alone."

"She won't hurt them. It doesn't have to be all bad. She can make it better too."

The girl reached for his hand. He didn't retreat. A tear frosted halfway down his cheek.

The dragon swiped my arm around Brai's middle and launched us both toward the river. The chill of the creatures clutched us as we passed through them. Brai cried out at the sharp sting and gulped a drink as we went under. We flailed to the surface, though our limbs were rigid with cold. I snagged Brai and hauled him toward the sunlight.

"Stupid boys!" the girl screeched.

The ghastly creatures soared overhead. They swooped, grasping with hollow, ragged fingers. The water crackled beneath their frozen beings. One snatched Brai's cloak. He kicked at its haggard face to no avail. The dragon helped me yank him free. The creature dove once more. We plunged and swam the last few yards into the sunlight halving the waterway. The creatures reared back, hissing, steam curling from their hoary beings. They swarmed along the edge of the shade as if around a hive.

Brai and I surfaced and paddled to safety on the opposite shore. I clambered up the steep bank first and hoisted Brai up. We flopped face down in the mud to catch our breath.

The girl's shriek flipped us onto our backs. She hovered above us, full in the sunlight.

"Stupid, *stupid* little boys!" she roared, slamming her feet to the ground in the air. "My mistress will find you again. She'll make you come, no matter how she has to do it."

I staggered to my feet. "We're not following you anywhere. Fly back to your mistress and tell her she can't have us."

Brai yanked me down before the girl shot into the air over my head. She vanished in a whiff of smoke, her piercing shrieks echoing along the cliff face. Her minions slithered to their hiding places in the fissures of the cliff and into riverbank graves.

I dropped beside Brai, panting. "Can't go in the sun, can she?" I snapped.

He gagged up a mouthful of river water. "The others couldn't. She couldn't get us alone."

I dusted the frost off myself and sat up. Brai's sopping hair had frozen into clumps, and the cold left his face ruddy and chapped. He moaned, soaked in all the warmth the sun had to offer, his fingers locked around his bow.

"What are those things?" I asked.

Brai sat up, combing his fingers through his clumped hair. "Ghastly monsters, is what. Some people just call them ghosts, but most call them Ice Shadows." He leaned closer. "They're the spirits of people killed by curses. They never find rest. They just wander and prey on living innocents." There was no ghost story exaggeration in his tone. He scanned the opposite banks with a shudder. "Skin and bones, what do they want with us?"

I stopped myself from imagining it. The child's vivid face hung fresh in mind. That was all I needed, a horde of undead haunters behind me. What more could happen between here and the Manor a few days' journey out of reach?

Brai flopped down when I reached to help him up. "Let's rest a moment. It's too nice right here." He spread himself out to dry, a faint smile cracking his mouth. "This is almost like Corandul. Almost. We have to take Emlyn there. She'd love it, I know it."

I dropped beside him, clutching my throbbing wound. His restless chatter would've been a comfort, but his consciousness slipped under the warm sun and thawing limbs.

A smack to my cheek woke me with a start. The rough hand stayed on my face until I blinked up at the scowling figure shading me.

"Ash and flame," Dair snarled. "Between the both of you, we'll reach the city by next winter." He balanced me on wobbling legs before he bent to wake Braidac.

Brai moaned behind his hands. "I *told* you there was something in the water."

Dair ripped him up as though he weighed nothing. "Glad there was. If it'd been one of your games, I'd have held you under the water myself." He moved down the riverbank a ways and gave a ranger's call. When a distant response came, he took up his staff and waved us along. "You're making your own way back. I'm not carrying either of you pups."

We followed. We kept to the grass far from the water, though the sun had shifted to shine along the ravine, leaving nothing to shade. Brai scrutinized our surroundings.

"We were here last night," he groaned. "How far did they drag us?"

"If you pick up the pace, we'll reach the others in another hour," Dair answered. "Who is *they*?"

Brai closed his mouth. The red heat in his face paled. I avoided Dair's silent demand and kept walking.

By the time we reached the ford where the creatures discovered us, the sun loomed toward the west, glinting red along the cliff face across the water. Dair led the way across, and Rodd and Athrú waited to pull us over the high banks. Athrú supported me the distance to the cavern the others had crowded into. A mage ranger lowered his glaze of green shield to let us pass. Oedolyn pounced on us, searched our weary faces, stripped off our cloaks, and sent us to dry by the fire.

Brai and I huddled around the minute blaze. Oedolyn gave us more than our fair share of supper. Everyone pried for Brai's fantastic tale of what had happened, and even Dair grumbled about his silence. He kept his mouth shut. I said nothing when he wouldn't.

The next few nights were quiet. The river slithered south. The ghosts never showed themselves again, and nothing suggested they spawned from the water, but Brai and I gladly strayed from it. The tan cliffs sloped to green hills, fragrant with heather.

Too often, our scouts returned to veer us off course before we sprang another trap. Hunters and mercenaries alike were prowling the wilderness, anticipating our every pathway. Our haphazard serpentine stretched what should have been a few more days' journey into another week.

Rodd turned us south. A rainstorm pelted us that night, perhaps the most pleasant part of our dismal journey. Gildio's valley sparked white with lightning. The mages raised a barrier overhead to keep out the downpour. Oedolyn cooed some song to ease Chamberlain through the storm. Long after the beast was snoozing, Brai requested another tune, and another, until Oedolyn drooped midverse. Athrú kept her close in the warmth of his cloak as they rested.

Dawn dispersed the clouds and hung a thin light across the valley. The scent of rain cooled the sweet air, adding a briskness to the late summer morning. We kept moving toward a towering hill to shield ourselves from the city's view and made camp at its foot. Athrú, Brai, and I scuttled to the top to look.

Straight down the gradual slope, less than a mile south, lay Gildio city. Within the walls, the small green mounds cradled the Manor. The city glowed gold from the east, and shadows crept across rooftops and followed the grid of streets, fingers stretching toward flattened brown farmlands beyond the walls. The light caught on the Gildian banners hanging limp on each of the castle's turrets.

"All right," said Brai. "Now what?"

CHAPTER 47

Rhys

The next dawn arose in a gray sky, alighting the feathery clouds with a blaze of scarlet and amber. As the misty light shrouded the valley, I slinked up the hill to study the land.

The others looked to me to devise the bulk of the plan, as I new the Manor and the city best. Undoubtedly, Vespar knew his various welcoming parties had failed and had doubled or tripled security inside and outside both the Manor and city walls, with another force scouting for us. I lay on my stomach at the crest of the hill and studied the city.

I squinted in the blinding sunrise. A turret guarded each end of the narrow wall to the north. A small gate, secured with a portcullis without and iron doors within, took up the middle. We hid too far away to see anything else well, but venturing closer deprived us of decent cover.

Having difficulties?

I grimaced. *You've been quiet.*

You have not needed me.

I would've liked a bit more help against those Ice Shadows. Or at least a warning.

I do not do well in water. The dragon shifted his face to me. *That is not the issue at hand.*

I hesitated. *I can't see the Manor well enough.*

A dilemma. He turned away.

Can you help me?

I can, but I do not know that I will.

Don't do that to me now. We're so close!

Too close. It is treacherous. Nothing you do will go unnoticed, whatever plan you contrive. Should I be so quick to lead us to our end?

We scared off an army thanks to you. We can take a few mages.

Perhaps, but can you best the strongest of them all?

I licked my lips. *I'll make you a deal.*

He looked at me sidelong, red eyes narrow.

I've been thinking about what you said, how we'll live a dragon's age, and we're stuck together forever, I said, still coming to terms with the fact.

Thanks to me.

Thanks to you. So if we're going to live with each other, we have to come to some agreement, yes?

Incredulity lined his scaled face.

If you help me now, I'll let you help me in the Manor. But only if you promise not to go mad like you did last time. And you let me choose what happens.

He laughed low in his belly. *You are the one who lost hold of the reins.*

Do we have a deal?

That is much to ask. You hinder me.

You want out so bad. This is how I'll compromise. Deal?

The dragon switched his barbed tail, debating. *Unfair. You cannot win double.*

Double? I scoffed. *You think I like you ripping through my skin?*

I will accept your terms with one addition. The dragon brought his head level with me, nothing sinister in his midnight dark features. He glowered, a look of resoluteness, not contempt.

My name.

The sincerity in his rumbling tone threw me. *You…want a name?*

I have one. I want you to use it.

I…didn't know, I said, feeling stupid. *What is it?*

A long silence, then he said, *Draas.*

I nodded. *All right, Draas. Do we have a deal?*

Draas swerved away. I called him back, beating my fist to the grass.

My eyes burned, like fresh ash tossed in my face. I rubbed the irritation away. I peered up—the wall, half a mile away, appeared to stand a few yards off. I focused on the armored sentinel on the eastern tower. Draas scanned the fields within the wall.

I centered my inspection on the castle. The bailey spread in full view, where the entire garrison marched under Swordsmaster Perreth's tyrannical eye. The castle blocked all but the southeastern corner of the garden and a few shaded Melys trees. I concentrated on my memory of the vast garden, identified where each gate stood, imagined the castle's ancient structure. The hedges, the pathway, the windows overlooking them, to which chamber each casement led.

Draas tossed his head at the plan formulating in my mind. *You leave too much to chance*, he growled.

Any better ideas?

No response. I slid down the hill. Draas withdrew his sight before we reached the others, and with a few interjections from the dragon, I related my plan. Rodd and his men set to dissecting the scheme. We spent the morning smoothing any mishap we could imagine, watching the city and the Manor, memorizing the guard rotation. A few rangers disguised themselves and scouted ahead. By late afternoon, we had agreed upon a plan of attack. We had until the next evening to devise our escape.

As early dusk shrouded purple across the valley, I clambered up the hill to look again. The glittering river cut through the city in the shape of a whip in motion. Far south in the Lower Side stood another ruined castle I'd never seen before. A street west of Brac's tavern, the tan bricks of the Mage Academy's four spires towered above three symmetrical rings of grass courtyard. Folks brimmed the streets, not knowing Master

Claytherdon had returned, thinking I was a fool boy who'd forsaken his people and blackened the Claytherdon name.

I didn't realize how I missed Gildio until I saw it again, counted the many black-and-green banners, watched the palace where I was born and raised. Nor how miserable guilt constricted around me, for what my people thought I'd done. Wishing they would understand, that they'd see what I did was, in part, for them.

Brai flopped down beside me, scanned the valley with half a smile. "It was Winter Dawn the last time I came through here. It's a nicer winter here than back home. You don't get snowed in. But Lleogren's not Ethelfled, praises be."

"You've been to Ethelfled?"

"Mm. It was spring then, but I had icicles hanging from my nose."

"Why on earth would you go there?"

"I've been lots of places," Brai said, peering down at the bow in his lap. "We're always on the move, you know. But I liked it here." He perked up. "I won a tournament here once. I can't remember what I won. Something nice. Was that where I got the...no, that was in Itis."

I shoved him. Brai's smile wasn't as easy as usual.

"I've just decided," he said. "I'm taking you to Corandul after this. Make our grand escape for the seashore. It's a long way, but worth every step. You and Emlyn will love it."

I frowned, turning away from the cityscape. "If we're not fighting a war before we get there."

"Isn't it strange?" Brai laughed sadly. "How something so small could upend the world? How one little girl can set great men at each other's throats out of fear and hate?" He smoothed a hand along the length of his bow. "What a terrible thing."

His dimmed eyes swept across the knolls to the southwest. Burial mounds glistened green there, with wavering specks of black eagles decking the field. Weathered stones marked the hillside openings of my forebears' resting places.

My chest clenched until I couldn't bear it. "Let's go."

Brai blinked. "Where? Down there? But—"

I hurried down to camp. Brai scrabbled behind me to Athrú's side.

"There's somewhere I have to go," I said.

Athrú's inquisitive look willed me to point toward the particular patch of mounds. "Rhys—"

"Please. Just for a moment."

Athrú looked to Rodd. The captain shook his head. "We can't risk our cover now," he said.

Brai studied me, frowning. "What's got you, hm?"

"Please."

Athrú sought Rodd's opinion once more, eyed the plea on my face. He sighed and ran a hand through his hair. "Not alone, I think."

"Brai's coming. You?"

Athrú cast a hesitant glance toward his sister, but followed.

When half the sun perched on the horizon, Brai, Athrú and I sneaked along the verdant ridges, spying the sentinels on the wall. I took them the long way behind the hills to cut down toward the faint dirt path south of us.

Mounds stretched far across the slopes, marked with aged stones and flagpoles. Banners morphed from reds to blues, each bearing the eagle insignia, the most recent generations waving black on green. A few oaks stood proud, as ancient as some of the tombs they guarded. Violet heather and white lilac sweetened the air, saving my forebears from looking quite so lonely.

Da's mound was indistinguishable from the others, rounded with over-growth and adorned with white wintercraft blossoms. A fresh Gildian banner tossed in the gentle breeze. Propped against the stone door rested a child's wooden sword.

"Da made that for me," I said. "I didn't know what else to give him. Vespar put a protective charm on it for me. It hasn't even aged."

Braidac laid his hood back, knelt on one knee, and clasped his bow to his chest. Athrú pressed a fist to his heart and bowed, as if greeting my father at his throne.

My throat thickened. Eyes misting, I groped to the stone, brushed the rainswept grime from the engraved eagle, scraped it out of the letters of his name. I dropped to my knees. I set my head to the stone.

"I'm trying, Da. I'm trying."

I slammed a fist to the stone. I needed him. Just one moment for him to rough my hair and call me his boy. To remind me how my mother had smiled when he kissed her, how she had emboldened him with the same strength he had empowered her. To grant me the courage he'd always exuded when standing against Vespar. It stole all my strength, left me bare and raw. He was my da. Why couldn't I have my da?

Why Flannery? Why them both? How did the world not stop when they did? How heartless of it. I faced it without them, misshapen, crippled, and alone. Could it not stop to let me catch my breath, let me get to my feet? No, it would dangle me over the edge of the earth and watch me beg.

I brought my head up. A sparrow alighted atop the stone door frame. It sang a few refrains, blinked at me, and flitted away.

I knelt there, staring where the bird had been. I'd forgotten the others were waiting for me until Athrú stepped reverently beside me. He took my arm and raised me up.

"Come on," he said. "Emlyn's waiting."

❧❧

Full dark shrouded the hills by the time we returned to camp. No one asked or spoke of our excursion, except Rodd mentioned he was about to send scouts after us. Athrú and Brai maintained a respectful silence, Athrú answering only his sister's worried frown. She squeezed my hand and sent me to rest.

As he did every night, Dair sat alone and whittled away at his staff.

I thought there'd be nothing left of it at this point, but the rod held strong. Dair beckoned me with a nod of his head.

"Miss your father, lad?" he said, gruff voice gentle.

I didn't answer.

Dair nodded. "Heard he was a good man. Had a spirit like yours, they say. Makes me wonder why he didn't get around to this before you."

"Vespar always stopped him," I said.

"Vespar kicked your rear out of your own realm, yet here you are. Then the question is, what's he got against you that he never had against your father? How did the heir threaten him more than the master?" Dair stowed his knife away, leaned his staff on his shoulder, and set his elbows on his knees. I crouched beside him. "If Vespar was of a mind to end the Hunt, he would have while your father lived. You know this. That's not what he's after."

I looked in the direction of the city, the hill concealing its spread of blinking magelights. "But how else is he supposed to keep Emlyn? What does he want her for?"

"What, indeed." Dair glowered, the scars across his face hardening. He jabbed a finger to my chest. "Think, boy. What was he rid of with you and your father, but gained from this girl?"

I considered, but I saw the comparison as clearly as I saw the city through the hill.

Dair clutched my collar, looked me in the eye. "Power."

I swallowed. Dair shoved me to the ground.

"Lord Cael said it himself. Vespar's after more than the kingdom he's taken from you. Why else would Cael and Rodd stick their necks out for you? Skin and bones, boy, did you think it was just about you and that girl?"

"No," I said. "But it is about Emlyn. Nothing happened until she came."

"Then think, you witless boy!" Dair smacked the side of my head. "Did Vespar need that girl to be rid of you? Does he need her to take Gildio for himself? Would a man like Vespar enlist a child, a comparative toddler, to whisk himself to the top of the heap?"

"No—"

"No. Then what does this girl have to offer? What power does he seek from her?"

"I-I don't know. He thinks her magic is strong—"

"Exactly. Then what more strength could this exceptional witch give the greatest mage in Caeradin?"

I gawked at him.

Dair cursed, pinched his eyes. "Rot you, boy! How can you fight a battle you know nothing about?"

"If I can't solve your riddles, will you at least tell me the answers?" I retorted.

"Solve this one, and you'll have all the answers." Dair jabbed me in the chest again. "What would make Vespar the most powerful man in Caeradin?"

Dair awaited an answer I had yet to find. Whatever came so obvious to him was not rearing its ugly head at me.

"Bah." Dair leaned on his staff and stood. "Everything has always been about power, and it will always be about power. All you have to determine is how much of it you're dealing with."

I stared up at him. He looked away from my despair, rubbed his eyes with a sigh. He clapped a hand to my face.

"At least it's a battle worth fighting."

I didn't watch him storm away, my heart pitted.

The camp sank to uneasy stillness. Brai and I took first watch. While the others dozed, Athrú lay awake, propped on his elbows to whisper to his anxious sister. She drifted, nestled with Chamberlain and his warmth. Athrú spread his cloak over her and settled down to sleep. All movement in the camp stilled.

The tension among the troops seeped into talkative Braidac. His eyes flickered across the others, focus sharpening his expression in the radiance of the high moon. I searched around with him, and after a while noticed what stirred him.

"Who's missing?" I whispered.

Brai slinked to his feet, bow in hand. We stole up the hill, the grass scarcely whispering under his feet. Chamberlain trotted after us and, noticing our wariness, began an investigation himself. Sweeping darkness cradled the knolls, except for feeble mageglow and firelight from the city. Brai squinted over the northern slopes.

"See it?" He gestured with the tip of his bow toward a slope to our left.

Draas peered out with me. The faintest light quivered in the shade behind the hill.

Chamberlain scurried ahead of us, nose to the ground. We crept behind him and weaved to the trace of light. Brai inched an arrow into place. I gripped my sword, motioned Chamberlain to stay. Brai and I exchanged silent glances, took a breath. We pounced.

No one was there.

The light emitted from a single candlestick, where a makeshift pavilion of a cloak shielded its brightness. It illuminated a disarray of spilled ink and parchments across a dirt patch. One sheet of paper smoldered.

Brai relaxed his bow. We stooped and sifted through the parchments. Brai plucked the quill from the ink puddle, retrieved the half-empty bottle, and held it to the candlelight.

"Knew we were coming," he whispered, twirling the stained feather between his fingers.

I straightened the pages on the dirt. I flipped them against my thumb and studied the first parchment while Brai peered over my shoulder. The scribe was unaccustomed to using a pen—the crooked scrawl of foreign letters was shaky and thick.

"Can you read this?" I asked.

Brai raised a brow without looking at the page. "If you can't, what makes you think I can, Sir Scholar?"

"I can't. I think it's—"

"Ethelfledian."

I blinked.

"It's Ethelfledian." He used the feather to point to a lowercase *a* with a long, downward tail. "That's their symbol for 'and.'"

"How'd you know that?"

"What, you didn't? Aren't you Gildian nobles supposed to know Ethelfledian?"

I ignored that. "So can you read it?"

"No." Brai frowned. "But some of the other rangers can."

I flipped through the pages again until I came across a thicker sheet. The same language covered it, this time drafted in straight, sharp calligraphy without a blot out of place. I held the page to the light and examined the familiar scrawl. It struck me when my right wrist tingled. Draas rumbled.

"This is Tylysk's writing. Someone's talking to him."

Brai paled. "Are you sure?"

"Yes, look at the—"

Brai snatched the parchment from my hand. Just as he looked, a few words scratched onto the sheet, letter by letter, with Tylysk's pen. Brai dropped the page as if it'd caught fire. When the writing stopped, he gathered the papers and tucked them into his cloak.

"We'll take these to Rodd." He stowed the ink and quill away. "He'll deal with this."

Chamberlain howled.

Something caught us both across our throats. Brai flung himself to the right, somersaulted to his feet, and raised his bow. I choked behind the strangling pressure. It yanked me backward and held fast. Draas snarled and, as caught off guard as I, struggled to catch his footing.

Braidac's dismay froze me against the throttling force. He stammered, but raised his bow.

"Get off him, Dair."

The staff scraped down my chin and settled deeper into my throat.

"Oh, my guard is low, is it?" I managed. "Or is that your mess down there?"

Dair stood his ground, even with Chamberlain poised and snarling at Brai's side. The staff dug so close, I couldn't swallow.

"I'll shoot." Brai's voice cracked. "I'll shoot. You know I will."

"Run along, pup," Dair rumbled. "You're not worth the mess."

"We've all seen you sneaking off at night," I grunted. "Get away to chat with Vespar's man? And we thought it was Master Corrick giving us away."

Dair tugged harder, the buckles of his jerkin mashing into my back. I stood on my toes to give myself room to breathe. Brai drew his bowstring to his cheek.

"It's bad enough it was one of us," he said, "but you, Dair? Everything you said back there, everything you've done. Put Rhys down, and this never happened."

Dair's heart pounded against my spine, his shaky breath hot on my neck. "Then do your duty before I do mine."

"I don't want to kill you, Dair. And you don't want to kill Rhys. Think of that little girl we came all the way out here for. Think what Lord Cael sent us to do." Brai shook his head. "Don't do this to us. Not now. Please, Dair."

White sparked across my vision. Draas staggered. My limbs wilted.

Dair wrenched back with enough force to break my neck. Brai's arrow flew.

Dair roared and twisted around, clutching the shaft embedded in his shoulder. The staff fell at my feet. I dropped and hacked for air. Braidac readied another arrow. Dair regained himself and lunged for the staff with his wounded arm. I jerked it from his weak grasp. Taking command, Draas clubbed the old ranger full in back, sent him sprawling to the ground. The arrow piercing him snapped under the fall. Dair howled, paralyzed with agony.

Brai rushed to Dair's side. He rolled the moaning ranger over. He pressured a hand to the gushing wound, the broken shaft between his fingers. Draas urged me to disarm the rogue ranger of every weapon I could find, though I wondered if Dair would have the strength to wield them again.

"If you'd just listened to me," Brai cried.

"If you hadn't hesitated," Dair spat. "Witless coward, always so trusting, so hopeful. Here you are again."

Draas moved my hand to redirect Dair's knife, but I stopped it from pricking his throat. "You are more a coward than he could ever be," I snarled.

We hadn't noticed the others slinking toward us, weapons raised, until one of the mages yanked Braidac aside to tend to Dair's wound himself. Athrú grasped my shoulders and urged me away, gripped my wrist to loosen the knife from my fingers. Oedolyn gasped and started for her satchel, but Brai caught her and sent her to tend to me instead. The developing bruise and the lingering burn of Dair's staff scraping my throat were my fortunate alternatives to a broken neck, and I wasted no time with her examination.

Rodd motioned for his men to stand down. Brai presented the evidence of Dair's betrayal and left the heated report to me. One of the mages conjured a light and held it for Rodd to read the pages.

Athrú swung on the traitor. "You knew about Righnách's ambush, didn't you? Did you know what would happen at the river, as well?"

Dair groaned as his healers sat him up. With the embedded arrow free, the mages set to binding the wound. Draas growled at the sight of it, thinking Dair deserved every pain that wracked him.

"Played your part well enough," I said. "Made sure to do something spectacular to save our skins. Did you tell those mercenaries to let you win?"

"And you stopped them from getting Oedolyn and Rhys before they could escape," Athrú asserted, motioning to his startled sister. He glared, a terrifying look on his subtle features. "You let them walk into Righnách's trap."

"Athrú," Oedolyn said softly. He clenched his jaws, but didn't stand down.

"And when that failed, you reported to Vespar's man, and he told you to lead us to those ghosts at the river," I spat.

"No one has any idea what happened to you there but you, your-selves," Dair said. "I had no part in that."

"That I believe," said Rodd. He perused the parchments as casually as reading a bit of trifling news. "There's nothing to suggest you had a hand in the incident at the river. You did, however, inform your cor-respondent of everything else, including when we intend to make our move. You didn't have time to reveal our strategy, but they know we're here." The captain's expression held professional contempt and no sur-prise whatsoever. "When everything else failed, you were told to stop Master Rhys yourself."

"But Dair found you two after the attack at the river," the mage at Dair's side said. "He had every chance to do something then. Why didn't he?"

Braidac stared at the wounded ranger, pallid. "He hesitated," he said. "How else could we have trusted him?"

"Better yet," said Rodd, "you had your doubts, so some of these exchanges show. Your contact had to persuade you with land and a title should you succeed."

No one was made more furious than Braidac. He took a step toward Dair, fists shaking. "You almost snapped Rhys's neck for some dirt? For a sickly, scrawny, puny little patch of *dirt*?" Then, broken, he said, "You were *Dair*. You were the warrior who took the javelin for Cael's father. Who's been the most respected ranger in the Elite. Skin and bones, the one who thought up this whole mission in the first place and told him it was worth it," Brai roared, jerking a finger at me. "And you blacken it all by betraying your comrades, your *friends*, to side with the enemy—and for what? Some filthy coin and a spit of land you won't even get now."

Dair laughed low through the pain. "Do your fairytales end with a man claiming his due? He can't live off praise and honor. If you fight a rich man's war, fight on the rich man's side, else you'll come home poorer. And if the rich man offers more than you can swallow, all the better—take a nibble and come back for more. Learn that now, boy. You'll get nothing here." Dair motioned to Rodd and me in turn, staring Brai down. "If I were your age and knew what I do now, I might not have thought twice about taking Vespar's land."

Brai paled with Dair's every word.

"Answer this, then," said Rodd. "How did this come about?"

A wicked madness glazed Dair's eyes. "Master Tylysk was dowsing for the boy while he met with the council. He showed up after in his pentacle, where he thought no one could see him. Well, I saw him, pentacle and all."

"Then you chose to abandon your duties and betray your liege lord to side with a foreign mage who would better reward your allegiance." Rodd shook his head. "It is indeed always about power and greed, isn't it, Sir Dair?"

No one could bring themselves to say more. Dair relished everyone's disquiet, triumphant, we far more wounded than he.

With the healers seeing Dair speedily on the mend, the traitor was bound. Rodd assigned five rangers to take him and the injured and return to Windborough, where the council would oversee Dair's trial. They stripped him of his hidden weapons, which Rodd distributed among us. He gave the departing rangers the parchments and evidence.

As they set off, the captain faced the rest of us. "Change of plans. We move now."

CHAPTER 48

Rhys

odd and Brai's silhouettes emerged from behind the boulder and shrub on either side of the road. Braziers from the city wall's high turrets brightened the way, spitting ash into the night air. Guards stood on each, sentries marched atop the barricade in two lines of six. With soundless signals to one another, the two rangers released their arrows. The fire pits on either end crackled as the darts entered. A count of twelve, and the watchmen slumped to unconsciousness.

Brai fastened another canvas pouch of white powder, prepared by our mages with Oedolyn's herbs, to an arrow. He secured his mask over his face before pulling the bowstring to his cheek. As a patrol turned to see the other guards had fallen, Brai loosed the arrow. The undetectable vapor fumed from the fire, dosing the sentinels to unconsciousness.

Rodd motioned his men forward. Three rangers darted and leaped onto the rough wall, masked against the fumes.

I grabbed Brai's arm. "Remember, take the main road south. It's on the west side. Don't cross the river."

He saluted.

The rangers jumped onto the wall, flipped the hatch, and leaped into the turret. Fifteen counts, and the sally port near the west turret opened.

Two minutes before the next patrol arrived. As we passed through the postern, Rodd and Brai each shot the fire pits once more. The fumes would linger long enough to incapacitate the patrol, but our mages doubted the men would lose consciousness.

We rushed down the low green slopes, spreading out to keep from being seen, Oedolyn's hand in Braidac's the entire distance. Vast braziers lit the Manor's limestone walls and sent a whiff of smoke into the night. Mage and Ordinary guards were statues between them.

A ranger took aim at a guard on the western wall. The pouch pounded into his breastplate, releasing the toxins into his unprotected face. He crumpled. A cry went up, and heads on the other two walls turned. An archer vanished into the shadows, then another watchman collapsed near the south side. Guards swarmed to the western wall, hurrying to aid their comrades below. We slinked to the east. The two rangers stayed low in the hills, luring the scrimmage away. Swordsmaster Perreth would be out soon, and once he ordered his men to advance, he'd follow four decoy rangers halfway across the city. We had to be in the castle before the chaos overtook the Manor.

Rodd disabled the guards at the east gate. He beckoned us on. Brai nocked an arrow, Oedolyn whispered a call to Chamberlain, and the three of them stole to the road. I drew Athrú away before he stared after them too long.

The rest of us, making eighteen, smashed ourselves to the wall and sneaked to the gate, where an eagle statue glared at us. A mage fumbled at the lock. Once inside, Rodd slinked behind the cover of the garden house, then the nearest hedge, where he took aim at the castle door. The watchmen dropped.

I ducked beside Rodd and pointed up at the windows. A thin break of light filtered through a seam in the drawn curtains of a casement above. We padded through the hedges to the back steps, mere shades in the piercing mageglow, lost to the garden fragrance and roaring men to the west. Calling on Draas's strength, I clambered onto the rough wall. Half the troop stayed below while the others crept toward the door and hid themselves until they counted six minutes.

I scaled to the left, sweat running down my back. I swung my legs up and balanced on the narrow ledge below the window. Back and soles of my feet flat to the wall, Draas keeping our balance, I crouched and glimpsed through the curtain's breach.

Mam's chambers—Vespar stood halfway through the bedchamber door, gripping the handle. Mam, robed in her nightclothes, huddled on her bed with Aria tight in her arms. The windowpane muted their hasty words. As my quivering ankles were about to throw me off the wall, Vespar closed the door behind him. Giving him time to move off, I inched Dair's knife from my boot, slid the blade between the window frames, lifted the latch, and slinked inside.

Mam clamped a hand over Aria's mouth. They spun around, wide eyed and blanched, Aria quaking with every need to bolt. I motioned to the antechamber, and the two rangers behind me moved to disable the guards. When Mam couldn't quiet herself any longer, I rushed to meet her embrace. Aria clamped her arms around me.

"It's all right, Mam. Did Lord Cael write you?"

She clasped my face in her hands. "He said you were safe, and he had some tasks for you, but—my love, not this."

"Master Rhys," Aria said, "Master Rhys, my lady—"

"Hush, Aria," Mam said, stroking her hair. She caught sight of the other rangers piling into her bedchamber. She held a hand to her head, breaths shortening.

"They're my friends, Mam. The Ranger Elite."

"Rhys," Athrú said, urging me along. He bowed to my mother. "My lady."

Mam was too astonished to respond.

Aria paid him no attention. She eyed the rangers, rare wonder blooming on her face. She soundlessly approached them. Mam called her name.

Hearing it, Rodd crept forward, extending an open palm. Aria jumped back, but regained her courage. A glance at me, and Rodd stooped to whisper to her. Aria gasped. The captain spoke more rapidly.

"Rhys, what is he..."

"It's all right. No one will hurt Aria or you."

She shook her head. "Please, you shouldn't have come. I missed you, darling, but this is too reckless."

"I'll be fine, Mam. We'll make it out."

She grasped my arm. "Listen to me. Much has happened since—"

"Two minutes," our timekeeper warned.

"Mam, you have to tell me where Emlyn is."

She clutched a hand to her chest, and the other slid from my arm to hold her head. I caught her as she fell from her bed.

"Mam, what's happened to you?"

She shook her head.

Then Aria returned to us, bolstered by Rodd's words, emboldened to her real age, a courageous thirteen-year-old with a new resolve in her soft green eyes.

"Emlyn has a room downstairs, next to Master Tylysk's. He's been taking care of her, and me and Isabelle help him."

Athrú interrupted my surprise with a hand on my shoulder. I gave him hasty directions to find Emlyn's rooms. He offered another bow and moved with the others into the antechamber.

Rodd roughed Aria's hair as he passed. She watched him go, falling to her childlike self, glassy eyed and crying.

Mam stopped me from rising. "Rhys, you must listen to me."

"I promise, everything will be fine." I kissed her cheek and squeezed Aria's hand on my way to the door.

The others crowded on either side of the far door. I stepped over the unconscious guards and joined the rangers. Rodd slipped out first and incapacitated the unsuspecting watchmen with ease. I led the way to the stairs. Athrú stole down the first set and disappeared down the left corridor. When nothing hindered us, we made to follow. A mage ranger outside willed the lock on the garden door out of place, and the others crept inside.

Draas tensed, impatient. He flung me around to the mage quarters corridor. Rodd halted his men.

Do not turn your back.

Vespar's chamber door creaked open. I braced myself—but I would never have guessed who stood there.

Master Heldran. The quiet, bookish Mage Master, Tylysk's school friend, and one of Vespar's favorites. Sallow and exhausted, he sagged where he stood. He faced the door, brows low, nodding to the others inside. We froze.

He turned. Terror squeezed a gasp out of him. Tylysk reeled past him, a crumpled messaging parchment in his fist. He whipped his dagger from its sheath and called for his master. Heldran stood petrified at his side.

The rangers released their arrows. Heldran ducked and clutched his cloak pin. A brisk flick of Tylysk's dagger erected a sheen of red shield between us. The shafts hung taut in midair before clattering at the mages' feet. Armored Ordinaries and mages careened from every passage, some swarming on the rangers downstairs. The archers skulking about the city had successfully drawn the foe off—the forces within the castle were few.

I glanced back. Athrú was gone.

Tylysk thrust Heldran out of his way and drew his sword. He snarled, his hideous scar blood red.

Vespar shoved past his men. A swift sweep of his arm propelled us into a heap at the edge of the stairs. Some tumbled a few steps, but each got to his feet.

Vespar readied his sword. He stared me down, face stony as ever, but with unnatural fire underneath. His gold ring glinted as lethally as his blade.

Then I saw it—the pendant resting on his heart. The hand on my hilt slackened.

I had come home to confront the Lord of Gildio himself.

A forward thrust of his arm, and a sparking green dart burst against my chest. Convulsions wracked through my limbs. I lurched into Rodd. The captain hoisted me up and ordered the attack. He stayed at my side to face Vespar's advance.

Vespar discharged curse after curse, too many to deflect. He pressed me, sweat beading across his brow. The onslaught of so many spells swirled my pounding head, sent the stench of bristled smoke through the castle, cracking louder than clashing blades. Draas tried to brace me but writhed against the pain.

Disregarding Rodd's defenses, Vespar drove me against the balcony railing. Another dizzying curse blasted me in the chest. I flipped, my back arched over the railing. I scrambled and clung to the iron bars. My sword fell among the rangers below. Rodd rushed to pull me up. Tylysk and Heldran slid through the chaos and bounded down the stairs.

"No! Rodd, stop them!"

Rodd lurched around to parry Vespar's hack. Draas and I strove to climb, but the polished iron gave me no grip. Vespar cut past Rodd and kicked at my hands. I sidled to the next bars. Rodd's sword crossed Vespar's inches from my back. I strained to swing my leg up to the ledge. My foot skidded off the lip. A curse grazed past my head. My hand slipped. Draas roared.

The wrenching agony weakened my grip. The wings ripped through flesh, arching me backward. They jostled me in midair, clumsily slowed my plummet. I landed on my stomach, disoriented, limbs splayed. The wings spread, crooked and ungainly as if I'd just crawled from an egg.

I rose and crouched on the balls of my feet. I grasped my sword, glared up at Vespar.

Rangers around me steered the guards off, but the soldiers were too terrified to approach a draconis. Rodd recovered from my distraction and took advantage of Vespar's shock. The mage twisted aside and heaped to the ground. Rodd met me halfway down the stairs. I pointed to the corridor where Tylysk and Heldran had disappeared.

"You have to stop them. They'll find Athrú."

Rodd grimaced. "Keep yourself alive." He charged down the passage.

I hurdled up the staircase. With the foe's forces dwindling upstairs, rangers retreated to aid their comrades below and barricade the stairwells. Vespar was alone among the fallen forms of his garrison.

Vespar staggered to his feet, clutching the wound in his arm, but steadied himself enough to parry my advance. He swung off my sword and hacked down. I bounced aside and slashed toward his shoulder. Vespar blocked, pressed, and raised his ringed hand. Draas's defenses collapsed against the spell, and he squirmed in pain. Vespar thrust me up to the wall, both sword and clawed hand directed at me. Blood trickled from his hairline down through his brow.

"Look what has become of Ioan's son," he cried, voice pained. "Look at this wretched creature, this beast! Where has that boy gone?"

Draas regained his footing. He launched us from the wall. Vespar thrust us aside, his spell never slackening, and bashed us into a pillar. My head lolled. The echo of the battle below lanced through my headache.

"How could he resign himself to this?" Vespar said. "How could he succumb to this monster?"

"Let me go. Give me Emlyn, and we'll leave you alone. I'll never come back."

The curse constricted around me. Vespar traced the tip of his sword along Da's jerkin, looked up into my face. "I stand by what I said. Had you brought her forward in the first place, it would have been for the better. There would have been no exile. You would have claimed your lordship. I would have helped in your ambitions if you had listened to me."

"If that were true, you would've helped me long before Emlyn ever came. How many innocents had to die before you decided she was good enough? What could you possibly think to take from Caeradin that you would turn your back on them when you knew nothing you taught me was true? What more could you possibly take from me?"

Vespar roared and cast me aside. I crumpled to the floor, sword limp in my aching hand. Vespar pricked his blade under my chin.

"She is mine," he snarled. "You will not take her from me, Rhys Ioan. Not you and your beast, not you and all the armies in Caeradin. She is mine!"

I swiped. Vespar parried, taking his sword from my neck. Draas sent him sprawling with a sweep of his wing. I scrambled to my feet. Vespar expelled another curse, an explosion of shocking blue, and staggered to stand. My blade hacked and thrust at every possible angle, parried the few projectiles and strikes Vespar managed around Draas's speed.

I pressed him toward the stairwell, he taking a backward step with every swing. Holding off another strike, Vespar dodged and retreated to summon a curse to lurch me toward him. He sidestepped. His blade hurled sideways into my back. I reeled forward to twist and land hard on my shoulder on the stairs. The gashed wings stopped the rest of the spill. The torn flesh stung and made my eyes water.

I made to snag Vespar's ankle with my foot. I misjudged the angle, and he staggered without falling. I got to my knees before he struck again. Draas steeled me. Our swords crossed, his above, crushing down on mine, doubling me over. I gave the slightest bit.

I moved with the motion of Draas's neck, the launch of a catapult. Vespar flew and struck the wall. I charged.

Vespar heaved for breath, but got his blade up. I swung, caught his sword by the cross guard, and sent it clattering out of reach. I jabbed the tip of my blade under his chin.

"Don't!"

Mam's plea clutched me. I stared at Vespar, my blade never wavering from his throat.

Do it.

"Don't, Rhys. Let him go."

Vespar glared. The flintlike spark in his eyes dared me to press a little closer with my mother watching.

"Look what he did to us, Mam. He destroyed us. He took Gildio—"

"I gave it."

I looked at her.

Vespar's spell thrust me aside and ripped my sword from my hand. He stood and tipped the blade to my chest. Draas snarled at my stupidity.

"No, stop!" Mam rushed between us. "Both of you, stop this!"

Vespar kept the blade poised. Mam faced him, arms widespread in front of me. "Orrtha," he said, meeting my eye, "stand aside."

"Touch my mother, and see what this beast will do."

"My lord, please," she begged. "Not my son. Not Ioan's only son. Not the little boy you once loved."

"He will not stand in my way."

"Then strike me down too. I will hinder you all the more if you touch him."

"He will not take her from me!"

"Look at you," Mam pleaded. "Both of you. You, who used to carry this boy on your shoulders. And you—" She turned to me, the sword at her back. "You who begged him to carry you, and to play your silly games and let you tag along wherever he and your father went." Again, she turned, showing Vespar tears. "You who raised him for me when I could not."

We glared at each other. Mam's words couldn't move me. The Vespar Da had known was gone. He would murder his best friend's son before I stood between him and his schemes. How could a broken past matter after all he'd done to me? How could I forgive him for my exile, for Flannery, for stealing Emlyn and Gildio?

Vespar's hand trembled. Rage pulsed in his clenched jaws, in his temples, but was drowned by the wide eyes I never thought could look so lost.

He bolstered himself, tightened his grip on my sword, all the fiercer. The same thought I had for him glinted in his eyes. I had changed.

"You can't win," Mam said, exasperated. "My lord, you cannot win. You can't best a draconis. He will overpower you. You must surrender."

I thought I saw tears in his eyes. "He won't take her from me. She is mine."

"If you strike, Rhys will kill you. Then Emlyn will never be yours."

Vespar's gaze never broke from mine. Yes, there were tears there, and he let them trickle down his face.

Mam laid a gentle hand on his arm. "Please. Let our boy go."

Vespar let her lower his arm.

Reaching for the hilt in his grasp, Mam looked to me. "Call your men off."

"Mam—"

Vespar seized her by the wrist and thrust her aside. Mam spilled to the floor, shrieking. Vespar raised the sword over his head. Draas whisked us out of range. I caught his arm, and he cried out as I wrenched the blade away. Draas cast him toward the wall. Vespar slumped in the rubble of a marble pillar. He didn't move.

I stepped toward him. Mam clutched my cloak, on her knees, crawling at my feet. "Leave him. You are better than this."

Do not walk away.

"No, my Rhys!" Mam held fast. "Listen to me. Do not be the beast Caeradin thinks you are. Show them this is not who you are."

My arm trembled. The sword quivered. "Everything was a lie, Mam. He never cared about us or Da. He took Emlyn, and now Gildio is his. How much more will he steal? How much more power will he claim before he's satisfied?"

"Then finish the task you came to do," Mam said. "You came for Emlyn, not to murder Master Vespar. Please, my love. Don't do this to yourself. Don't do this to your father."

Finish it now.

Mam cupped her hands around the fist on my hilt. She claimed my gaze, her misting hazel-brown stare steady. She guided my hand to sheathe the blade.

Draas rumbled at her, a furious smoke curling from between his jaws.

Mam rushed to her feet to embrace me. "Be careful, my love. Take care of Emlyn. We will miss her. All of us," she said, casting a glance at Vespar's slumped form. She kissed my face. "Go. There will be scouts out before light."

Mam urged me away with a hand to my back. I stared at her, watched her shed no tears and radiate the strength I had forgotten was in her, wishing I had the same. Wishing I had the courage to face Vespar again. To tell Mam she was coming with me, and that I wouldn't leave her in the hands of this despicable, false lord of Gildio.

"Go, my Rhys."

I stepped away, blinking back tears.

Once downstairs, I ordered the rangers to retreat. I counted them as they limped from the battle. Looking for the last of them, I spotted two dark ranger cloaks fallen amid those of Gildian green. The remaining foe pursued, forcing us to abandon them.

Rodd had Tylysk cornered against a pillar. Tylysk had lost his sword and blocked the captain with his dagger. I cut between them, let Tylysk see the rest of the beast that had given him that scar. His snarl slackened. He kept his dagger raised. I gripped my hilt.

"Run and scrape up your master, dog."

His glare fell to sheer astonishment. "You can't. You didn't—"

"Shall I finish you now? My dragon wasn't done with you before."

Tylysk retreated. Stumbling backward, dagger directed at me, he roared, "You won't win. We will find you. Lord Vespar will burn you out, whatever it takes." He sprinted away.

We escaped through the silent garden, crisp and chilled after the tumultuous heat of battle and magic. The sliver of moon hung high, and the late night shielded us. Beyond the Manor walls, the eastern half of the city lay awake, scarred with the rangers' mischief to lure Swordsmaster Perreth from the castle.

Without a sound, Draas withdrew his wings. Dizziness made the street whirl and tilt. Rodd steadied me and motioned his men on. The rangers scattered, each to make his own stealthy way to our hiding place, as our horde of strangers would not have gone unnoticed. Rodd stayed at my side.

We trudged on, bone tired, aching, coming to terms with everything after Dair, the raid, the two comrades who would never leave the Manor. The fact that I might never see my mother again.

The west lay asleep, unaware of the disaster in their lord's manor. After the battle din, my ears rang in the stark silence. Rodd and I slinked as fast as we dared under the lamplight. At last we found the sign, its yellow knife visible through the dark. We scurried down the alley to the tavern's back door. Rodd gave three short raps and a ranger call. The handle clicked.

I fell on the steps, pulling Rodd down with me. He hefted me through the door.

Don't do this to me now, I pleaded. *Emlyn's in there!*

It is your feeble being that causes this, Draas said. *Do not blame me for your fragility.*

His gigantic frame wheeled around, his neck craning to face me, and he burst forth a merciless torrent of flame.

You are a fool, Rhys Claytherdon.

CHAPTER 49

Athrú

Their intrusion hadn't yet disturbed this wing of the Manor. Slumbering stillness kept Athrú on the balls of his feet, and his heart seemed to course along his spine with every pulse. He tried not to think—move, go, next footstep. But no other place could shake him like this, and no other task could steal his courage as this one did. He felt as if he were sprawling on his back after someone had whisked a carpet from under him, and any moment he would look up and stare his murderer in the face.

He'd forgotten how magic thrummed in Gildio. How its hundreds of thousands of threads weaved, all different hues and strengths, patterned into a whirring hive. The entire city exuded it. The Lord Mage's Manor was bad enough alone, but—and Athrú shuddered—the Academy, brimming with mage students from across Caeradin, practically glowed with the power within its walls. Magic's potency scrambled his mind and upended his courage like an hourglass.

Athrú padded down the corridor, the magelights casting glassy white glares across the tiled floor. In the next moment, ringing steel and erupting spells echoed behind him. He slammed to the wall, peeked around the corner, and swerved left into the second empty corridor. The second door on the right, Rhys had said. Athrú pressed his ear to it. Sucking a deep breath, he forced the lock out of place. The door swung wide. He thought a protective charm slowed him at the threshold, but he passed through it.

He hadn't expected an antechamber, nor for the room to be lifeless. By the spread of parchments on the table and the boots near the door, someone else shared the little girl's chambers. Athrú slinked around the table, glancing at the two doors ahead. He chose the nearest and listened before testing the handle. It clicked open. The faint shimmer of a green shield rising an inch from the floor didn't slow him this time.

Not a sound. Nothing leaped at him. A tiny orb of feathery sky-blue light bobbed over a nightstand at the far end of the room, giving off an arc of light. Athrú held his breath, but one of the two beds was unoccupied. He ventured farther, waiting for someone to jump him.

Emlyn tossed in her sleep, flung over with a whimper. She sat up, scrubbing her eyes. Athrú went shadow still when Emlyn peered up at him.

"Heldran?" she squeaked.

Athrú risked another step. "No, but I'm here to help you."

Her blue-violet eyes shone wide in the magic light. She charmed the orb to grow, and the light swelled toward Athrú. Emlyn scuttled into the wall beside her bed. She hid behind her knees. "Don't take me away. *Please* don't take me away! Master Vespar says you can't!"

"Shh, Emlyn. I'm not here to hurt you."

She peeked up. In another panic, she scrambled through her blankets and pillows. Athrú glanced at the floor, where a rumpled doll lay in a lopsided heap. He picked it up.

"Is this what you're looking for?" He held it out to her.

Emlyn eyed him as if he might crush her precious doll in his bare hands. "Give Laela back," she whimpered.

Athrú sat on the edge of the bed, heart thudding against his ribs. He rested the doll near her. Emlyn snatched it away, curled into the corner of the wall, and buried her face in its hair.

"I'm Athrú. I'm here with Rhys."

Her head shot up. Athrú hadn't expected her look of terror.

"I'm his friend. I promised to bring you to him. Let's hurry. He's going to meet us soon."

"Master Vespar said he wouldn't come."

Athrú inched closer. Emlyn's back hit the wall. "We have to go," he said. "Let's find Rhys."

"No, I can't! Master Vespar needs me!"

Athrú cringed, but said, "Rhys needs you too. He's doing all he promised you he would. He needs your help." He hesitated, watching her crumple. "What Master Vespar wants will hurt more people."

Emlyn looked as though he'd struck her across the face. "How do you know what Master Vespar wants?"

He shook his head. He extended a hand. "Come, now. We have to hurry."

"Not till you tell me."

"I don't know for certain," he said, only partially lying, he thought. "But Rhys believes whatever he's planning will do more harm than good."

Emlyn hugged her doll, eyes glazed. She inched to the wall, out of reach of Athrú's hand. "Master Vespar lied to me? But he promised. And Tylysk said…" She stared at him, messy with tears. "They're going to kill Rhys, aren't they? He came back, and he's a monster, and they have to."

"Shh." Athrú dared to creep to her side and held her tiny, quivering hand. "They won't, little one. Don't be afraid. Rhys is not a monster, and he will be fine if we go now."

Emlyn stopped herself from pulling from his grasp. She studied him, scrubbing her tears on her shoulder. Athrú watched her addled thoughts try to steady in her weary eyes. How could she give up this new, lavish, safe life with those she'd come to trust? Rhys hadn't expected to find Emlyn living like a lady herself.

Athrú wasn't surprised.

Then a stranger, filthy and rank with weeks of travel, calloused and fatigued, who promised hard ground for a sleeping place and an exhausting roam across the country, meant to steal her away. Unless she loved Rhys as much as he claimed, why would she choose them over the life she had here?

Emlyn uncoiled herself from the corner. She hesitated, but laid her palm flat on his. Athrú closed his fingers around her tiny hand. Emlyn bit her lip.

She extended her charm. It crept through her fingertips into his, delicate and warm and bright as sunshine, a tender hand reaching to caress him. Athrú closed his eyes. He let it.

And, for once, was whole.

Athrú reached to meet her spell. Hers flickered, but remained. Her charm's hand was as tiny as her own, her fingertips brushing the edge of his palm. But he couldn't deny the raw strength behind it.

Emlyn withdrew, wonder glowing in her eyes. Athrú held out his arms. "Let's find Rhys."

She gathered her doll and crawled to him. Athrú scooped her up and moved.

He froze in the bedroom doorway. Light from the corridor silhouetted the figure he first thought to be the Lady's. The girl in the door gasped, rushed to start a magelight.

"Emlyn—"

Little Emlyn put a finger to her lips, and the girl quieted. She glared at Athrú, shut and blocked the door. "Put Emlyn down."

"It's all right, Isabelle," Emlyn said. "It's Rhys! He came back!"

Athrú recognized her from Rhys's descriptions—those absorbing brown eyes widened at him. Her ferocity melted to shock, then to suspicion.

"Why isn't he here instead of you?"

"He's preoccupied at the moment, my lady, if you haven't heard the noise outside."

Isabelle scowled. "I don't believe you. Give her to me. I won't let you hurt her."

"I would never hurt her, milady. Master Rhys trusted her to me, and I won't betray him. If you don't believe me, go and look. You'll find him fighting for his life."

Emlyn fell still. Isabelle paled. She swallowed and shook her head.

"You have to help us." Emlyn's voice quivered. "I want to see Rhys."

"If you're really here with him," the Mistress said, "leave Emlyn with me, go scrape him out of that mess, and run. Don't put this over Rhys's head on top of everything else." Her shoulders raised with each desperate breath. "You don't understand. Vespar might let the exile slip, but he will never stop looking for Emlyn. Don't do that to them."

Athrú had no doubt Vespar wouldn't let the exile breach go unpunished. He would be at their throats by morning, if they succeeded. The thought shook him to the core.

Emlyn clung to his cloak and avoided Isabelle's eye.

"What about Heldran?" Isabelle said. Emlyn's lip quivered. "And Aria, Mistress Orrtha. And Tylysk—you'll miss him." She laughed a little. "He won't know what to do without you."

Emlyn hid her face on Athrú's shoulder. "Master Vespar lied to me. I won't help him anymore. He doesn't want to take care of me."

"We've talked about this, Emlyn. It's not that simple. Now that he's lord—"

"What?"

Isabelle frowned at Athrú, relayed what had happened since Rhys's banishment. Lady Orrtha's abdication, Vespar's lordship, his guardianship over Emlyn, the Gildian council's summons to be held the next day.

Athrú held Emlyn tighter. Vespar had already made his critical moves. Gildio was his, Emlyn secure under his influence. Rhys had broken his exile, the perfect excuse to finish him off.

And Athrú so close, lying in the palm of Vespar's hand.

"Then we won't allow it," he said before his courage deflated. "I'll defend him. Rhys is under Lord Cael's protection, and the Ranger Elite stand at his side." Isabelle's eyes widened. "Don't underestimate him, milady. His head is full of more plans than either of us know."

Isabelle stared, a smile flickering the corner of her lips. "Yes," she said, "that I believe."

Emlyn joined in Athrú's plea, facing the Mistress once more. Isabelle faltered, gazing between them, the weary sorrow bearing her down. But her scowl returned, giving her strength. She jerked her hands to her hips with a huff.

"Fine. This way."

Athrú followed her into the hallway. Isabelle crept close to the wall, slinking on tiptoe. Emlyn covered her ears at the battle raucousness echoing off the walls. Bitter smoke wafted over their heads, charged with magic. Isabelle waved Athrú back as a horde of servants escaped down the adjacent corridor. She took a breath and moved on.

"Tell Rhys he owes me," she hissed.

Isabelle slid behind a pillar as Athrú opened his mouth. Shadows blotted the magelight glow on the wall, hurrying toward them. Isabelle glanced around, thinking fast.

"Down the hall, right side, through the double doors. Take the staircase to the right. The windows in the back lead to the garden. You should be safe that way."

Athrú nodded. Isabelle squeezed Emlyn's hand and sped on. Emlyn clung her arms around Athrú's neck. He ducked behind the pillar and inched close to the wall.

"What's going on up there?" Isabelle demanded from down the hall.

"Where's Emlyn?" two men's voices came at once. Emlyn jumped at their ruthless tones. Athrú hid her on his shoulder.

"I was going to sit with her, but I heard—"

Isabelle gasped. One of the men cried out. Athrú glimpsed around the pillar at the sound of ringing steel. Rodd rushed the armed mage, Tylysk, he guessed, seeing the scar down his face. The other mage seized Isabelle's wrist and dragged her from the skirmish to the nearest corridor. Athrú's heart stopped.

The Mage Master glanced back as he passed their hiding place. He halted and jerked around. Isabelle tugged his arm, but he stood fast. Dismay and rage contorted his face. One hand went to his cloak pin, the other tensed to attack—then, as he met Athrú's eye, his face fell open to unhindered awe. He reached tentatively for Emlyn. Isabelle cut between them and refused to budge when the mage grasped her shoulders to pry her aside. His eyes never fell from Athrú's.

Without thinking, Athrú careened around the corner and surged toward the double doors. The mage stammered, then stumbled over leaden feet and sprinted after them.

"Wait, please, stop!"

Athrú couldn't. Not when Emlyn started to cry, not when the mage's voice broke to ragged, desperate barks. He lay in the hollow of Vespar's palm, and the fingers were closing over him.

Athrú heaved the door open and slammed it shut behind him. Swarming darkness swallowed them, the memory of magelights blinding them. The stale air was trapped, tightly enclosed, stuffy with mildew. The squashed silence smothered Emlyn's sobs. Athrú faltered forward a few steps, turned to the right. His foot met wall. He groped along it until it cornered.

The door screeched open. Light flooded the entry of the gigantic room, and the sight of its shaded immensity startled Athrú. The momentary brightness guided him to the stairwell. He bounded up, the mage and Isabelle at his heels. Magelights burst to life behind him, willed awake as he passed.

Athrú loped down the narrow aisle between ceiling-high bookcases toward the back wall. Emlyn begged him to wait. Isabelle pelted the mage with reason and pointless assurances to no avail. Athrú rushed to the nearest window at the end of the aisle, set Emlyn down for the briefest moment to open it. She scampered, but Athrú snagged her as their pursuer overtook them.

The Mage Master held up his hands, heaving for breath. "Please, wait. Sir, please, you can't take my sister."

Athrú's heart dropped. Of any way to complicate matters, why *this*?

Weary resignation and the reminder of Oedolyn slackened his grip on Emlyn's arms, but he kept hold of her. The girl dangled in his grasp, exhausted by her tears.

Isabelle stepped beside the mage. "She'll be safe, Heldran. Rhys will protect her."

"And you would put my sister in a draconis's hands?" Heldran growled at her. "Please, sir, I beg you. She's all I have."

Athrú glanced at his escape route. "I'm not Master Rhys," he said. "And I wouldn't trust Emlyn more to any other hands. He's more disciplined than any draconis has ever been. And that he would break his exile for her should tell you where he stands."

Heldran shook his head. "I know who you are. And I ask you, beg you, please, stay here with Emlyn. Please, my master—"

Isabelle stopped him with a delicate hand on his arm. "You don't want Master Vespar using Emlyn any more than they do. Trust Rhys. Let them go. I know you—"

"Do you?" Heldran swung on her. "Did your servants sell your baby sister to a tinker? Did you walk to her empty grave every night? Did you return to your master to learn she was alive and turned the greatest household in Caeradin upside down? Don't touch me!" Heldran stalked nearer, clawed fingers grasping for his sister. "Give her to me!"

Athrú lifted a hand. The mage recoiled and threw his hands up. Emlyn cowered inside her rescuer's cloak and cried, horrified. Heldran blanched, realizing it, and sank to the floor. The magelight overhead shone on the tear down his cheek.

"Emlyn…Emmy, I'm sorry. Emmy—"

"Is that why you're here?" Athrú assumed the commanding tone the mage no doubt expected. Heldran cringed, but faced him. "Are you here for your sister or your master?"

Athrú paused long enough for Heldran to speak, but hadn't expected an answer. "Emlyn is…sir, you must understand—"

"I understand you are as much bound to your orders to protect her as you are determined to do so as her brother. What takes precedence, your sister's welfare, or your master's wishes?"

Athrú loathed the role he had to assume. Heldran must have felt like the smallest being alive. He stammered, bolstered himself. "Everything I do is for her welfare."

"Then do this for her welfare. Let me take her to Master Rhys. Unless you would see Gildio fall and Emlyn lose all she loves, including you."

Heldran shook his head. "Lord Vespar will not let Gildio fall. He swore to protect us. He won't betray us."

"Then you have chosen a side, and it isn't Emlyn's."

Heldran was stricken. Emlyn gave a tiny gasp, catching his eye. A sob squeezed from his throat.

"Emlyn, tell him. Tell him what I do for you. You can't leave me again."

She clung to Athrú's cloak, huddled tight against his leg. "But, you said…"

"Tell him to stay. Tell him you want to stay with me. *Tell him.*"

She looked between the three of them, cowering, a tiny bird among lions. She twined her arms around her head and hid behind her doll. Isabelle crept behind a bookcase, unwilling to be a factor in her choice. Athrú took his hand from Emlyn's head. He wouldn't sway her one way or the other, though he dreaded to think what he'd have to tell Rhys should she refuse him. Dreaded the choice he himself would have to make.

Heldran stayed on his knees, arms extended to his sister.

Emlyn unwound herself. Tear streaked, but steady, she stepped away from Athrú. Heldran let another sob escape, this time in relief. But Emlyn stopped halfway between her brother and her rescuer.

"Come with us, Heldran."

His outstretched arms stiffened. He dropped on his heels.

"Come on, Heldran. I can't leave you if you come with me."

His arms lowered to his sides.

Emlyn dropped Laela, seized Heldran's hand, and strove to pull him to his feet. He wouldn't budge. She leaped and clamped her arms around his neck, smothered her pleas in his chest. His hands stayed leaden on the floor.

Athrú glanced at Isabelle. She heeded him and gingerly gathered Emlyn up, warning them about time. At last, Heldran moved to stammer and embrace his sister. He kissed her face, begged, grasped for her, glassy eyed. Emlyn struggled as Athrú lifted her out of Heldran's reach, but, exhausted and heartbroken, she wilted on his shoulder.

Athrú looked down at Heldran, regretting every word, hating the role he had imposed on himself, guilty for being the lever to pry them apart. Heldran and Emlyn mirrored him and Oedolyn: brothers doing all they could for their helpless sisters when they were too young to set their upended worlds aright. When smiling devils caged them and robbed their brothers of all the precious good in their lives.

But Heldran had a choice; Athrú never did.

Athrú faced him, dropping his callous act, and awaited Heldran's word. The Mage Master gazed dazedly over Athrú's shoulder. His eyes flicked to match Athrú's.

"Sir," he said, "don't go."

Athrú stepped away.

Isabelle grasped the mage's hand. Heldran let her raise him to his feet. His eyes glazed again, never blinking. The Mistress stooped for Emlyn's discarded doll and extended it out to the girl. Emlyn refused to take it. Isabelle clutched it to her chest, biting back her own tears. She showed Athrú a determined frown.

"Be careful with her."

Athrú nodded. "I swear," he said, meeting Heldran's eye, "I won't fail her. You will see her again."

Heldran made no sign that he heard. Isabelle led him away, promising to buy the refugees time to escape.

Athrú shifted Emlyn onto his back. She sniffled in his ear, arms loose around his neck.

"Why won't Heldran come? He said he'd always…"

Athrú had no answer, nor did he have the heart to speak one.

He made sure the girl was secure before he peered out the window. Not a soul was wandering the garden or the wall, no guards to snare them. They were off hunting phantom rangers or contesting a draconis.

Athrú hoisted himself through the window and crouched on its ledge. Emlyn clung to the front of his cloak. He stroked her arm when she whimpered. "I won't let you fall," he said.

He scaled the uneven stones to the grass below. A thread of moonlight illumined what lay beyond the reach of the mageglow lamps. A briskness clung to the breath caressing Emlyn's hair, startlingly fresh after the stale library had suffocated them. Athrú cleared his lungs of the mustiness and realized how little his fear let him breathe.

As soon as his feet touched ground, Athrú made for the nearest gate. He ducked into the long passage, slipped through the iron threshold, and locked it behind him. He pinned himself to the wall to catch his breath and watched for patrols.

With Emlyn tight in his hold, he ran for the road, moving south to the next path, and wove through the backstreets. As they neared the city's west wall, he veered south.

The main street was quieter than he'd anticipated. A few late-night drinkers staggered out of taverns or collapsed on shop steps, too engrossed in intoxicated humor or bickering to notice Athrú and Emlyn's passing. On the next road, a tipsy crowd loitered at the front deck of a tavern, belting a garbled rendition of "One, Three, Two" under the direction of a man waving a bottle around. Athrú glanced at the sign under the lamplight—the Golden Rogue.

Athrú ducked into the alley, stole past the inn's stables, and rapped on the door. A tall, broad man, trimmed with a red beard and decked in a stained apron, cracked the door open. The sight of Emlyn granted them entry. Athrú stepped into the sweltering kitchen. Another rabble roared beyond the door to the common room.

Brac the tavernman led them to the far end of the kitchen. He rolled away two barrels and scraped a crate across the floorboards to reveal a narrow hatch. Brac stooped, gave three uneven knocks. After a pause, the hatch flipped outward. Grinning Braidac stood below, peering up from the dark cellar.

"That was fast," he whispered.

Athrú knelt and lowered Emlyn through the hatch. She clung to him, but Braidac lured her attention with a friendly gasp.

"Hullo, lamb!" He grinned and held Emlyn on his side. "My, you're *much* prettier than Rhys said."

Athrú stayed on his knees and watched Braidac carry Emlyn out of sight. He looked up at the tavernman towering over him. He raised an open hand. "We can't thank you enough, sir."

Brac grunted and ignored Athrú's handshake. "Where's the master?"

"On his way," he said, refusing to think anything else had come of Rhys and the troops. "He'll have several others with him."

Brac sighed. He waved Athrú away. "Get down. Keep quiet." He lowered the hatch behind Athrú.

Barrels, crates, and sacks had been shoved aside in high stacks about the cellar, making room for their unwelcome accommodation. The kitchen hearth above warmed the dank space. Pebble-glass windows near the low ceiling scattered no moonlight, as the view showed little above a passerby's ankles. A handful of candles dispersed the thick dimness. More than suitable, and more than they deserved for dragging the unsuspecting innkeeper into their plot.

Emlyn drooped on Braidac's lap as they sat with Oedolyn on a bed of spare blankets and empty canvas sacks. Oedolyn inspected the girl for any harm, though both she and Athrú knew she would find none. Emlyn let her, consoled by tender whispers and gentle hands. Chamberlain plopped beside them and savored the girl's shy strokes. Braidac had already gotten her to smile.

Athrú moved to join them, but staggered. He leaned against the wall to catch his breath, slid to the floor. Eyeing him, Braidac tousled Emlyn's hair, lifted her off his lap, and joined him.

"Have a nice stay at the castle?" he asked.

Athrú rolled his eyes. A glance at Emlyn postponed the miserable report. "Did Brac give you trouble?"

Braidac shrugged. "Not bad. Oedolyn convinced him." He beamed at her, winked, and turned back. "How are the others coming along?"

Oedolyn glanced sidelong at them. Emlyn seemed not to have heard and promptly asked when Rhys would be there. "They'll be along," Athrú said.

"Don't worry, lamb." Braidac went to pinch Emlyn's cheek. "We're not leaving without Rhys."

They left it at that. Once satisfied that Emlyn was in fact better off than any of the rest of them, Oedolyn tucked the girl into the blankets. Smiling and wrinkling her nose at Braidac, she complied with his request for a lullaby. It lulled the ranger as much as Emlyn, and he lounged beside her. His bow rested in a tight fist on his chest.

Emlyn stared across the cellar at Athrú. She seemed content, nestled with the others, but he saw her shy want for him. Her silent charm caressed him, soft as the brush of eyelashes on his skin. It touched his face, traced the lines of his features, memorized them. Gossamer and warm, beautiful in its purity, young and brilliant.

Athrú met her touch. Their hands came together, palm to palm. He curled his fingers around hers. Emlyn smiled at him. It gripped him more than any smile ever had.

She drifted to the rhythm of Athrú's spell on her cheek. He let it falter once she was slumbering.

As he saw her at last, her youth stunned Athrú more. She was small for her age, light enough to carry awhile, just starting to lose her teeth.

How could It be this cruel? Why would It ask this of a child, Its Chosen? Nothing could be more heartless.

Athrú watched her slumbering. For a moment, Vespar had almost won. There they stood, side by side, all the Lord Mage sought, his hand closing around them. And for a moment, Athrú's life lay in the hands of a distraught though dutiful Mage Master. Had he not shaken Heldran, Vespar would have succeeded.

Emlyn hummed in her sleep. Athrú brushed her face with a tender spell. Savored her presence, the wholeness it brought. Yet, at the same time, sensing her strength, the enormity of her power, housed in her tiny being. Emlyn's magic was immense and terrible.

So was Athrú's.